A one-time legal secretary and director of a charitable foundation, **Susan Meier** found her bliss when she became a full-time novelist for Mills & Boon. She's visited ski lodges and candy factories for 'research', and works in her pyjamas. But the real joy of her job is creating stories about women for women. With over eighty published novels, she's tackled issues like infertility, losing a child and becoming widowed, and worked through them with her characters.

Suzanne Merchant was born and raised in South Africa. She and her husband lived and worked in Cape Town, London, Kuwait, Baghdad, Sydney and Dubai before settling in the Sussex countryside. They enjoy visits from their three grown-up children and are kept busy attempting to keep two spaniels, a dachshund, a parrot and a large, unruly garden under control.

MOTHER OF THE BRIDE'S SECOND CHANCE

SUSAN MEIER

CINDERELLA'S ADVENTURE WITH THE CEO

SUZANNE MERCHANT

MILLS & BOON

First published in Great Britain 2024
by Mills & Boon, an imprint of HarperCollins*Publishers* Ltd,
1 London Bridge Street, London, SE1 9GF

www.harpercollins.co.uk

HarperCollins*Publishers*, Macken House, 39/40 Mayor Street Upper, Dublin 1, D01 C9W8, Ireland

Mother of the Bride's Second Chance © 2024 Linda Susan Meier

Cinderella's Adventure with the CEO © 2024 Suzanne Merchant

ISBN: 978-0-263-32136-4

08/24

This book contains FSC™ certified paper and other controlled sources to ensure responsible forest management.

For more information visit www.harpercollins.co.uk/green.

Printed and Bound in the UK using 100% Renewable Electricity at CPI Group (UK) Ltd, Croydon, CR0 4YY

MOTHER OF THE BRIDE'S SECOND CHANCE

SUSAN MEIER

MILLS & BOON

CHAPTER ONE

JULIETTE MORGAN STOOD in a grassy spot a few feet away
from Dene Summerhouse in New York City's Central Park.
She'd been summoned here by Antonio Salvaggio and her
heart thrummed with anxiety.

Her daughter, Riley, had been dating Antonio for a few
months, but they'd broken up. Juliette hadn't heard that
they'd gotten back together. But Riley was a marriage proposal planner, and she scheduled a lot of the events she put
together in this very gazebo. Wouldn't it just be like an Italian playboy to rashly propose instead of simply calling her
daughter and apologizing?

She glanced at Antonio's grandmother, GiGi, and his
dad, Lorenzo. They both looked like cats who'd swallowed
the canary. Though Lorenzo was an extremely handsome
man with his dark hair and compelling dark eyes—explaining where Antonio got his good looks—Juliette was not
amused by the antics of this privileged family. When she'd
been hustled here by Riley's videographer, she'd barely
been introduced to the Salvaggios, let alone been given
time to ask them what was going on.

Because she'd been shushed. *Silenced.*

It had been so long since someone shushed her that she
didn't know whether to be amused or infuriated.

Infuriated was winning.

She glanced around. The beginning of the second week of November, the park's trees had lost most of their colored leaves. But the sun was warm. The day bright. It was a perfect fall day—

Oh, God. It *was* the perfect day for a proposal! She just knew that impulsive billionaire was going to ask her daughter to marry him.

Off in the distance, Juliette heard Riley's assistant Marietta's voice. "This way."

Riley said, "Really? I thought Dene Summerhouse was that way."

The Salvaggios laughed.

Juliette's suspicions heightened.

Marietta said, "You can get to it a lot of ways."

They emerged from a bank of trees. As they walked up the path to Dene Summerhouse, Antonio appeared behind the gazebo, still not visible to Riley but Juliette could see him. He wore a suit and tie and looked his absolute handsomest.

Marietta and Riley reached the gazebo and Marietta gave Riley a nudge. "We can't see much from back here. Why don't you go check out the inside, see if you can tell what the contractors will be changing or repairing."

Juliette frowned. What was Marietta talking about? There was no scheduled maintenance on Dene Summerhouse.

Riley did what she was told, ambling up the steps into the pavilion like a person so confused they just went with the flow.

Juliette's heart squeezed. Not only was Antonio going to propose, but Riley didn't know. Marietta had lured her here with a ruse!

Before Juliette could figure out a way to rescue her

daughter, three violinists appeared out of nowhere, playing something soft and romantic.

Riley turned, clearly baffled, but Juliette wasn't. Her breath stuttered as Antonio climbed the steps. They'd broken up. They hadn't made up as far as Juliette knew. But the real bottom line was they didn't know each other well enough to get married.

This was all wrong.

The only hope she had was that her extremely logical daughter would say no.

Antonio got down on one knee, pulled a ring box from his pocket and said, "I love you. Will you marry me?"

Juliette held her breath.

Riley leaned down to kneeling Antonio and whispered something.

Antonio rose, slid his arms around her and pulled her close enough that he could whisper in her ear.

Riley eased back, studying his face as he kept whispering.

Clearly, Riley wasn't sure—might have even said no—and he was talking her into it.

He bumped his forehead against hers.

Riley pressed her lips together.

Juliette pressed her lips together. This was it. Her smart, logical daughter was going to say no.

Antonio opened the ring box and slid the ring on her finger.

No longer whispering, Riley said, "It's a different ring."

Antonio said, "The other one was for a fake proposal. This one is very real."

Riley smiled. "And it fits."

Then he kissed her. Riley kissed him back passionately, apparently with no thought to taking off the ring.

Juliette's face fell in disbelief. Where the hell was her smart, logical daughter?

Antonio broke the kiss, and the sound of the alleluia chorus filled the area. Thirty singing judges danced their way onto Dene Summerhouse and made a circle around them. GiGi and Lorenzo began to applaud. Marietta and Jake, the videographer for Riley's company, stood off to the side, applauding too.

Juliette stared at them. What the hell had just happened?

She calmed herself. She didn't dislike Antonio. He was a nice guy. And he made her daughter happy. What she objected to was their getting married without really knowing each other. Still, they weren't *getting married* today. They had gotten engaged. No big deal. They could be engaged forever.

Or at least a year. Most people needed a year to plan a wedding. People in Manhattan needed two, sometimes three to reserve a good venue. In that time, her smart, logical daughter would see Antonio's flaws, his quirks, and she'd be wise enough to break it off with him, if the flaws and quirks were god-awful.

They might not be. Rich, handsome, suave Antonio Salvaggio could be a great choice for a husband for her daughter—after they'd been engaged awhile and knew each other better.

There was no reason to panic.

"Aren't you going to congratulate your daughter?"

Juliette pasted a smile on her face and turned to Antonio's father, the equally suave and handsome Lorenzo Salvaggio. "Yes. Sure. In a minute."

He frowned. His nearly black eyes grew serious and sincere. "Something troubles you?"

"No." Something troubling her was the last thing she'd

admit. These people were rich, pampered, accustomed to getting their own way. If they supported this engagement, she'd have to be careful what she said to them. "I think I will go congratulate the happy couple."

Lorenzo said, *"Sì."* He put his hand on the small of her back and directed her to Dene Summerhouse.

She stiffened, but not from offense. Owning a home nursing agency, she worked with a lot of older doctors, who believed taking a woman's elbow or putting a hand on the small of their back was gallant. Those kinds of gestures never bothered her.

It was the zing that traveled up her spine when his fingers touched her that almost made her shiver.

Ridiculous really.

He kept his hand on her back the entire walk. When they reached Riley and Antonio, Lorenzo's mother, GiGi, was hugging them.

"I am so happy for you." The older woman glowed with happiness.

Not for the first time, Juliette noticed the scarf on her head. She knew GiGi had breast cancer. The last she'd heard from Riley, GiGi had been refusing treatment. If she'd begun the treatments in the time Antonio and Riley had been apart, that was good.

Riley stepped away from GiGi to hug Juliette, who squeezed her tightly. Even her successful business wasn't her greatest accomplishment. Riley was. Juliette loved her beyond what she had ever believed possible.

Though she thought it too soon for her daughter to be getting engaged, she wouldn't ruin this moment. She pulled back and said, "Congratulations!"

"Thanks, Mom."

Antonio came over and hugged Juliette.

"And congratulations to you too," Juliette said. "You'd better take good care of my daughter."

Riley groaned. "Mom, that sounds so outdated."

"Oh, I don't think so. I don't expect him to wait on you hand and foot or even to buy you chocolates and write poetry. But I know you want kids. I hope he's aware of that."

Antonio laughed. "That's what we both want. Two or three children we can raise in the villa."

Juliette's heart stuttered.

Her daughter would be moving to Italy? To live on a villa…when Riley's company was in Manhattan?

She faced her daughter. There were so many questions and cautions Juliette wanted to issue. But this was a little too public. She would wait until they were alone when the conversation could be honest.

Antonio put his arm across Riley's shoulders. "That's why we're getting married in January."

Juliette's eyes bugged. Good God! Was it not shocking enough that her daughter was actually engaged and eventually moving to Italy…but so soon?

"January?"

"We don't want our wedding to be too close to the holidays. We want the day to be ours."

"First we make the commitment," Antonio said, smiling at Riley. "Then kids."

Juliette worked to find her voice. "Just like that?"

Antonio and Riley laughed joyfully, as if they were the two happiest people in the world. "Just like that."

GiGi left the small group to sit on a bench, and it dawned on Juliette that her health was poor enough that Antonio and Riley might be rushing the wedding to please his grandmother. It was noble to be sure. But a smart person didn't make a lifetime commitment to please someone else.

Marietta and Jake stole Riley's attention to congratulate her.

Juliette's thoughts jumped into overdrive trying to put all this together as her brain was bombarded by the terrible problems her daughter and her Italian playboy apparently had not considered.

"They're not kids."

Lorenzo's voice came from behind her, and Juliette turned. "No. They aren't." She sucked in a breath. "But a heads-up would have been nice and a chance to remind my daughter that she's got a company to run—here in Manhattan—also would have been appropriate."

"I understand that she's relocating most of the administrative work to Tuscany and leaving Marietta behind to continue work in the States."

Juliette gaped at him. "You know this?"

He frowned. The corners of his eyes crinkled. Juliette's breath stuttered. Good grief the man was gorgeous.

"It came up in casual conversation."

"Really? Riley hasn't been in Italy for weeks. How did it come up in casual conversation?"

He shrugged. "Maybe I also read between the lines a little bit." He smiled. His dark eyes sparkled with humor.

She swore if a person could blind others with their good looks, he'd be the one.

She took a breath. "She hasn't actually told you?"

"I guess not in actual words. But it's the logical thing to do and your daughter is nothing but logical."

Juliette's gaze strayed to her daughter. "She usually is."

"Look, I understand your apprehensions."

She faced him again. "You do?"

"You think the marriage is too soon?"

"I think the engagement is too soon, but I could have

handled that if they'd spent enough time being engaged to get to know each other a little better."

"*Sì.*"

The first bit of hope filled her. "You agree that they should be engaged longer?"

He laughed. "Of course I do."

"What are we going to do about it?"

Riley and Antonio walked over again. Antonio addressed his father, "Are you ready to go?"

Lorenzo looked at his watch. "We have about three hours before the plane takes off." He caught Riley's gaze. "That gives you a half hour or so to pack."

Riley said, "Okay." She leaned in and kissed her mother's cheek. "I love you, Mom. I'll see you later." She turned to leave but stopped suddenly. "Actually, I was hoping you could fly to Italy this weekend, and we can start planning the wedding."

GiGi was suddenly beside her. She caught Juliette's hand. "*Sì!* We would love to have you. Stay at the villa. We'll have every waking minute to plan the perfect wedding."

Lorenzo saw Juliette's expression fill with dread, as his mother outlined all the things they had to plan and how they'd be having the ceremony at the villa.

He swore the woman was going to faint or hyperventilate. Obviously accustomed to being the one in charge—as anyone who owned a business was—not being able to voice her opinion was killing her.

He understood. He knew how it was to raise an only child. He knew she felt a certain proprietary interest. Which was foolish. Once a child became an adult, they grabbed on to the life you'd so carefully nurtured and took it for a spin like a shiny new convertible. Various careers and lovers. A little travel. A lot of wine.

Though it seemed Juliette realized she couldn't voice the only dissenting opinion, she was still having trouble processing everything.

She said, "Sure, that's great," to Riley's invitation that she come to Italy. Then Riley, Antonio and GiGi headed out of Central Park to the limo.

Juliette stared after them.

"You wouldn't happen to be able to give me a ride to the airport, would you?"

She spun to face him. Her eyes still spoke of confusion, but he suddenly noticed how green they were. The prettiest green he'd ever seen.

"You need a ride?"

He laughed at the incredulity in her voice. "I was kidding. They might have taken my limo, but I can call a cab." He smiled at her. "I have about an hour if you'd like to go to a coffee shop to talk this out?"

That seemed to knock her out of her shock. Her eyes sharpened. Her full lips lifted into a fake smile. If he hadn't negotiated with world-class businesspeople for the past thirty-plus years, he wouldn't have realized the smile was fake. He wouldn't have seen the determination in those eyes.

"No. Thank you. I'm fine."

He snorted. "I'm sorry, but thirty seconds ago you looked like you were going to faint. I know it's difficult when you feel left out of your child's decisions—"

"Feel left out?" She gaped at him. The fire in her eyes could have set Central Park ablaze. Her shoulders were back. Her breathing became ragged. "This morning, my daughter was snarfing down a doughnut, telling me she was considering giving up on men forever. Now she's engaged and flying to Italy? Yeah. I'm definitely out of the loop."

"Then come with us."

The eyes that had been filled with fire narrowed. "Oh, you'd love that, wouldn't you?"

"This isn't war. There's no need to think I'm planning a sneak attack. We're going to be organizing a wedding." He smiled. "Join us."

She huffed out a sigh. "No. Thank you."

She turned and stormed down the path to the street, leaving him standing at Dene Summerhouse in Central Park. When she was out of range of hearing, he let himself laugh.

She was magnificent when she was angry.

Still, unless he wanted to risk her doing something she might regret when she eventually did come to Italy, he was going to have to keep an eye on her—

Which, actually, wouldn't be a hardship. She was very pleasant to look at. He liked her eyes. He loved her hair. Yellow. Shiny.

And, no, he hadn't missed that she had the figure of Venus.

CHAPTER TWO

JULIETTE CAUGHT A cab back to her office and rode the elevator to the fifth floor, knowing she needed a few minutes alone to think this through before she said anything to anybody. Lorenzo had said this wasn't war and there was no need to think he was planning a sneak attack?

Huh!

She burst out of the elevator and charged down the corridor to the private entry to her office.

That was because his side was winning! He might not be plotting against her but there was a clear strategy in the works. He'd love for her to capitulate, fly to Italy and be the sweet mother of the bride, thrilled because her daughter was marrying above her social status—

She closed her office door and leaned against it.

Dear God. She hoped that wasn't what was really bugging her.

She sat on the tall-backed chair behind her desk and spun it to face her unremarkable view of Manhattan. Her business made lots of money, but she didn't waste it on a showy office with a view. She also shared space and a receptionist with Riley's company.

She was smart. Frugal. Did everything right.

Why? Because Riley's dad's parents had kicked her out of the condo she shared with their son when Greg died unexpectedly. From old money, they'd called her a gold digger, an upstart, and refused to acknowledge Riley.

Instead of being hurt, she'd gotten angry. She'd used that anger to make something of herself. More than something. She now had lots of money. She was well-known. Respected. No supercilious billionaire would ever look down on her again.

She sucked in a breath. All that was true. It was actually a source of pride. Who wouldn't be happy that they were a success?

But was that also why she so desperately mistrusted Antonio's family? Because they were rich the way Greg's family had been?

No. The real question was: Was that why she didn't want Riley marrying into the Salvaggio family?

Juliette tossed a pencil to her desk. No. That wasn't it either. The truth wasn't about the Salvaggio family. It was about *her*. She'd fallen for Greg too quickly. Then she'd gotten pregnant, and they'd made plans to marry…but he'd never married her.

They'd lived together for eight years. At first, getting married just seemed like nothing more than confirmation of what they already knew. They were in love. Then, as the years passed, she had to admit she had wondered why it was never the right time for them to tie the knot. She had no family, and his family wouldn't have wanted to witness them get married. They could have easily gone to the courthouse and gotten married in a quick ceremony.

But they never had. Greg always had a reason. It wasn't until he'd been dead ten years that she'd realized his "reasons" were actually excuses.

He hadn't wanted to marry her.

If she was worried about Riley, it was because she was

worried Antonio would hurt her daughter the way Greg had hurt her. Greg made her feel like the most important person in the world, but he wouldn't commit—

Had he grown tired of her?

Was that why he didn't want to marry her?

Her phone buzzed. Her office assistant's voice came through the speaker. "Juliette, the weekly reports were emailed to us from the accountants. I printed them for you. Do you want to see them now or should I hold on to them?"

She rose from her desk and walked out to Jane Fineman's office. "I'll take them now."

Jane studied her face, then her brow wrinkled. "Are you okay?"

"I'm fine. Riley got engaged. That's the reason I was rushed to Central Park this afternoon."

Jane clapped her hands together. "Oh, that's wonderful!"

"Is it? She hasn't known Antonio very long."

Jane batted a hand. "I didn't know my husband long before we got engaged."

"Engaged is one thing. They want to marry in January."

"*This* January? It's already November. That's only a little over two months from now."

"I know."

Jane sucked in a breath and obviously tried to be diplomatic. "Well, lots of happy marriages begin spontaneously like that."

Juliette smiled to let her assistant off the hook. "Yes. That's true. We'll hope for the best."

She maintained that attitude, pretending to be happy, the rest of Monday and all day Tuesday, but by Wednesday morning, keeping up the pretense wore thin. She called Pete Williams, her second in command, into her office and told him she was going to Italy.

"Don't forget we have meetings with two huge doctor groups on Monday. Recommendations from them could substantially increase our business."

She rose and began organizing her cluttered desk. "I'll only stay until Sunday." She found her briefcase, opened it and slid a bunch of reports inside. "With the time difference, I'll be back on Monday morning. Email all the information I need to read before our meetings."

She went home, packed a bag, called the airline, went to the airport and was in Italy eighteen tiring hours later. Adding the hours of the flight, then a train ride and factoring in the time difference, she arrived in Florence at three o'clock in the morning Italian time.

She'd lost a whole damned day.

Luckily, she caught a cab and could check in at her hotel. She'd gotten the name of the place Riley had stayed at when she visited Antonio and arrived bleary-eyed and exhausted. As she walked through the lobby, she saw that the bar with the glass wall had only a few patrons, all of whom looked about ready to call it a night.

The desk clerk, however, was fresh as a daisy. She cheerfully checked Juliette in as if accustomed to having exhausted Americans show up in the middle of the night and then Juliette headed for the bank of elevators.

She crashed on the bed in the tiny hotel room, then slept until noon Italian time...or six o'clock in the morning Manhattan time.

Groaning, she rolled out of bed to shower and dress for the day, then debated calling Riley to let her know she was there. In the end, she decided to wait until after she ate to give herself time to think of a reasonable excuse for why she'd flown to Italy early.

She could make it look like she was so excited to start

wedding planning that she'd arrived a day early. When really, she wanted some time to talk to her daughter. Alone. She wanted the chance to explain why she should at least delay the wedding until June or July or even November of the following year so she and Antonio would have a real opportunity to get to know each other.

She would have to be crafty about spiriting Riley away for a private talk when the Salvaggio family seemed to be completely on board with this wedding—

Except Lorenzo.

He'd agreed with her that it was all too soon, and maybe she could work that to her advantage.

Lorenzo had spent the morning with his friend and business associate Marco. Though Marco was Italian, he now lived in Paris. He stayed at the same hotel every time he was in town, and usually insisted on having lunch there.

"Don't you love this place?"

Lorenzo gave Marco a sideways glance. "It's kind of Americanized."

Marco spread his hands. "So?"

"I like the United States as much as anyone, but I'm not a fan of a hamburger for lunch."

Even as he said that a pretty woman walked past the big glass wall that separated the restaurant from the lobby.

He stared for a few seconds, taking in her yellow hair and the way her blue jeans hugged her butt, then said, "You're not going to believe this but that looks like Antonio's future mother-in-law."

Marco squinted. "Oh…well, I see where Riley gets her good looks." He straightened in his chair. "Maybe you introduce me?"

Lorenzo's voice soured. "No!"

"Oh, so *you're* interested."

"No. Not because she isn't pretty, but because I think we have some trouble on the horizon. In fact—" he rose from his chair "—I might just check to see if that is her. She's supposed to be coming to help plan the wedding this weekend. There's a good possibility she decided to come a little early."

He paid their bill and raced out of the restaurant. She was nowhere in sight. Enough time had passed that the woman could have already caught a cab or rideshare. But when he returned to the lobby, he saw her at the concierge desk.

"Having a problem?"

She turned. "Lorenzo! What are you doing here?"

"My friend Marco stays here when he's in town. Though I can sometimes persuade him to go to a better restaurant for dinner, this is where he insists on having lunch."

She laughed.

He blinked. She was magnificent when she was angry, but happy she was stunning. Clearly, Riley had gotten her timeless beauty from her mother. Smooth complexion, soft eyes and the kind of mouth that teased men every time it formed a word.

He cleared his throat. "Sorry. What were we saying?"

"You were telling me about your friend Marco."

"He's in the restaurant, about to go to his room to do some work, which means I have time, if you'd like to drive out to the villa with me." He winced. "I assume you're going to the villa?"

"Actually, because of the time change, I slept all morning. I haven't had breakfast yet. I walked out of the hotel, then came back in to get a recommendation from the concierge."

"I can recommend somewhere to eat, and I will be happy to accompany you."

For a second, it looked as if she'd say no. Instead, she

smiled again. "Sure. But nothing big. A bagel, croissant or doughnut would be fine."

He scoffed. "Doughnut? Really?"

"Hey, I'm just looking for enough calories to get me to dinner."

He laughed and directed her to walk to a nearby bistro. When they reached the outdoor seating, he said, "Outside or in?"

"It's a bit brisk."

"It always is in November." He motioned to the door. "Inside it is."

They chose a small table, and a server came over. Juliette ordered a croissant and coffee. He ordered a bottle of water.

As she walked away, Juliette said, "I get it. You're a health fanatic."

"Nope. I'm a person of balance. Tonight, at dinner, you will see me enjoying wine. I am able to do that because I eat right and drink water nearly all day."

"Ah, a smart guy."

She said it teasingly, but there was nothing that turned her on more than a person who looked after themselves. She watched her weight, worked out, worked hard on her business and read to keep her mind sharp. If he told her he'd read any of the recent bestsellers, she'd probably swoon.

But she couldn't swoon. She needed this guy. If one of them suggested the wedding was too soon, Riley and Antonio could brush them off. But if they had a united front, the kids couldn't ignore them.

The waitress came with her food and his water. When she was gone, Lorenzo said, "You know, I wasn't sure you'd show up this weekend."

She stopped her croissant halfway to her mouth. This

could be her opening, but she'd let him talk first. See what he had to say. "Really?"

"You weren't happy about this engagement and marriage."

"I wasn't. But if I remember correctly, neither were you."

He sighed. "I think it's too soon."

"Then why aren't you fighting this?"

"Because Lorenzo is a grown man, and your daughter is also an adult."

"Meaning, we just let them make mistakes?"

"What would you like to do? Devise an evil plan?"

She laughed. "It doesn't really have to be evil." She sighed. "I'd just like twenty minutes alone with my daughter. You could also spend twenty minutes alone with Antonio and express your concerns. Or maybe we could talk to them together?"

He sat back. Juliette surreptitiously studied him. Expensive suit, white shirt, fabulous dark hair. For the first time it struck her that his hair wasn't short and business-like as Antonio's was. It was longer, to his collar, and a little ragged, a little rough around the edges—very sexy.

"Won't that make them feel like we're ganging up on them?"

"You think we should divide and conquer?"

He snorted. "I'm still in the camp that thinks we should let our adult children make their own choices." He paused. "Though, while planning the wedding, items might come up that make them realize waiting a few months might be better."

She set down her croissant. "Such as?"

He toyed with his water bottle. "The temperatures are cold in January. They want to be married in the vineyard. They're so excited right now that it probably hasn't crossed either of their minds that they'll need to wear coats to their ceremony. No strapless dress for Riley."

She smiled. This was the better plan. "And she looks so good in a sweetheart neckline."

He chuckled. "There will also be no reception outside. Which is a shame because GiGi recently redid our outdoor space. In the summer, it would be perfect for a wedding."

"Mentioning that might get GiGi on our side."

He winced. "Don't count on it. She's a tough nut to crack. Right now, she's envisioning a blissful holiday followed by a fabulous wedding in her own backyard. All that stuff grandmas love."

She laughed. "Okay, so what are you not a fan of? Holidays or foo-foo stuff?"

"Don't get me wrong. I like celebrations. But most things are better unplanned and natural." He took a swig of water, set it down then smiled at her. "Like a woman in bed."

Dear God. Sexuality was like breathing to him. Unplanned and natural.

Her chest tightened. Her heart rate had gone wild.

She was fifty. Not dead. And he wasn't much older. He was fifty-five, tops.

He was also gorgeous. And she swore that "unplanned and natural" comment had been flirting.

The server returned with their check. Lorenzo took it and pulled a few bills from his wallet, telling her to keep the change.

Finished with her croissant, Juliette tossed her napkin to the empty plate. "Want to explain that last comment?"

"It's just an expression." He finished his water. "You don't have to worry about me making a move on you. Imagine how awkward holidays would be if you and I had a torrid affair, then split up. We have to be together for baby births, baptisms, birthdays…and all holidays." He rose. "Cute as you are, I've decided you're off-limits."

CHAPTER THREE

LORENZO MOTIONED FOR her to precede him out of the bistro but as soon as they were outside, she turned on him. "First, no one decides anything for me. Second, cute? Seriously? I'm *cute*?"

He pulled out his phone and texted his driver. "What did you want me to say? Your beauty blinds me with its splendor?"

"Now you're just being ridiculous."

He slid his phone back into his pocket. "*Cute* implies young and perhaps impish. You might not want an evil plan, but what we are about to do is devilish."

"Okay. Fine. Whatever. Think what you like. I'm not here to have a fling with you. Just as you said, it would get awkward."

The limo arrived and he motioned for the driver to stay inside and opened the door for Juliette himself.

They slid onto the bench seat, and he pulled the door closed. "So you have flings?"

"You don't?"

"I'm Italian. It's expected of me."

"Meaning, you think an American businesswoman is too what? Too busy? Too uptight to have an affair?"

He caught her gaze. "I don't really know you. You could be."

She gaped at him. "Seriously?"

Right at that moment, he would have given his life savings to kiss her. Her expressions could be so thunderous he knew that kissing her would be explosive—and real. She would give her entire self to a kiss.

Since that was wrong, for all the reasons he'd mentioned, he yanked himself out of that fantasy and shifted to look straight ahead. "Doesn't matter. We are parents of the bride and groom. We have responsibilities. *You* want to delay the wedding. We shouldn't even be thinking about kissing."

An awkward pause followed. Juliette said, "*I* wasn't."

He sucked in a breath. That was a bit of a slipup. But technically there was no harm done.

As pretty as she was, as magnificently energetic and passionate as she was, his assessment was right. There could be nothing between them.

Juliette ignored him for the duration of the ride to the villa, entranced by the raw and beautiful landscape of Tuscany in late fall. She might have asked him what was being harvested in the groves of hills they passed, but he had her too confused.

He agreed about the wedding, but he wasn't going to help.

He decreed that there would be nothing between them when she hadn't suggested there should be.

He told her they shouldn't be thinking about kissing—

When no one had mentioned kissing.

Meaning, he'd been thinking about kissing her. Even as the idea stole her breath, her brain became righteously indignant. He was a bit full of himself.

Of course, he was rich, good-looking, suave—

And he'd thought about kissing her.

The limo eased down a long driveway and stopped.

Within seconds, the driver opened the back door, and she got out in front of a grand three-story yellow stucco mansion. The vineyard behind it was bare but somehow still beautiful in this resting phase. The blue sky looked down on Tuscany lovingly.

"Wow."

Lorenzo put his hand at the small of her back again. This time, knowing that he'd thought about kissing her, the jolt of electricity that flashed up her spine nearly set her sweater on fire.

"This property has been in our family for generations."

Remembering she needed him, she forgot all about the electricity and the fact that he'd thought about kissing her. A compliment could get them to a better place. And, really, that was her goal. Keeping him on her side.

"It's amazing. It's also clear your family takes loving care of your home."

"Thank you. We see it as a responsibility."

There was that word again. *Responsibility.* He thought they had a responsibility to their kids. He had a responsibility to his land.

It was interesting. She might have believed he went a bit overboard, except his sense of responsibility, maybe even duty, fit him.

Greg hadn't seen himself as having a responsibility to anybody or anything. His focus had been on making money.

It certainly wasn't on her or Riley.

That might set Lorenzo apart from Greg, but she couldn't forget that this man who was almost poetic in his love of his vineyard was cut from the same cloth as the family who had kicked her and her innocent child out on the street.

Her sense of reason restored, she allowed Lorenzo to

lead her to the front door. Inside the beautiful foyer, he called, "GiGi!"

Juliette looked up, expecting to see his mother appear at the top of the grand staircase. Instead, Riley said, "We're in here."

She turned in the direction of the voice, but Lorenzo caught her shoulders and looked her in the eyes. "Are you ready for this?"

His dark eyes held hers, giving her a second to take them in and enjoy their sharpness. But she didn't stare long. He'd already thought about kissing her and she didn't want him to get the wrong idea. Plus, his question was actually encouragement of a sort. He wanted her to succeed.

"I think so. I'm going to make your weather the villain in a January wedding."

He laughed. "Good way to look at it."

"I am a fairly successful businesswoman." She slid out from under his hold. "I know how to help my staff see things the way I want them to." She took a few steps toward the room then paused and looked back at Lorenzo again. "I've also been known to charm a banker or two."

Hoping he was following her, she walked through the doorway into a room that could best be described as a family room. Bookshelves, a wet bar and lots of couches and chairs filled the room.

Riley jumped up and hugged her. "Mom! Why didn't you tell us you were coming early?"

GiGi smiled. "*Sì!* We could have had a feast tonight."

Lorenzo finally entered. His jacket gone, his tie loosened, he strode over to the wet bar. He pulled out a bottle of water. "Anyone else?"

There was a general round of refusal, as Juliette eased farther into the room to the sofa where Riley sat surrounded by open books displaying bridal gowns. Unexpected tears formed.

Her baby was getting married.

She stopped the flood of emotion. She could cry all the happy tears she wanted if Riley and Antonio waited until summer to make sure they were doing the right thing.

"I see you're looking at bridal gowns."

GiGi patted the cushion beside her, indicating Juliette should sit. When she was settled, GiGi handed one of the thick books to her. The pages weren't glossy like a magazine or catalog. They were designer drawings. Riley's gown would be an original.

Because she was marrying into a family swimming in old money.

"These are beautiful."

Riley laughed. "I would have been happy to buy something off the rack since time is so limited...but GiGi insisted we needed an original. A gown in a style no one else has ever worn."

Juliette ignored the shout of caution that exploded in her brain because Riley's comment opened an interesting door for another reason to delay the wedding. "Are you sure you'll get the gown by January?"

"Sì," GiGi said. "I will see to it."

"How?"

She laughed. "Money talks."

Discomfort stiffened Juliette's spine. Riley spoke so affectionately of this family that it was clear she didn't see the pretense all around them. Still, this wasn't the time to bring that up. Not when she could use all the issues surrounding the dress to make yet another good argument.

"Technically, as mother of the bride, I should be buying the dress." She glanced around. "Actually, doesn't the bride's family pay for the whole affair?"

GiGi batted her hand. "Don't be silly. With the wedding at the vineyard, it is our honor to foot the bill."

That hadn't worked, but it had opened another door. "The wedding's outside?"

"Just the ceremony," Riley said.

"It's cold in January. That means you're restricted in the kind of gown you can get."

"No! Look!" Riley peered around the sofa until she found the drawing she wanted. She handed it to her mother. "Don't focus on the gown. Just the white velvet cloak." She smiled dreamily. "Look at that hood. I'm going to look like Maid Marian."

Lorenzo finally spoke. "From *Robin Hood*?"

"The remake with Kevin Costner was amazing," Riley gushed.

Staring at the cloak, Juliette reluctantly said, "It *is* beautiful."

Riley handed her drawings of three dresses. "Picture these with the cloak over them," she said helpfully, sounding so happy that Juliette's heart sank.

After another hour of discussing the three gowns, Riley wasn't able to choose from among them and they came to a stalemate. GiGi told her that they'd have the designer do quick versions of all three gowns that she could try on.

Without a pause, GiGi then showed Juliette three menus. She explained that the reception would be in the ballroom, which was down a long hall that she'd be happy to show Juliette.

In the enormous room, Antonio's grandmother pointed to spaces that would be occupied by musicians for dinner music and a band for dancing.

Walking up the hall to return to the front room, Riley talked about flowers from a local florist that she'd interviewed for her Tuscan proposal events. Marietta would be coming as a bridesmaid. Maybe the maid of honor? She hadn't yet decided how big her bridal party would be.

As Juliette took her seat on the sofa again, menus, flowers, music, gowns, cloaks, the ballroom and even the weather tumbled around in her brain like towels in a dryer. And somewhere in the mess, her wish to postpone the wedding kept getting lost.

Every time she tried to think of a way to get Riley alone or simply edge in the thought that the wedding would be prettier, happier, nicer in the summer, someone showed her a wineglass or potential napkins or a swatch of material that might become bridesmaids' dresses.

She bounced from the sofa. "You know, you guys have been looking at all this, planning things since Monday." She forced a smile. "You might have even started on the jet home."

GiGi laughed. "*Sì*, we did!"

"I need some time to catch up."

Riley's face crumpled. "Oh, Mom! I'm sorry. I didn't mean to make you feel left out."

GiGi clutched her chest. "We are so sorry."

"It's fine. Your planning isn't the problem. It's me," she assured them. "I'm jet lagged." She motioned around the coffee table filled with lists and drawings. "There's a lot of stuff going on here for a person to take in all at once." She sucked in a breath. "I should probably go back to the hotel, soak in a bubble bath, maybe go to bed early…"

GiGi frowned. "You are staying at the hotel?"

"Yes. I don't want to impose."

"It's no imposition!"

Lorenzo rose from his seat across the room. He hadn't

said a word in twenty minutes. She'd almost forgotten he was there.

"I think what Juliette is saying is that she will probably be video conferencing with her staff, keeping up with her work while she's here. It's better she have a room in a hotel."

"And the jet lag," Juliette reminded them, trying to mitigate appearing rude. She needed time to regroup.

"You are not staying for dinner?"

"I will tomorrow. I promise. Honestly, I'm simply tired." Riley hugged her.

GiGi warmly said, "We will see you tomorrow," and Lorenzo got her out of the house.

"They overwhelmed you?"

"Yes."

The limo pulled up. Juliette was so flummoxed she hadn't even noticed him texting for it. He opened the door. She slid inside and he followed her.

"I'm sorry. I hope I didn't offend your mother."

"She's a tough old girl. It takes more than that to faze her."

She leaned back on the beach seat. "Not only did I not get any of my points across, but I made myself look like a fool."

"You were fine until GiGi started talking about the flatware, then I think your brain was too full to take in anything else."

"They planned the whole wedding."

"They came up with *ideas* for the whole wedding. Tomorrow when your jet lag is gone, you can give your opinions. Talk things over with Riley, as any mother would when she and her daughter are planning her wedding."

"You think?"

He glanced over. "You don't?"

"Even though I'm trying to delay this—and disagreeing with their choices could start the ball rolling in that direction—I don't want to be that pushy mother who wants everything her way. Plus, I would like to be a part of things if I can't get them to wait until June."

"Makes sense. But it might be fun to see bossy Juliette come out and go toe-to-toe with GiGi about the musicians or the flowers."

She laughed. "No. It wouldn't. And I'm not always bossy."

He gave her a sidelong glance again. "You sure?"

She snorted. "Yes."

"I like your bossy side. I'm guessing it comes from years of running a company."

"It does. Before that I was a sweet, naïve girl. I lived with Riley's father for eight years and we never had a cross word."

"Wow. My wife and I were together for less time than that, and she used to throw dishes at me."

Juliette laughed.

He pointed at his temple. "I've got a wicked scar to prove it."

"Why'd you marry her?"

He sighed wistfully. "Ahh, she was *pretty*. And really something at parties. Everyone adored her. After we got married, I realized she was always effervescent and bubbly because she was always buzzed."

"Close to drunk but not quite there?"

"Yes. Thus, her ability to still be able to toss a dish." He sucked in a breath. "Didn't figure out she had an alcohol problem until after Antonio was born."

She shook her head. "You act like your life together

was no big deal. But I know how hard it probably was. I run a home nursing agency. We've dealt with our share of addictions."

"I knew the marriage was over when Antonio was only two years old. It wasn't difficult to lose her when the time came and that made me sad." He peeked at her again. "What happened to you and Mr. Perfect."

She sniffed. "He wasn't perfect. We just seemed to fit."

"But…"

"But he died."

"Oh, I'm sorry! I remember Riley telling us that. I shouldn't have mentioned it."

"Yeah, well, that's how I ended up becoming tough. His family kicked us out of our condo, refusing to acknowledge Riley and calling me a gold digger." She snickered. "Their hate motivated me to become the best and in my own way I am."

"We sure have a lot of baggage between us."

This time she full belly laughed. "Because we've lived longer than single people in their twenties or thirties." She nudged his shoulder. "But I bet we have better stories."

He leaned down and whispered, "I bet we do."

Time froze. It had probably been the jet lag that caused her to open up to him, but it didn't feel wrong. Riley had obviously told Antonio's family about her father, which was a perfectly normal thing to do. It was the closeness between her and Lorenzo that threw her. He'd all but said he'd thought about kissing her and now here he was, his lips only a few inches away.

The longing to kiss him rippled through her. She told herself it was nothing but curiosity and debated. A kiss did not have to mean they would start something—

But would a kiss be enough? He was gorgeous. His voice

was smooth like a silk scarf running along her skin, raising goose bumps. Plus, she dated. She'd had months-long relationships that were sexual.

But while those guys had great careers and made big salaries, they were not in Lorenzo Salvaggio's league.

Kissing him opened too many doors to temptation that could end up hurting her. And that was reason enough to stay away from him. Particularly since being near him had the whisper of destiny.

Of course, so had her relationship with Greg—the high-society guy who couldn't quite bring himself to marry her.

Yeah. She couldn't forget that.

She eased up on the seat and scooted a few inches away from Lorenzo, refusing the temptation.

He cleared his throat and straightened up too. She took that as confirmation that he agreed with her.

But when they got to her hotel, and she was walking through the lobby, the weirdest sense haunted her. Being around Lorenzo did have a feeling of destiny about it. He was fun, good-looking and charming. Much more so than the men she'd been dating—

Was ignoring this chance really smart or was it a missed opportunity?

CHAPTER FOUR

FRIDAY MORNING, Juliette had just finished dressing when her cell phone rang. Fastening her earring, she raced to answer it, hoping it was Riley, wanting to talk. She and Riley had been close, like girlfriends, most of their lives. They'd lived together until Riley had gotten her proposal planning business on its feet. Now they shared office space and discussed every aspect of their respective companies.

Yet, suddenly, they had no time alone. No time for mother and daughter to talk things out. No time for Juliette to tactfully, respectfully, tell her daughter to wait a while before she married her handsome Italian.

She peeked at the caller ID and sighed with relief. "Riley?"

"Hey, Mom."

She sat on the bed. "What's up?"

"I think you and I need to talk."

She winced. "I'm really sorry about bugging out yesterday."

"And I'm really sorry that we seem to be planning the wedding without you. That's not at all how I wanted this to happen. In fact, I've been thinking you should leave the hotel and stay at the villa for a few weeks. We can all plan together and you can see Antonio and I are the real thing.

You like him, Mom, and I love him. All you need is a little time with us to see that."

Her worst fears melted into a puddle of love for her daughter. Her smart, successful, cautious daughter. She thought of her conversations with Lorenzo the day before. Remembered that she didn't want to be the pushy mother of the bride. Remembered the look of love Riley wore every time Antonio was around.

"Oh, sweetie. That's—" She swallowed, suddenly feeling like she'd panicked prematurely. Riley *was* smart, successful, cautious. No matter how shocking that proposal had been, Riley didn't make decisions lightly. She wanted to marry Antonio. And as her mom, Juliette should be helping with the wedding, enjoying one of the happiest times of a mother's life.

"You know what? Staying at the villa is a good idea. But I can't spend two weeks in Italy until I put everything in order at work. Pete and I have a meeting on Monday with some influential doctors. I can't leave that to him alone. So how about this? How about I go back to Manhattan, go to that meeting and spend time with my staff to arrange things so that everything is set for the weeks I'm away?"

"You promised GiGi you'd have dinner with us tonight."

"I probably won't be able to get a flight out until tomorrow morning anyway. I can still have dinner with the Salvaggios tonight. I'll leave tomorrow and be back on Tuesday or Wednesday. Probably Wednesday considering the hours of travel and the time difference."

Riley's voice perked up. "That's perfect. We'll hold off on planning anything else until you return."

The hotel room phone rang. "Sweetie, the phone is ringing. I'll see you at dinner tonight."

"See you tonight."

Happier than she'd been in weeks, she disconnected her call with Riley and answered the hotel phone. "Hello?"

"It's me. Lorenzo. I came to town an hour early so I can take you to breakfast."

Even in the morning, his voice was as smooth as good whiskey. She instantly shifted from mother of the bride to woman attracted to an extremely sexy guy. Their almost kiss in the limo the afternoon before popped into her head. The sense of destiny. The fact that she could be missing out on something wonderful by ignoring all these feelings.

And the fact that she was about to spend two weeks living in his house.

This time next week, she'd be staying in his villa, enjoying being mother of the bride. She did not want to be distracted from that. Besides, he'd already said, and she'd already agreed, that anything romantic between them was off the table.

"You don't have to do that."

"I insist. Besides, I'm already here. Would it be so terrible to spend time with me?"

His voice and accent caused her hormones to shiver. She shook her head at her own foolishness. Maybe if she spent some more time with him, she'd get accustomed to him, and her unwanted feelings would go away before she found herself spending twenty-four hours a day in his company?

"Why don't we meet at the restaurant in the lobby?"

"I'm already here. I'll get us a table."

"I'll be right down."

She hung up the phone. Grabbing her purse, she left her room then rode the elevator to the lobby. She entered the restaurant and saw Lorenzo seated at a table in the back. He waved her on and rose as she approached.

"Good morning."

He pulled out her chair for her. "Good morning. I see I didn't call too early." He motioned to her soft blue sweater and jeans. "You're already dressed."

He looked cosmopolitan and sexy dressed for work in his black suit and red tie, especially with his dark hair. But she ignored the sizzle of interest that raced through her. They were nothing more than parents of the bride and groom.

"Yes. I was just finishing when you called." She positioned herself in her chair.

"Good. I wouldn't want to disturb your sleep."

Part of her would happily allow him to disturb her sleep anytime he wanted. The other part was smart enough to agree that as parents of the bride and groom, they shouldn't get involved, if only because they would be connected *forever*. They'd spend holidays together. They'd be together for the birth of every grandchild. Then they'd be together at every birthday party for those grandchildren.

If they started something and it fizzled, the rest of her life would be spent with a guy she might have been attracted to but a guy she'd broken up with. That would be amazingly awkward.

"No worries. But maybe it's good we're getting a chance to talk. Riley called this morning. She invited me to spend two weeks at your villa."

He winced. "Since you're not asking me to send a limo for your things, I'm guessing you're not okay with that."

"Actually, I am. I'm dropping my concerns about their wedding to become mother of the bride. I need to go home for a meeting on Monday, and to make sure my business can run without me for two weeks, then I'm coming here to be part of planning the wedding."

His eyes narrowed. "Really?"

She sighed. "Riley is very smart. She's also a good decision-maker. If she wants to marry your son, she's thought it through."

"Ah. You're going to let your adult daughter make her own choices."

Her goose bumps turned to porcupine quills. "You don't have to make me sound like an overprotective mama bear."

He pressed his hand to his chest the way GiGi had the day before. "I didn't mean to! It was a joke."

Her brain froze. He hadn't said or done anything to warrant her snapping at him. But for as sexy as he was, he was a billionaire. In the same class with Greg. Combine sexy and billionaire and the self-protection instincts she should have had with Riley's dad came popping out.

She sighed. "I'm sorry. I'm short. I'm blond. Everybody thinks I need a keeper. My motto is never show weakness."

He chuckled. "You are anything but weak. In fact, your strength is part of what makes you so intriguing."

She felt herself blushing. Men found her formidable, sexy, even a challenge. But no one ever said she was intriguing and damned if that didn't please her a little too much.

She reminded herself that he was in Greg's world, not hers, but even if he wasn't there were plenty of other reasons she couldn't get involved with him. "You know my story. People disappointed me. I had to become strong."

He picked up one of the menus sitting on the table and began perusing it. "I get it. But I'm still sending a limo for you tonight for the dinner you promised GiGi you'd have with us."

His tight tone made her feel a little silly for reminding him she was strong. "I apologize again. I think deciding to spend two weeks planning the wedding has me all wound up and I'm even more feisty than I usually am."

"Feisty." He pondered the word. "I like that."

"I've been told more than once I can be overassertive."

"Honestly? You being you doesn't bother me. After a few decades of running a business, I learned a lot about the importance of getting to know the real person…not the facade they present."

She leaned toward him conspiratorially. "I know! It's amazing how many people are fakes, isn't it?"

"It was the first thing I taught Antonio." He snorted. "The boy is good-looking, rich and smart. I didn't want him to be taken in by someone with a smooth line. Yet he made the same mistake I did and married a trophy wife, who took him for a bundle when he divorced her."

"Riley lived with three guys who weren't right for her."

The server arrived and poured coffee before she wrote down their breakfast orders.

When she walked away, Lorenzo said, "It took a while for me to realize Antonio didn't learn from my mistake because I protected him from his mother."

"Protected him?"

"I was careful about his visits with her when he was a child and even more careful when he became a teenager. His mom was such a party girl that I worried she'd introduce him to more than wine."

Julie gasped. "Oh, my goodness!"

"I did a lot of worrying and watching. Luckily, Antonio was basically a good kid. Head down in school, working toward good grades, knowing the family business would be his responsibility someday."

She nodded.

"Then there's GiGi and her love of people. She's let many a stranger spend weeks at the villa." He shook his head.

"I love her kindness when someone needs a helping hand. But she can't seem to separate the needy from the grifters."

"She has a good heart."

"Yes. And she has me to make sure she doesn't run into trouble with any of her rescues."

From the way Riley had talked, Juliette had believed GiGi was the head of the family, but ten minutes of conversation showed her Lorenzo was. GiGi might rule like a queen, but Lorenzo was the person in the background who saw everything and kept their lives on track. It was equal parts of sexy and confusing. She did not like anyone telling her what to do, yet being the boss was clearly part of his personality.

"I had to gently guide Riley about the first couple of people she hired. She loves everyone too. But every person a manager hires has to be able to do the job. I was lucky that she appreciated my advice."

"It sounds like we're two peas in a pod."

It did…but they weren't. She might have a good life, but he had wealth, power and status beyond what she'd ever know.

She pulled back. "I think you and I are very different."

He laughed. "I have more money, maybe. But you're doing okay."

She nodded. "I am. In fact, I'm doing very well. I came from nothing and became something. I'm a bit of a scrapper."

He chuckled. "Are you telling me that a junkyard dog will beat the purebred?"

"No. Because we're not fighting."

He chuckled softly. "Establishing ground rules, then?"

"Maybe." She'd made the mistake of thinking the differences in her background and Greg's meant nothing. Older, wiser, she knew they had. And that was an error she would not repeat.

The server arrived with their breakfast, and their conversation stopped except for a few comments about their food and the weather. As they finished eating, a tall, dark-haired gentleman walked up to their table.

Lorenzo rose. "Marco! I didn't expect to see you this morning. I thought you had breakfast with another supplier."

He said, "I did. But I spoke with Antonio and he told me you were having breakfast with Riley's mom." He faced Juliette. "You do not look old enough to have a daughter Riley's age."

She laughed at the flattery. She didn't know who this guy was, but he was as smooth as Lorenzo. "I can assure you I am Riley's mom."

"Juliette, this is my *former* friend Marco."

Marco chortled as he faced Lorenzo. "After my meeting, I tried to call you to see if I could get a ride to your office with you. When you didn't answer your phone, I called your house."

Lorenzo winced. "I turned my phone off."

"I see why."

Ignoring the comment, Lorenzo glanced at Juliette. "You are fine on your own this morning?"

Knowing he was only asking out of politeness, not because he thought she was helpless, she picked up her purse and started to rise. "Absolutely."

Marco offered a hand to help her. She took it with a smile. The way Lorenzo's face contorted surprised her, but she ignored it. She had to arrange to go home the next day and should make notes about what things needed to be done while she would be in Italy. She'd be too busy to need a tour guide or someone to eat lunch with.

Which was good. She might have decided he had to be off-limits because he was too much like Greg, but she couldn't talk herself out of being attracted to him.

Still, that was a problem for later. She was a strong enough woman that she could behave so well not one person would even guess she was attracted to him.

"Gentlemen. If you'll excuse me."

Marco gallantly said, "Of course," and let her pass.

Lorenzo said nothing until she was out of sight then he turned on Marco. "What are you doing? I called your office to let you know I wouldn't see you until this afternoon."

Marco shrugged. "Didn't get the message. Besides, some of what we have to do today can't wait till this afternoon."

Lorenzo took a long breath and headed out the door. "You could have told my staff that. Not let me think you'd barged in on our breakfast to meet Juliette."

"What would have been the fun in that?"

His suspicions tripled. "You *did* want to see Juliette!"

He shrugged. "So? You said yourself you aren't interested."

"There's enough stress in this family right now without you playing Romeo."

"I wouldn't play Romeo! I would *be* Romeo."

Lorenzo rolled his eyes. "She wouldn't fall for that."

"Really? Maybe we will see?"

Jealousy set his blood on fire, but he stopped it because Juliette was leaving the next day and Marco would be back in Paris before she returned. The chances of them running into each other again were small.

They walked outside and got into Lorenzo's limo. Marco immediately began discussing business, but Lorenzo only half listened. He wasn't jealous. He really did want Marco to stay out of the picture to prevent even more drama in his family, but damned if it didn't rub him the wrong way that Marco was interested in Juliette.

He tried to comfort himself with the knowledge that anybody would be interested in Juliette. She wasn't just gorgeous. She was smart and strong. As he'd told her, she was intriguing.

And she was the perfect age. They had similar life experiences. He and Juliette could talk honestly and understand each other's perspective—

That was the problem. He wasn't merely attracted to her. He saw something *more* in her. Not just a few dates or an affair...but *more*.

The thought shook him to his core. The guy who'd lived through the marriage from hell was thinking about *more*?

It was foolishness. He had learned his lesson about *more*. If his interest in Juliette went beyond a couple of months of being together for fun, then anything romantic between them really was wrong.

Fun? Fling? Romance? All fine.

Commitment? Seeing her as something more? *Wrong.*

His feelings for Juliette sorted, he forced his attention to what Marco was saying. From here on out, he would redirect conversations with her to the wedding. No more personal chitchat.

When the limo arrived to pick her up that night, Lorenzo was in it. Juliette almost made a comment about how they seemed to spend a lot of time in the back of a car like two teenagers but wasn't sure he'd get the reference. And, if he did, it might not be smart to think about that.

"How was your day?"

She leaned back against the seat. The intimacy of the

space instantly reminded her of how attracted she was to the man sitting next to her, but she didn't let it show. When it came to controlling her emotions, she could have the strength of Hercules.

"I spent it going through digital files and making lists of things I need to discuss with Pete, my second in command, when I get back to the office. I won't leave any stone unturned."

He laughed. "The things we do for our kids."

She snorted. "Tell me about it."

"You really are okay with this wedding?"

"I just needed to remember that my daughter doesn't do anything rashly. I trust her."

"I trust Antonio too."

"They might end up being the happiest two people in the world."

He laughed. "Because they are acting on instinct."

His beautiful accent sent warmth shimmying through her. The instincts it inspired were every bit as tempting as what Antonio and Riley were feeling. Again, she controlled it. Especially when a quick peek at Lorenzo revealed nothing. She might be feeling things, but he was fine.

"Not all instincts are supposed to be followed through on."

"Yes."

The back seat got quiet. The scent of his aftershave drifted to her, and she stifled a sigh. This wasn't a fair fight. He was gorgeous. He smelled great. His accent could charm the angels and he wasn't a bossy, jump-to-conclusions person. He thought about other people. Wanted to see everyone happy. But while he liked her feistiness, he seemed to not be fighting the same attraction she was. Which was a relief. Really. Knowing his attraction to her was dimming as they spent time together would help her stay in line.

The limo stopped in front of the villa. Lorenzo exited and helped Juliette out. They walked into the foyer and were greeted by a gentleman who took their coats.

Lorenzo's head tilted when he saw her pretty blue dress. "You look lovely."

After how neutral he'd been in the limo, she took the compliment as merely a polite acknowledgement from a gentleman. "The way your mother talked, I got the sense that your dinners are semi-formal."

He shrugged. "Sometimes."

"Is tonight one of those times?"

He put his hand on the small of her back to direct her into the living room. "Probably."

She laughed, but with his hand on her back, the sound was strained. Everything about him appealed to her. But he no longer seemed interested.

Because they had kids who were getting married.

Not only did he not want to do anything to jeopardize the fragile peace they'd finally found about the wedding, but they would be connected for years after the wedding. If they started something that ended badly, every holiday would be strained. They couldn't risk it.

He'd said it and now he was behaving appropriately.

It made perfect sense and she would work harder to do the same.

GiGi rose when they entered the room. She wore a scarf over her head that matched her simple green dress. She appeared tired, as if her chemo treatments were wearing her out. When Juliette reached her, she caught both of her hands. "How kind of you to join us."

"Your invitation was kind."

Motioning for Juliette to sit beside her on the sofa, GiGi said, "I understand you're going home for a few days then coming back for two weeks for wedding planning."

"Yes," Juliette said. "I'm very excited."

"So is Riley. She's put everything on hold until you get here." She squeezed Juliette's hands. "I'm so glad you will be staying with us!"

The future bride and groom entered from a doorway in the back. Both were grinning. Antonio said, "Good evening, everyone."

GiGi said, "Antonio! Riley!"

Lorenzo walked to the bar. "Who wants a drink?"

He filled beautiful crystal glasses with white wine and distributed them, then he sat on the big chair on the right of the sofa. Antonio sat on the big chair to the left, with Riley sitting on the chair's wide arm, as if she loved being close to her new fiancé.

Another layer of peace filled Juliette. There wasn't a ripple of discontent. No disturbance in the air. She'd never seen Riley so happy.

The doorbell rang. Not one person in the living room even blinked, as someone from their staff answered it.

After a few seconds, Marco walked in.

Antonio said, "Marco! Thank you for joining us."

Marco grinned. "Thank you for inviting me."

GiGi and Lorenzo rose. GiGi clasped his fingers the same way she had Juliette's. "It is wonderful to see you."

Lorenzo shook his hand. "Yes. *Wonderful*."

Juliette glanced from one man to the other. Marco looked like a guy who'd pulled off a great coup. Lorenzo looked like someone had stolen his lunch.

Marco headed for the sofa. "Juliette! Lovely to see you!"

Just when Marco would have sat beside her on the sofa,

Lorenzo intercepted him. "Please. You're a guest. Take the chair." He pointed at the chair he'd been sitting in and blocked the way to the sofa.

Marco paused. Juliette swore he was about to argue, then he smiled broadly and said, "Thank you."

He sat on the chair. Lorenzo sat beside Juliette on the sofa.

She peeked at him from her peripheral vision. He'd clearly not wanted Marco to sit on the sofa—

A laugh bubbled up and she swallowed it.

He was jealous.

All this time she'd been so worried about controlling her own feelings, she hadn't seen his weren't as simple and handled as he'd tried to make her think.

Then Marco had shown up.

And calm, cool, collected Lorenzo was jealous.

CHAPTER FIVE

HE WAS NOT JEALOUS.

Lorenzo told himself that as they ate dinner. He reminded himself of that when they sat in the living room with dessert.

When everyone was finished, Antonio and Riley excused themselves. They had plans with another couple in town.

After they exited, Marco rose. "This has been wonderful," he said to GiGi. "But I need to get back to my hotel." He faced Juliette. "We're staying at the same place. Shall we ride together this time?"

Lorenzo's nerves crackled. They shouldn't have. Not only had he decided that he and Juliette couldn't be romantically involved, but also it made sense for Marco and Juliette to leave at the same time and share the limo. Plus, there was no reason for him to ride into town again, except he liked Juliette's company—

And that was dangerous territory. Something he should be avoiding.

Still, he didn't like the idea of Marco romancing her. She was a good person who'd been hurt once. Marco could hurt her again. God only knew what could happen in the darkness and privacy of the back of the limo—

Oh, Lord. Why had he let himself think about the darkness and privacy of the back seat of a limo? He knew exactly what could happen!

She started to rise. His nerve endings renewed their crackle—

But GiGi stopped her. "Stay a bit, Juliette." She caught Lorenzo's gaze. "You too." Then she rose and walked over to hug Marco. "It was lovely seeing you."

He kissed both her cheeks. "You too, GiGi."

He faced Juliette. "Maybe you and I can have breakfast tomorrow?"

"She's leaving early tomorrow." The words were out of Lorenzo's mouth before he even thought about them. But they were true. She was leaving town. She'd be back in a few days but there was no reason for Marco to know that.

Marco inclined his head. "Then I'll say goodnight."

He left the room, and silence hung in the air like a cloud of doom. He wasn't sure what his mother wanted to discuss with him and Juliette, but she rarely asked for privacy.

She took the big chair and motioned for them to sit across from her on the sofa. They sat simultaneously like two bad kids who'd been sent to the headmaster's office.

"Juliette, I'm so happy that you are going to be spending time in the villa."

Juliette smiled. Lorenzo sat back on the sofa. Juliette had told him she'd be staying at the villa, but that fact suddenly hit him full force. He would see her breakfast, lunch and dinner. Of course, he could spend a lot of time in his office and if need be he could hide out in the den. But he wasn't a coward. Surely, he could get control of his attraction to her.

"There are many things we have to plan for the wedding."

GiGi said, "*Sì*. But I also want this time to get to know

you. We'll be spending a lot of time together over the years."

"Yes. We will."

"I want you to be comfortable in our home. I almost feel like we should dedicate a suite to you so that you will know you are always welcome anytime."

"You are extremely kind. But I don't want you to go out of your way for me."

"It is no trouble. Though I'm sure you'll want Riley and Antonio to visit you in Manhattan—especially once the grandkids arrive—holidays might be easier here."

Juliette nodded. "It would be simpler for me to fly here than it would be for Antonio and Riley to pack up kids and Christmas gifts and whatever else just to even the score about who visits when."

Lorenzo glanced at her in surprise. When she said she thought something through, she thought it through the whole way. And extremely honestly. Selflessly. She could be arguing to get at least one holiday in her home. Instead, she thought of Riley and Antonio and their future kids.

Something his ex would have never done.

GiGi said, "Which is why I think assigning one of our suites to you permanently might make the whole transition easier."

Juliette hesitated, then she inclined her head. "It might. But the truth is everything is happening so fast that I feel like maybe we should just let some things work themselves out."

GiGi laughed. "I'm an old woman who has very happily gotten new life in her home again. I want everyone to be happy with what we decide."

Lorenzo said, "We will be. But I think Juliette's correct. We have so much to do with the wedding that we can figure the other things out later."

"Okay." GiGi agreed but she sighed and rose. "Sometimes I know I fuss too much. But it gives me great joy to have a future with my family again. Now, if you'll excuse me, I've worn myself out today."

Lorenzo kissed his mother's cheek before she walked out of the room and to the elevator that would take her to her second-floor suite. When she was gone, he faced Juliette. "I hope she didn't offend you."

"I hope I didn't offend her, but you have to admit things are happening so fast we're getting ahead of ourselves."

"Yes and no. You have an uncanny ability to put us back on track."

"Right. Yesterday, I got overwhelmed. Today, I nixed the idea of getting a permanent suite in your house when GiGi might be right. But it just seems off to be planning the next twenty years of our lives."

"GiGi isn't planning twenty years. I think she simply wants everything settled so she can enjoy it in the last years she has left." He laughed. "Besides, there are people who would pay good money for a permanent suite here."

"I'm sure." She rose with a sigh as GiGi had. "Honestly, it's been such a long day and tomorrow I'm flying out again. I should get back to the hotel."

He stood up too. "Okay."

Juliette headed for the foyer, and he walked out after her. He took her coat from the butler and helped her slide into it.

She faced him with a smile. "I'll see you when I return?"

"Actually, you're not done seeing me today."

She smiled slyly. "Are you afraid of me being alone with the limo driver?"

Oh, Lord. She hadn't missed his maneuvering with Marco. "No. Marco took the limo. I'll be driving you back to the hotel."

* * *

Juliette blinked. She hadn't thought anything of it when Marco left, but even if the Salvaggios had an extra limo, there probably wasn't a second driver on duty.

Lorenzo led her to a huge garage to the right of the house. They walked in through a side door, and he hit a button that caused a cascade of lights until the entire garage was lit. Unlike the garages she'd seen in her neighborhood when she was a kid, this one was open. Cars weren't parked in a straight line. They were angled as if they were being displayed.

And why not? She saw a Bentley, an Aston Martin, four sports cars she couldn't name, and various SUVs and sedans, probably for everyday use.

"Holy cow!"

"You've never seen a garage before?"

"I've never known anyone who owned…" She paused to count. "Fifteen cars."

"Antonio is the car guy. Now that I've done with my years of speeding on the A1, I'm happy with a limo and an SUV." He motioned around the room. "What's your pleasure?"

She didn't even hesitate. "I love the Aston Martin."

He walked to the back, where he used a keypad to unlock a room. A few seconds later he emerged with the car starter. He opened the passenger door for her and scooted around the front to get behind the wheel.

She caressed the leather. "This is beautiful!"

He laughed. "We like it."

He started the car and drove to a garage door that opened automatically as he approached, then they headed out into the night. Accustomed to city lights, she was amazed at how dark it was when they reached the country road.

The beautiful night and beautiful car were so romantic that she struggled with her attraction again. After short stretches of time with his family, they always seemed to end up alone. But the chat with GiGi reinforced what they both already knew. They would be together, as family, forever now. A romance between them was out of the question.

The car sputtered oddly. Lorenzo muttered, "What the heck?" Then he looked down at the console and sighed. "Antonio and Riley must have taken this car out for their errands today."

He turned the vehicle to the side of the road. The car sputtered some more then slowed to a stop on the berm.

Lorenzo faced her. "We're out of petrol."

"Well, that's not good."

"We're not even a mile from the house." He opened his car door. "Consider it a stroll in the moonlight."

He closed his door and disappeared into the darkness. Juliette opened her door and found him walking around the back of the car, on his way to help her out. She displayed her pale blue high heels. "These aren't walking shoes, buddy."

He took her hand, nudging her out of the car. "Don't tell me you've never spent a day running around Manhattan in those beauties."

She scowled. "I have. But it's not the same as walking on the side of the road."

"You can walk on the road. Pretend it's a sidewalk."

She sighed and they made their way to the pavement. She could feel the shale and dry dirt taking chips out of her pretty blue shoes. But she didn't say a word or even sigh. Things like cars running out of gas happened.

"I never even thought to check the gauge."

"Because you have staff who does that?"

"Well, yes."

His billionaire mindset sent another ripple of warning through her. He could be so open and congenial that she sometimes forgot how wealthy and pampered he was. How different his life was from hers.

He sighed. "I'm guessing Antonio and Riley returned after the maintenance guy went home for the day. He probably would have filled the tank first thing in the morning."

She glanced up at the wide-open sky. The stars were bright. The crescent moon looked like a shiny sliver of glass. He might be pampered but she wasn't. Pretty shoes or not, she wasn't afraid of a little walk, especially on such a beautiful night. "The sky is so clear."

He peeked up. "I know."

She took a long breath of the air that held the scent of the soil and the plants it nurtured. It was all amazing, but it was also dark. So dark she could barely see where they were going.

Half of her was tempted to nestle against him. Now that the thrill of the beauty of her surroundings was gone, her courage began to desert her, and she started to wonder if Italy had bears…or wolves…or snakes. Did snakes sleep at night? Or did they prowl?

She shuddered.

"Are you cold?"

"No. Letting my imagination run wild. You don't have bears or wolves around here, do you?"

He laughed. "You really are a city girl."

She lifted her chin. "Nothing wrong with that."

"Nothing at all," he agreed with a chuckle. "I love Manhattan and I like your city-girl sophistication."

"Okay. Let's see. You find me intriguing. You like my

sophistication. You like that I'm feisty. Anything else I should know?"

"I wanted to ask Marco to shut up and stop stealing all your attention at dinner."

She laughed. "I picked up on that."

He snorted but said nothing and she winced. GiGi wanting to assign a suite to her really had brought home how connected she and Lorenzo would be in the future. If he was fighting the same attraction she was, this was something they needed to discuss.

"Don't clam up now."

"Why not?"

"Because we need to talk about this. Marco monopolizing the conversation annoyed you because you were jealous, and it might be smart if we got it out in the open so we could deal with it."

"Deal with me being jealous?"

"In a way, we've already sorted all this. We're not good for each other. Our kids are getting married. Our lives will be connected forever. If we give in to our attraction, then every holiday, baby baptism and birthday could be awkward. GiGi wanting to give me a permanent suite in your house really brought that home for me."

"Which makes me right. It's pointless to talk about the fact that I'm so ridiculously interested in you that I got jealous."

She casually said, "Yeah," but the feeling racing through her wasn't as simple as agreement that he was correct, or disappointment that they were wrong for each other, or even flightiness like the sense of destiny she'd had about him when she first met him. The feeling that lodged in the pit of her stomach was somehow different. The sense that being logical was the wrong move here.

He took her hand in the darkness. "This isn't a pass. This is for guidance. It's dark out here."

His hand felt so good wrapped around hers. "And there might be bears."

Even as she said that, her foot missed the pavement and fell another three inches to the dirt. Her ankle gave, but so did her heel. When she heard a slight snap, she prayed it was her shoe.

She stopped.

"What's up?"

"I either broke my ankle or my shoe."

"If it was your ankle you'd be crying."

He stooped down, took her foot in his hands. The way he gently turned it from side to side almost felt like a caress.

Tingles of arousal formed where pain should have been. Her ankle definitely wasn't broken.

"It's your shoe. You no longer have a heel on your high heel."

She swallowed, almost willing him to slide his hand from her ankle up her calf. It felt so wonderful to have him touch her.

But it was wrong. It had to be wrong. Babies, baptisms, birthdays had to be considered. Plus, they were worlds apart as she and Greg had been. And she knew how that ended.

She swallowed again. "So, my shoe is broken?"

"Yep. The good news is you can see the villa lights from here. I told you we hadn't even gone a mile."

"Well, the bad news is my hobbling on one shoe will slow us down."

He laughed. "I could always put you on my back. Like the piggyback rides I used to give Antonio when he was a toddler."

She sighed. With the way her thoughts kept going back

and forth it was not wise for her to be that close to him. "Or I could take my other shoe off and walk barefoot."

"It's cold."

She rubbed her arms. "I know. And the longer we stand out here talking about it, the colder it gets."

He lifted her second foot and removed the other shoe. "Okay, but if you change your mind—"

She laughed. "I won't." She couldn't. His being jealous had tickled her a little too much. Still, she could talk herself out of that. She could also keep the attraction at bay by sheer force of will. But she wouldn't tempt fate by putting them into any closer proximity than they already were.

They walked a bit with her feet feeling both the cold and the stones. The lights of the villa buildings got closer and closer but when they reached the lane to the house, she realized they weren't actually home yet. There was at least a quarter mile to walk down the long lane to the house.

He paused. "Okay. We're done with you showing me how tough you are." He presented his back. "Hop on."

She sucked in a breath. With freezing feet that had been bitten up by stones, she couldn't argue. She walked over. Balancing her hands on his shoulders, she hiked first one knee against his side, then the other.

He handed her shoes to her then put his hands beneath her butt and hoisted her up higher. "You settled?"

She burst out laughing to hide the sizzle of attraction that zipped through her. "Yes."

"Do you want me to whinny or snort or something? Antonio seemed to particularly enjoy that when he was four."

She laughed again. "No. Let's just get back to your house."

But the temptation arose to snuggle against his back, nuzzle her nose in his shaggy hair, sniff his aftershave.

Just the thought tightened her chest, so she stopped herself, keeping herself a few inches away from nestling against him—or even leaning against him.

She couldn't even imagine what he was feeling with her thighs against his sides and her dress riding up almost to her hips.

There simply was no graceful way to ride piggyback.

Two steps before they would have turned to walk down the lane, car lights approached, illuminating their path as the vehicle drove by.

"Well, that's about ten minutes too late."

Juliette said, "Yeah. Are you sure you're okay carrying me? I could probably tough out the walk down the lane."

"I'm fine. You're not exactly heavy."

Right in that moment she thanked her lucky stars that she worked out regularly and rarely indulged in the doughnuts Riley liked so much.

As she'd assumed, the remainder of the walk took fifteen minutes. Fifteen long minutes of temptation. Especially after the scent of him wafted to her naturally. It seemed a shame that they were from such different worlds and also had a future of potentially awkward holidays to consider.

When they reached the stairs to the stoop in front of the door, he slid her down and punched in a code to open it. She eased her scrunched dress down her thighs and desperately tried to regain her dignity as she forced herself to forget the feeling of being so close to him.

He opened the door and she gingerly walked inside, removing her coat and hanging it on the newel post of the stairway. "My feet are probably filthy. Can you get me a cloth or a towel, so I don't leave footprints all over the place?"

He laughed and walked away, returning with a wet cloth

and a dry one. Then he headed for the sitting room. "I don't know about you. But I think this calls for bourbon."

She finished wiping her feet. Whether he was tired from carrying her or as flummoxed by their proximity as she was, it didn't matter. A drink was definitely in order. "I think it calls for bourbon too."

She walked into the room to find he'd lit a fire in the stone fireplace. The warmth of it reminded her how cold she was. She padded over to him. He handed her drink to her. "Thanks."

The fire illuminated the small section in front of the sofa. They sat and she sighed with relief.

He took a sip of his bourbon, then sighed too. "What a night."

She laughed. "I know."

He pulled a throw from the back of the sofa and tucked it around her, leaving the hand holding her drink free. "I don't think you and I have ever had a normal time together."

She snuggled into the throw. "Breakfast the day I got here was pretty normal."

"You mean the day we were talking about our evil plan?"

She laughed.

"I hate to tell you this, but that's not normal."

He lifted the corner of the throw and eased under with her. "You know, things like this aren't supposed to happen to suave rich guys."

"So I've heard."

He leaned against her, sharing her warmth. "But maybe this is part of what makes you so intriguing."

She almost snorted bourbon through her nose. "Usually when a guy tells a woman she's intriguing it means she's stunning, sleek, sophisticated. Not trouble."

"Oh, I don't know. Sometimes trouble's fun."

She glanced at the elegant, controlled guy beside her. "Were you ever really in trouble?"

He shrugged. "All kids push a boundary or two." He glanced over at her. "I'll bet you did."

"Believe it or not, I didn't. Being on my own after my parents died, I couldn't. And I stayed that way. I don't throw temper tantrums or complain out loud."

"Just in your head."

"Just in my head."

"That doesn't give a guy a chance to argue his case."

She pondered that. "Never thought of it that way."

"What else don't you do in Manhattan?"

"Walk barefoot. Anywhere. Ever."

He gasped. "That's a shame. There's nothing like the feeling of soft grass under your feet."

"I sort of remember from my childhood." She took a drink of her whiskey, then sighed. "Anyway, as much as I'd love to just sit here and watch the fire, I need to get back to the hotel."

"Why don't you stay tonight?"

She slowly turned her head to look at him. He was such an open, honest person she couldn't believe he was hinting at something. But she didn't know him well enough to assume he wasn't. "You're not asking what it sounds like you're asking, are you?"

"I wish I could. But we both know anything between us is a potential landmine in the future. That means we're not looking at this as just fun. We both know there could be something more and we both know that doesn't work for us. Otherwise, we wouldn't care. We'd jump into bed and never think of it again—except fondly."

She laughed, but the truth of that rumbled through her. She might have thought the similarities between his life and Greg's were what bothered her, but that wouldn't matter if she was simply thinking about an affair. Just like him, she realized there could be something more between them. And *that* was where the trouble lay.

"Yeah. I get it."

He thought for a second, then said, "All that is true, but you know what? I don't think it's fair that we never even get to kiss, to get a taste of what we're missing."

With him so close, the heat of him keeping them both cozy and warm, it did seem a shame that they'd never kiss.

She set her bourbon on the coffee table and leaned toward him. He leaned toward her. Their mouths met softly, chastely, then he pulled away.

She caught his shoulders and brought him back. That was not the way he wanted to kiss her or she wanted to kiss him. She opened her mouth over his and after a quick second of shock, he put himself into the kiss.

Tingles of arousal poured through her. She slid her hands up his shoulders to his nape to feel his hair. He deepened the kiss again, his tongue sliding across hers, raising goose bumps. She wiggled closer, pressing against him, making herself sigh with pleasure. If they ever got the chance to make love, she would drown in him.

The thought brought her back to her senses. She pulled away and they stared at each other.

Then he smiled sexily. "I knew it would be worth it."

That brought her out of her haze. If she stayed another ten minutes with this guy, under this blanket, they'd end up doing things they'd agreed they weren't going to do. Gloriously seductive, his kiss had drawn her into a place she hadn't been in decades. She'd felt the sweet sensation of connection, along with that cursed feeling of destiny.

The connection she could deal with. That sense of destiny was nothing but trouble. He might like trouble, but she didn't.

She rose from the sofa. "Let's get me to the hotel."

He groaned. "Really?"

She busied herself picking up the throw they'd snuggled under and neatly folding it. "Yes. I have a plane to catch tomorrow."

He gave her a confused look. "You're ending our night when it feels like we're just getting started?"

"You're incorrigible." She marched to the foyer where she found her coat and shoes but only one was wearable.

He leaned against the doorway. "You're going to have to walk into a lobby, past a noisy bar, with only one shoe."

She sucked in a breath. "Better late at night than in the morning when people are sober and wide awake."

He laughed. "Perhaps. But let me suggest that you stay overnight and tomorrow you can borrow a pair of your daughter's shoes. We can put you in a suite and call it yours permanently, the way GiGi wanted."

She sighed. "I really do need to get back to the hotel. I haven't even changed my flight yet. Then I'd like to get at least a little sleep, so I don't arrive in Manhattan like a zombie."

"Okay. But you wait here. Let me get the car."

"All right."

He arrived a few minutes later with a big black SUV. She raced outside and opened the door before he could.

By the time they reached her hotel, she'd decided to toss her shoes in the trash, so she didn't have to carry them—all but suggesting people look at her feet—as she walked through the lobby without shoes.

He laughed as he parked the car. "At least let me walk in with you so your bare feet aren't so obvious."

"You think people won't notice I'm barefoot if I walk in with you?"

"I think people won't care that you're without shoes. They'll look at us, wonder what we're doing in a hotel, wonder if we're married, or having an affair."

She laughed and shook her head. He was probably right. "Whatever."

They walked into the hotel and through the lobby as if nothing was amiss. She knew people noticed them. She knew they wondered who they were just as Lorenzo had suggested.

When they got to the elevator, she giggled. "That was sort of fun."

"Affairs with me are *always* fun."

She didn't doubt it for one second.

He pressed the button for the elevator. The doors opened slowly. She started inside. "Thanks for dinner, the ride to town and mostly for the piggyback ride."

He laughed, caught her hand and pulled her out of the elevator again. Before she could stop him, he kissed her deeply, then looked into her eyes.

"I want you to dream about me tonight."

She walked into the elevator shakily. Good grief! Either he was the most suave, sexy guy in the world…or he had some of the best lines.

The doors began to close. He smiled at her.

She stared at him. When the two panels met fully, she blew her breath out on a long sigh.

Wow. Just wow. She hadn't had feelings like these *ever* in her life. She'd thought falling for Greg was romantic and it had been. But this was beyond that. Warm. Tingly. And connected. There was something wonderful about being with him. Almost like they understood each other.

And maybe they did? They were well versed in the game of life. They knew the realities of sex and relationships. And they still wanted it.

They both wanted it. Each could feel that coming from the other. She couldn't hide it any more than he could.

But it was a complication. Their lives were such that they couldn't have anything but an affair. They couldn't "date." Whatever they had would lead nowhere. So...

They would have to have a secret affair. That way there would be no mess when they broke up and still had to see each other for their grandchildren's baptisms and birthdays—

After the thrill of the short walk to the elevator, a secret affair didn't merely seem possible...it felt romantic. And after that kiss she wasn't sure if her thinking was correct or if a secret affair simply felt so right that she wasn't thinking at all.

Which made it good that she was going home. She'd be back in a few days to spend two weeks at the Salvaggio villa and the temptation would be overwhelming. She definitely needed some distance to clear her head.

They both had to be on the same page. Secret affair. No talk of the future. Just fun for however long it lasted.

If they didn't agree, then they had to be adults and stop flirting.

She laughed. She wasn't entirely sure Lorenzo knew how to stop flirting. But she did. Sexy or not, he wasn't irresistible... He was close. But she was the one who had taught Riley had to be a strong, smart woman.

She could handle this.

Though it was late, she called the airline and changed her ticket before she showered and packed to return to Manhattan. She woke early, dressed and headed out. If she hurried, she had just enough time to get to the airport, check in and grab a bagel at a coffee shop in the terminal.

Happy with her plan, she rolled her suitcase to the door and opened it. A box fell into her room. Confused, she bent down and picked it up. A note was taped to it.

I couldn't find a shoemaker to fix your heel, but my assistant did find these this morning.

She opened the box and found a pair of blue shoes identical to the ones she'd broken the night before.

She laughed out loud, then packed the shoes in her suitcase and left her room to check out. It was definitely time to leave. The man could charm the birds from the trees. At home, she would develop a plan to resist him.

CHAPTER SIX

SATURDAY MORNING, Lorenzo woke knowing he wouldn't see Juliette that day. She was returning to New York, but when she came back to Italy, it would be for two weeks—

And she'd be living in his house.

Decisions needed to be made before then So maybe it was a good thing she'd left for a while. These days apart gave them a cooling off period. The next time they saw each other, their kisses wouldn't be so fresh in their minds, and they could behave like adults about it.

Which was wise.

Smart.

Because getting involved with each other might not be the good idea he had thought it to be the night before when they were snuggled under the blanket. In the light of day, he remembered that they had babies and birthdays and holidays to consider. No one wanted things to be awkward between them, ruining festive events for everyone. Especially not him. Or Juliette. She'd said no at least three times the night before, when he would have thrown caution to the wind.

As much as he liked her, an affair between them clearly wasn't a good idea.

He pondered that as he was driven to work to catch up on things best handled on Saturday morning when his office was quiet. The limo now reminded him of Juliette. Reminded him of how sassy and funny she could be. Reminded him that in a world of people who wanted something from him, she didn't give a damn who he was. She spoke her mind.

Sleeping with her would probably be as honest and real as it was fun.

To get those vivid images out of his brain, he read contracts all morning and by noon he was exhausted and sick of legalese. After lunch with GiGi, he went to the den where he found a sporting event on the television and relaxed in a recliner to watch it.

Just when he was getting into the game, Antonio walked in. "Funny thing."

Lorenzo sat up. "What?"

"Gino told me you sent him down the road this morning to get the Aston Martin."

"Because you used all the petrol, and the car conked out when I was driving Juliette back to her hotel. It was no big deal."

Antonio flopped on a chair. "Gino said it was over half a mile down the road. How'd you get back to the villa in the dark?"

"Walked."

"You walked?"

"Yes."

"Interesting."

He gaped at his son. "Why is that interesting?"

"Because one of the staff said they heard someone say that they'd seen someone walking along our road with a woman on his back."

He sputtered upright. "The heel broke off her shoe! And since when do you listen to someone who says they heard someone who heard someone else say something? That's usually gossip."

"But you admitted it."

"Okay. This time it wasn't gossip. But I taught you better than to listen to rumors."

Antonio laughed heartily. "I'd have paid to see that. You're both such sticks in the mud—"

Righteous indignation roared through Lorenzo. "I'm not a stick in the mud!"

His son batted a hand. "I don't remember the last time you did something foolish."

"It's called being an adult."

Antonio took the remote and focused his attention on the TV. "Whatever."

He said it simply, ending the conversation and the teasing, but a sharp jab of reality stabbed through Lorenzo. His life had gotten predictable and boring. Now fate had sent Juliette to him, and he was arguing?

He pulled in a breath, pretending to fix his attention on the TV again, but Antonio was too damned right for him to focus. Where was his spunk? His fire? He was wild about Juliette and lusting after her like a schoolboy. Not so long ago, he wouldn't have talked it to death. He simply would have initiated an affair. After what would undoubtedly be the best sex of his life, he would have reminded her it would be prudent to keep their relationship to themselves. Because if no one knew they were sleeping together, then no one would be awkward at birthdays and baptisms and whatever the hell else they would do together.

The only two people who would know if they were sleeping together or had broken up would be him and Juliette. And they'd already proven they could keep a secret—

And be mature after a breakup. Despite his horrible marriage, he never spoke unkindly about his ex for Antonio's sake. And despite her horrible situation with Riley's father, Juliette didn't speak ill of him.

They were the perfect candidates for an affair.

Sunday at noon, Juliette's phone rang just as she was struggling with her takeout lunch, her briefcase and the key to unlock her front door. Traveling the day before had been exhausting enough that she'd spent what was left of Saturday recovering from jet lag. But that morning she'd called Pete, her second in command, and arranged to meet him at the office to begin sorting through the work he would be handling for the next two weeks. In four hours, they had put a significant dent in the projects he would oversee while she was gone. But, not wanting to overwhelm him, she'd stopped at noon, then gone to a deli for a good salad because she was starving. Whoever was calling they were going to have to wait.

The lock gave and she entered her condo, racing the distance to her kitchen island to rid herself of the salad and briefcase.

Out of breath, she rummaged through her purse for her phone and answered, "Hello?"

Lorenzo's laugh drifted to her. "Working? On a Sunday? We *are* the two most boring people in the world."

Her heart stuttered. She hadn't thought she would miss him—or that beautiful voice—but the sound of it filled her with pleasure. "You know I had to come home to prep Pete to work without me for two weeks."

She slid out of her coat, then curled up on her sofa, her toes under her butt. Just hearing his voice had zapped her tiredness and while she should probably be careful about that, she needed this break.

"Exactly. That's boring."

"Oh, yeah. What did you do today?"

"Today is my second day of reading contracts."

"Ugh! And you called me boring! There is nothing more boring in the world than reading contracts." She paused only a second, then said, "So what's up? Nothing wrong with the kids, is there?"

"No. They're still gloriously happy and looking forward to your arrival."

"I thought they'd be wedding planning."

"No one is even talking about it. Riley said she wants you in on all that fun, so no one is even permitted to mention a potential appetizer."

She laughed.

"You really do have a good relationship with her."

"And you have a good relationship with Antonio."

He paused. His voice was cautious when he said, "That sort of brings me to the reason I called."

"The fact that we're good parents?"

"Yes. We're such good parents that we want to do all the right things for our kids. But I think denying ourselves the pleasure of an affair goes above and beyond what good parents would do."

Her heart rate plunged then shot up again. "You think we should have an affair?" The memory of their kisses flashed through her brain and her chest tightened, her breath stuttered.

"Yes."

"You're willing to risk the weirdness that could follow when we end it?"

"That's the beauty of my plan. If we don't tell anybody about it, there won't be any weirdness."

"Except between us."

"I don't think so. We're older. Smarter. We've both been

hurt. We know good sex isn't love and even if we did fall in love, we know love doesn't last. We also know what's important in life. Our kids. Neither one of us would do anything to hurt them. So we'd always be cordial when the family is together."

She bit her lower lip. She understood what he was saying because she'd considered a secret affair herself. But something hovered on the edges of her brain, a warning that was more of a feeling than a fact.

"So, what are your thoughts?"

She took a breath. Even as every nerve ending in her body tingled at the possibility, her brain held back.

"As much as I want to say yes, I need to think about it."

"Okay. You're working until Tuesday. By the time you leave for Italy it will be Wednesday. Plenty of opportunity to think about it."

She hoped so because on Wednesday night they'd both be living in his villa, seeing each other every day—

It was no wonder he'd brought up the possibility of an affair. Spending that much time in the same space, their attraction would be off the charts.

Unless they controlled it. Or satisfied it. Giving in behind closed doors meant not fighting it twenty-four hours a day.

It also meant closeness and happiness with a guy who was charming and fun.

She swallowed. She hadn't wanted something the way she wanted this in years. "Okay. I'll think about it."

"Good. We'll talk when you get here."

She almost said goodbye to him, glad he wasn't going to belabor the issue, then she remembered the shoes. "Wait! I forgot to thank you for the shoes!"

He laughed. "Ah, yes. The shoes. I'm afraid I can't take credit. My assistant got them."

She frowned. "How did she know I needed them?"

"That I can take credit for. I phoned her on the way back to the villa that night to tell her what had happened and mentioned that I wanted you to have replacement shoes first thing in the morning. She volunteered to find them immediately so you could take them home with you."

"That was very kind of her. But they were at the hotel when I left for the airport. That couldn't have been more than four or five hours. She had to order them in the middle of the night."

"Probably."

"She lost sleep over my shoes?"

He laughed. "She loves her job and makes an extremely generous salary. She also likes to keep me happy. It wasn't a big deal."

He might not understand it, but it *was* a big deal. Still, she didn't say anything more about it, just said goodbye when they disconnected the call.

But at least now she knew what the negativity haunting her was all about. Telling her about the shoes, he'd sounded so much like Greg that their different stations in life stood out like neon signs.

Still—

Did it really matter that he had more money than some small countries, when they were only considering an affair? She'd wanted to marry Greg. She did not want to marry Lorenzo.

Just to have some fun.

She glanced around her silent living room. Because he was right. She wasn't entirely sure *he* was boring, but her life had definitely gotten quiet and predictable.

Still, her only daughter was about to marry his only son. One slip could ruin their wedding, and with them living in the same house the opportunities for slipups were too great. They would have no privacy. No space where it wasn't possible for someone to barge in on them. The very thing that made an affair seem like a necessity also made it an impossibility.

Her priority in Italy had to be wedding planning, not romancing the groom's dad.

Tired of thinking about it, she picked up the remote and turned on the news to distract herself. Monday morning, she and Pete attended the meeting with the doctor group and Tuesday she worked furiously, so she wouldn't have time to think about Lorenzo or the wedding or anything but the tasks she needed to accomplish. Then she caught a late-night flight on Tuesday night so she could sleep on the plane.

With the train ride, she arrived in Florence on Wednesday night. Her heart fluttered just thinking about seeing Lorenzo, who had said he was coming with the limo to pick her up, but being eager to see him was wrong. An affair might be fun, but if they were discovered it could ruin Riley's wedding.

She saw the limo just as her phone pinged with a text.

Something unexpected came up. Didn't come with the limo. I will see you when I get home. Lorenzo.

Her heart rate nosedived, but she scolded herself. She wasn't on board with a romance between them. So maybe not seeing him until they were in his house, around other people was a good thing?

Her phone pinged with another text. This one from Riley. She was in the limo only a few feet away. With things returning to normal with her daughter, thoughts about Lorenzo all but disappeared. She rolled her suitcase and duffle bag to the limo, smiling. Her daughter was getting married! Tomorrow, they would begin planning.

The driver opened the door. "Good evening, ma'am."

She smiled. "Good evening."

She slid inside and reached out to hug Riley. "It's so nice to see you!"

The driver closed the door.

Riley laughed. "It's nice to see you too."

"You didn't have to meet me. It's bad enough we're keeping the driver from going home and getting out of the cold."

Riley batted a hand. "He doesn't mind. He's paid extremely well."

Juliette glanced at her daughter. That was almost exactly what Lorenzo had said when they'd discussed her shoes and his assistant losing sleep to get them to her—the thing that reminded her of the huge gulf between her standard of living and the Salvaggios'.

She almost said something but decided against it. She didn't want to disturb this wonderful time with her daughter. Plus, the billionaire lifestyle was foreign to her. Maybe the Salvaggios really did pay their staff enough that they didn't mind doing personal favors in the middle of the night? She also knew nothing about the hours chauffeurs worked. This guy could be handling the night shift.

The nudge of discomfort wiggled through her again. She really didn't know anything about this world. She was a fish out of water. She didn't know about life on a vineyard, with a villa, and servants. She knew Manhattan. She knew doctors. She knew how to be the best at providing services for her clients.

She didn't know how billionaires lived. Having been so cruelly judged by Greg's dad at the funeral, she could be too sensitive about the Salvaggios' behavior. She needed to keep an open mind about Riley's prospective in-laws. Not make unfair comparisons.

After the driver tucked her suitcases in the trunk, they drove to the villa, chatting about the things Riley and GiGi had discussed before they'd put a moratorium on wedding planning, waiting for Juliette's arrival. Excited to hear everything, she forgot about the Salvaggios' station in life and even about feeling like a fish out of water. These two weeks would be all about her daughter.

Walking into the foyer, they removed their coats, which were taken by a man Juliette now assumed was the butler because he was there to take her coat every time she arrived. She'd simply accepted his presence the first two times she'd been to the villa. Today, realizing she'd be here for two weeks and needed at least a rudimentary understanding of how this household worked, she paid attention to what was going on.

Riley directed her to the sitting room. As they entered, GiGi rose. "We waited dinner for you."

Juliette walked to her, took her hands and kissed her cheek. "Thank you. I have to admit, I am starving. I slept on the plane, then wasn't hungry until I got off the train. I think it's the time difference."

GiGi and Antonio laughed. GiGi said, "Our Riley had no trouble adjusting to the time difference."

Juliette didn't even take offense at GiGi claiming Riley as her own. GiGi was a wonderful woman who only wanted to make everyone happy. Even Lorenzo knew that.

She smiled. "Riley *is* younger, but if I remember correctly, she also had several trial runs last summer. What was it? One weekend in Italy. The next in Manhattan?"

Everybody laughed.

"They didn't see that they were falling in love," GiGi said. "But I did."

"You're a wise old woman," Lorenzo said from the bar.

His voice startled Juliette so much, she spun to face him. In his dark suit and white shirt, he looked his usual yummy self. She might have decided against a secret fling, but that didn't stop the warmth that shimmied through her or the way her breath bottomed out.

She told herself that was only because he was good-looking.

He motioned to the bar. "What can I get you to drink?"

"If everybody's having wine, wine is good with me."

His dark eyes held her gaze. "You know you're allowed a before-dinner cocktail. Just because we make wine, doesn't mean we're purists."

She laughed. No one else did.

With a quick glance around the room, she realized GiGi, Antonio and Riley were so wrapped up in their own conversation they weren't noticing her and Lorenzo.

She said, "Wine is fine," but her voice came out deeper than it should, sexy, as if her hormones had taken over.

He smiled, poured her wine and brought it to her. As he handed it to her, he whispered, "You don't know how badly I want to kiss you right now. I missed the hell out of you."

Her stomach fell.

"Please, Juliette," he said, his voice back to normal volume. "Have a seat."

GiGi heard that and she gasped. "Where are our manners! I didn't mean to leave you standing there."

Juliette smiled. There was no way to tell an eighty-something woman that Juliette had been standing in the middle of the room mesmerized by her handsome son. And also no way she'd expected the kiss remark or her reaction to it.

All her good intentions about not having an affair wavered.

Still, she was a strong New York businesswoman. She could handle this.

She primly took a seat in one of the chairs flanking the sofa where Antonio, Riley and GiGi sat. Lorenzo took the chair across from hers, so they were looking at each other.

"I'm sorry I couldn't come with the limo to pick you up. Today was a day from hell for me. I barely got home in time to shower and change for dinner."

"Oh." He didn't have to explain himself to her, but it was considerate that he had.

He smiled and her heartbeat stuttered.

Seriously. The guy was gorgeous and suave and so sexy her nerve endings perked up every time he was around. Just as he said that it was a shame they'd never get to kiss, it suddenly also seemed a shame not to explore what was between them.

Couldn't they just sleep together once?

She was about to say no, that she didn't want to do anything that might make a mess of the wedding. But her romantic side cut her off, telling her an entirely different version of what might happen. One time of sleeping together couldn't mess up the wedding. Soon everybody would be so busy with the planning that they wouldn't notice anything but dresses and dishes and floral arrangements. They probably wouldn't even notice if she and Lorenzo behaved differently.

Though she didn't think they would. They weren't giddy teenagers, or twenty-year-olds or even rambunctious thirty-year-olds. They knew how to act—

"Mom?"

Her head snapped up. "I'm sorry. Did you say something?"

"We were all wondering about your flight."

Across the coffee table, Lorenzo smiled knowingly at her.

"It was fine." She cleared her throat. "I had my laptop. After I slept, I did some work."

Antonio said, "Riley tells us you barely ever take a break."

"Running a small business is a lot different than running a conglomerate." Her wits restored, she immersed herself fully in the conversation. "I keep an eye on everything."

Lorenzo said, "We keep an eye on everything too."

"But it's so much more," Riley said, her voice dripping with awe. "You should see the things these guys manage, Mom."

The sense that she was out of the loop hit her again. She was accustomed to running something about the size of their winery. They managed that and God only knew what else. Obviously enough to impress Riley.

Lorenzo's phone buzzed. He glanced down at it, then rose. "Dinner is ready."

Antonio motioned for GiGi and Riley to walk before him. Lorenzo stealthily wound up beside Juliette. He whispered, "You look ravishing tonight. I love you in red."

Her body was covered in goose bumps. How could she not want to take advantage of this chemistry? Once. Just once.

"It's a sweater and jeans." She winced. "No time to dress for dinner."

He leaned closer. "I would have only imagined myself undressing you anyway."

His husky whisper tickled her ear. A shower of tingles fluttered through her. It appeared that if she really wanted this night, it could be hers. But it had to be on her terms.

CHAPTER SEVEN

WHEN THE CONVERSATION at dinner turned to the wedding, Lorenzo almost groaned. He did not want to get into that mess that could take hours and delay showing Juliette to her room.

Unfortunately, he knew Juliette was enjoying this. She'd realized she needed to participate fully in this wedding because this was the rest of her life. First, coming to Italy to help plan the wedding. Then coming to Italy for the wedding itself. Then visiting after the wedding to be part of the family her daughter was marrying into. She looked so calm about it that it appeared she was happy with her choice. If that was the case, that meant they could talk about gowns and bridesmaids and whatever else they had to choose tomorrow.

Tonight, she was his.

When they finished dessert in the sitting room, Antonio and Riley left through the back entry to go to their suite, taking GiGi with them so they could help her to the elevator, and he motioned for Juliette to precede him into the foyer. Just as he'd instructed the staff, her suitcase and duffle awaited them.

"What's this?"

"I wanted to be the one to show you to your room."

Her face scrunched as if she had no idea how to take

that and he motioned her to the second elevator. He walked in behind her, carrying her duffel and rolling her suitcase. The door closed.

As the little car began to climb, she faced him. "I've been thinking about what you suggested in our phone conversation."

He almost smirked, hoping she'd spent all her time in Manhattan dreaming about him, but he realized that nothing with her was guaranteed. She could have been nearly seduced in their phone call and changed her mind on the flight over.

"And?"

"And I have an amendment to your suggestion."

He laughed. "Really? Formal negotiations?"

She sniffed. "We're too smart not to lay out our expectations."

"True. What are you thinking?"

"One night."

He turned to gape at her. "What?"

"One night."

"And we'll see how it goes?"

She laughed. "No. One night. You're too sexy to resist completely. But a woman's gotta know her limits."

He chuckled. "You think I'll be too much for you?"

"No. Our situation is too delicate. I don't want to ruin the wedding if our relationship is a bust." She peeked over at him. "You have to agree with that."

"I don't. We'll be keeping this a secret, remember? No matter what happens between us, the wedding won't be ruined because no one will know. Plus, you live in Manhattan. I live here. Anything we start could be over every time one of us gets on a plane and returns home."

She frowned, thinking about that. "Every time we're to-gether would be like a one-night stand?"

"I suppose."

Her frown became a smile.

For some reason or another that smile grated on his nerves. "You like the idea of not being attached to me?"

"I have my reasons." She laughed. "You're the one who suggested we keep everything a secret. I could be insulted by that, but I'm not."

"That's the best way this works."

"I thought you said no attachments, just fun was how this worked."

"They mesh together. Put secrecy with no attachments and any margin for error has been taken care of."

She considered that, her frown returning, then as if she'd run through all the options and decided his reasoning was sound, she laughed. "I think you're right."

"I *am* right. These next few weeks have to be about Riley and Antonio. But that doesn't mean we can't enjoy some private time."

"Agreed."

The elevator door opened. He directed her to step out into the hall. "No more reservations about the wedding now?"

"It all hit me last weekend. Coming to Italy, becoming part of your family, is the rest of my life." She caught his gaze. "It's also why we have to be smart about us."

"Exactly."

He motioned for her to walk to the right. "There are three guest suites on this floor. I would let you have your pick, but I think you should take the first one."

She frowned.

He pointed to the end of the hall. "That door leads to

my suite." He pointed at the door closest to it. "If I put you right beside me... Well, maybe no one would notice, but putting you here—away from my room—prevents anyone from questioning."

She rose to her tiptoes and kissed him. "You overthink."

He caught her elbows, keeping her close to him. "After the discussion we just had setting terms for something that happens naturally for most people, you have no room to talk."

"Are you really concerned that someone's going to question that we're on the same floor?"

"When Riley came to live with us, we moved Lorenzo down to the second-floor suite, which has a kitchen and sitting room to give them the option of eating alone or watching television alone sometimes. All the rooms up here are empty now. People should consider it the logical move."

She tilted her head. "There isn't a free room on the second floor?"

"Of course, there is."

"No one will wonder why I'm not by my daughter?"

He sighed. "Now who's overthinking?"

He opened the door onto a suite decorated in blues and pale greens and filled with flowers. Vases of bouquets sat on every flat surface. Tall vases. Short vases. Roses. Carnations. Lilies. Mums.

She faced him. "Pretty sure of yourself."

He caught her by the waist and hauled her to him, kissing her the way she deserved to be kissed. Thoroughly and without reserve. No one would see. No one could comment or care.

This was the moment he'd waited for.

She slid her arms around his neck. This time when he pulled her close, he felt her softness—through clothes. Not at all what he wanted. Without any hesitation, he reached for the hem of her sweater, as he kicked the door closed.

"Seems a shame to get rid of this. You look so good in it. But right now, I want to feel your skin."

The flutter of his fingers against her belly sent wave after wave of arousal through Juliette. She had never been so hot for someone. Probably because of the element of forbidden fruit, but she didn't care.

Knowing she had to distract herself or she'd melt into a puddle of need, she unbuttoned his jacket and let it fall to the floor. His tie followed suit and so did his silky white shirt, as he undid her jeans and she stepped out of them.

Standing before him in a red bra and panties, she admired his flat stomach, his chest, his muscular arms. But not for long. With a growl, he pulled her to him. Their bodies met and her heart shimmied, as their mouths merged in blissful union, tongues twining.

He reached around and unsnapped her bra. She reached down and unbuckled his belt. More clothes drifted away. His hand slid under her panties and along her bottom. She groaned with pleasure.

Without missing a beat in his kiss, he eased them to the bed. The feeling of being stretched out together almost overwhelmed her. But he didn't give her time to think. All she could do was feel. The roughness of his skin beneath her palm. The way his hand glided along her smooth thighs. With all thought gone and only feelings guiding her, she touched and tasted to her heart's delight. When they joined, she was so ready the heat of it was like an explosion. And when they reached the summit and tumbled over, her breath caught then drifted out on a moan of pure pleasure.

After a few seconds for each to recover, Lorenzo rolled

away and flopped down on the pillow beside hers. "Only once you said?"

Her breaths came in ragged puffs. "Yeah, I said that, but your way is better."

He snorted. "We're gonna be sneaking away from the family to meet up for this every chance we can get."

She laughed.

He rolled over and pinned her to the bed. "Now, can we stop analyzing and let things happen naturally?"

She grinned at him. "I seem to remember you like things that happen naturally."

"Yes. I do."

He kissed her before she could say anything else. The kiss went on and on, warming her blood and her heart. Her blood could catch fire and she wouldn't care. It was the heart that worried her. She did not want her heart engaging. She wanted to maintain the distance she kept in all her relationships. No need for her heart to get involved. Given that she continually noticed ways they were different, and the horrible feeling of not belonging that filled her every time she did, she knew there was no way this could ever be permanent.

But as long as they were just having fun, seeing every goodbye as a potential end of anything between them, she didn't have anything to worry about.

Two hours later, Lorenzo woke up and looked at the clock. Skimming his hand down his face, he took a long, slow breath. Juliette roused.

He rose from the bed. "Sorry. Go back to sleep."

She eased into a sitting position. "Are you going to your room?"

He stepped into his trousers. "Yes. I get phone calls at all hours of the day and night. I don't want to disturb you."

As he slid into his shirt, she smiled. "Back to overthinking again?"

He bent down and kissed her. "No. The truth is I don't really overthink. I figure out ways to make things work." Socks in his jacket pocket, he stepped into his shoes. "Like this," he said motioning between them. "Just try to stop me from making love to you again."

Rather than argue, she busied herself straightening the bed sheet. "Well, if you insist."

"I'm going to do more than insist. After your two wedding planning weeks are up, we should fly to Paris."

She gasped. "That's the kind of thing that could get us caught."

He shrugged. "I don't see how."

"I've never been to Paris. I'll talk about it. I'll slip up."

"Then maybe we save Paris for after the wedding." He sat beside her on the bed. "I want to show you the city."

She smiled. "Okay. After the wedding."

She said it through her smile, but Lorenzo sensed hesitation. "You don't think we'll last that long?"

"You're the one who said every goodbye might be permanent. I'm just keeping it real."

He headed for the door. "Okay. You keep it real, and I will be the dreamer."

"It's all about balance."

He laughed. "I suppose it is."

He walked out of her room and headed down the hall to his suite.

No one had seen. No one had heard.

And he had no fear that Juliette would slip up. She was too concerned about her daughter not to monitor her every word.

That unexpectedly gave him pause. She really did overthink everything. He wasn't worried she'd zap the fun out of their relationship. Her overthinking sometimes made him laugh. Maybe it was male pride, but he wanted her to be as out of control with him as he was with her.

But she'd held something back as if she was afraid—

She was only afraid of hurting her daughter, messing up the wedding somehow, and he would see to it that they wouldn't.

He opened his suite door. Once she got comfortable with the idea that they wouldn't get caught, she would come around.

CHAPTER EIGHT

JULIETTE WOKE TO an empty bed the next morning. She yawned and stretched feeling wonderful, then a sense of foreboding shimmied through her. The man was a billionaire. Technically, she was a commoner, the way she'd been with Greg—

She ignored her thoughts. She and Lorenzo were having an affair. Nothing about their relationship was serious and certainly not permanent. If she was thinking of marrying the man, she might be panicking right now. But she wasn't. It didn't matter that how he lived was different than how she lived. All that mattered was that Lorenzo was sweet, handsome, sexy and so romantic she could still swoon from things that happened hours before.

She took in all the flowers in her room and laughed. He was such a charmer. Actually, he was such a charmer that he might have overlooked the fact that whoever helped him with this would tell the rest of the staff—

No. As head of the household, he'd probably sworn that person to secrecy. He was too certain they wouldn't get caught to ask someone to help him and not make sure they wouldn't spill the beans. He was also a very responsible guy. He'd told her about raising Antonio, about watching out for GiGi. He took his responsibilities seriously.

However he'd gotten these flowers in here, he'd been careful.

Which was one of the things she liked about him. He was a smart guy.

She glanced at the clock and sat up with a smile. It was only a little after seven. She was getting better about adjusting to the time difference. Which, technically, was her first hurdle. And she'd aced it.

She reached for her phone and saw that Riley had texted her.

In all the confusion last night, I don't think anyone told you breakfast is at eight in the dining room where we ate dinner last night.

She threw off the covers. Not only was she awake before noon, but she had time to dress for breakfast. Things were going her way.

Dressed in jeans and a peach sweater, she took the elevator to the first floor and easily found the dining room.

Walking in, she said, "Good morning, everyone."

Gentlemen, Lorenzo and Antonio rose. Both wore suits because they would soon be leaving for work, but Riley and GiGi were dressed comfortably.

Second hurdle down. Not only had she awoken on time, but also she'd dressed appropriately.

Then she caught Lorenzo's gaze and her stomach fluttered. He always looked yummy in a suit and tie, but today his eyes had a special sparkle.

The urge to smile at him almost overtook her. Instead, she pulled her gaze away and headed for the empty seat... right beside him.

No need to panic about his nearness. She could handle it.

"Thanks for the text, Riley. I had just awoken."

As she reached the chair, Lorenzo rose to pull it out for her. His hand grazed her forearm as she sat. Memories of their night before flooded her, but she ignored them.

GiGi said, "Breakfast is always at eight, though you don't have to be here if you want to sleep in. The kitchen staff will be happy to accommodate you."

All thoughts of Lorenzo fled. Making staff work to accommodate her didn't sit right, but something tapped the toe of her shoe. Her gaze nearly flew to Lorenzo, but she stopped it. She should have guessed he was the kind of guy who would play footsie.

"I like to get up early..." She cleared her throat when her voice came out scratchy. "Breakfast at eight will suit me."

Antonio gave her a confused look, but GiGi kept on talking. "Lunch is whenever we decide. Dinner is typically based on when these two—" she pointed at Antonio and Lorenzo "—get home from the office."

"There's fruit in the kitchen," Riley added. "Snacks. Crackers."

"And cookies," GiGi said with a laugh. "In case you need a little something to get you to dinner. Please help yourself."

The guy who usually took her coat walked in pushing a cart with plates of French toast, eggs, bacon and regular toast.

"This is Gerard, our butler," Lorenzo said. "Gerard, this is Juliette, Riley's mother."

He actually bowed. "Pleasure to meet you, ma'am."

Juliette froze. She had no idea if she should stand and shake his hand. A person always rose from their seat and shook the hand of a new business acquaintance, but this man was the butler.

Too much time went by for her to rise. She smiled and said, "It's a pleasure to meet you too."

He nodded before setting dishes on the table in front of Lorenzo, serving breakfast family style. Lorenzo handed a dish to Antonio and one to her, as Gerard left the room.

Luckily, her plate contained scrambled eggs, something she loved so she could occupy herself with that and forget about the uncomfortable situation. She took two spoonsful and passed them to GiGi.

In short order, all the plates made their way around the table. Juliette had taken only eggs, bacon and a piece of toast.

Lorenzo pointed at her food. "That wouldn't keep me until ten."

She cautiously caught his gaze. "I'm a light eater."

He smiled at her. Her breath stalled.

Riley said, "She always eats like a bird. It's how she stays so small."

"Not like this one," Antonio said, pointing at Riley, "who likes doughnuts."

Riley laughed. GiGi laughed. If Juliette had made a faux pas in how she'd reacted when being introduced to Gerard, no one had noticed…or cared. They didn't seem to be real sticklers for protocol, so maybe she could relax?

Or maybe she needed to do some research. Before they got down to wedding planning this morning, she would go online and research household etiquette when there were cooks, housekeepers and butlers. She knew all the normal things a person needed to know when dealing with business associates—including eating out at fancy restaurants—but she'd never personally interacted with a butler before—or lived in a house filled with servants. She would think this through and research accordingly.

They finished breakfast and Lorenzo and Antonio rose. Antonio bent down and kissed Riley who gave him the most wonderful smile.

Lorenzo caught her gaze as if telling her he wished he could kiss her, and she yanked her eyes away and got up from the table too. "I have a few things to do in my room, then I'll be down to start the wedding planning."

GiGi rubbed her hands together with glee. "I can't wait."

She left the dining room. Rather than take the elevator, she ran up two flights of stairs, the exercise helping her to release the odd mix of feelings she'd had at the dining room table. Her potential faux pas. Being so close to Lorenzo that she could smell his aftershave. The fight to keep her reactions normal around him—

And there he stood at the top of the stairs.

As soon as she'd taken the last step, he scooped her up into his arms, kissing her deeply. "Good morning."

She wanted to scold him. She should have scolded him for the flirty smile and the footsie. Instead, she blinked. "Good morning."

"I hated having to leave last night."

"If we want to keep this a secret, we need to take appropriate measures. And speaking of that—how did you get those flowers into my room without anyone seeing?"

"Everyone saw."

She gasped.

"Relax. I told Gerard that you wanted all the flowers so you could see your options for bouquets and centerpieces."

She stared at him.

He snickered. "As a cover story I thought it was pretty damned good." He kissed her again. "You are such a stickler for propriety."

She stepped back and crossed her arms on her chest. "Because I don't want to risk ruining the wedding."

"And I am careful."

"Playing footsie when everyone is in the room is not careful."

He sighed. "Fine. You are right. I will behave."

She shook her head with a laugh. "You're such a charmer that I think you're having a little trouble holding that back."

"Or maybe you bring out the charmer in me."

Her heart melted. He had a way of making her feel special, but not like a princess, more like an equal. Which was probably why he was getting to her. She wasn't a princess, so she could shrug that off. But she was an equal. Maybe not in money. But she worked as hard as he did. She'd made the best out of her life the way he did.

That's why it was so easy to forget his life was different. In a lot of ways, they were alike.

He left for work, and she headed for her laptop to investigate etiquette with maids and butlers, chauffeurs, even the maintenance people. Twenty minutes later, proud of herself for getting on top of this, she left her room and walked into the sitting room. Riley sat alone, leafing through a book of floral arrangements.

Thinking of Lorenzo, she held back a laugh, and lowered herself to the sofa beside her. "Have you made any choices?"

Riley laughed. "A lot of choices. No final decisions. Though I understand you asked for some samples."

"Yes. I didn't so much want to see bouquets," she said, expanding on Lorenzo's story. "As I wanted to look at different kinds of flowers. Remind myself of what's out there."

Riley nodded, then she frowned. "It's a bigger job to pick something for yourself than it is for other people. Most of my clients are pleasantly surprised by what I choose. But I've got a hundred options they didn't even know were available."

"Don't stress!" She squeezed Riley's hand. "Let's just have fun."

"Agreed." She bit her lower lip, then drew in a long breath. "There's something else I'd like to talk about before GiGi gets here. I know you weren't happy with our engagement, and I just want to make sure you really are okay with everything."

Juliette smiled and squeezed Riley's hand again. "I'll admit I was a little taken aback when you first got engaged. But now, I'm getting caught up in things. The wedding. Your future children." She laughed. "*My* grandchildren. And all the lovely holidays we'll have together."

Riley blinked. "You really don't mind coming here for holidays?"

"It would be ridiculous for you and Antonio to drag your kids to Manhattan, when I can more easily get on a flight and come here." She glanced around at the beautifully appointed sitting room. "Being here is not exactly a hardship."

Wide-eyed, Riley said, "Wow. You totally changed your mind?"

"Totally."

Riley laughed "I've never seen you do that."

"I'm not unreasonable. When I'm wrong, I never stubbornly dig in my heels."

The perfect example was her relationship with Lorenzo. She'd thought one night…he disagreed. Now, she agreed with him. What they started could go on for a while. As long as he really could keep his feelings under control when they were in public.

She wished she could tell Riley that. They always discussed their relationships. But Riley had held back a bit about Antonio. Of course, their relationship began as pretending to be engaged in the hopes of lifting GiGi's spirits enough that she'd start her chemo. Juliette was keeping Lorenzo a secret because they'd made a deal knowing secrecy was the only way this worked—and she agreed with him.

She smiled at Riley. "You really love this guy?"

Riley rolled her eyes. "Remember the three I lived with?"

Juliette grimaced.

"Well, what I feel for Antonio is totally different. It's complete. It's overwhelming sometimes. He's thoughtful and kind. A hard worker who takes his responsibilities seriously...yet he's still romantic."

Juliette understood that perfectly. Still, this was her chance to make sure Riley did. "You don't think it's just infatuation? The guy *is* gorgeous and charming—"

Like his dad. With a room full of flowers, replacement shoes, compliments and suggestions that made her toes curl—Lord, no wonder Riley fell like a ton of bricks.

"And charming, gorgeous guys are very easy to fall for."

Riley shook her head. "No. This is real. We've talked about everything. Kids. Where we should raise them. Where we should live. What we want out of life." She sighed. "He's felt empty for a long time. So have I."

Her heart tweaked. She'd already realized that sometimes her life seemed hollow too. Lots of work. No deep emotion. Breakfast while she raced to her office. Takeout dinners alone. She understood what Riley was saying. Sometimes she wanted more. Then she would remember Greg dying and his dad telling her she was an upstart and remember that "more" frequently came with heartache and trouble.

"You and Antonio want the same things?"

"We want to be happy. But we also want to be fulfilled. You know the Salvaggios are committed to their land, their legacy."

Juliette nodded. "Lorenzo has mentioned it a time or two."

Riley perked up. "Antonio said you two were getting friendly."

Given what they'd done the night before, they were a lot more than friendly. "Yes. I like him. I like his sense of responsibility. If Antonio has that same sense, he's a good a guy."

"He really is, Mom. And we make each other happy."

Trying to be subtle, she said, "You realize you've changed the entire trajectory of your life for a man."

"No, I changed the entire trajectory of my life for love. For a purpose. For a future. Besides, I'm not abandoning my business. I'm expanding it. Someday, I'll be offering proposals all over the globe."

Juliette laughed. "I hope."

"I *know*. And not just because I'm strong. Because Antonio and I are a team."

"That's good."

"It *is* good. I finally don't feel alone."

Remembering the difficult years after Greg died, with his family disowning them and no other family to speak of, Juliette caught her daughter's hand. "You were never alone. You always had me."

"I know." She sighed. "But this is another level. I wish you could find this."

Juliette groaned. "Are you kidding? I'm too set in my ways. Plus, I like being the boss. I don't think I'd do compromise as well as you do."

Riley laughed.

But Juliette suddenly saw that this was why neither she nor Lorenzo wanted a future. They'd both been burned, but more than that they'd both been alone too long to think they could suddenly become part of a couple.

Disappointment tightened her chest. She ignored it. Riley and Antonio wanted a future. They had space in their lives to compromise. They had space in their lives to grow. Lorenzo had duty and responsibilities. She had a company to run and a home in one of the most beautiful cities in the world. It had taken her decades to get here. To be satisfied. To be the boss. To have everything she wanted. What Riley and Antonio sought wasn't right for her anymore. And she didn't want to risk being hurt...or getting into a relationship that was wrong for her. In Manhattan, she was at the top of her game. Here, she'd had to research how to deal with a butler. She liked being at the top...being the one in control...better.

GiGi stepped into the room. "Great! We are all here. While you were upstairs, the designer arrived. I took him to the second-floor sitting room. He hung rough versions of all three dresses there. They're waiting for you to try them on."

Riley raced upstairs and GiGi led Juliette to the elevator that took them to the second floor. When they arrived in a big room that looked like another living room, Riley was in the adjoining room to the right. After a few minutes, she came out, wearing a simple white A-line dress, the designer, Pierre, following her.

As Juliette and Antonio's grandmother took seats on a sofa, GiGi said, "Do you like it?"

Riley smoothed her hand along the material. "This fabric for the real gown will be silk…" She paused. "But the fit is nice."

Juliette laughed. "If it's *nice*, it's not the one."

Riley returned to the adjoining room and came out in a second dress.

GiGi frowned. "Is it me or do both of the dresses look too plain?"

"I think the velvet cape is throwing you off, Riley," Juliette said. "Because it's so pretty you're letting it steal the show. But you won't have it on in the ballroom. You need a pretty gown. Let the cloak shine through the ceremony, but you're going to want something stunning for the reception. All three of these dresses are too simple."

GiGi nodded. "I agree."

"Do you have the book with your renderings?" Juliette asked Pierre.

"Of course." He went into the dressing room and returned with the book.

Juliette took it and flipped through Pierre's designs. When she saw the perfect dress, she said, "Ahh."

GiGi leaned in. "Ahh."

Riley raced over. She glanced down, then she laughed. "I think you're right."

GiGi smiled at Pierre. "Can you make a mock-up of this one for us?"

Lorenzo could tell something was up at dinner from the way Riley glowed, GiGi giggled and Juliette looked pleased. Not one of the three of them mentioned anything that should have caused so much excitement. They'd finalized a menu, made changes to the bouquets and flowers for the ballroom and put together a list of songs for dinner music to be played by the string quartet.

None of which should make his mother giggle.

Something was going on.

When it was time to retire for the night, no one even noticed that he and Juliette entered the elevator together. GiGi had long ago gone to bed and Antonio and Riley were headed to the sitting room of their quarters to watch a soccer match.

In the elevator, he waited a second before he casually said, "So I take it the wedding planning went well today."

"We got a lot done. It's very convenient that we'll be having the wedding in the vineyard and the reception in your ballroom. No one to call to reserve space. No one to tell us no."

"There is a freedom to it."

"And GiGi showed me your outdoor space." She shook her head. "I wish they would wait until June so we could have the reception out there."

"That sounds like you haven't given up trying to persuade them to change the date."

She laughed. "Lord, no. That was just wishful thinking. They know what they want." She paused a second. "It might be because they're older than I was when I committed to Greg, but Riley and Antonio have talked about things that it never occurred to me to discuss with Greg. We were in love. We were pregnant. I felt the hand of fate. We simply moved in together and made a life. And Riley and I both saw how that turned out."

The elevator door opened. "Are you saying Antonio and Riley might have done everything right?"

She smiled. "Maybe."

He frowned. "Are you looking for guarantees?"

"Nope. I'm just experienced enough to know that no one does *everything* right."

His laugh filled the third-floor hall. He loved laughing with her. He loved having someone he didn't have to measure his words with. He loved hearing her perspective, even if it sometimes didn't match his.

It felt so good to be himself.

She opened the door to her suite, and he followed her inside, closing the door behind them.

When he gathered her into his arms and kissed her, she didn't argue or question. She simply melted. She had his clothes off before he managed to get hers off but once they were on the bed, he didn't care who was taking the lead. He just wanted to hold her and touch her and taste her until they were both so far gone, they forgot what day it was.

The only thing that marred the perfection of sleeping with her was not actually getting to sleep with her. He had to re-dress and go back to his suite. Before he reached it, he realized he was hungry and glanced at the stairway. By now, Riley and Antonio's game should be over, but it didn't matter. They were in their own room.

Not that he cared. This was his home. He could go to the kitchen for a snack. What could they say if he ran into them?

He ambled down the stairs and into the kitchen for some crackers. Deciding to take the entire box to his room, he left the kitchen and almost walked into Riley.

"Hey!" She glanced at his suit. "What have you been doing for the last two hours?"

He felt his face redden. *This* was what they could say! Normally, he would have changed out of his suit and into sweats or even pajamas and a robe once he went to his room. Yet here he was still in his suit. It was one of those mistakes he'd promised Juliette he wouldn't make.

"I was talking on the phone with a friend. He called right as I got to my room. I didn't get a chance to change."

Antonio popped out and joined Riley. "Oh! What friend?"

"Frank."

"You don't know anybody named Frank."

He snorted. "Antonio. You do not know everybody I know! Frank's from the States. He and his wife are in Florence on vacation."

Riley said, "Oh! That's nice."

Antonio smiled approvingly. "You should invite them here to see the vineyard."

He gaped at his son. Being in love was making Antonio incredibly kind and generous.

Unfortunately, Frank wasn't real.

Thinking quickly on his feet, Lorenzo said, "They're going home tomorrow. Which was why he called tonight— to say goodbye." He displayed his crackers. "And I'm saying good night to you."

As if not hearing him, Riley frowned. "If you spent two hours on the phone with him, you could have gone into town and had a drink together," she said. "And taken my mother. She could use some fun."

Lorenzo knew for a fact she'd had plenty of fun that night.

Antonio said, "You know, Marco will be at the wedding."

Lorenzo worked to hide a scowl. He did not like the idea that Antonio planned to fix up Juliette and Marco. Still, he avoided the topic by saying, "I should hope he'll be at the wedding. He's your godfather." He headed up the stairs. "But right now, I'm going to bed. Good night."

On the second floor, he turned to the left to climb the rest of the stairs to the third floor and his suite. At the top, he pulled out his phone. As he walked down the hall, he texted Juliette.

Ran into the kids in the hallway. Told them I was on the phone with a friend all night. You don't really need to know that because you were in your room and wouldn't know that I'd talked to a friend—

He sighed and deleted the text. She really didn't need to know that. Getting accustomed to keeping this a secret really was going to be harder than he'd first thought.

He loosened his tie, then opened the door of his five-room suite that was more of an apartment. Loneliness hit him in a wave, but he knew why. He wasn't so much lonely as he was hungry for Juliette's company.

He wanted to sleep with her. In his big bed.

That probably made him a chauvinist…at the very least politically incorrect. But he was too tired to care.

In the morning, he would probably kick himself for letting those emotions seep in. He told himself it was just exhaustion, took off his clothes and fell face-first on the soft comforter.

When he awoke late, he didn't panic. He simply showered and went downstairs to breakfast. Antonio and Riley were finished eating and getting ready to start their day. GiGi dawdled over coffee.

He wanted to ask where Juliette was. Instead, he said, "What's on the agenda for the day, GiGi?"

"More wedding planning. Juliette will be down in a minute. She slept in."

He hid a smirk. He was not the only one who'd been tired out the night before. "She slept in?"

"Yes. She texted a few minutes ago, said she'd shower and be right down."

He almost laughed. He thought it was cute that she had trouble adjusting to the time difference and even cuter that they tired each other out so thoroughly that they'd both slept in.

He told himself to stop having thoughts like that. Dreamy, sexy things were good…but thinking them cute? That had too much of a feeling of connection to it. Still, he might not want forever with her, but he did like her. He liked her a lot.

And he intended for them to completely enjoy what they had, while it lasted.

CHAPTER NINE

THE DAY BEFORE Juliette's two-week visit was over, Antonio and Lorenzo were in his office in Florence immersed in creating a five-year plan for a new project when his phone buzzed.

They glanced at each other.

"Didn't you tell your assistant to hold all calls?"

Lorenzo sighed. "I did." He hit the button to answer. "Yes?"

"I'm sorry, Mr. Salvaggio," his assistant said, her voice coming through the phone's speaker. "But Annabelle Lindstrom is here to see you."

At the mention of his ex-wife's name, Lorenzo held back a groan. But, remembering she was Antonio's mother, he simply handed the visit off to his son. "Go talk to your mom."

"I'm sorry." His assistant's voice came out of the speaker again. "But she's here to see both of you. She was very clear about that. Do you want me to take her to the conference room?"

Antonio glanced at Lorenzo, obviously gauging his father's mood before he said, "Yes. Ask her if she'd like coffee. Because we might need a minute before we get to her."

Lorenzo rose. "We don't need time. Take her back to the conference room and Antonio and I will be right there."

As Lorenzo disconnected the call, Antonio said, "Are you sure?"

He snorted. "Antonio, your mother might be a thorn in my side, but she's your mother. We always treat her with respect."

Antonio said, "We do."

"Okay, then. Let's go."

They walked to the conference room and entered through a side door. Annabelle was already there, staring out the window at the streets of Florence. Her shiny dark hair gleamed in the sunlight pouring in, despite the cold morning.

She turned as they entered. "Antonio!" She raced over to hug her son.

Antonio returned her hug.

Lorenzo studied her, not quite able to put his finger on what was different. She pulled away from Antonio and faced Lorenzo.

"It's nice to see you too, Enzo."

He snorted. It really had been a while since he'd seen her. No one except GiGi called him Enzo anymore. Hearing her say it sent waves of memories through him. None of them good.

Still, he said, "It's nice to see you, Anna."

"You're probably wondering why I'm here..."

Lorenzo wasn't. She undoubtedly needed money—

Except she usually called him for that. They hadn't had a visit in forever.

She faced Antonio with a smile. "I heard you got engaged."

Antonio grinned. *"Sì."*

"Is your fiancée here?"

"She doesn't work here. She has her own company."

"In Florence?"

Antonio motioned for his mother to sit on the couch of the sitting area in the corner of the big room, then sat beside her. "Yes, she is moving her corporate offices here." He laughed. "Her name is Riley. She's American."

"American!"

"*Sì*. She's beautiful and kind and everything I've ever wanted."

Anna took her son's hands. "That's wonderful."

"The wedding's in January," Lorenzo said carefully.

She gasped. "So soon?"

"Yes. We are happy. We want to have children. We want to start our life together now. No waiting."

She smiled prettily—

And Lorenzo realized what was different. She was sober.

Weird sensations cascaded through him. He had no idea what to say. What to ask. Why she wanted to see them. Except that she probably wanted an invitation to the wedding. She *had* known Antonio had gotten engaged. She hadn't come to congratulate him. She'd come to insinuate herself into his life again.

Antonio said, "The wedding's here at the villa. So is the reception."

She squeezed their son's hands. "It's cold in January for an outdoor wedding."

Antonio laughed. "We know. We don't care. Your invitation will have the details."

She clutched her chest as if surprised. "I'm invited?"

Antonio said, "Of course!"

"I don't know what to say."

Lorenzo leaned against the windowsill. "Antonio, why don't you see what's taking my assistant so long with that coffee?"

He gave Lorenzo a confused look, but nodded and left the office.

Annabelle caught his gaze. "You're not happy I'm here."

A statement not a question.

"Annabelle, Antonio has never been so on track. His fiancée is the sweetest woman I've ever met. They know what they want. And they are full of prewedding joy. Do not screw this up for them."

Her chin rose. "I'm sober now."

Foreboding sent warning after warning through him. Annabelle might not have made an actual demand for anything and might have stayed congenial, but she'd gotten what she wanted: an invitation to the wedding. He vividly remembered this kind of behavior from her. It was usually the calm before the storm. Play nice until she was back in his good graces, then push for something else. Whatever that was this time, she would be sneaky about getting it. Maybe even approach Antonio privately.

His blood heated with anger. Still, he remained calm. "I'm glad you're sober. But it doesn't change the fact that you will do irreparable damage to your relationship with your son if you ruin his wedding."

Annabelle happily said, "I won't."

How many times had he heard that?

Antonio arrived with the tray of coffee. "Since I was headed this way, I decided to save Maria a trip."

Having said his piece, Lorenzo headed for the door. He didn't have to be here for the rest of the mother and son time together. "I have a lunch appointment." Not true. Just an excuse to leave without offending her. "But you two enjoy your visit."

Annabelle protested. "No! Stay! I want to hear how you are too."

"I'm fine," Lorenzo said easily, casually, and even managed a smile. "You two are the ones who need to catch up."

Outside the conference room door, he ran his hands down his face. He hoped her sobriety lasted forever. He hoped, for Antonio's sake, she was ready for a real relationship. But he knew the drill. This visit was only the beginning. He would not let his guard down for thirty seconds around her, and he would watch her like a hawk at the wedding.

As he returned to his office, he considered calling Juliette, if only to talk this out. He even pulled his phone from his pocket—

But he paused.

Their little fling was exactly that. A fling. He would not in any way, shape or form burden her with the vagaries of his life or share his troubles.

If he called, it would be to hear her pretty voice or laugh about something. There would be nothing serious between them.

Ever.

For both of their sanities.

So maybe the reason he reached for his phone was because he just wanted a chance to hear her laugh? To think about the fun, happy things he always thought about when he was with her.

For that, he wouldn't call her. He would take her to lunch so his excuse to Annabelle wouldn't really be a lie.

Maybe he should call GiGi and try to find her? Juliette had mentioned something about sightseeing that morning. But she hadn't said where. GiGi would know.

Juliette spent the first few hours of the morning playing gin with GiGi. When Lorenzo's mother tired out and went upstairs for a rest, she had the driver take her to town to look for a wedding gift for Riley and Antonio, then have lunch somewhere interesting.

But riding in the limo to go shopping, she'd felt ridiculous. She was a capable driver who should have simply used one of the cars in the big garage. It was weird to be driven to shop for a few hours. Especially since she might be part of the Salvaggios' extended family, but she wasn't actually one of them.

She refused to forget that.

She walked along Via Tornabuoni, looking at the offerings in the artisan boutiques, but nothing felt like a wedding gift. Realizing she'd probably end up buying a gift for the kids online, she shifted gears and became a sightseer, enjoying the way the city could be quaint in some places and sophisticated in others. The sights and sounds—and the scents of food and freshly baked bread and treats—all gave her a sense of being somewhere unique, somewhere wonderful.

She pulled up the collar on her coat. The first of December air was freezing, making her think about how cold an outdoor wedding would be in the middle of January.

Her phone rang. The busy street almost drowned out the sound but she'd caught the phone before it stopped ringing, ducking under a canopy to answer it.

Seeing the caller was Pete, she winced. "What's wrong?"

"I know I promised I wouldn't call you, but something happened late yesterday that was weird."

Realizing it was six o'clock in the morning in Manhattan and he was already in this office, she knew this was serious. "Weird? What does weird mean?"

"Your ex's parents' doctor called to arrange for our services."

At first, she froze, then her business instincts kicked in. "Are you sure they are who you think they are?"

"I did the usual investigations that we do on all potential clients, financial, criminal, and personal."

Those checks were run to determine what level of services the client could afford, and also to ensure they weren't sending an unsuspecting nurse into a bad situation.

"Not only do they have the same last name—Finnegan—but they had a son Greg who died."

Her stomach plummeted. "Okay. That still could be a coincidence."

"Juliette," Pete said sympathetically. "The timelines match up. Riley's age now and the age she was when her father died were my guidelines."

Her muscles froze. They probably were Greg's parents. She had to face that. Handle it. "Okay."

Pete continued. "Apparently Mrs. Finnegan is suffering from dementia. She's not that far gone, but her husband is ten years older than she is and can't care for her at all."

Juliette mumbled, "I never knew about their age difference." She basically knew very little about them. Greg rarely spoke of them. She'd always believed there was a rift of some sort between them. After he died, she realized she'd been the rift.

Pete very kindly said, "Should we say we're too busy to take the job?"

"No. We are in the business of taking care of people. Call the doctor and say we'll be doing our usual intake visit before we commit and arrange a date with him for that. Normally, I would be the one to do it, but they probably need help now and I'm in Italy another day, then the day I get back to Manhattan I'll be jet lagged. You'll need to do it."

He said, "Okay, boss."

They disconnected the call, and Juliette glanced around the quaint street that had so enthralled her and tried to get back her happy feelings. She refused to let the past ruin her afternoon. Even if these were Greg's parents, too much time had gone by to harbor anger or bitterness. She would treat this couple like any other clients who needed the help of the nurses she employed. Nothing more. Nothing less. Simply people who needed help that she could give.

But a weird heaviness followed her as she walked out from under the canopy. Refusing to give into it, she ignored it, once again huddling into her coat to protect herself in the freezing December air. She thought of Riley's wedding again, trying to figure out what to wear so she didn't shiver through the ceremony. Even a long-sleeve gown wouldn't provide enough protection—

It didn't matter. A January wedding in a very cold vineyard was what Riley and Antonio wanted. That's what they would have.

She wouldn't let herself make the connection of how she respected her child's wishes and how Greg's parents had walked all over his. Because she didn't know that for sure. It was one of the things that had haunted her after he died. He could have married her hundreds of times. She hadn't wanted a big wedding. Only him. But they'd never made it official, making it easy for his parents to kick her out because she'd been too stunned by his death to fight them.

She'd never even tried to get child support because she'd been so damned determined to make it on her own and part of her was glad. She was as successful as she was because of needing to prove she wasn't an upstart.

And she had.

On her way up the street, scouting for a restaurant, she saw a black limo, one that had the Salvaggio Vineyards logo on the rear bumper.

She took a few steps closer. The back window slowly

lowered. Lorenzo said, "Hey, know any beautiful women who would like to have lunch?"

All her thoughts of the past disappeared. Her heart lifted. "I was just looking for a restaurant."

He opened the limo door and eased out. "Where would you like to eat?"

"I'm a stranger here. You choose." Remembering her jeans and sweater under her navy pea coat, she added, "And make it somewhere I'm dressed appropriately for."

He stopped in front of her and kissed her. "To me you're always beautiful."

She laughed. Dear God, the man could pull her out of any unwanted mood. "Seriously? Flirting on a public street?"

"I enjoy wooing you."

Yeah, she liked it too. But they *were* on a public street. She glanced around. The old stone buildings had a lot of windows. Anybody could be watching them. "Where are Riley and Antonio?"

"Riley's working from the villa and Antonio's at the office. We're fine."

Her phone rang. Worried it might be Pete again, she dug it out of her purse and glanced at the caller ID. Not recognizing the number, she considered it might be the Finnegans' doctor and gave Lorenzo the *hold on one second* signal as she answered.

"Hello?"

"Hello, sweet Juliette," GiGi said.

She laughed with relief. "Hello, GiGi. What's up?"

Lorenzo frowned at Juliette, as she said, "You know, it's funny you called. I've been shopping in town and the cold is brutal. That made me think about what I'd be wearing to the wedding ceremony. What do you suggest for a coat for me? I'm wearing a gown, so I'm half tempted to do something like a cloak too...the way Riley is." She listened while GiGi talked. "We could make it a theme."

His frown disappeared as she laughed again. He loved her laugh, but more than that, he loved how good she was to GiGi, treating her like a friend. His mother had lost a lot of her friends. Juliette was a good fit.

"Okay. So, we're all wearing cloaks and there's an engagement party this weekend."

His eyes widened. *Engagement party?*

She batted her hand, giving him the universal symbol to simmer down. There was nothing to get excited about.

Then she said, "Goodbye. I'll see you this afternoon sometime."

She disconnected the call and tossed her phone into her purse again.

He stared at her. "An engagement party?"

"Antonio and Riley just decided they wanted one, and Antonio called GiGi. She called me."

He shook his head and directed her to walk up the street. "I know why. Antonio's mother visited this morning."

She met his gaze. "Is that unusual?"

"Yes. They rarely see each other. And you know how he's been lately...the world's a beautiful place and people are wonderful."

She chuckled. "That's the love hormones."

"Exactly. Anyway, he invited her to the wedding."

She winced. "She *is* his mother."

"I know. And realistically I want her there but she's a problem. I'll probably spend most of the wedding keeping an eye on her."

She squeezed his forearm. "I know. It's what you do."

"I had hoped to dance with you." He caught her gaze. "If only once."

"We can dance at the engagement party."

"No. She'll be there too. That's why Antonio wants a party. I'm guessing he's giving her a trial run to make sure a big gathering isn't too much for her sobriety."

Juliette's eyes widened. "She's sober? That's great news!"

He took a breath. He hadn't wanted to burden her with all of this, but she would be at the engagement party and wedding. She had to know what to expect.

"If we are lucky, maybe this time it will work for her."

"Let's hope so."

Her reaction was so calm and kind that his spirits lifted a bit. Not only was she good to his mother, but she wasn't the type of person to panic over potentially bad news. She thought of Antonio first. Which made it nice to talk to her about it. He was almost glad that GiGi had called. Having her to sort it out with, it all seemed smaller somehow.

They reached the restaurant and he motioned for her to enter before him.

She laughed. "A pizza place?"

"Real pizza," he said, then led her to a booth in the back. After giving the server their orders, he leaned across the table. "I'm sorry I had to tell you about Annabelle. I like our relationship to be about fun. But you need to be prepared."

"I'm fine. In fact, whatever you need, I'll help you."

"That's the other reason I'm glad I could tell you. I'll probably need someone to help me keep an eye on her." He took her hands. "Thank you."

She said, "You're welcome," then she grimaced. "I actually have something I wasn't going to tell you either."

He glanced at her. "Really?"

"Greg's parents' doctor called my agency. His mother needs a private nurse."

The server returned with their drinks, giving him a moment to absorb that news.

As she left, Juliette looked at a picture of the pizza on the menu. "This isn't so different from ours. The crust's a little thicker."

"There's also no sauce. We use real tomatoes."

"Oh."

He wasn't sure if she was trying to distract him, but he hadn't forgotten what they were talking about when their drinks had arrived. "You were saying your ex's parents are about to become your clients?"

She set her glass down. "It's what my company does. We help people."

The thought of her being kind to the parents who had evicted her burned through him like hot coals. "They hurt you."

"They are old and sick now. My company's mission statement is that we provide good care and human kindness to people who need it. That mission would be meaningless if I turned someone away."

He leaned across the booth and kissed her. "You are a good soul."

"Yeah, and it might just come back to bite me in the butt."

Wanting to support her, the way she supported him about Annabelle, he thought that through and said, "Or you could get the opportunity to show them what they missed."

"I'm not a hundred percent sure it's them, but it would be a hell of a coincidence if it wasn't. Still, they must not have recognized my name, or they would have shifted their doctor in another direction. If they don't remember me, there's no reason for me to tell them who I am. Pete's doing the intake interview. I'll let him figure out what they need and assign staff, then I'll trust my extremely talented nurses to do their job. I won't even have to see the Finnegans."

He smiled at her. She was probably the most levelheaded person he knew. "Look at us… I'm rooting for my ex to stay sober so she can have a relationship with my son and whatever grandchildren he gives us, and you're being the most generous woman in the world."

She shook her head. "Not hardly. Just adhering to my mission statement."

He could see from the determination in her eyes that she believed that, but he saw more. So much more. He saw enough that his heart stumbled. He didn't think he'd ever met anyone like her. She was certainly Annabelle's polar opposite. Antonio's mother always wanted the spotlight. Never helped anyone because she never thought about anyone but herself and having fun.

Warmth filled him. "You know…maybe we get our pizza to go?"

"And eat it at your house?"

"And eat it in the nice little hotel you stayed at the first time you were here. We could spend the afternoon together."

She laughed. "Eating pizza in bed?"

He grinned. "This affair is about fun… We both just had a weird morning. We need some fun. Plus, you're leaving tomorrow. I don't want you to forget me."

She laughed. "As if I could."

They got their pizza in a to-go box and strolled up the street to the limo, which took them to her former hotel. When they registered, he asked for champagne to be brought up to their room. It arrived only a minute or two after they'd stepped inside.

He poured two glasses, and they sat on the bed and sipped indulgently.

"This is great."

"I told you affairs with me were fun."

She laughed. He took the glass from her hand and set it on the bedside table of the small room so he could kiss her. She had no idea what a wonderful person she was. How kind. Even having reservations about her daughter's wedding, she'd listened to Antonio and Riley, watched them and come around to their way of thinking. Now she'd be taking care of Riley's grandparents, who'd not only kicked her out of her condo; they'd never acknowledged Riley.

If he wanted to spend a few minutes enjoying her company, thanking the heavens that she was in his life, he was not going to stop himself. She deserved to be pampered.

They could go back to having fun when she returned from Manhattan for the engagement party, but today he wanted to love her.

CHAPTER TEN

Two hours later, Juliette kissed Lorenzo and walked into the bathroom as if she were the happiest woman alive, but once the door closed behind her, she leaned against it with a sigh.

Making love after their difficult mornings had been wonderful. She'd never felt so close to anyone. Her heart had swelled with ridiculous emotion. She would call it love but they didn't know each other well enough to be in love. Even Antonio and Riley had known each other for a few months. She and Lorenzo had basically just met…

A little over two weeks ago.

It wasn't love.

She'd promised herself she would not let her heart get involved, but having someone to talk to about her life was a little too nice to ignore. Yes, she talked to Marietta and Pete, but they were employees and there was only so far a boss could go with her confidences to maintain enough distance that she could be a good employer. She didn't want to burden them with her troubles, but talking to Lorenzo didn't feel like burdening him. It felt like confiding in a trusted friend.

And she'd loved him confiding in her too. He trusted her. Not in the one-friend-trusting-another way. In that deep down, almost spiritual way that two people could when they really understood each other.

After washing her face, she walked out of the bathroom and swooped her jeans off the floor. "Are we going back to the villa separately or together?"

"Did you make arrangements for one of the drivers to pick you up?"

"Yes. In a half hour in front of Gucci."

He grabbed his watch from the bedside table and winced. "I'll get you there with my limo." He rolled out of bed. "Then I'll go back to work, telling Antonio I ran into a friend."

She laughed. "Let's see… So far, you've been continually running into friends and had a two-hour phone conversation with a guy you made up… What was his name? Frank?"

"I should have never told you that."

"I can say I was shopping all day. But you may need to come up with a better excuse."

He laughed. "I could say I ran into *you* and we had lunch and shopped together."

She grimaced. "Maybe next time."

"Why?" He walked over and slid his arms around her. "It's a reasonable excuse for why I didn't come back to work. Instead of shopping, we could say we got pizza and were talking about the wedding." He stopped and grinned devilishly. "Or I could say I was telling you about an investment that might interest you."

She bit her lower lip thinking, then said, "I do have investments."

"See! Now we can take the same limo home."

She shook her head. "You are a conniver."

"No. I am always thinking of ways to make things work."

She had to give him that. She canceled her ride, and they took his limo back to the vineyard. The foyer was empty when they walked inside, so they could share the elevator to the third floor without raising suspicions. She told herself to stop worrying because no one was paying attention to them. No one was even there to see them.

But the next morning, Juliette wasn't surprised that she needed to go to Florence for her flight at the same time that Lorenzo needed to go to work. Still eating breakfast, GiGi, Antonio and Riley said quick goodbyes, seemingly accepting the excuse that he would be dropping her off at the train station on his way to work.

Walking to the limo, she considered saying something about his casual way of doing things, but just as her worries about arriving home together the day before had been for nothing, their kids and his mom had taken it as no big deal that they were riding into town together.

He walked her inside the terminal and stopped in front of her and straightened her scarf. "Sleep on the flight, if you can."

"That works coming to Italy, but I think it might backfire on the way home."

He chuckled. "No. It pretty much works both ways. But you're still going to have some jet lag."

"Yeah. I did the last time."

He glanced around then gave her a quick kiss before he walked away. He turned to wave goodbye, then quickened his steps to walk back to the limo.

She shook her head. He thought he was being careful, but she always thought of cities as being like small towns in some ways. You never knew who your waitress or cab driver knew and anything you said or did in public could become gossip. She rarely said anything significant in a public place.

He thought a quick look around handled everything.

She arrived in New York a little before nine o'clock. Though it was the middle of the night in Italy, it really wasn't even bedtime in Manhattan. At her condo, she caught up on emails.

The third one from Pete made her frown.

Finnegan appointment pushed to Thursday morning.

If she wanted to, she could handle it.

Confusing thoughts bombarded her. She made herself a bourbon and told herself to forget it, let Pete do the intake as planned, but she couldn't. If nothing else, she was curious about the people who'd rather be alone than acknowledge their only grandchild.

With a sigh, she returned to her computer and emailed Pete that she'd be doing the intake visit with the Finnegans.

The time difference and her nerves conspired to keep her up all night, so at seven o'clock, she showered and dressed, then left her apartment to find a bagel before she headed for the Finnegans'.

When the elevator door opened on a big sitting room, she saw why the building's doorman had punched in a code rather than tell her their floor number. The elevator was the front door to their penthouse. She also saw that the area needed a good cleaning. Dust had accumulated on lamps and end tables. She swore there was a cobweb on the top valance of the drapes.

She winced. The place was also hopelessly out of date, as if it had been frozen in time—

Her heart stuttered. Maybe they'd stopped caring when Greg had died?

Doctor Art Jenkins walked into the sitting room, his hand extended to shake hers. "Thank you, Juliette. I appreciate this."

"I'm happy to be here."

"It's why everyone loves your company. It's more than a job to you."

She said simply, "Yes," as the feeling of having traveled back in time enveloped her.

He motioned for her to follow him from the formal sitting room into a family room. She could see the old-fashioned French Provincial dining room furniture against the backdrop of Manhattan displayed through a wall of windows. A sense of their loneliness and desolation filled her. She understood perfectly. For years, she had missed Greg too.

As they entered the family room, an old man rose. Greg's dad. She'd only seen him at the funeral, but she'd spoken to him afterward. She easily recognized him as an older version of the man who'd humiliated her.

"This is Walter Finnegan." He faced Walter. "Walter, this is Juliette Morgan."

She offered her hand to shake his. He took it with a weary smile. "I'm sorry. I just can't care for her."

He looked barely able to care for himself.

Upstart. No social climber will benefit from my son's death.

She released his hand, let the memories drift away as her work personality easily kicked in. "Please, Mr. Finnegan. Your situation isn't unusual, and my staff is more than capable."

The doctor motioned for them to sit.

"If you don't mind my saying this, I think you could benefit from a little help too."

He snorted. "I wouldn't mind some assistance."

She smiled kindly, as she glanced down at the intake sheet. The man was ninety. He might have a cook and a negligent housekeeper, but those kinds of employees didn't do personal things like assist with dressing or showers. Plus, once her employees were on staff, they could add a little accountability for the housekeeper.

They talked for ten minutes, and then she was taken back to Greg's mom's bedroom. Rachel Finnegan sat on a chair by the window, toying with her long hair, staring out at the city.

Art Jenkins said, "Rachel?"

She turned with a smile. "Good morning, Doctor." She glanced at Juliette and frowned. "Do I know you?"

Juliette shook her head. People with dementia frequently asked questions like that. Not for one second did she think Greg's mother recognized her.

"No. I'm with a home nursing agency. We'll be coming in to help you from now on."

"Help me what?" she demanded. "Help me lose my jewelry? Help me spend my money?"

Walter faced Juliette. "I'm sorry. The dementia turned her into a totally different person."

"Don't be sorry," Juliette said. "This is part of her disease."

Greg's parents were old and helpless. Their cook might feed them, but they needed help with hygiene and maybe someone to read to them or play games with them to keep their mental acuity as high as possible. Juliette's staff could make their final years much more comfortable.

The doctor walked her to the elevator. "Your company can take them on?"

"Yes. We probably should have been called sooner." The elevator arrived and the doctor got on with her. "How long has she been like this?"

"Two years."

The doors closed and they started down to the lobby. "It looks like two years since she's had a haircut."

He shook his head. "Walter just kept being positive, thinking she'd bounce back, and she would want to take care of it herself."

"We're glad to help. My staff will contact your office to set up the bulk of the arrangements, including a schedule. You will also need to give us authorization to look at their medical reports so we have the full picture." Though she knew the answer, she asked, "There are no other close relatives who could sign papers or make arrangements?"

"Just me."

"You're a relative?"

"Not a relative. I was their son's friend. I have power of attorney."

She took a quiet breath but didn't react. Yet another person Greg hadn't introduced her to.

"He died and because I was their doctor I sort of stepped in."

The elevator doors opened. "That was kind of you."

"No. That's life."

Didn't she know it.

The doctor stayed on the elevator, obviously to return to the Finnegan penthouse.

"You'll hear from my staff."

She left the building not quite sure what she was feeling.

She hadn't hated Greg's parents her entire life. She hadn't let herself think of them.

If she felt anything it was sorrow that they were so alone when they hadn't had to be. Riley could have filled the empty spaces in their lives, but they had preferred for them to remain empty.

Confused about her feelings for them, Juliette threw herself into work when she returned to her office. At the end of the day, she was seated at her desk with a full view up the hall to the reception area when the main door opened, and Lorenzo walked in. Wearing a black cashmere overcoat and black leather gloves, he looked every inch the sophisticated gentleman that he was—with a little bit of bad boy thrown in when his unruly hair shifted along his collar when he moved his head.

Her mouth lifted into a smile. Her whole body began to tingle—

Then she remembered that there could still be stragglers in the office and any one of them could call Riley and tell her anything that happened between her mother and soon-to-be father-in-law. Whatever his reason for being here she did not want anyone on the staff of her company *or Riley's* to hear it.

She rose and scooted around her desk, then changed her mind. It was close enough to seven o'clock that she could also leave for the day. She grabbed her coat and purse and raced up to the reception area as quickly as she could.

"Lorenzo!" she said, walking past the empty receptionist desk. Sissy would have gone home at five o'clock.

Lorenzo faced her with a smile. "Juliette—"

"I was just on my way out," she said, catching his elbow and steering him toward the door again. When they were in the empty hall on their way to the elevator, away from any employees who might still be in the office, she said, "Why are you here? Did the kids break up? Oh my God, is there something wrong with Riley?"

He laughed. "Riley is fine. I just…" He cleared his throat. "My house is wedding central. Gifts are beginning to arrive."

The elevator came and they stepped inside. When the doors closed, he smiled. "And I missed you."

"I haven't been gone long enough for you to miss me."

"Maybe not, but it was long enough for my sitting room to fill with gifts."

"Isn't it early for gifts?"

"Wedding's about five weeks away. People who can't attend are beginning to send gifts."

"And you don't like your peace disturbed?"

"I'm not *that* bad."

"No. But you like your world comfortable."

"I do. Riley and Antonio are fabulous. I love living with them."

"But…"

"No buts. I love living with them."

"Well, they are filling your house up with gifts."

He sighed and relented. "Okay, the house is different with them there. I want them there. I really do. But I honestly left because I wanted to see you. Our affair is limited. Once they marry, we really will see each other only a few times a year. I feel like these weeks before the wedding are our chance and we should be allowed to make the best of them."

He said it in such a simple, honest way, that she saw his point. Though she'd worried that she was getting feelings for him, there might not be anything to be concerned about.

After the wedding, they'd see each other four or five times a *year* at most.

Even if she fell madly in love with him, they'd drift apart simply by virtue of the fact that they lived on two different continents and their feelings would lessen naturally.

The elevator stopped and they got out. Lorenzo pointed out the glass door. "I have a car on the street."

"Okay. But my condo's not that far."

He batted a hand. "We'll take the car anyway. Then I can send the driver back to his company."

They got into the car and were driven the few blocks to her condo. Using his phone, he paid the bill. The driver retrieved Lorenzo's black duffel bag from the hatch, and they headed into her building.

They entered the lobby with its sleek midcentury modern décor and walked to the elevator. She pushed the button for her floor and the doors slid closed.

She thought of their last night together but actually took herself back the whole way to that afternoon with pizza in bed. They'd talked about important things, and she'd felt a connection that had scared her. But she'd worked all that out in her head and after the confusing morning she'd had, it was great to see somebody who understood her. She might not tell him about the intake visit, but she didn't need to. She simply needed a few hours of being herself, not caring about the past or the future.

And he would provide it.

The elevator doors reopened. She led him out and down the hall to her condo.

They walked inside. He dropped his duffel bag on the floor and gasped. "Wow. Look at that view!"

"I'm sure you've had a similar one in hotel rooms other times you've been to the city."

He laughed. "Yes. But there's something different about a hotel room view. It's always temporary. This view is yours."

She acknowledged that with a tilt of her head. "True."

He slid out of his overcoat and laid it across the back of her white sofa, then removed his suit jacket.

"Want a drink while I find takeout menus so we can get dinner?"

He winced. "Probably not. I stayed up on the plane so I could get on Manhattan time and bourbon might put me to sleep."

She laughed and pulled a handful of menus out of a drawer in the kitchen of her open floor plan living area. He might live in a mansion, but she'd paid a pretty penny for this condo then completely remodeled it. The dark bamboo flooring gave a cozy feel to the space and complemented her white sectional sofa with two yellow throws, as well as the white cabinets in the kitchen.

"Here you go." She handed the menus to him, walked to the smoky-blue-colored tile fireplace and pressed the button that turned on the gas. A small fire sprang to life.

Lorenzo loosened his tie and unbuttoned the top two buttons of his white shirt before he flipped through the takeout menus. "What's your preference?"

She loved how relaxed he looked, especially since he appeared perfectly at ease in her home. Actually, he fit. For as much as he belonged in his villa, he also fit in her condo.

"I skipped lunch so I'm starving. Wanna get burgers?"

"You sound like Marco."

"What then?"

"It's cold. How about soup?"

"I know just the deli."

She walked to the kitchen island, got her purse and

rummaged for her phone. As she dialed the number, he glanced around, smiling with approval. Though his opinion shouldn't matter to her, it gave her great pleasure that he liked what he saw. Particularly since she'd done all the decorating herself.

She ordered soup with some breadsticks. When she was done, she offered him a bottle of water. He took it happily.

"So?" She sat on the sofa. "Who's doing your work while you're away?"

"I can do a lot online, but Antonio had meetings scheduled with our lawyers here in Manhattan." He chuckled. "I made it seem like I was doing him a favor by taking them so he could stay in Florence with Riley."

She gasped. "You devil."

"Hey, I *am* doing him a favor." He eased onto the chair across from her. But she didn't care that he hadn't sat beside her. This gave her a good chance to look at him. The comfortable way he sat forward, elbows on his knees, hands folded in front of him. While she'd ordered their soup, he'd rolled up the sleeves of his white shirt and now looked like the businessman that he was, sleeves out of his way so he could get down to work.

"He also didn't argue about taking a bit of my work while I'm away."

She laughed. "That just makes sense."

"Especially since it ensures he gets private time with Riley."

She laughed. "And that makes even more sense."

When Juliette's landline rang, Lorenzo watched her push herself off the sofa, walk to the kitchen and answer it. She said "Okay" a lot, then reached for her purse again.

"That was the doorman. Our soup is here. He'll bring it up."

A minute later, there was a knock on the door. The doorman entered with two brown paper bags. She tipped him and closed the door.

He rose. "Where do you want to eat?"

"You're tired. Let's sit on the sofa."

"It's white."

"That's what the throws are for."

"They're yellow."

"I'll wash them."

He laughed. "You're so casual about these things."

"Because I know how to use a washing machine."

She set the soup and breadsticks on the center island. As she pulled the breadsticks out of the bag he said, "So, are you going to tell me what's happening with Greg's parents?"

She said, "Nothing. Really," but she slid a breadstick out of the bag and took a big bite.

He sniffed. "Stress eater?"

"No." She winced. "Maybe." Looking like a lost lamb, she eased down to sit on one of the stools in front of the island. "I don't want to burden you. Mostly because it was nothing."

"*What* was nothing?"

"I did the intake interview."

"Oh." He'd suspected she wouldn't be able to send someone else to handle that meeting if she'd arrived in time to go herself. Curiosity overwhelmed him and he sat on the stool beside hers. "What happened?"

She rose and went to a cupboard and opened it, leaving her back to him. "We keep the interviews short. We don't overburden the potential clients. I spoke with both Walter and Rachel—just long enough to assess their conditions and what they'd need." She walked back to the counter with two soup bowls and filled both with soup, then handed one to him.

"And what did you think?"

She walked away to retrieve soup spoons and he realized that she needed to be doing something—not looking at him—to be able to talk about this.

Because it confused her? Because she was embarrassed to talk about it? He didn't know.

"My analysis was that they're old and sick." She sat on her stool beside him. "And alone."

He caught her arm to get her attention. "Hey, that's not your fault. You would have happily let them into Riley's life."

"I would have. Even if they didn't want anything to do with me, I would have let them love Riley."

"And it confuses you that they didn't want that?"

"Yes! I was alone after my parents died. I would have given anything to have family in my life. When Riley was born, I finally had a connection again."

He said, "Yeah. I get it."

They ate a bit of their soup in silence. Then she sighed. "Did you ever wonder why fate showed you something?"

"You mean you think it's fate that yours is the agency their doctor chose?"

"Yes."

He shrugged. "I have two thoughts. First, your agency is very good. That's why their doctor thought of you. And second it only means something if you make it something. What if it really is a coincidence that you are connected to them again…and what if you try to make it something that it isn't? The only thing you will accomplish is lost sleep."

"I never thought of it that way."

"Well, think of it that way. Sometimes a coincidence really is just a coincidence."

He tossed his napkin on the counter. "That's enough serious talk. Time for a break. What do you say we dance?"

Her eyes widened, then narrowed, as if she wasn't sure she'd heard him correctly. "What?"

"Dance." He retrieved his phone and pulled up a playlist. "Surely you've heard of it."

"Yes. But…dance? In a kitchen?"

"Kitchen, living room, bathroom. What does it matter? When someone needs cheering up, who cares what room you choose?"

She laughed. "I can cheer myself up."

"Ah. Why would you want to do that when dancing is so much fun? For once, give yourself a break. Stop worrying and wondering and just dance." A slow romantic song floated into the room. He offered his hand to her.

She sniffed. "That sounds like a line."

"I never use lines. I always say what I think." He offered his hand again.

"Well, if it's not a line—" She took his hand.

He pulled her close. He almost said, "There. Isn't that better than trying to figure out everything?" But holding her felt so good, he decided to let the moment speak for itself. He genuinely believed it was a coincidence her ex's family had hired her firm, but he also understood how that could open emotional doors for her.

With the size of her open-plan area, he could maneuver her away from the island into an uncluttered space between the kitchen and the living area. The music drifted around them. He felt the stress of the day and his tiredness melt away.

"This is better."

He smiled down at her. "I do have a good idea or two every once in a while."

She laughed, easing closer and laying her head on his shoulder.

He tightened his hold on her to accommodate her. Her softness pressed up against him and his eyes closed. He allowed himself to feel every sensation, absorb every scent, enjoy every word and note of the song.

Her hand cruised up his back. His hand slid up hers then down again.

There was a natural intimacy between them, something he couldn't deny, even if it sometimes baffled him. They'd known each other for a few weeks and he felt like he'd known her forever.

Juliette felt like she was floating. As a woman who kept her boyfriends and lovers at a distance, she didn't have moments like this. Quiet intimacy. Not because she liked Lorenzo more than the rest, but because there was something different between them. More than lust, not as unreliable as love, it was sort of a bond—a link—something unique and wonderful.

The music stopped. She looked up. He gazed down at her with such longing that her heart stuttered. Their lips drifted toward each other naturally and met warmly. But in seconds, the kiss heated. She slid her hands along his silk shirt, luxuriating in the feeling of the fabric and muscles beneath. Sweet arousal rippled through her. Her entire body begged for attention. As if reading her mind, he deepened the kiss. With the increase in tempo came an increase in need. His hands raced down her back and up her sides.

Still kissing, she guided him down the hall to her room.

They undressed and fell to the bed like two people so attuned to each other they could anticipate every move.

It wasn't as hot as their first time had been or as emotional as their afternoon at the hotel eating pizza on the bed and talking about their lives. This time, they seemed to find that perfect combination of familiarity and excitement. Naked and happy in her own bed, she let herself play to her heart's delight, until Lorenzo took the lead. His hands cruised her curves, heating her skin and igniting her blood. When he finally rolled her to her back, hiking her hands over her head and pinning them to the pillow, he caught her gaze and smiled at her.

She couldn't help smiling back. Everything between them was always wonderful. How could she not smile?

She suddenly realized she would miss him when the wedding was over. When she only went to Italy for holidays and birthdays or the birth of a baby.

Still, this was how she liked her life. Uncomplicated. Controlled. No chance to be hurt.

CHAPTER ELEVEN

THE NEXT MORNING, she woke in his arms. She yawned and stretched and wiggled enough that she could get out of bed to shower. He finally woke when she returned to the bedroom, dressed and ready to leave.

Taking a long drink of air, he levered himself onto the pillow. "My meeting's not for an hour."

"I have coffee and a coffeemaker. Or there's a little coffee shop about half a block down. You can get a bagel or a doughnut or a breakfast sandwich." She raced over to him and kissed him. "But I have to go. I'll see you tonight." She frowned. "Unless you work late?"

He laughed. "Are you kidding? This is like time off for me. I'll make sure the meetings end before three, so we can have the whole night to ourselves." He turned to slide out of bed. "Is there anything you'd like to do?"

She didn't hesitate to be honest because even if he disagreed, whatever she said would be a starting point to finding something they both wanted to do. They didn't argue or compromise; they figured things out. Which was so comfortable, so honest, even that added to her ease around him.

She never felt she was being pushed into a corner.

"I wouldn't mind a nice dinner."

"I did notice you eat a lot of takeout." He kissed her. "So nice dinner out it is."

"Thanks."

She ran out and he glanced around with a smile. These next few days could actually be fun. Or he could even extend his stay until the following Wednesday when they had to return to Italy for the engagement party. There was always something to do with lawyers. They liked billable hours and he wanted to stay in Manhattan for a while.

That night he planned the kind of dinner that they had to dress up for. He'd even had a tux delivered to her condo and a limo waiting in front of her building. She'd swooned a bit when she'd seen him in the tux, and he had to admit she looked so good in her little black dress that he'd swooned a bit himself.

Saturday night they went to a Broadway play, then had dinner at Jupiter and returned to her condo to make love. Sunday, they walked to Central Park and fed the pigeons. He wouldn't let her work, though she wanted to. He insisted they both needed a break. The air was crisp. The sky cloudy and moody. But the pigeons were hungry and the people watching—something he'd never taken time to do—was more interesting than he would have ever believed. His brain rested, he went back to the law firm with his list of things he wanted to accomplish and damned if he didn't get some real work done.

She headed out every morning around six thirty, to be at her office when her nurses went on shift at seven. He spent leisurely mornings in her condo drinking coffee and eating pastries that he would buy the day before.

By the time Wednesday came around, he was rested and ready to return to a villa filled with gifts and noise, and she was tired enough from all her work to look forward to having several hours in the air when no one could reach them.

They couldn't catch a flight out to Italy until that night. With the time difference and the flight time, they arrived at the villa early in the afternoon on Thursday. Preoccupied with the engagement party, no one even questioned their arrival at the villa together. GiGi was too joyful over having Juliette back to question anything.

Gerard reached for their bags.

Lorenzo said, "Juliette will be in the same room she stayed in last time."

Gerard said, "Very good," and headed for the elevator.

Antonio said, "So why were you in New York so long… what's going on that you're not telling me?"

Though Juliette pretended great interest in digging for something in her purse, Lorenzo didn't miss a beat. "Antonio, your wedding is about four weeks away. You shouldn't be questioning what I do or who I see. You should understand that I'm trying to come up with a wedding gift."

Antonio grimaced. "Right! Sorry!"

"If you bug me too much, I could end up giving you a butter dish instead of what I have planned."

Riley laughed. GiGi shook her head. Antonio winced and said, "Sorry," again. "I'm not usually the one to ruin a surprise."

Lorenzo shook his head. "That's typically my mother's job."

GiGi gasped and swatted him. "I'm sharp as a tack. I don't leak secrets."

Juliette smiled and said, "If no one minds I'm going up to my room for a shower."

"No! Go ahead," GiGi said. "We want you to feel like this is your home too!"

Juliette said, "Thanks," and walked up the foyer stairs.

Lorenzo waited a few minutes before he, too, excused himself. He found her in the room he'd assigned to her the last time.

When he stepped inside, she walked over and kissed him. "I'm not sure if we're getting better at this with practice or if we're just really good at fooling people."

He laughed and lowered his head to kiss her, but Riley came running into the room. Juliette bounced away from him. The move was so fast, and Riley was so clearly focused on whatever had brought her upstairs, that Lorenzo was fairly certain she either hadn't seen her mom pressed up against him or she hadn't registered what she'd seen.

She walked to Juliette. "You dropped this." She handed Juliette her phone. "We didn't even notice it on the foyer floor until it started ringing. It stopped, of course, because I don't have your password to open it. But if it was Pete or Marietta, I'm sure they left a message."

Juliette quickly checked to see who had called, but Lorenzo noticed Riley's attention shifting. Now that the urgency of giving the phone to her mom was gone, she glanced around, taking in everything she saw.

"Nice suite."

"Prettiest one we have," Lorenzo said casually, giving a reason for why he'd put Juliette on this floor. "So, we're a couple days away from your engagement party..." he said, changing the subject.

"Yes! It's a great way for me to meet a lot of your relatives and business associates all at once before the wedding. Plus, I'm excited to meet Antonio's mom."

He didn't overtly react. He could not refuse Antonio the right to have his mother at all his wedding celebrations. But that didn't mean he had to like it.

Or even pretend he liked it. Particularly since Annabelle could behave perfectly at the engagement party and come to the wedding stone-cold drunk and curse at anyone who tried to talk to her.

He didn't worry for himself. He would simply have her escorted off the grounds if it was up to him. He worried for Antonio. His son was happy. His expectations were high. If his mother did something, it would devastate him.

With Lorenzo and Riley chatting in her room, Juliette walked from the sitting room into the bedroom to return Marietta's call.

"I'm at the airport in Rome."

Juliette blinked. "What?"

"I flew into Rome. Now I think I take a train to Florence but I'm not sure."

Juliette sat on the bed. If she and Lorenzo hadn't been so secretive about him being in Manhattan, Marietta could have flown with them. Instead, it appeared she'd taken another flight out.

"Yes. Take the train to Florence." She bit her lip, thinking things through. "I don't know if the family is putting you up here in the villa or if they have you in a hotel. Before I come get you, I'll ask."

"*You're* coming to get me?"

"Sure. I've been from Florence to the villa lots of times." And it was a good way to get out of the house for a few hours and put some distance between her and Lorenzo so they could adjust to the fact that they weren't in her home, where they could do anything they wanted. "I know my way. And I've been driving since I was a kid. The train ride will take an hour and a half. That gives me time to get a shower, then ask about your arrangements and drive into town. Text me the time the train leaves so I'm not too early or late."

"Okay."

Juliette disconnected the call and returned to the sitting room of her suite where Riley and Lorenzo were still chatting. "Marietta's at the airport. She's about to take the train to Florence."

Riley clapped her hands with glee. "Yay!" She faced Lorenzo. "Should we send somebody to get her?"

"Actually, I told her I'd be driving to town to pick her up."

Both Lorenzo and Riley faced her.

She shrugged. "I know the way. Besides, she and I can talk business, then when we get here, we'll be all yours."

"Okay!" Satisfied, Riley pivoted and raced out of Juliette's suite.

Lorenzo crossed his arms on his chest. "You're going to drive in Florence?"

She laughed. "I've got to do it sometime. I've been back and forth a few trips and I'm actually a very good driver."

"Let me go with you."

"No." As she had with Riley, she kissed his cheek. "We need some distance, a chance to shift our behaviors from how casual we were in my condo. I'll be fine. I have GPS on my phone."

"Better make sure to set it up before you leave."

She teasingly said, "Yes, boss," and grabbed her suitcase to roll it back to the bedroom. "Now leave so I can unpack. I want to shower before I get her."

He started out of her suite but stopped. "Take the big black SUV when you go. That's got GPS already set up."

In the bedroom, she began pulling clothes from her suitcase and tucking them into drawers or hanging them in the closet. Without time to shop for a new dress for the engagement ball, she'd brought a red silk sleeveless gown that she'd worn to at least four Christmas parties. Elegant in its simplicity, it always made her feel beautiful. Saturday night, she'd be the mother of the bride, officially for the first time, and she wanted to look her best.

She smiled dreamily. It might not have happened the way she'd expected, but her daughter was getting married to a wonderful man who had a fabulous family. Everything was going well. Without anyone overwhelming her, she felt part of everything—

Mother of the bride. Happily involved with the groom's gorgeous father. Caring for Greg's parents.

The last one popped into her head of its own volition, causing a horrible feeling of dread to shuffle through her. She couldn't understand why the thought of Greg's parents ruined the moment or even popped into her brain at all. They were clients. Nothing else.

Given that Antonio's family was wonderful, Lorenzo made her happy and the wedding filled her with anticipation, Greg's parents should be the last thing she'd think about. Caring for the sick and elderly was her company's bread and butter. There hadn't been any angry words when she'd gone to their home, and they clearly hadn't recognized her. She'd also managed to stay neutral after a few stray memories when she saw the condition of their home.

She would not let thoughts of Greg's parents, the decades-old insults, the shaming, get to her. Not when this weekend could be one of the happiest of her life.

She refused.

She wasn't simply smarter than to do that. She was stronger.

In fact, she was the strongest person she knew.

A few memories wouldn't take her down.

* * *

Over three hours later, Juliette stepped into the foyer with Marietta Fontain following her. Both glowing. Both giggling.

Lorenzo had overheard GiGi telling Juliette that arrangements had been made for the maid of honor and best man to stay at Riley's hotel—the name they gave to the hotel in Florence where she'd stayed while she and Antonio were falling in love. So, Lorenzo wasn't surprised Marietta didn't have luggage. They'd probably stopped at the hotel to drop it off.

The tall, wispy redhead impulsively hugged him, and he laughed. "It's nice to see you too, Marietta."

She winced. "Sorry. I'm just so excited I can't contain it."

"We're pretty happy too," Lorenzo said. With Juliette standing beside him, he almost slid his arm around her waist to bring her close to him, and he stopped cold. Not because he worried that people would see. But because the gesture had been so natural. The kind of thing a man does with a woman he considers his partner, the woman he loves.

If he'd thought his reaction to almost sliding his arm around her waist was bad, the word *love* nearly choked him.

He wrestled it to the back of his mind. Tonight, he and Juliette would sleep together. They'd have the whole nine yards. A lovely evening with family and friends, followed by a passionate night.

He had plans and would not let a few random thoughts ruin them.

His phone buzzed with a text. He pulled it out of his pocket and sighed. "Rico is here."

Juliette said, "Rico?"

"Antonio's best man. He wants to know where to park his car."

Juliette laughed. "He's never seen your auto showroom?"

Lorenzo rolled his eyes. "At least he didn't need GPS to find the place. Let me go out to greet him and tell him what to do."

He directed Marietta to the living room. "I believe bridesmaids gowns are being discussed in there." Riley had excitedly told him they were taking advantage of everyone being in Italy for the engagement party to choose bridesmaids' gowns and tuxes.

Then he addressed Juliette. "You've been around enough that you can be in charge of wine...or mixed drinks."

She winked at him. "We'll be fine."

As he turned to go outside, the urge to kiss her goodbye came so naturally that he barely caught himself. Walking to Rico's Bentley, he shook his head at the slipups that kept confronting him that day. It had to be the excitement of guests arriving and a party being planned around him that had him off his game. Normally, he wasn't so careless that he nearly made mistakes. But now that he was aware, he would watch what he said and did.

Rico stepped out of the car. Tall and thin, the dark-haired British coffee merchant looked perfectly at home in a T-shirt and jeans with a black leather jacket. He caught Lorenzo in a big hug the way Marietta had.

"Good to see you, old man," he said, slapping Lorenzo's back, his British accent smooth and clear in the crisp air.

Lorenzo snorted. "I'm far from an old man."

"I know. Rumor has it you've got a new lady in town."

Lorenzo gaped at him. "What?"

"I know. I know. It's a secret. The way all your relationships are."

"Not all my relationships are a secret." Actually, they were. "Just drive up to the garage door and one of the maintenance guys will park your car inside. We can text them to get it for you when you're ready to leave."

Rico tossed his car starter in the air with a sarcastic laugh. "Evading the question about your mystery woman." He shook his head. "Same old Lorenzo."

Rico said "same old Lorenzo" as if there was something wrong with that. There wasn't. His life was good, happy, because he kept his most intimate company private. One friend of his son's, no matter how close to the family, wouldn't make him feel weird.

But he addressed it with Juliette that night, when dinner was over, and the kids had decided to go to the wine tasting room and join the tourists for music and dancing. With no one to notice, he and Juliette had gone to his room.

"Do you ever get hassled over keeping your private life private?"

She considered that as he brushed her hair aside so he could unzip her dress. When it was down and the garment slithered to the floor, she sighed. "Yes and no. The people who count, Riley and Marietta, know they'll get the scoop when it's over, so they don't ask and jeopardize their access to the juicy details. Anybody else just gives me significant looks if I come to the office doing the walk of shame."

"Walk of shame?"

"You know—in the same clothes you had on the day before."

He laughed heartily. "This is why I—"

Love. He almost said *why I love you*! What the hell was wrong with him?

Luckily, Juliette stopped his talking by standing on tiptoes and kissing him. In only yellow panties and bra, she brushed a kiss across his mouth, then began unbuttoning his shirt. With one quick move of her hands under the clothes at his shoulders, she removed both his shirt and jacket.

Reaching for his belt, she frowned. "You always wear too many clothes."

He laughed and shoved aside the weirdness that kept sneaking up on him by changing the subject. "I love you in yellow."

"You seem to love me in most colors."

"I prefer you *out* of most colors," he said, sliding his hand under her bra strap as he kissed her.

She all but purred with contentment, the sound hitting the part of him that responded to her naturally and happily.

They made love then she fell asleep nestled against his side. Given that no one was around, he'd persuaded her to sleep with him. She'd agreed but he suspected she would sneak off if she woke in the middle of the night. Which was fine. He only wanted to fall asleep holding her.

For as much as he longed to nod off, he forced himself to stay awake for a few minutes to enjoy the moment. Something was happening between them. He didn't know if that meant it was time to break it off or to wonder if after all these years real love was finally finding him.

He'd been so sure with Annabelle, though, that he knew he wasn't always the best judge of these kinds of situations. His feelings were one thing. The truth of what was happening was sometimes another.

Which was why it was smarter to stay the course. Stick with his normal romancing routine. No more thoughts of love meant no more questions bouncing around in his head.

Besides, she wanted a temporary relationship too. Any decision otherwise might be met with a swift breakup. He absolutely didn't want to lose her until he had to, so he wouldn't bring up anything serious.

He slid down onto the bed, his head now on the pillow.

Even if he was falling in love, he should ignore the potential problems and enjoy it until the inevitable chips fell because they always did. He might usually be the one to break things off, but Juliette was strong, smart, knew her own mind. He had to be ready for the day she said she wanted to move on.

Actually, he should begin preparing for it now. He should stop being so casual and be more intentional about everything he said and did.

Also, as she'd mentioned that afternoon, a little distance between them was necessary when they were here, at the villa. He might be thrilled having her in his home, but he needed to remember their relationship was about happiness. Not love.

Love had never made him happy.

CHAPTER TWELVE

THE FIRST THING Juliette became aware of as she woke was that she was in a different bed. Which was actually her new normal, given that she now spent so much time at the villa—

Except she wasn't in that room. And she was waking up with Lorenzo. She smiled before she opened her eyes and saw him looking down on her.

"Good morning."

She stretched as far as she could with him wrapped around her. "Good morning."

"I have a coffeemaker up here."

It wasn't what she'd expected him to say, but in some ways it was the most romantic thing anyone had ever said to her.

She purred against him. "Sweet talker."

He laughed and rolled out of bed. She'd expected him to initiate another lovemaking session. When he didn't, she realized being on the same floor, in the same room, with everybody else a whole floor below them—or maybe even in the dining room by now—they had all the time in the world.

He gathered her clothes from the floor and set them on a chair. "If you'd like, you could leave a pair of pajamas or a robe here."

"I probably should go to my room and get a toothbrush."

He opened the door to the exquisite, spa-like bathroom

she'd seen in the middle of the night. "No need. There are extra toothbrushes and several kinds of toothpaste in the cabinet."

She walked toward him. "I don't suppose you have my favorite cinnamon coffee."

"I might have taken note of the pods on the coffee carousel in your kitchen and instructed staff to get some."

She laughed. "Are you trying to get me to stay forever?"

"Just being a good host."

She slid by him to get into the bathroom and use one of those extra toothbrushes so she could kiss him after. "A very good host."

She opened the cabinet, looking for a toothbrush, and found two white terrycloth robes instead. One was clearly Lorenzo's size, the other was smaller and fit her like a glove. She'd think he'd had it placed in his room, as he had with her favorite coffee, except Lorenzo was a gorgeous, wealthy man. He might live with his family, but he had a private apartment.

She was not the first woman he'd brought here.

Brushing her teeth, she told herself that didn't matter. He wasn't the first guy she'd had an affair with.

Except he was the first guy in a long time that she'd had these over-the-top, happy feelings for. Their relationship was more than just stolen nights or afternoons. They talked about things—they liked each other.

She shook her head, reminding herself that a big part of her extreme happiness was a result of her joy over her daughter getting married. She was planning with Riley and GiGi and had laughed herself silly with Marietta the day before as she'd driven them along the roads from Florence. She was having fun. *Real fun.* Fun that had nothing to do with work or success. She was enjoying herself.

Enjoying life.

Wow. She couldn't remember the last time she'd done that.

After her final mouth rinse, she noticed her hair was sticking out all over the place. She tried to fix it with her fingers but failed.

"Let it be." Lorenzo walked into the bathroom and kissed her. "I like it a bit messy. It reminds me of everything we did last night. I can take that image to work with me."

The shimmer of happiness over the lovely things he always said to her was tempered by the mention of work. She groaned. "You have work?"

"It is Friday, and I did spend over a week in Manhattan with you. Plus, you'll be doing wedding planning so we wouldn't see much of each other anyway. Your coffee's on the kitchen island. I have to get dressed."

She almost asked him if he was going to shower, then thought the better of it. If he had time for shower sex, he would have suggested it. She gave him a quick kiss goodbye, then went on a mission to find her coffee.

In the morning light, his quarters looked bigger and fancier than what she remembered from the night before. A butter-brown leather sofa and recliner dominated the main living space with the big-screen television. Natural wood cabinets and geometric print tile in the kitchen area were complemented by dark countertops. The place was extremely masculine, yet rich and expensive looking.

She knew exactly how expensive from having recently finished decorating her own condo. She found her coffee and turned on the television, not surprised when she was able to find a morning show in English. She listened to the news, drinking her coffee, and rose when he finally came out of his bedroom, dressed for work.

"I need to get going."

She smiled and nodded. "I should go too. I want to shower and dress before breakfast."

He adjusted his cufflinks. "Since Marco's in town for the engagement party, I'm meeting him for breakfast. Then the goof will probably keep me in meetings all day." He rolled his eyes. "You'd think he was my only supplier. Except he uses the time to pick my brain so he can do bigger and better things with his own company. I swear last summer I all but wrote his corporation's five-year plan."

She laughed.

He kissed her quickly, then headed for the door. "I'll see you tonight."

He left so fast the whole room shimmered with confusion.

She took her cup to the sink, then went into the bedroom to gather the clothes she'd worn the night before. The sense of foreboding that she'd managed to sidestep the past few days tiptoed through her. Alone in his bedroom, after the rushed way he'd left her, a horrible thought struck her.

What if the thrill of their relationship was gone for him?

She took a breath, left his bedroom and snuck into the hall then to her room. She didn't need to sneak. No one saw her. He really did have perfect privacy on the third floor, all by himself.

But maybe that was part of what had taken away the mystique for him? With everyone focused on some facet or another of the wedding, no one would notice or care that they were on this floor together and, in a way, she wasn't forbidden fruit anymore.

She thought about that as she showered, telling herself she was making too much out of nothing—

Except if another man treated her this way, that would be her signal to end it before he did.

Was this her signal to end it?

She never let anyone dump her. She never let herself get so involved that her feelings might be hurt. Her subconscious could be telling her she should be planning her escape. Not just because she didn't want Lorenzo to break up with her at the engagement party or before the wedding, when things really could get complicated. But because she was having *feelings*. Bigger feelings than what she usually had for the men she had relationships with.

Of course, if *she* broke up with *him* before the engagement party, wouldn't she be doing the same thing she was worried Lorenzo might do?

She sighed. Maybe this wasn't the time to make that decision?

Particularly since today was the day to choose bridesmaids' gowns.

Caught up in the excitement of the day, Marietta wanted to go into town to the boutique to try on bridesmaids' dresses, but GiGi had exhausted herself the day before. Not wanting to leave Antonio's grandmother out, Riley called to see if the gowns could be brought to the villa, and an hour later Rosalee Agosti arrived, sample dresses in her van.

Gerard helped her unload the clothing rack and wheel it into the living room before he eased himself away from the noisy group.

As maid of honor, Marietta surveyed the gowns, examining every dress as Rosalee pulled it off the rack.

"I like the pink one," GiGi said from the sofa.

Juliette laughed. "I do too, but it's a winter wedding being held outside in a resting vineyard. I think you need a gown as dramatic as the setting."

Riley considered that. "What are you thinking?"

As if catching on to Juliette's suggestion, GiGi said, "The same dress but in a wine color like burgundy."

"Or a stunning red," Juliette said.

Everybody seemed to like that idea.

Rosalee spoke up. "Let me check to see which of these dresses comes in red."

"Remember we have only about four weeks to get them in," Riley said.

Rosalee nodded. "They will be special ordered."

The boutique owner spent a few seconds tapping on her electronic tablet, then she smiled. "These three all come in red."

Riley took the three samples off the rack and she and Marietta retreated to a private room in the back to try them on.

Juliette sat on the sofa beside GiGi. She caught her hand and squeezed it. "This is fun, right?"

"So much fun," GiGi said with a laugh. "Imagine how much fun the rest of our lives are going to be…" She met her gaze. "With you being here for every holiday and birthday."

She didn't want to burst GiGi's bubble but that was really only a few times a year. Christmas. Easter. And the birthdays of Antonio and Riley's kids—who weren't born yet. She was not going to see as much of the Salvaggio family as GiGi made it seem. Which was why her affair with Lorenzo would end when their lives went back to normal after the wedding.

Her stomach plummeted. It all suddenly felt very real—

Except, it seemed that he was already tiring of her. And she refused to stay in a relationship that was clearly over. That was how women got hurt. That was how Greg had hurt her. She felt the sting every time he'd made an excuse for why they couldn't get married. She should have left him after the third or fourth refusal. Instead she'd stayed and ended up alone and humiliated.

So, rather than be sad that her affair with Lorenzo would end naturally after the wedding, she should be glad that their romance had an end date. She wouldn't be hurt. She'd be too busy working. And they'd both walk away with happy memories.

That was what was important. That she could come back, visit, celebrate without any odd feelings between her and Lorenzo.

She squeezed GiGi's hand again. "I'll be here for every holiday."

GiGi smiled. "I consider myself lucky to have you as part of my family."

"It's fun for me too." Juliette wasn't really lying to GiGi. Her relationship with Lorenzo had nothing to do with her being a part of family celebrations. When it ended, she would still be Riley's mom, Antonio's mother-in-law, grandmother of their children. Right now, she was doing exactly what she was supposed to be doing. She shouldn't be thinking about Lorenzo at all.

She enjoyed her friendship with GiGi.

She loved planning the wedding.

She was thrilled that Riley was happy.

The other feelings? The concerns she had about her relationship with Lorenzo? Those feelings—those worries—had no place here.

After having Marietta try on all three dresses that came in red, Riley chose a long-sleeved gown for her, and Rosalee ordered it on her electronic tablet.

Giggling with happiness, Riley and Marietta decided to take the SUV into town to get lunch. They invited Juliette and GiGi to join them, but GiGi declined.

Juliette glanced at her, saw her tired eyes and said, "I think I'm going to bow out too." She hugged Riley. "You guys have fun."

"Yes," GiGi said. "Your mom and I should go down to the ballroom and discuss decorations for the engagement party."

"Exactly," Juliette said.

With Gerard's help, Rosalee packed up to leave, and the bride-to-be and her maid of honor shuffled off to Florence, their big black SUV following behind Rosalee's van.

When the room was quiet, Juliette said, "Do you really want to look at potential decorations for the ballroom? Won't your staff do that?"

"The decorations, yes," Lorenzo said, entering the room. "But we have several different kinds of silver and at least ten options for tablecloths."

Juliette started at the sound of his voice. "I thought you were at work?"

"I was. Marco met a woman last night so he's busy, and everything else I had to do today could wait. I came home to help."

Her heart lifted. But she stopped it, suddenly realizing the truth of what she'd thought only minutes before. Her feelings for Lorenzo had no place when they were around other people in the villa, working on wedding things. She had to stop letting her feelings for Lorenzo as a lover mix into her feelings for him as Antonio's dad and GiGi's son... Riley's future father-in-law.

This was the problem. Not that she liked Lorenzo too much. But that she wasn't separating her romantic feelings for Lorenzo from her feelings about the wedding and the new life she was creating as an in-law.

GiGi rose shakily. "Let's go take care of the necessities for the ballroom."

Obviously seeing her exhaustion as Juliette had when the girls asked them to join them in town for lunch, Lorenzo waved her back down. "Juliette and I will handle this. When we get back, we'll all have lunch."

Juliette rose. "Yes. Lorenzo and I can do this."

GiGi sat with a sigh. "Page Gerard. He knows what we have and what looks best with what."

They headed out of the front sitting room and down the hall. When they were a safe distance away, Lorenzo said, "Nothing made me happier than getting that call from Marco saying he was busy today."

She laughed. "Competition for me has officially been ended?"

He snorted. "I won that weeks ago. I'm talking about the fact that I can now spend the day with you."

Her heart wanted to fill with happiness. But she tempered her emotions, testing out her theory that she had to think of him two different ways, as a lover and as Antonio's father. Walking through a main floor corridor to a ballroom, about to choose linens, she should be treating him as Antonio's father.

"Trust me, buddy," she said, bringing their conversation to the place where it belonged. "We have enough work to do this afternoon that you're going to wish you were with Marco."

He laughed and opened the door to the ballroom. They walked through the enormous space and into a room in the back that was filled with dishes and utensils. Gerard was already there, waiting for them.

"Wow."

Every time she came to Florence, something reminded her she was a fish out of water. She felt foolish being squired around in a limo. She'd had to read up on how she was supposed to deal with household staff. She knew what fork to use. She had good manners. But their lifestyle was beyond the commonsense of her world.

Now here she was again, in a situation that was over her head. Mostly because she didn't have any idea what the criteria was for choosing from among all the different patterns of china and silver, tablecloths and chair covers, and vases—hundreds of them. She had good china and everyday dishes. Good silver and everyday silver.

She did not have thirty patterns of china and neither did she have a ballroom. She did not, *could not*, entertain hundreds in her house.

Because there was no reason to.

Gerard suggested two patterns of flatware and china. She absolutely wanted one over the other but deciding to let the guy familiar with all these things choose, she smiled brightly but said nothing, deferring to Lorenzo who laughed.

"I could not possibly care less about the dishes. You choose."

She hesitated. Up to now, she'd managed to sidestep any real disasters. So maybe she should just pick a plate style and flatware and hope for the best?

As if reading her mind, Gerard laughed. "There is no poor choice, ma'am. Everything in this room fits the occasion."

"Okay, then," Juliette said, pointing at her favorite. "I think these are beautiful, the prettiest dishes I've ever seen."

Gerard half bowed. "Excellent."

She picked simple white linen tablecloths and white tufted chairs for around the tables, then she and Lorenzo left the storage room and walked into the ballroom. It was so big their footfalls echoed around them.

Gerard made her choices so easy that being a part of

making those decisions could have been one of the most interesting experiences of her life, except for the nagging realization that wouldn't leave her alone. She'd never really thought about what being a billionaire actually meant.

It was more than a big house and fancy cars. It was twenty choices of tablecloths, employees silently cleaning or cooking or setting things up for you before you walked into a room. It was also adherence to etiquette and social conventions—things she didn't have to worry about in her world. All she needed was a firm handshake and the normal manners everyone needed to eat at fancy restaurants and seal deals. The bolder she was the better. And she could be pretty bold, pushy even, about getting her own way. A scrapper. That was what Lorenzo had called her. A junkyard dog—

Her chest tightened with anxiety. Was this what Greg's parents had seen when they'd considered her as a potential match for their son? That she didn't have the refinement needed to plan charity balls or Christmas parties—

Good Lord. *Was* that what they had seen? Her inadequacies? How she would embarrass them until she caught on?

She looked around the ballroom as she and Lorenzo walked the final steps to the door. She was raised blue collar. A nurse, who'd edged her way into a life that suited her. Comfortable to be sure—

But not this.

Realistically, the things she was noticing today could also be only the tip of the iceberg of differences between her life and Lorenzo's. She'd never been on a yacht, never been to Paris, never hobnobbed with royalty, but she would bet GiGi, Lorenzo and Antonio had.

What in the name of all that was holy was she doing here?

CHAPTER THIRTEEN

THE NIGHT OF the engagement ball, Juliette stepped out of her suite into the third-floor hall two seconds before Lorenzo did. He looked so good in his black tux that her breath caught as he walked over to her.

He gave her sleeveless red silk gown a quick once-over then caught her elbows and pulled her to him for a kiss. "You are ravishing."

She returned his kiss. "Thank you." Two days had gone by since her thoughts while choosing the dinnerware for the engagement party and she'd spent that time reducing her foolish fears to rubble. It didn't matter if she'd never been to Paris or ridden on a yacht. Her life and Lorenzo's were separated by an ocean. Their affair could end after the wedding. There was no reason to stress.

Though she absolutely adored Lorenzo, realizing their different places in the world only solidified the temporary nature of their fling. She would enjoy it for however long it lasted, then she would be Riley's mother and Antonio's mother-in-law, and she and Lorenzo would be great friends. He might even let her ride on his yacht someday, but she had no illusions about fitting into his world. She didn't want to.

Satisfied, she linked her arm with his and they walked down the first flight of stairs to the second floor, but they didn't continue down that route to the foyer. Lorenzo pointed out a private stairway and they ended up in a waiting area just outside the ballroom. The noise that ebbed and flowed from the room indicated that guests were arriving.

She turned to Lorenzo. "I thought you'd have a receiving line."

"Meh. Some people do. We're not that fussy."

She smiled and nodded just as Antonio and Riley entered. Wearing an ivory gown, with her dark hair piled on top of her head, Juliette's daughter looked every inch the wife of a billionaire that she was about to become.

Juliette hugged her. "You're gorgeous."

Pulling away, Riley sucked in a breath. "Thank you."

"Nervous?"

"It just seems like time is flying to our wedding."

There was enough of a catch in Riley's voice that Juliette swore she heard fear. The noise of the crowd, the ballroom dripping with finery and all the well-dressed people were enough to make Juliette feel antsy...and she wasn't the bride. All the worries Juliette had about fitting in were probably nothing to what Riley felt as the one marrying into this family.

She wanted to take her daughter aside and remind her there was time to pull out of this. But before she could say anything, Riley turned to Antonio with an expression of love. "We can't wait."

Antonio kissed her. "No. We can't."

Juliette blinked. The catch in Riley's voice hadn't been fear? It had been excitement? Totally the opposite of what Juliette was feeling staying in this huge villa?

Confusion made her glance around. Usually, nothing fazed her. Usually, she loved a challenge. That's what she saw in Riley's eyes—the confidence to take up the challenge of being a wonderful wife to Antonio.

She didn't have to worry about her daughter. She had made too much of the catch in Riley's voice because of her own odd feelings the past few days. It was no coincidence that this home—the Salvaggio wealth and position—reminded her of Greg. Of being unwelcome in his world, and then kicked out of their condo after he died. But she'd learned that lesson. That was why she was being careful about her feelings for Lorenzo.

She took a breath.

There was nothing to worry about. After all, she didn't have to be the happy bride-to-be, only the happy mother of the bride. The house and ball might be big, but her role was small. She could weave in and out of the crowd thanking people for coming, introducing herself as Riley's mother and simply have fun meeting the people close enough to Antonio and Lorenzo to get an invitation to this posh affair.

Then she would go home and return for the wedding to be the same sunny mother of the bride she would be tonight.

Nothing more.

And, no. This was not faking it. She'd been Riley's mom for decades. She was thrilled her daughter was getting married. That was reason enough to be happy, charming and welcoming to guests.

Dressed in a tuxedo, Gerard entered the room. "If everyone would line up, the master of ceremonies is about to introduce you."

He arranged Marietta and Rico, the maid of honor and best man, as the first in line.

"You and Ms. Morgan next," Gerard said to Lorenzo. "Then Riley and Antonio."

Juliette took her place in front of her daughter, beside Lorenzo with a smile. He caught her hand and squeezed it.

Juliette realized Riley had seen. But the master of ceremony's voice interrupted the noise of the crowd, which instantly settled down. He announced Marietta and Rico, then Lorenzo and Juliette.

She smiled, happy to be Riley's mom, and she and Lorenzo walked into the spotlight that led them to the formal table that was just elevated enough that everyone could see the bridal party.

Still holding her hand, Lorenzo helped her up the three steps, then guided her to their places, one on each side of Riley and Antonio, with the bride and groom's chairs empty between them. When Riley and Antonio were introduced, the crowd erupted in applause.

They entered the ballroom and climbed the three stairs. Then Riley and Antonio took the two chairs between Juliette and Lorenzo.

She breathed a sigh of relief seeing she and Lorenzo were separated. Not that she minded being paired with Lorenzo, but the way they'd been introduced almost announced them as a couple. Plus, he'd held her hand. People had seen that.

She tried not to care. Tried to make excuses. But if they told the world they were dating everything would change. She wouldn't simply be Riley's mom anymore. A guest. She'd be the woman Lorenzo was dating.

Riley said, "So…anything you want to tell me?"

Overwhelmed thinking about how everyone would look at her differently if she were the woman Lorenzo was dating, Juliette needed a second to bring herself back to reality. Then, she smiled and said, "I suppose I should have said congratulations on a beautiful party."

Riley rolled her eyes. "This isn't about me! It's about you! Holding hands with Lorenzo?"

Her fears shot back like a lightning bolt. "We're friends.

Plus, I needed him to help me keep my balance as I walked up the stairs."

Riley considered that. Juliette could see from the expression in her eyes that her daughter was skeptical. Still, she said, "Okay," before she faced Antonio who had taken the mic to say a few words to the crowd.

Juliette winced. She never could fool her daughter. Luckily, Riley was being introduced by her betrothed. She rose and stood beside Antonio as he thanked everyone for coming and instructed the group to enjoy themselves because he intended to.

The crowd laughed. People in dark trousers and white shirts began serving salads.

Riley took her seat talking. "I also heard, Cinderella, that you got a new pair of blue shoes after a piggyback ride in the dead of night."

Juliette almost spit out her lettuce. "My heel broke."

"That's the going gossip. Because you are gossip."

"You think I *wanted* to ride on somebody's back on a freezing cold night?"

Riley shrugged. "Could be. I've seen how you flirt."

"That wasn't flirting!"

"Okay."

Antonio said something to Riley, who looked away from Juliette.

She sighed heavily before catching Lorenzo's gaze and nudging her head toward Riley.

Lorenzo had no idea what she was trying to tell him, but she could explain after dinner. They ate a new dish the chef specially prepared for Antonio and Riley and even named after them.

Juliette smiled at that, the way a mother of the bride

was supposed to, but her nose wrinkled the littlest bit, the way it always did when confronted by something in his life she hadn't expected. Like the roomful of china and silver. The very fact that she thought some of those things pretentious made him laugh. Sometimes his life *was* pretentious. Even he saw it.

Which was why he loved her condo in Manhattan. Gorgeous, but also a sort of private oasis.

Dinner ended. Many people made after-dinner toasts, including him. They laughed about the fake engagement that became real love and some of the women in the crowd sighed with envy.

For the first time since this whole deal began, Lorenzo realized he was a little jealous of his son. Antonio's happiness caused Lorenzo to think back to his idealistic self, what he'd thought real love and marriage would be and something warm and soft floated through him. He glanced at Juliette and suddenly realized what he felt for her mirrored what he'd thought love should be.

Antonio and Riley left the platform to mingle before the band began to play. He walked to Juliette's chair and pulled it out for her. "Ready to meet some new people?"

She smiled. "Sure, I'm game."

He laughed. "You don't think very much of all this, do you?"

"Actually, I think it's beautiful."

"But pretentious?"

She chuckled. "Pretentious has nothing to do with it. It's who you are. But I also think it explains your mom's impeccable manners and longing for her charity work, even as it explains why Antonio was lonely."

He walked down the three steps and turned to take her hand. "You see us as being alone in a crowd, huh?"

She paused before easing down the steps. "Not alone in the crowd. You're with your people."

"*My* people?"

"Wealthy. Sophisticated. People who summer in the south of France and go on ski vacations for Christmas. If anyone's alone in this crowd it's me."

He smiled up at her. "You're not alone when you're with me."

"Easy, Skippy." She started down the stairs. "Talk like that takes us somewhere we don't want to go. And you should really pull back on the hand-holding. Riley's on to us."

In that second, Lorenzo didn't care. Too many thoughts were jockeying for attention in his brain. The fact that he didn't care if everyone saw them as a couple. They *were* a couple. The fact that his feelings for her mirrored what he'd believed love should be. The fact that he didn't have to be anyone or anything except himself with her. The fact that he agreed about the pretentiousness of his life. The fact that he understood why Antonio was so happy and so ready to start this new phase with someone he adored. He could see how Antonio's life would be bigger, happier with Riley. And how his life had been richer and fuller these past few weeks with Juliette.

"Lorenzo?"

He turned when Annabelle said his name. Everything he'd been thinking as he helped Juliette down the stairs evaporated as other emotions hit him like a punch in the gut. Failure. Misery when he realized how wrongly he'd judged Annabelle's character and what a love-struck fool he'd been not to see what was really happening.

"Annabelle…"

His ex glanced at Juliette, then brought her gaze back to

his, not really dismissing Juliette, but he noticed she hadn't asked for an introduction.

"Antonio hasn't suggested it, but I thought it would be nice…a show of good faith…if you and I could dance together when they introduce the bridal party."

He frowned. "I think Antonio wants me to dance with Juliette. She's mother of the bride, I'm father of the groom…"

Annabelle's chin lifted. "*I* am Antonio's mother. You and I should dance."

"But Juliette and I came together."

"Only because she's staying here. It's not like you're a couple. She can dance with someone else. Marco's here. It would be nice to get him on the dance floor anyway since he's Antonio's godfather."

Juliette just stared at beautiful Annabelle. Lorenzo had said she was pretty. *So pretty.* And she was. What he hadn't said was that she looked like royalty. For all Juliette knew, she might be. Tall and slender, shoulders back, an air of something about her—as if she knew she belonged here—

Actually, she *did* belong here. That was what she was saying. She was Antonio's mother. Probably born into wealth and privilege the way Lorenzo had been, she rearranged things with the confidence of a person who had every right to interfere with whatever she wanted because she knew the way things should be.

She behaved the way Juliette did in Manhattan. Running her business. Doing the right thing for her clients. Managing staff. Because in her own world, she was the leader. The strong one. Just as in this world, Annabelle was the leader—

The strong one.

Lorenzo told Annabelle he would take care of things and walked away. His ex stared at Juliette.

"I suppose you're his latest floozie."

Juliette laughed. "I'm Riley's mother. I'm also a business owner in the States. Not really a floozie anymore."

She thought her joke could lighten Annabelle's expression. Instead, it became thunderous. "Joke all you want, pretend all you want, but I know Lorenzo better than anyone ever has. I know when he's sleeping with someone. And he's sleeping with you."

Juliette sighed. "I'm not sure what difference it makes. This party is about my daughter and your son. Let's all just be happy."

Annabelle blew out her breath as if Juliette were tiresome. "Of course, you're happy. Your daughter is marrying up." With that she turned and walked away.

Upstart. Gold digger. Trying to raise your station in life by marrying above it.

Suddenly, the things Greg's dad had shouted at her took meaning. She'd never completely understood it before. Maybe pride had blinded her. She'd wanted to make something of herself, and she had, but that was nothing to these people who only saw pedigrees and the sophistication that came with old money.

As Juliette watched her go, Lorenzo returned. "No matter what she said, ignore it. The woman is a piece of work."

The master of ceremonies began to introduce the bridal party. After Marietta and Rico, the MC introduced Annabelle and Marco. "The mother and godfather of the groom."

Juliette spun to face Lorenzo who grinned. "She pushes but I don't always comply."

A burst of laughter overrode her feelings of not belonging, as the master of ceremonies introduced her and

Lorenzo as mother of the bride and father of the groom.
Lorenzo swept her into a dance hold and maneuvered them
out onto the floor.

A person would never know Annabelle was furious because she smiled happily, dancing with Marco.

"See? Everything worked out."

Juliette glanced at Lorenzo. "Because this is her world,
and she knows how to behave."

"In public," Lorenzo clarified. "In private, that's not always the case."

"But isn't that part of it? Knowing when to talk and when
to stay quiet. When to sulk and dig in her heels or let go?"

"I suppose." He pulled her close. "Let's not ruin a good
dance talking about things that don't matter."

She eased back slightly. "I told you, Riley suspects we're
more than friends."

He laughed.

"All right that might be funny, but Annabelle figured it
out too. She called me your floozie."

He snorted. "She would know all about floozies." He
sighed. "And here we are talking about her again, when I
want to dance and focus on you." He took a breath. "You
know what? If you and I were to behave like a couple tonight, then everybody's suspicions could be confirmed and
then it wouldn't matter who said what."

She gaped at him. "Are you serious? What about all the
awkwardness when we break up?"

He waited a beat then cautiously said, "What if we don't
break up?"

She frowned.

"Juliette, I can't see myself ever growing tired of you."

Her voice failed her for a second. Then she very skepti-
cally said, "Are you asking me to marry you?"

"No!" He paused. "At least not now...but I have to be honest and say that's where I see us heading. Of course, if you're dead set against marriage, we don't have to get married...but we are a couple. A happy couple. As good to each other as Riley and Antonio. We fit."

It took a minute to find some breath in her frozen lungs so she could talk. "No. We don't. We do not fit."

"How can you say that?"

"How can you not see it? Lorenzo, I've never seen so many dishes before or been with a man who has a house big enough to have a ballroom. Hell, I've never even been on a yacht." The song ended and she pulled away from him, her head spinning. "You're just in the happiness portion of a shiny new affair. And you're trying to make it into something it isn't."

"No. I've been unhappily married. I've had my share of affairs. This is different." He held her gaze. "You know it is. That's why you're fighting it."

Her ire rose. "I'm fighting it because I don't belong here."

He snorted. "Why don't you let me be the judge of that?"

"Because you're not looking at us correctly anymore! Take off your happiness glasses and see the truth!"

"It's you who doesn't see the truth."

He walked away and the band began to play a second song, a song meant for guests to join in the dancing. She smiled her way past the couples pouring onto the dance floor as she struggled to get off, to get away.

Recognizing her role as mother of the bride, she sucked it up and made her way from table to table, saying hello and thanking people for coming, especially Marietta's parents who appeared to be the only people Riley invited.

The horrible sense that her daughter was being absorbed into the Salvaggio family competed with the frightening feelings Lorenzo had inspired while they danced. She couldn't believe he could see them getting married. She couldn't believe anyone who'd had as bad of a relationship as he had—and she'd had—would even for one second consider committing again.

After an hour of avoiding Lorenzo by dancing with Rico and Marco and chatting with more guests, Juliette almost bumped into Riley when they both reached for a glass of champagne being distributed by a passing waiter.

Her face flushed with joy, Riley said, "Hey, Mom!"

"Hey, sweetie. Are you having a good time?"

She laughed. "The best. I love Antonio's friends."

Juliette glanced around. "I'm guessing a lot of these people are business associates."

"And GiGi's friends."

"Where are *your* friends?"

"The wedding and engagement party are too close time-wise. Most of my friends can't come to Europe for both. But *everybody* will be here for the wedding."

Juliette sipped her champagne. The sense that she was making too much out of nothing filled her again. Riley was happy—

She was the one who wasn't. And she suddenly knew why. She liked her life where she was the ruler of her world. Where she didn't worry about eight different sets of dishes or flatware or have all these feelings of inadequacy.

Because, she realized as she left the ballroom, Lorenzo's talk of forever hadn't scared her as much as it had made her long for something that couldn't be.

Even if she were head over heels in love with him, it wouldn't matter. She did not belong in his world.

She knew that because she *did* belong in her own.

CHAPTER FOURTEEN

LORENZO GAVE JULIETTE a good hour to get her bearings after their discussion on the dance floor. He knew he'd been suggesting something that she would need time to adjust to, but he also knew he was correct. What was happening between them wasn't a short-term fling. It was permanent. Real.

And the best relationship he'd ever had because she was honest, innocent in a way, worldly in others. She was one of the first people he could be himself with. A mere ten minutes with Annabelle had reminded him of how important that was.

As if thinking her name had summoned her, his ex-wife was suddenly by his side. She made a pouty face. "I think I might have insulted Riley's mother."

"She's tougher than she looks."

Her pouty face got even poutier. "She might be, but she doesn't belong here. She and I both know it."

Lorenzo's heart stuttered. "What did you say to her?"

She straightened regally. Her pouty face was replaced by a look of strength and stubbornness. "I am Antonio's mother. Do not think you and that prissy upstart from America are going to edge me out."

"No one wants to edge you out—"

"Oh, Lorenzo, you're so innocent when it comes to women. Of course, she wants to edge me out."

"She feels sorry for you."

Annabelle gasped.

"Because she's a good person. She doesn't want your place in Antonio's life any more than she wants a place in mine."

The truth of that hit him so hard, he almost buckled over in pain. He wanted her in his life, but she didn't want to be in his.

Why would she?

His family had all but taken over the wedding. His ex-wife, Antonio's mother, was an unmitigated snob. His whole world dripped with money and pretense, and she was a worker bee. She made her own place in the world. She'd made herself who she was.

The very reasons he loved her were the reasons she believed she could never love him.

He waited until the engagement ball was almost over before he looked for her again. He wasn't sure time would fix the gap between their ways of thinking, but he tried to be an optimist. Once he found her, he could take them back to their normal relationship. Then he would wait to mention the possibility of them being together for longer than they'd originally assumed. He would use time to show her they belonged together. Everything would be fine. He simply had to be patient.

His hope dimmed when he didn't find her anywhere in the ballroom. As the guests left, the crowd thinned until he found himself alone in the huge room, listening to the sounds of silence.

It dimmed even further when he walked up to the third floor, sliding his tie from around his neck, and saw the door to her quarters was open. It was a sign to the housecleaning staff that a guest had gone, and they should clean the room.

She'd gone.

He stood staring at the beautiful sitting room, thinking how ridiculous he was to be standing there, looking for her. She wasn't there. The room itself meant nothing without her in it.

His life stretched before him every bit as empty as her room because he was fairly certain that leaving was her way of breaking up with him.

He wasn't sure what he'd tell Riley, but the next morning he discovered that he hadn't needed to worry. Juliette had texted her and told her that her office had called with an emergency, and she had gone back to Manhattan.

Antonio, GiGi and Riley didn't think anything of her packing up and leaving. But he knew what had happened. He'd scared her.

Or his life had scared her.

But the bottom line was, she wanted no part of him.

He'd never been so hurt or so confused. When he'd divorced Annabelle, he'd never been so relieved. He'd begun to see breakups as happy things, but Juliette leaving him gutted him.

Monday evening, Lorenzo said goodbye to Marietta in the foyer before Riley and Antonio left with her to take her to the train station. GiGi sighed, saying she was tired and heading to bed.

In two minutes, he was alone in silence. Just as he'd been in the ballroom after everyone left the engagement party. He almost went to the sitting room to pour himself a bourbon but decided it would be easier to simply make himself a drink in his room where he could find a movie and relax.

The weekend had been filled with noise and people, the way Antonio wanted the house to be forever, teeming with kids and laughter, and though it was one kind of wonderful, it certainly wasn't restful.

Still, GiGi and his father had been just fine with him and Annabelle living with them after they married. Of course, Antonio's mom hadn't lived with them long. In a few short years, it had been him and Antonio with his parents, and his mother had taken over the role of mom to Antonio. It had worked out really well because he had needed their help, and they happily gave it.

But Antonio and Riley wouldn't split up after a few years. They would go the distance. They would fill this villa with kids—

He would be a fifth wheel.

Telling himself he was being overly dramatic, he walked up the stairs to his suite, but the sense that he didn't belong here wouldn't leave him. If Juliette had agreed with his proposition at the engagement party, they could live here as the doting grandparents to Antonio and Riley's kids. Somehow that made sense. But him living here alone... damned if it didn't seem wrong.

In his sitting room, he found a movie and sank into the soft sofa with a sigh of relief. He took a sip of bourbon, then another, through the film's opening credits, thinking about Juliette. It didn't insult him that she wanted no part of his life. He understood. She had built her life from the ground up and it was a good life. She wasn't just fulfilled; she was happy.

And she'd done it all on her own. He understood the pride she had in herself.

The movie began. He hunkered down to watch but after a few minutes, he glanced around his place. They hadn't spent a lot of time together in his suite but he could sense her presence.

Or maybe he just missed her?

He did miss her. But not in the way he'd expected. He thought he'd be remembering her in his bedroom. Instead, he thought about dancing with her in her condo. He laughed remembering lying to Antonio, saying he'd gone to Manhattan to arrange for a wedding gift for him. And laughed some more thinking of how they'd had the entire third floor to themselves—

Still, Juliette had told him that Riley had figured it out. That had been the beginning of the end. That had been when he'd suggested that they should just tell everyone and be a couple at the engagement party and she'd refused—

Of course, she'd had a private chat with Annabelle right before that. And his ex could be mean when she didn't get her own way.

Sheesh. No wonder Juliette didn't want to live in his world.

He sat back, combing his fingers through his hair. His house felt empty. Even when Antonio and Riley returned, it would feel empty. His life had been routine and boring for a while. He'd tolerated it because it was a good life.

But now he didn't want it anymore. God only knew what he wanted. He could have just about anything. He was wealthy. That had always given him choices and right now he was considering two changes.

At the end of his movie, he returned to the downstairs sitting room. When the foyer door opened an hour later, he rose and called Antonio and Riley in to join him.

Antonio said, "What's up?"

"Remember how I went to Manhattan to look for a wedding gift for you?"

Riley sat on the sofa. "You're going to tell us you went to see my mom."

He laughed as Antonio sat beside Riley. "Yes and no. I did go to see her, but the visit also helped me figure out what I wanted to give you as a wedding gift."

Antonio raised one eyebrow. "It did?"

"I'm making you CEO."

"Of what?"

"Of everything. I'm going to trade jobs with you."

Antonio laughed. "Really?"

"I'll be taking on all the legal work that requires you to go to the States."

Riley smugly said, "Especially Manhattan?"

He laughed. "Save your suspicions. Your mom made it very clear that she doesn't want to have anything to do with me."

Antonio said, "That surprises me. You two really got along well."

He wasn't about to tell Antonio that it had been his mother who'd said whatever she'd said to make Juliette reconsider the good thing they had. He also wouldn't tell him that in Manhattan he'd have opportunities to run into Juliette and maybe change her mind.

He simply rose from the sofa, said, "Good night," and went upstairs to pack and make travel arrangements.

Juliette settled Pete's problem on Tuesday morning, then crashed in her condo out of sheer exhaustion. At work on Wednesday morning, she opened her laptop to find a message from Greg's parents' doctor that Rachel Finnegan had passed a few days before and that the services required from her company would be changing. The doctor asked to meet her at the penthouse to discuss Walter Finnegan's needs, and she called to let him know she would be right there.

This was what she did. Helped people. She needed the reminder of who she was and why she loved being who she was. Clients and doctors depended on her.

That's what gave her strength and purpose. She wanted to be herself. She did not want to be the pretty woman on Lorenzo's arm. The queen of the romantic villa in Tuscany.

Thoughts of the villa and Lorenzo made her squeeze her eyes shut in lonely misery. But she had understood what he was saying even if he didn't. He might love her, but it was on his terms.

The last time she'd loved a man on his terms, she'd lost him in the worst possible way and been scorned and ridiculed.

She would never do it again. No matter how tempting. Or how much she missed him.

She arrived at Walter Finnegan's building, and the doorman met her, explaining that their doctor had instructed him to input the elevator code so she could go right up.

When the doors opened on the front room, Art was waiting for her. He took her to an office where they spoke briefly about Rachel's peaceful passing then discussed Greg's dad.

"He's been happy having someone to help him shower and dress for the day. Even happier to have company at breakfast and someone to play board games with him for a few hours in the afternoon. Those services should continue."

"If you don't mind, I'd like to talk to him to get a feel for what he really needs. He's aware enough that he should be the one directing his care. Having us at least consult him should give him a sense of normalcy."

Art rose from behind the big desk. "I understand that. But I also believe he needs more help than he thinks. We might have to guide him to make the right choices."

"Agreed."

They left the office and Art led her to a small sitting room with a wall of books and a television. Walter sat in a recliner watching—of all things—a game show.

"Walter," she said, walking toward him, her hands extended to clasp his when he rose. She couldn't forget this was the man who had shamed and humiliated her at Greg's funeral. Yet, she also couldn't forget this lonely man had just lost his wife.

"Juliette."

A little surprised he remembered her name, she smiled. "I'm sorry for your loss."

He motioned for her to sit.

The doctor's phone rang, and he turned away to answer it. After a few seconds, he left the room.

Walter said, "Must be important."

She nodded. "Must be."

"But maybe it's good we got a minute alone." His eyes closed and he sighed before he opened them again. "I know who you are."

"I'm sorry?"

He swallowed. "I know who you are. Oh, you don't look the same. But I'm an old businessman who has always trusted his instincts. Your name nagged at me for a couple of days, then I hired a private investigator."

She gaped at him. "A private investigator?"

"I checked you out, and while Art's out of the room it's a good time to tell you that this—" He motioned around the room. "Won't work. If you think a few weeks of kindness will cause me to put you or your bastard child in my will, you are mistaken."

Torn between the urge to tell him to settle down, she didn't want his money, and the urge to stand up, take her nurse and go—right after she told him to go to hell—she sat there staring at him.

"Oh, you were so clever, giving us your best nurses, pretending to like us when you interviewed us." He shook his head. "Do you think I haven't dealt with a hundred women like you who came sniffing around after Greg, or a hundred upstart businessmen who tried to get on my good side?" He snorted. "You're even more witless than we thought."

All the times she'd felt sorry for him popped into her head, along with the way she'd thought his wife had been the rude one. A million biting comebacks rose to her tongue, but she stopped them. He was alone. He was old and at the end of his life. If he wanted to drown in his own vitriol, that was his choice. Because money did not give anyone the right to be condescending and hateful.

She thought of GiGi. Her warmth. Her kindness. The way she always opened her home.

She thought of Antonio, learning the family business but also creating a family. Building a life.

She thought of Lorenzo. He carried as much weight on his shoulders as Walter did, but he trusted people. She'd never seen him be disrespectful.

Walter didn't need to be either. He *wanted* to be.

She rose. "Walter, you were rude and thoughtless thirty years ago. You are rude and thoughtless now. My nurse will be out of here at the end of her shift. I'll give Art the names of two other nursing agencies who are as competent as mine. I won't leave you in a lurch, but I won't take this from you anymore."

She headed out of the office.

He yelled, "You're still no one. A little money doesn't give you class."

She stopped and looked at him. "You're right about that. Money certainly didn't give you any class. Or any smarts. Riley, your granddaughter, is the nicest, most wonderful woman. Knowing her would have brought you great joy. You live in an empty penthouse with only servants to keep you company. Riley would have loved you."

She turned to walk out, and he sputtered something, but she didn't hear him. She didn't care to hear him. The world and the obvious had suddenly opened up to her. None of her confusing relationship with Greg had ever been about her. It had always been about the Finnegans. Were she to guess she would say they'd somehow kept Greg from marrying her.

Which was every bit as sad for Greg as it was for her. He'd loved her. But he couldn't go against his parents' wishes. She'd always wanted to believe that. Now she did.

Still, that didn't make her a good match for Lorenzo. She had to be who she was, and she could never be herself with him.

In fact, if Greg had married her and she'd become part of his life with his parents, her life would have been hell.

Maybe, by not marrying her, he'd actually done her a favor.

She finished her workday with no residual anger toward Walter and finally accepting that she and Lorenzo weren't right for each other. It hurt. Not because she'd always wanted love but because she'd wanted real love and once again the man she'd found would draw her into a life where she couldn't be herself.

Looking up as she got out of the elevator on her condo's

floor, Juliette stopped as if she'd hit a brick wall. There, sitting on the floor by her door, was Lorenzo. He pulled himself up as she approached. Rather than his typical suit and tie, he wore jeans and a black leather jacket over a polo shirt and tennis shoes. In case she'd thought she was attracted to him because he made sexy businessman look yummy, she had now been proven wrong. No man was as handsome as he was to her.

"I think you and I need to talk."

She nodded. Though there was nothing he could say to make her change her mind, she did realize he had a right to hear and understand her side of the story.

She punched her code into the pad beside the door and invited him to follow her inside.

Her heart pounded from the longing that washed through her just looking at him. She reminded herself that wanting him was wrong, though right at that minute she didn't think so. She might not have allowed herself to admit she loved him, but she'd never had feelings this strong for anyone before. Not even Greg. She simply knew better than to enter another relationship where she didn't fit.

He closed the door behind him, as she tossed her briefcase onto the island in the kitchen area.

"I owe you an apology."

She looked at him. "You owe *me* an apology?"

He rubbed his hand across the back of his neck. "I was feeling all kinds of happiness at the engagement party. I spoke too soon about us being together forever." He sucked in a breath. "But now that it's out there I don't want to take it back."

She slid onto one of the stools and offered the one beside it to him. Lord, she wished he would take it back. She wished they could return to their affair, to being happy, to not worrying about tomorrow. Because tomorrow for them wasn't a very happy prospect for her. Leaving Manhattan. Being someone's wife…not being herself anymore.

Still, she wouldn't burden him with that. She'd stick to the obvious reasons committing to each other was wrong. "Lorenzo, we don't know each other very well."

He sat on the stool. "I disagree."

She went to argue, and he stopped her with a kiss. All her feelings bubbled up, not surprising her with their intensity. Her feelings for him were strong and real, but wasted on two people who didn't belong together.

He broke the kiss. Holding her gaze, he said, "What we don't know is the future. I'd like to think we'd be together forever, but I realized I can't make it so by rushing it." He sucked in a breath. "First, because as it stands there are more than a few things you don't like about my life."

She squeezed her eyes shut. "Lorenzo, don't. This is hard enough without trying to fix things that can't be fixed." She sniffed a laugh as she opened her eyes. "Today, I had a meeting with Greg's dad."

He winced. "And you're laughing about it?"

"His mom had died."

Lorenzo's eyes bugged. "Again, not really funny."

"Well, I needed to reevaluate the care Greg's dad would need, given that he is now on his own. When his doctor left the room, Walter told me he knew who I was. He accused me of running a con, trying to ingratiate myself to him to get myself or Riley into his will."

Lorenzo groaned. "Just because Greg's family foolishly threw you away—"

"No. No one threw me away. I finally set things right today. I didn't change the facts or try to fix them, I set Walter Finnegan right. Though I managed to keep myself from telling him to go to hell, I did quit. I gave his doctor the names of two of my competitors and pulled my nurse from his penthouse this afternoon when her shift was over. We are done."

He grinned. "No kidding."

"Hey, I'm nice and I'm fair. But no one accuses me of the things he did without repercussions. He's lucid enough that I knew he understood what he was saying. So, when I quit, I decided to go the whole way. I finished the conversation we'd had at Greg's funeral. I told him it had been his loss that he didn't want to get to know Riley. Then I left." She sucked in a breath. "And it felt good."

"That's because you've spent most of your adult life repressing your feelings about what happened after Greg's death."

"I was busy making a life."

He glanced around her condo. "A good life."

She followed his lead, looking at her beautiful home, knowing she'd worked for every floorboard and lamp. "It is a good life."

"Would you be willing to take in a boarder?"

She shook her head. "Why would I need a boarder?"

He put his hands on her shoulders. "Because I would like time to get to know you. All the time I can get. Us living together should show you that I'm right. We're perfect for each other."

"You are a billionaire who grew up in a villa—"

"Which my son and his soon-to-be wife will be taking over completely. I don't want them to feel like they live in my home. Or that I'm watching them. I want them to have their own life."

His consideration didn't surprise her. She knew he was like a guardian taking care of things behind the scenes.

She also knew he saw more than he said. It was one of the reasons she liked him so much.

And now here he was, homeless, on her doorstep.

Her heart thrummed. "Are you saying you're leaving your life for me?"

"Yes. I want the chance to get to know you…the chance to have the happiness that's always eluded me. I found it with you. I want it forever."

She searched his eyes. He was giving up a lot for her—for them. "We'd live together?"

He smiled and her hope blossomed. He might be accustomed to running things like a business, but a relationship wasn't a job. It was life. It was making a life.

"I don't need the big house. I can take over most of the legal things Antonio does with our law firm here in Manhattan—"

"Meaning, you would be working here?"

"And living here…except when we want to visit the kids."

"And grandkids."

He nodded. "And grandkids." He took her hands. "When I realized how much I'd pushed you, how often my family takes it for granted that our way is the right way, I finally saw how much compromising Antonio and Riley had done. Because sometimes you have to compromise to have what you want. I would like to do that with you."

She squeezed his fingers. Her hope was so strong that her voice vibrated. "I would like to do that with you."

"So should we get a pizza?"

She laughed and bumped her forehead against his. "How about a nice dinner out?"

He looked a little disappointed, but said, "Okay."

"That was a test! What I'd really like is about two hours

in bed with you, followed by Chinese food that we have delivered."

"I could get on board with that."

She brushed her hand over the front of his soft leather jacket. "It looks like you might be wearing more clothes than I am again."

He shrugged out of the jacket and tossed it into the living room. "I never did like that coat."

"If you're going to live with me, you're not allowed to just throw clothes around."

"What if I hire a maid?"

"What if you don't? What if we live like two Manhattanites, go to a Broadway show or a museum every weekend, eat at fancy restaurants, maybe ice skate in Rockefeller Center?"

"Sounds great."

"It *will* be great." She leaned in and kissed him, and he kissed her back. Their attraction popped. But her heart engaged. This time she let it. If she was ever going to take a risk with someone, it would be him.

It *was* him.

Because when she kissed him, it didn't feel like a risk at all. It felt right. The whisper of destiny that rose up was suddenly welcome.

They were going to go the distance. They were simply going to take their time about it.

EPILOGUE

CHRISTMAS MORNING, Lorenzo and Juliette walked down the stairs, through the foyer toward the sitting room.

He caught her hand. "Ready?"

She brushed her hand along the front of his cashmere sweater. "As ready as I'll ever be."

"The kids knew I was going to Manhattan to see you but since we got in so late last night, this is our first meeting with them knowing for sure we're a couple."

She laughed. "They guessed."

"Yeah, but they haven't really seen us behave like people in love."

"I guess they will this morning."

He caught her hand and they walked into the sitting room, which had been decorated for the holiday. Tinsel had been strung across the fireplace mantle. A huge tree sat in front of the big window facing the circular driveway. Christmas carols drifted out from the speakers around the room.

Riley saw them first. "Mom?" She raced over and hugged Juliette. "I didn't think you were coming!"

"You thought I'd miss Christmas?"

She stepped out of the hug and Lorenzo took Juliette's hand again.

Riley blinked, but she didn't say anything.

Juliette laughed. "Yes. You guessed right." She smiled at Lorenzo. "We're an item. Lorenzo is officially living with me in Manhattan."

Antonio walked over. "Wow. We didn't have any idea things had gone that far."

Juliette smiled. "We're having fun."

"And it's glorious," Lorenzo said as he headed for the bar.

"So, you're living together in Manhattan?" GiGi asked from the sofa. Then she sighed. "I loved Manhattan. The park. Broadway. Wonderful restaurants."

Lorenzo said, "It's convenient for my new job."

"But we might not just live together forever," Juliette said, smiling at him. He winked.

Catching on long before the Salvaggios did, Riley's gaze flew to Juliette's hand and bounced back to her face when she saw the ring. "You're engaged?"

"Nope. It's a promise ring."

Antonio frowned. "What's a promise ring?"

Juliette took the glass of wine Lorenzo handed her. "It's a promise that we'll have a future."

Riley groaned.

Lorenzo laughed. "We're being unconventional. Both of us tried being normal and got stung. So, we're doing everything differently."

With everybody's curiosity satisfied, he changed the subject to Antonio's first week as the new CEO. Antonio had a lot to say, questions for his dad, the man he'd replaced.

Juliette took a seat by GiGi, who hugged her and filled her in on some new wedding details. Riley started distributing gifts from under the tree.

The ease of it suddenly hit Juliette and she swallowed hard. She hadn't had a real family since her parents died when she was eighteen. Now she had one. A great man, a future son-in-law and a sort of mother-in-law who actually liked her.

In a year or so, there would be a grandchild and who knew how many after that. She and Lorenzo had already discussed going to Paris. He'd told her about having fun with the tourists who frequented their wine tasting rooms. He'd mentioned a yacht.

But all on her timing.

The rest of her life was going to be a blast.

* * * * *

If you loved
Mother of the Bride's Second Chance,
why not read the first book in
The Bridal Party trilogy?
It Started with a Proposal,
available now!
And look out for the third book,
One-Night Baby with the Best Man,
coming soon!

And if you enjoyed this story,
check out these other great reads
from Susan Meier:

Fling with the Reclusive Billionaire
Claiming His Convenient Princess
Off-Limits to the Rebel Prince

All available now!

CINDERELLA'S ADVENTURE WITH THE CEO

SUZANNE MERCHANT

MILLS & BOON

For Saffet and the staff of the pansiyon at Simena,
who welcome their guests with unfailing warmth
and hospitality.

CHAPTER ONE

NO ONE KNEW where Jensen Heath had gone. And that was exactly how he wanted it. Five weeks earlier, when he'd walked through the prison gates a free man, declared the victim of a miscarriage of justice, he'd contacted nobody. Returning to his city penthouse, he'd stood at the wide glass windows and studied the view. A new building had altered the skyline in the past year, but far below, the grey ribbon of the Thames had continued to wind its timeless path towards the sea. The vista was virtually unchanged, and yet to him it would never be the same again. He'd become a different man, one who viewed the world through a lens distorted by anger and bitterness.

He'd turned away, packed a cabin bag with a few essentials and called the concierge, asking for a taxi to Heathrow.

The rattle of the chain and then the splash of the anchor hitting the water sounded thunderous, disturbing the still of the night. Jensen returned to the wheel in the cockpit and shifted the gears into neutral, allowing *Sundance* to drift astern until the metal spikes dug into the seabed and tugged her to a gentle stop. The throb of the engine, a muffled counterpoint to the soft wash of the sea on the beach, died away as he hit the 'off' button.

Jensen exhaled into the almost-silence, listening for anything out of place. An owl hooted somewhere in the belt of trees behind the beach, and the water, which he knew would be like warm silk on his skin, lapped at the hull. He was tempted to slip over the side for a swim but chose instead to simply absorb the atmosphere.

This was the place he'd dreamed of when the nights had been disturbed by the clang of a metal cell door, the snapping shut of a grille, voices raised in argument somewhere nearby. It felt miraculous that he'd found his way back, sailing solo from Piraeus in Greece; that he'd plotted his course to bring his boat to the narrow entrance between two embracing headlands on the Turkish coast, and then slipped her through the gap, into the cove he'd come to think of as belonging to him.

Managing the forty-foot ketch on his own had been a challenge, at times. Some of the sailing had been hard, and the way he'd pushed the boat to her limits had taken its toll, not just on the boat but on his body, too. Yet he'd relished the days when the wind and weather had demanded his full attention, leaving no room for the memories of his unjust incarceration, and the anger they stirred up, at times when he had space to think.

He stood and stretched, aware of the slight stiffness that had crept into his muscles and joints over the past few weeks. An old injury made his left shoulder ache. Twenty-five years ago, shouting the odds on the trading floor, he'd been supple and strong, working hard all hours of the day and playing even harder in the few left at night. Success and wealth had allowed him to slow down a little. And yes, he admitted wryly to himself, age had played its part.

He tidied the cockpit and then dragged his thin, rolled-up mattress from the locker on the foredeck. Stretching out on his back, his hands behind his head, he watched *Sundance*'s masts describe an arc against the starry sky as her hull rocked in the slight swell. There was a luxurious double berth in the cabin below, but after a year of imprisonment he didn't know if he'd ever be able to sleep in a confined space again.

The cramped cell, the constant noise, and the lack of decent food or exercise had been no surprise, he thought. But the psychological impact had shocked and shaken him. He'd considered himself to be mentally tough and resilient, and to find those strengths called into question had been frightening. Doubt had eroded his self-belief, making him question his worthiness. Losing the love of his family, friends and, most devastatingly of all, his daughter had seemed like confirmation that he no longer mattered in a world that had moved on without him. The frustration of being wrongly accused, and of not being believed, had been almost unbearable.

As he'd grown used to the prison routine, his confusion and disbelief had crystallised into anger. He'd kept a grip on his sanity through the long days and nights by planning the voyage he would take when he won his freedom; by imagining how it would feel, guiding *Sundance* through the narrow inlet, into these calm waters again.

In the solitude of this safe anchorage was where he wanted to be. *Sundance* had taken a battering and it would take weeks to repair some of the damage and make her properly safe again. He'd treated her gently over the past few days, aware that another gale might be more than she could withstand.

The prospect of being forced to spend a month or more in this magical place was soothing. Here, he could confront the recent past with a level head and clear mind. While he worked to repair his beloved yacht, he could work on his own recovery, too. He needed a plan to put his shattered life back together in some sort of shape that would fit his changed future.

Beth Ashton put the copper coffee pot on the hob and ignited the flame beneath it. Then she padded in her bare feet across the tiled floor and slid the glass doors open, breathing in the scent of the herbs she'd planted in pots on the terrace and the ones that grew wild beyond it.

Two cups of Turkish coffee per day were her self-imposed limit, but the one she relished was the first one in the morning, sipped on the stone terrace as the sun rose over the headland to the east, reliably ushering in another perfect day. Wrapping her hands around the mug, she stepped out into the warm morning, and stopped.

Something was different. She placed the mug on the table and listened. Scanning the tree-covered slope that dropped away towards the beach, she tried to identify what had changed. Then it came again: the unmistakeable metallic tapping of metal rigging against a mast. Coffee forgotten, she peered through the scrubby trees and dense bushes, but one of the beauties of this place was the way the beach remained hidden from view until the last moment, when the stony path ended and the azure water and pristine shore burst into sight, dazzling in their perfection. She couldn't see anything.

During the weeks she'd spent at the villa, she hadn't seen a single vessel in the cove. The entrance, almost hidden, was narrow, requiring a level of navigational skill beyond most holidaymakers who might have hired a boat for the day. There were other bigger, easy-to-reach beaches up the coast.

Curious, and a little irritated at the interruption to the habitual rhythm of her day, Beth pulled the sarong she'd left by the pool around her, knotting it at the front. She slid her feet into her flip-flops and began to pick her way down the path towards the beach.

The tap-tap sound of the rigging grew louder but there were no accompanying voices, or the splash of swimmers. She slowed, and stopped in the shade of the pine trees that fringed the beach.

The yacht was elegant. Its sleek white hull, punctu-
ated with portholes, swung gently on an anchor chain. She
thought the design, with the foremast taller than the aft,
meant it was called a ketch. The sails were tightly furled
and there was no sign of life on the deck. Had the occupants
already swum ashore and scrambled up the path, past her
villa while she slept? A knot of unease tightened in her abdomen at the thought. She stepped out from under the trees
and raised a hand to shade her eyes, wishing she'd thought
to pick up her sunglasses.

A movement made her draw back sharply. A man, tall
and wide-shouldered, had risen from the deck and now
stood looking, or so it seemed, straight at her. She held her
breath, hoping he hadn't seen her, not wanting to be noticed.

The only interactions she'd had since arriving five weeks
previously had been with Omer in the village shop, rely-
ing heavily on the use of her phrase book, and the young
girl who brought her lemon tea at the outside tables of the
little café. The thought of a conversation with a stranger
troubled and unnerved her. She squinted to see if she could
recognise the flag at the stern of the boat, but it hung, limp
and unmoving, in the early light, hiding its identity and,
presumably, that of the owner of the vessel.

He, if he was the owner, remained motionless for a little
longer. Then he moved to the stern. He extended his arms
above his head and dived, in a graceful arc, cleaving the
water with hardly a splash, and disappeared.

Something about the powerful lines of his silhouette and
the clean execution of the dive kept Beth riveted to her spot.
She scanned the glassy surface of the water but when he
emerged it was in a completely different place from where
she'd anticipated. The sound of his deep intake of breath
carried to her across the water and she saw a shower of
droplets sparkle in the low rays of the sun as he shook his

head and then swam slowly back towards the ladder that extended down the side of his boat.

Was he alone, she wondered, as she watched him haul himself up the ladder onto the deck and lean against the foremast, looking towards the shore again. Surely a boat like that required more than one person to sail it. Perhaps his companion, because he must have one, was still asleep. Perhaps there was more than one. She imagined a noisy, young crowd plunging into the water, swimming ashore and playing raucous games of volleyball or cricket on what she thought of as *her* beach.

Or perhaps, she thought, trying to put a positive spin on this intrusion, they'd move on when they realised there was nothing here for them. No ice cream or kebab sellers, or even a supply of fresh water. She shrank back into the deeper shadow of the trees and turned towards the path. She'd stay at home this morning; skip her usual morning swim in the sea and take it in the pool instead. By this afternoon, when she ventured back to the beach, she hoped she'd find solitude restored to the cove, with all trace of the unwelcome yacht and its crew erased.

Her coffee was cold. She threw it out onto the grass and began the process of making a fresh cup. She sipped at it, seated on the terrace, inhaling its intense, rich aroma, but the serenity she'd fought to cultivate over the past weeks eluded her. She'd arrived at the villa with her nerves in shreds, her life upended in a way she'd never anticipated, and her self-confidence pulverised.

The basic supplies she'd picked up at the airport had lasted a couple of days and it was hunger for something other than cheese crackers that had forced her to visit the village. There was a bicycle in the storeroom, the comprehensive villa notes told her, for cycling along the rough track to Sula. How long was it since she'd ridden a bicycle?

Decades. She'd doubted she'd be able to balance for more than a few seconds. Balance was an important ability to maintain as one aged, and she practised it assiduously in her weekly yoga class and when pulling on her tights or socks in the mornings. But the idea of balancing on a bicycle had felt daunting. If she fell off onto the stony track and broke something, who would find her?

For the first time, she'd questioned the wisdom of accepting Janet's offer of the empty villa, 'for as long as you need it, Beth'. Had Janet simply been trying to move her on from the guest room she'd occupied for three weeks while her life imploded? She knew that wasn't true, but since everything had begun to go wrong, she'd had difficulty in seeing the positive side to anything. If there was a positive side to being unexpectedly homeless and shockingly unemployed, she personally had failed to find it.

The house in Islington, where she'd lived, first with her parents, although she could barely remember her mother, and then with her father and stepmother, was no longer home. It seemed her father's dying promise that it would eventually be hers carried no weight with her stepmother. She'd bequeathed it to her only daughter, Beth's half-sister, who now intended to sell it.

It shouldn't have mattered. It would have freed Beth up to move in with her lover; to take their relationship to the next level; to commit to each other fully. Only that hadn't suited him at all, because it turned out he was fully committed already, to a wife in New York, on the Upper East Side.

The company where she'd steadily climbed the career ladder for twenty-five years, until she was appointed PA to a senior partner, had no longer felt like a safe place. How had she been so easily taken in? She'd resigned, with immediate effect, but as the heavy glass doors had swung closed behind her, she'd been engulfed in panic. Her home would soon no longer exist, and she'd left the job that had given her identity for so long. She'd felt invisible.

Fumbling for her phone with numb fingers, she'd called her best friend, Janet.

Several days after arriving at the villa, the thought of biting into a crisp slice of one of the watermelons she'd seen, stacked like footballs at roadside stalls, in the taxi ride from the airport, got the better of her. She'd wheeled out the bicycle and launched herself on a few trial runs across the dry grass behind the house. The bike had wobbled alarmingly, but she hadn't landed face down in the dust, and so she'd loaded a shopping bag into the basket on the handlebars and set off down the track in search of food.

The enjoyment of her solitude had grown with each day and now the idea of having to engage with the visitor to the cove filled her with unease. How, she wondered, had she come to this? Had the crushing of her expectations and the loss of her job crushed her personality, too? Reluctantly, she admitted the truth. The energetic carer she'd been to her aged stepmother, and the capable PA in a challenging role, had turned into an indecisive, anxious shadow. She was supposed to be using this time to rebuild her life, but so far all she had done was withdraw further and further into herself, with no idea of how she was going to move forward. What would happen when she had to leave and return to London? She pushed the thought away and drained the coffee mug. Janet had said she could stay here for as long as she needed, and it was only early July.

But she made a decision to log on to the Internet later and start searching for a new job. Even though she had no plans to leave soon, she had to confront the reality of her future. And the more immediate reality of confronting the broad-shouldered man on the boat was too unnerving to contemplate just yet.

CHAPTER TWO

THE INTENSE HEAT of the afternoon had begun to fade, and the light had softened when Beth ventured down to the beach again. The thought of being seen in her cherry-red bikini had almost made her change into her black one-piece swimsuit, so, just in case she met anyone, she'd pulled a thigh-length cotton kaftan over it. If the boat had gone, as she really hoped it had, she'd be able to have a swim in private and not care about exposing her body to the eyes of strangers.

Janet had bought the bikini for her, placing it, still wrapped in tissue, on top of her clothes in the suitcase.

'I saw it and thought of you, Beth,' she'd said, moving a pile of underwear from the chair so she could perch on the edge of it. 'It's your colour, and you deserve a treat.'

'Do I?' Beth had lifted the silky bandeau top from its wrapping and shaken her head. 'I've never worn a bikini, Janet, and I can't start now.' She'd glanced down at her body. 'I'd be so self-conscious.'

'Why?' Janet had sounded surprised. 'You've got a gorgeous figure.'

Beth had run a hand over the curve of her hips. 'I'd gained a little weight recently, although I've probably lost it now...'

'You were too thin before. You're perfect just as you are

now. And anyway, you'll have the pool and probably the beach all to yourself. There'll be no one else to see you, so be daring. Wear the bikini!' Janet had given her a quick hug. 'You have nothing to be self-conscious about at all.'

As she picked her way down the rough path a dislodged pebble rattled ahead of her, and she paused, tugging at the hem of the kaftan. Should she return to the villa and dig out the old one-piece, after all? But Janet's words echoed in her head, and she lifted her chin, took a breath and carried on.

The ketch had not gone.

It floated, on its own perfect, upside-down reflection, in the middle of the cove, and it appeared to be deserted. The air was so still that even the tap of the rigging had been silenced. Earlier, as she'd dozed on the shady terrace, Beth had heard the putter of an outboard motor, but it had sounded distant, through the heavy afternoon air. Now she wondered if the crew of the mysterious boat had taken to a dinghy and motored up the coast, in search of a livelier neighbourhood.

She stepped out of the shade of the trees and onto the beach. Her eyes had been fixed on the boat so she didn't notice the man floating on his back in the water until it was too late. He stood, water streaming from his broad, bronzed body, and began to wade out of the sea towards her. She froze, fixed to the spot, wanting to turn away but determined to stand her ground.

'Good afternoon.' The voice was deep and slightly roughened, as if rusty from lack of use. Apprehension sent goosebumps racing over her skin. She was sharply aware of how isolated and vulnerable she was. She shifted her balance on the pebbles beneath her flip-flops. She'd have to kick them off if she had to run…

He was silhouetted against the low evening sun, but she recognised him immediately as the man she'd seen dive into the sea earlier. His broad shoulders were square, his stance upright and, when he stopped a little way in front of her, he folded muscled arms across his chest.

'I hope I didn't startle you.'

She raised her eyes, squinting into the sun, even though she was wearing her sunglasses. Her heartbeat, which had leapt into overdrive in response to a shot of adrenaline, steadied to something more like normal and she tried to quieten her breathing.

Beth swallowed. 'I… Good afternoon. I haven't met any strangers here before. I'm just…surprised.'

'I apologise.'

Putting on the kaftan had been the right decision.

He stood at least six inches taller than her own five feet eight, and his clipped, cultured English was at odds with his slightly piratical appearance. His dark hair, threaded with silver, looked as if it hadn't been cut for many weeks and he raised one hand and shoved his fingers through it, slicking seawater down his back. Thick dark stubble, lightened with grey, roughened his jaw. If there were lines at the outer corners of his eyes, they were hidden behind his Ray-Bans. Big hands rested on the muscles of his upper arms.

She dropped her eyes, aware that she was staring. He had the sort of suntan that resulted from weeks of exposure to the weather, not a few days at a beach resort. Dripping-wet board shorts covered his thighs. A livid gash ran from his left knee down his shin and although the cut had healed over, the bruising surrounding the injury looked angry.

'What happened to your leg?' If she'd intended to say anything, that wasn't it, but the sight of the laceration had shocked her into speech.

He glanced down, shaking his head. 'I tripped over a line on the deck and caught it on a cleat.'

'It looks nasty.'

'It was a nasty moment. Price you pay for sailing a forty-footer solo in a force eight.'

Beth's eyes shifted beyond him, to the ketch. Her white hull was tinged with the pale gold of the sinking sun. She looked elegant and serene.

'Solo? You don't have a crew?'

'No. Not this time.' He turned away from her, following her gaze. 'It makes the sailing harder, but the solitude is the pay-off.' His voice had dropped.

A little flash of hope warmed Beth's insides. When he discovered this was her cove, he'd move on to somewhere he didn't have to share.

'You won't be staying long, then,' she said to his back. 'There's nothing here.'

He glanced at her over his shoulder, one eyebrow raised. 'I know that.' He shrugged. 'That's the appeal. I took the RIB down the coast this afternoon. The shop in the village stocks everything I need.'

'Oh. Do you know the area?'

'This coast? Like the back of my hand. But it's been a few years since my last visit.'

Beth thought she heard the grate of anger in his tone, and she moved away a little, wary, and anxious to put him off.

'Things change,' she said. 'If it's solitude you're after, you'll have to find somewhere else, because I come to this beach every day, and I like my privacy, too.'

She felt the satisfaction of seeing his mouth tighten. If she'd been able to see his eyes she felt sure they would have registered surprise.

'Every day?' he said. 'How do you get here? You don't have a boat and it's a tough walk along the track to the village.'

'As I said, things change. There's a villa up there now.' She indicated the tree-covered slope behind them. 'It belongs to a friend of mine and I'm there for…for the summer,' she said, firmly.

'So it was you, this morning.'

'I didn't think you'd seen me.'

'You moved, and then your shadow didn't fit with your surroundings.'

In the silence that followed, Beth was aware of the quiet slap of the sea on the pebbles and the sigh of a breeze through the pines. He held himself very still. She wished he'd remove his shades so she could read his expression more easily but remembered that she still wore her own.

'A villa?' He sounded incredulous, and not a bit pleased. 'Is it big? How many of you are there?'

'Big enough, but it's just me.' Mentally, Beth kicked herself for telling him she was on her own, but it was too late. 'It's only been finished a couple of months. My friend's husband, Emin, is half Turkish and they intended to spend the summer here with their family. But work commitments have kept them in London.'

She saw some of the tension leave his shoulders.

'What,' he asked, 'made you opt to spend several months alone at the end of an almost impassable track?' He shook his head. 'At the height of summer.'

'Possibly,' she said, 'something similar to what made you decide to undertake an obviously hazardous voyage—' she looked down at his injured leg '—solo, in search of solitude.'

'Touché.' A line between his dark brows deepened. 'It seems we're both annoyed at having our space invaded. Perhaps we can reach an agreement.'

'Perhaps you can find another isolated cove. Your home is mobile. I can't move anywhere else.'

He unfolded his arms and pushed his hands into the pockets of his shorts. 'No.' He shook his head, once. 'I can't move, either.' He looked across the water at the boat.

'I pushed her, too hard, to get here. There're repairs which need to be done before she'll be safe to sail anywhere else.' He glanced down at his injured leg. 'And I'm tired.' He rotated his left shoulder. 'And hurt. I need to recover. And this is the place I want to be. I need...'

Beth felt a bubble of frustration expand in her chest. He was unreasonable. 'Surely there must be somewhere...' she began, but he raised a hand and stopped her.

'We've established one thing. Neither of us is going anywhere. What we need to do is work out how to avoid each other. When do you prefer to use the beach?'

Beth wanted to use the beach when she felt like it. She had fallen into the habit of swimming in the cove after her first coffee and before breakfast, before the heat climbed to a level that made being on the beach uncomfortable. Then, in the late afternoon, she'd stroll down again and swim while watching the sun sink in the west and the sea and sky turn from blue to aquamarine to indigo. When Venus appeared, always the first gleaming jewel to adorn the evening sky, she'd climb the path back up to the villa for the evening. She nibbled at her bottom lip, trying to suppress her annoyance.

'Usually in the mornings...'

'I presume you don't spend all day on the beach.' She felt his scrutiny travel over her and thought about the sprinkling of freckles that dusted her nose, in spite of her addiction to sunscreen. 'You obviously protect yourself from the sun.'

'Too much exposure to the sun is dangerous.' She lifted her chin. Even at this time of the afternoon, she could feel her legs burning. 'Perhaps you should consider that.' She cringed at the primness she heard in her own voice.

Unexpectedly, he smiled. Even white teeth gleamed in his bronzed face.

'Perhaps I should.' He pulled a hand along his jaw, the

stubble rasping under his palm. 'I'll string an awning up over the deck for some shade.'

Beth felt colour rising into her cheeks at the faint note of teasing in his tone. She raised a hand and lifted her heavy hair off her neck, wishing she'd tied it up.

'I come to the beach early in the morning and in the late afternoon, to avoid the most intense heat of the day.'

'That's easy, then,' he said. 'I'll avoid the beach at those times. We need never speak to each other.'

'But…you'll be watching me, from the deck, waiting for me to leave…'

'That's a problem?'

If only you knew, thought Beth furiously.

She wouldn't be able to wear the red bikini anymore. Not if she thought someone—*he*—was watching her. Anxiety, which she'd managed to bury under the calm, measured routine she'd imposed on herself, stirred, reminding her it might have retreated but it had not gone away.

'I wouldn't be able to relax,' she muttered, turning away from him and starting to walk towards the beginning of the path.

'Hey.' His voice behind her was softer and a little warmer. She hesitated and turned back. 'I… I'm sorry. I've invaded your space and your privacy.' He raised a hand and pulled his shades from his face, pinching the bridge of his nose between his thumb and finger. 'And yes, I understand you'd feel uncomfortable if you thought I was watching you, so I promise that I won't. It's just that I'm stuck here, the same as you are, until she's ready to sail again.'

His eyes were dark, she now saw, dark blue, and troubled. His hands were back in his pockets, his knees and shoulders braced as if he was holding fatigue at bay by sheer willpower.

An unexpected wave of sympathy for him washed over

her. She appreciated his apology and identified with his position. Something had driven him to reach this place and it hadn't turned out as he'd expected and now the impetus had faded. He looked sad and drained of energy.

'Thanks.' She nodded. 'I appreciate that.' It occurred to her that he might need help, but she dismissed the thought. How could she be useful to a man like him, who sailed single-handed and relied on his own resourcefulness for survival? And anyway, he'd said he wanted solitude. She turned away, but his voice came from behind her.

'I don't know your name.'

'Since we're never going to speak to each other again you don't need to,' she threw over her shoulder.

CHAPTER THREE

IT WAS THREE days since Jensen had watched her walk away into the trees and disappear up the slope. The set of her shoulders had been stiff and she'd held her head high. It looked as if she was making an effort to appear offhand.

He hadn't seen her again.

The plan worked, he thought.

Solitude was what he wanted; what he craved. He didn't plan to expend any energy on thinking about a woman who wished he were somewhere else. Why, then, did he feel a little uneasy?

He hadn't exactly looked for her, in the mornings and evenings, when she could have been on the beach or swimming in the crystalline waters of the cove. But he'd noticed that she wasn't there.

He hadn't meant to frighten her off, if that was what had happened. The little twinge of guilt he felt surprised him. This was why, he thought, the days of tough sailing had been so good. So *welcome.* On those days he'd been in sole control of *Sundance*, and his own destiny. There'd been no time or space for feelings and emotions. He'd learned to keep them fiercely battened down while he'd been imprisoned but now found he had little control over them, when they chose to ambush him when he least expected it.

It was the morning of day three. Jensen leaned on the

rail of *Sundance* and scanned the curved shoreline, narrowing his eyes as he searched the fringe of trees that bordered it. The heat was already building, promising a scorching day. Perhaps she had come down for a swim before the sun had risen.

He dismissed that idea as impossible. Even if she'd tried her best to avoid his attention, the splash of her wading into the water would have alerted him. He was acutely attuned to the rhythm of the movement of the sea, and he would have noticed a change in it at once.

He was certain she hadn't been onto the beach since their exchange of words, and that niggle of guilt stirred his conscience, again. He'd probably made her feel insecure... maybe even unsafe. He'd appeared out of nowhere, as far as she was concerned, invading her privacy. She was alone, in an isolated place, and the last time he'd glanced at his reflection in a mirror, he'd looked far from friendly or even civilised. The realisation that he'd most likely frightened her bothered him.

To his disappointment, he hadn't been able to relax as completely as he'd expected. He'd been on the move for a month, he told himself, with reaching this place his one goal. It'd take time to adjust to staying still. *'I wouldn't be able to relax,'* she'd said, and now he couldn't, either. He suspected it was because he knew someone else—the woman in the thin cotton kaftan, which did a bad job of hiding her curves and the red bikini she wore beneath it— was somewhere up there, behind the trees.

If he knew her name, would he be able to put their encounter behind him, neatly tidied away where he didn't have to think about it again?

He straightened up, dragging his fingers through his hair and shutting down those thoughts. Her name and her curves were irrelevant, even if, in the past—the quite recent past—the latter would have sent a dart of anticipation and appreciation through him. He was beyond any of that. Those days were behind him.

He'd rather she wasn't there, and he knew she felt the same about him. If she'd chosen not to visit the beach, it was her decision. From the deck of *Sundance* nothing about the secret cove had changed and the solitude he craved was intact.

He'd go for his morning swim and then put the awning up over the foredeck, as he'd said he would. When he'd finished, the shade would be welcome as the temperature climbed towards forty degrees and he'd get on with the list of repairs he needed to make to *Sundance*.

When she realised that she'd read the same paragraph three times, Beth closed her book and dropped it onto the paved terrace beside her sun lounger.

Even a thriller set in the snowy wastes of Alaska couldn't distract her from the heat. She swallowed a mouthful of water from the glass at her elbow. The ice had melted, and the drink was tepid.

She stood and walked over to the pool, stepped carefully onto the Roman steps and sat down. The water was too warm to be refreshing and she longed for another swim in the sea. However hot the day grew, the sea temperature remained just cool enough, but she no longer wanted to venture onto the beach.

Each morning, she heard the telltale chink of the rigging tapping against the mast, reminding her that the boat was there.

She sighed and stretched her legs out in front of her, wriggling her toes. The opalescent polish on her toenails looked pretty against her pale gold skin. Despite keeping to the shade when at all possible, she'd acquired a light tan, even on her feet. Bracing her arms, she leaned back and studied the rest of her body.

Her thighs and tummy looked toned, which must be a result of all the swimming she was doing and the cycling trips to the village. The heat had been intense earlier and she'd taken a cool shower and had a siesta when she'd returned with fresh fruit and vegetables in the basket of the bicycle. Those last few weeks in London had been confusing and chaotic and her exercise routine had been forgotten, but she felt better now that she'd established it again.

From the time her father, his health failing, had charged her with the care of her stepmother and half-sister she'd begun to accept she'd never have the freedom to meet a partner, fall in love, or have children. The fairy tale didn't happen for everyone. Her role had been to work to provide for them, and she had fulfilled it. Her father had left them the house to live in with the promise that it would be hers, one day, but not much else.

There had been no reason why her future shouldn't have been exactly as she'd expected it to be, until she'd been foolish enough to believe she could be special to someone.

She wriggled forwards and sank into the water. She'd swim some laps to work up an appetite for her evening meal and then eat it out on the terrace. With luck, a light breeze might pick up to take the edge off the heat.

The stranger from the boat had not disturbed her, at least not physically. She'd thought curiosity might have driven him to climb up through the trees to see the villa, but he'd respected her desire for privacy, as she had his. His look of exhaustion, though, and the memory of his injured leg, plagued her thoughts. He'd turned down her tentative offer of help, but she'd like to know he was all right. Then she thought she'd be able to put him out of her mind.

Swimming was supremely calming. The measured

strokes of her arms, the kick of her legs and the steady breathing all combined to create an even rhythm and, once she hit her stride, she could continue indefinitely.

Twilight had descended by the time she took a deep breath, dived beneath the surface and swam the final length of the pool underwater. As she emerged, in a rush of exhaled air and with water streaming down her face and throat, she heard someone call.

Sinking back into the water, Beth pushed her hair back from her face and peered across the shadowed garden, apprehension snaking up her spine. But the shape of the man who stood on the grass, between the pool and the trees, was instantly recognisable. It felt as though she'd conjured him up with the power of thought.

'Hi.' Her greeting was guarded. She stayed in the water as he walked towards the pool.

'I'm sorry to disturb you. I know you don't want company. I just…'

Beth shook her head. 'That's…okay.' She remained where she was, with only her head and shoulders above the water, as he stopped at the edge.

She allowed her eyes to travel from his bronzed, bare feet up his legs. His injured shin looked inflamed, she thought. Faded shorts rested low on his hips. His hands were shoved into the pockets, but he pulled one out and ran it through his untidy hair, the movement drawing Beth's attention to the flex of his biceps, and the bunching of the muscles of his chest. His body looked hard, his abdomen tight and toned. The light smattering of dark hair, mixed with grey, did not hide the gleam of his tanned, smooth skin.

She felt an unfamiliar, and unwelcome, stirring somewhere deep in her body, and a sudden constriction of her lungs stopped her from taking a breath deep enough to quell the little tingle of awareness that shivered through her.

'I'm sorry,' he said, again. 'I just wondered if you're all right. You haven't been to the beach.'

'No. I—' Beth realised she was staring. She made an effort to drag her eyes away, but it felt as if there was nowhere to look, apart from at him.

'But I can see that you're fine. I'll leave.'

'I just haven't felt comfortable about the beach. I'd be intruding on your space.'

'We made a plan.'

She shrugged. 'Actually, you made the plan. I decided it didn't really suit me.'

'I promised not to watch you.'

'You did. But...'

'But you didn't trust me to keep my word.' He nodded. 'I get that. Why would you?'

'Oh. It's not that. I know you came here looking for seclusion, just as I did, so I didn't want to disturb you. You haven't disturbed me, either.'

'Until now.'

His eyes met hers and then he raised his head and stepped back.

'You're not disturbing me. I've finished my swim.' She felt suddenly self-conscious, remembering that she was wearing the revealing bikini and that within a few minutes the underwater lighting of the pool would come on automatically. She'd be lit up like a fish in a tank. A fish with too many curves, wearing a too-small, look-at-me, bright red bikini. She'd have to get out before that happened. 'But as for being alright, your leg looks as if it should be seen by a doctor.'

He glanced down at the injury. 'Yeah. You're probably right. It doesn't feel too good. Do you know if there's a clinic in Sula?'

'The information pack in the villa will probably include

details of local medical facilities. I can have a look if you like.'

She began to move towards the steps, eyeing the distance to her sarong, which she'd dropped next to her book on the terrace. If she could reach it and wrap herself up, she'd feel a whole lot better.

'That's very kind. Thank you.'

Beth felt for the steps and put her feet on the lowest one. As she straightened her legs the upper part of her body left the water. Acutely aware of the smallness of the bikini and how it was more revealing wet than dry, she sank down again.

His eyes rested on her for a moment and then he turned, covering the distance to the sunbed in three strides. In a matter of seconds, he'd gathered up her sarong and skirted the pool. He stood at the top of the steps, holding the length of fabric stretched out between his hands.

'Here you are,' he said quietly. 'You can get out now. But if you'd rather I went away, I'll go.'

'It's…okay.' In spite of the warmth of the water and the evening air, she shivered.

'Are you cold?'

'No. Not cold. It's just…you surprised me a little. I wasn't expecting a visitor.'

'I didn't want to frighten you. I heard you swimming, and so I called out.' He shook the sarong gently. 'Would you like to come out? Or if you'd rather I left, I'll go.'

Beth climbed up the steps, hunching her shoulders and focussing on her feet. As she reached the edge of the pool, her eyes still fixed on the ground, she felt the feather-light sarong settle over her shoulders. She grabbed the edges and pulled it around herself, bunching the fabric in her fists under her chin.

'Thank you.' Her voice felt tight and strained.

The pool water was running down her back, puddling at her feet. She wanted to squeeze her hair and wring it out but she didn't dare loosen her grip on the fabric that was shielding her.

'Do you want to go and get dressed?' He'd turned away from her and was studying the villa.

Beth nodded. 'I'll be back in a minute.' She transferred the sarong to her left hand and wiped the water from her eyes, pushing her hair off her forehead.

In the fading light his profile was becoming blurred, but she could make out his strong, slightly Roman nose and straight, dark brows. She wondered what his mouth looked like, beneath the scruff. And were his eyes really that dark or was it simply the lack of light that intensified their colour?

As if on cue, the pool lights came on, casting a watery glow over the immediate surroundings.

'Half past six,' she said, gesturing towards the pool. 'That's the time the lights come on.'

He nodded. 'And what do you usually do at six-thirty? Have a drink? Cook a meal?' She wondered if he was teasing her. 'You seem to keep to a set timetable, even here in the wilds of Turkey.'

'It's how I live. How I've always lived. Making the best use of my time.'

A little flare of anxiety ignited in her chest. She'd managed to curb it by establishing her routine here and this man had already upset it once. Over the past three days she'd made adjustments, allowances. The changes weren't perfect, but she could manage while he remained.

Keeping to her routines meant she had her life under control, superficially, at least.

He lifted his shoulders and dropped them again, his hands back in his pockets. 'Time is irrelevant here. Accepting that fact is liberating. And a great luxury.'

To her surprise, Beth felt the burn of anxiety fade a little. She'd regarded this intrusion as a threat, not only to
herself personally, but to the way she'd chosen to live here.
But he wasn't dangerous. He'd come, he said, to see if she
was all right.

It felt like a long time since anyone had asked her that.

Janet had taken her into her home and supported her
while her life had unravelled around her. *'You'll get through
this, Beth. You'll be all right,'* had become her refrain during those fraught weeks.

Everyone had always assumed she'd be all right. She was
dependable. Strong and organised. The thought that she
might not be okay was unthinkable. But what if she wasn't?

Facing her vulnerability and accepting it had been hard,
but she knew it was the first step towards moving on with
her life.

Suddenly, she didn't want this man to walk away into
the gathering darkness. The chance to have a conversation
with someone felt like one she would like to take.

She glanced down at the puddle that had formed around
her feet. 'Will you wait?' She nodded towards the table and
chairs on the terrace. 'I'll be right back.'

Jensen chose not to sit down. Instead, he walked to the edge
of the terrace and looked out over the tops of the trees. The
two headlands that sheltered the cove were visible as darker
masses against the paler sky. The air was heavy and still,
with no hint of a breeze.

He exhaled, trying to relax his tense muscles, then
breathed in, relishing the aroma of the herbs that grew
nearby, as they released their scents onto the warm air after
the heat of the day.

He heard her light footstep on the terrace and turned.
She'd changed into a loose cotton, long-sleeved midi dress

in a shade of dark green. It floated around her as she walked, masterfully disguising her shape. The most vivid imagination wouldn't have conjured up the gentle curves he knew were hidden beneath it.

Irritation at his thoughts made him slap them away. He felt under-dressed and wished he had a tee shirt on, at least. Sucking in a breath, he strolled towards her.

'Shall we start again?' He held out his hand. 'Jensen.'

Her hesitation was slight but noticeable. Then she put her hand in his, briefly, before withdrawing it abruptly.

'Beth.'

For the first time, in the soft lighting of the terrace, he saw that her eyes were green, fringed with dark lashes and faint smile lines at the corners. She must have rubbed her hair dry because it was no longer dripping, and she'd twisted it up into a loose knot.

'Pleased to meet you, Beth.'

'Oh, I don't think you are, Jensen.' The slight lift of the corners of her mouth softened her words. 'You wish I weren't here. Or the house, either.'

'That is true. Just as you wish *Sundance* and I would sail away into the sunset, leaving you with your own private beach.'

'*Sundance*? Is that the name of your yacht?' She placed a small brown glass pot on the table.

'It is.' He nodded. 'And the sun set a while ago, so that option has gone for another day.'

She shrugged. 'Maybe tomorrow...?'

'Maybe not.' He shook his head. 'And you?'

'The furthest I'm going in the near future will be Sula.' She put her hands on the back of one of the wooden chairs. Her fingers were long and slim. No rings, he noticed. 'Would you like to sit down? For a few minutes?'

Jensen hesitated. 'I wouldn't want to interrupt your plans for the evening.'

A dimple indented her left cheek, but it faded as quickly as it had appeared.

'I think I can spare the time. My plans can be flexible. A little.'

She pulled out a chair and he followed, seating himself opposite her, across the table.

'How,' he asked, with genuine interest, 'do you get to the village? I remember the track and it's a tough walk, especially in the summer. Some bits of it are steep and there's no shade, to speak of.'

'There's a bicycle that comes with the villa. It's not an easy ride but I've grown used to it now and I rather enjoy the challenge. I go early, to avoid the worst of the heat. It's helping to keep me fit.'

'You need help with that?'

'Here I do, yes. In London…' She stopped, leaning back in the chair and putting a hand up to her hair, as if to check it was still in place.

'You live in London? I suppose you belong to a fancy gym where you run on a treadmill and lift weights.' He looked around, thinking of the state-of-the-art gym and swimming pool in the basement of his former office building. 'A far cry from here.'

'Yes.' She nodded. 'That is, yes, I live in London. Or I did. But I've never belonged to a gym.' She reached out and nudged the glass jar towards him. 'Rub this on your shin. It's comfrey cream. Excellent for bruising.'

He picked it up and studied the printed label. 'Thank you. I'll try it.' His eyes found hers. 'Do you know of other herbal remedies?'

'Plant uses interest me, both in cooking and for medicinal purposes. I'm going to do...was planning to do a course in herbology.'

Some change had impacted on her life, he thought, but he pretended not to notice her slip. It would be wrong to probe and anyway he didn't need to know the details. He'd just wanted to know she was all right.

'I should probably go.'

Beth nodded. He felt better knowing her name. She seemed to feel a lot more relaxed since she'd returned, wearing that dress.

'I had a look at the file. Apparently Omer at the shop will be able to tell you where to go for medical help. He's the cousin of the owner of the villa and he seems to know everything and everyone. Will you go tomorrow?'

Jensen nodded. 'I will. I'll take the RIB.'

'I've heard an outboard motor a couple of times.'

'Has it disturbed you?'

'Not at all. Before I knew you were a lone sailor, I pictured a rowdy crowd of twenty-somethings roaring off to find the latest beach party.' She shrugged. '*That* would have been disturbing.'

'I brought the RIB up onto the beach. If I'd thought I was going to be sitting down at a table in such a civilised way I would at least have put on a tee shirt.'

He liked the sound of her quiet laugh. It was gentle and musical and he thought he'd like to hear it again. She tipped her head back, exposing the smooth column of her neck.

'I haven't entertained anyone here before. I haven't even *spoken* to anyone, apart from Omer in the shop and Ela at the café. That's why I like to cycle over there quite regularly. Otherwise, I might forget what civilised looks like.'

'Let me tell you, then, that, from the point of view of someone who has been sailing single-handed for over a month, civilised looks very much like this.' The gesture of his outstretched arm encompassed the terrace, the pool and the smiling woman across the table.

'Thank you.' She looked down at her hands, clasped loosely together on the table in front of her. 'Would you…?'

'I should go…'

'I was going to ask if you'd like a slice of watermelon. I bought one this morning and it's perfectly ripe.' Her words seemed to come out in a rush, as if she'd been uncertain about saying them and had then let them out before she could change her mind.

He'd been about to stand up, but he relaxed back into the chair. He nodded. 'If you're sure, I'd love some.' Then he wondered if he should have refused her offer. The longer he stayed, the more comfortable he'd feel, and he didn't want comfortable companionship. He wanted to be alone.

But Beth had already disappeared in the direction of the kitchen. She returned with plates, paper napkins and slices of pink watermelon in a bowl.

'Help yourself. It's delicious.'

It was. It was crisp, sweet and so juicy that their hands were soon sticky. Jensen couldn't remember anything ever tasting quite so good.

'Thank you, Beth.' He pushed his chair back and stood. 'I didn't intend to take up so much of your time.'

'Thank you for checking up on me.' She stood and stretched out her hand. He took it, feeling her slender fingers, sticky with watermelon juice, against his rough palm. She pulled her hand away and laughed again. 'It's impossible to eat watermelon and not get sticky.'

'Thank you for this.' He pocketed the pot of comfrey. He swung around and headed off into the darkness, finding his way to the place where the path tipped down the steep slope towards the cove. Before the shadow of the trees and scrub swallowed him up, he looked back. Beth stood where he'd left her, watching him leave. He raised an arm, hoping she'd be able to see him in the gloom, and when she gave a quick wave back he felt a small hit of satisfaction.

He needn't worry about her. She was fine.

Beth watched him—*Jensen*—leave. Meeting him again and learning his name had transformed him, in her mind, from the interloper to someone more approachable. She still wished he'd go away, or that he'd never come at all, but at least she knew he wasn't going to disrupt her quiet existence more than he had done already.

She watched as he dropped his arm and turned away into the darkness of the trees, then she went into the villa and pulled the sliding glass door closed, shutting out the dark and the hum of insect nightlife, which formed the background noise to every evening.

What had made her ask him to stay, even for a few minutes? To share the enjoyment of something as simple as a slice of watermelon? Although strength and self-reliance were the outward qualities that struck her first about him, it had been his underlying tentativeness that had made her look at him a little more carefully. There was an elusive quality of uncertainty about him, which she thought he probably wasn't even aware of himself, as if he needed her to recognise something in him and respond to it.

Was it as simple as him needing company after his solo voyage? If that was the case, why did he insist on being alone? And if he valued his privacy so much, why had he come to check up on her?

Nobody had ever needed her for herself and she wondered how that felt. Was that what she glimpsed in Jensen? A need to be understood and accepted for himself, and himself alone, whoever that might be?

The open-plan living area of the villa had been designed

to accommodate large groups. She imagined Janet planning get-togethers here, with family from England and Turkish cousins filling the house with laughter, the terrace echoing with the shrieks of young people enjoying the pool. It was the perfect place for reunions or celebrations.

Upstairs, the cool, calm bedrooms would accommodate couples and their children.

Beth shook herself mentally and pulled open the door of the large fridge, extracting a bottle of wine from the rack. She half filled one of the heavy, stemmed glasses and stretched out on a sofa from where she could see the terrace and the pool, and the trees beyond.

She thought about what she might have for dinner. Taking a sip of the cold, crisp wine, she relished the feeling of it in her mouth and throat. She'd briefly thought of inviting him to stay for a meal, but was glad she hadn't. Neither of them wanted company and it would have felt awkward. She'd given him the comfrey cream and they'd enjoyed a few minutes together. That was enough.

She pictured him steering the RIB across the dark water towards *Sundance*, climbing aboard and then perhaps turning to look back at the trees, where he could now imagine her at the villa.

The images were disturbing, along with the faint regret that accompanied them. She reached up and released her hair from the untidy knot, irritably shaking it out around her shoulders.

Perhaps it was time to cut it short. Working long hours had meant it was convenient to be able to put it up in a severe, neat pleat rather than to have to style it every day.

She'd seen a Turkish barber in the village. Perhaps they'd cut it for her. She'd enquire tomorrow. She wondered if her phrasebook would stretch to 'bob'.

CHAPTER FOUR

THE GIRL AT the café, whose name she'd discovered was Ela, brought Beth a tray of tea without her having to order it. She'd come to anticipate the morning tea ritual, on the days when she visited the village, almost as much as she craved that first cup of Turkish coffee first thing in the mornings at the villa.

She loved the silver pots, containing the brewed tea and hot water, the delicate, slim-waisted tea glasses and the plates on which they rested. A spoon, for lifting up the tiny lemon wedges, lay at the side. Today, Ela placed a small bowl containing squares of baklava at her elbow, waving away Beth's protestations.

Beth flipped open her laptop and logged onto the café's Internet. There was Wi-Fi at the villa, but it was unreliable, and this morning had been non-existent. Besides, she'd found she enjoyed sitting in the shade outside the café with the buzz of village life in the background. She opened the file containing her CV.

It was orderly and utterly dull. The only bit of it that caused her spirits to lift, slightly, was where she'd listed her hobby as 'gardening'.

Apart from a few temporary jobs, after she'd left her secretarial college, she'd worked for the same company for twenty-five years.

It had been a safe, predictable job, at least to begin with. She could walk to the offices in the City from the house in Islington, passing a supermarket on the way home.

The document on the screen in front of her showed her steady progress up through the ranks of the administration staff, with regular promotions that had brought added responsibilities and benefits.

What changes could she make to it that would cause a possible new employer to take notice? And what positive spin could she put on the facts so that her abrupt departure would seem like a good thing?

She poured tea into the pleasing glass and topped it up with hot water. From her table under the shade cloth that stretched over the rickety veranda of the café, she watched the morning unfold in the village square. A heat haze already shimmered above the roofs of the market stalls.

Across the square, a knot of men gathered outside the barber shop, waiting for it to open. She was glad she'd pinned her hair up again this morning, leaving her neck and shoulders open to any breeze that might stir. But the idea of walking into the barber's and trying to explain that she wanted her hair cut off felt daunting. She'd draw attention to herself, be the subject of rapid-fire conversation between the other customers, some of whom would potentially express a loud opinion, which she would not be able to understand.

Perhaps she could wait until there was a quiet moment, between customers. Or break the habit of a month and come into the village later in the afternoon, after the siesta and before the locals took their evening strolls.

She must try not to overthink everything. The habit added layers of unnecessary worry to every day. How much easier life would be if she could be spontaneous, and not care about what other people thought.

The aroma of the hot, lemony tea permeated her senses as she took a sip, closing her eyes to concentrate on its full impact.

When she opened them, she saw Jensen cross the square and enter the shop, his broad frame pausing briefly in the doorway, before disappearing into the dark interior. She closed her laptop.

A minute later, he emerged, with Omer at his shoulder, pointing across the square and looking at his watch. Beth stood up as Jensen began to walk in her direction.

He hesitated when he saw her and for a second she thought he was going to greet her and then simply carry on walking, but he stopped, a smile lifting the corners of his mouth.

'How is your leg?' She glanced down at his shin, which looked shiny. 'You've used the comfrey?'

He nodded. 'I have. And Omer has given me directions to the clinic. It opens in an hour.'

'He seems to be the lynchpin on which everyone depends.'

'He does.' He took another step towards her.

'Would you like to join me?' She indicated the second chair at the small round table. 'I'm having tea but if you'd prefer coffee...'

Jensen signalled to Ela, who was wiping down a table nearby, and ordered Turkish coffee. 'Are you working?' He glanced at her laptop.

'No. More like looking for work. But...' she pushed the laptop a little to the side and lifted her tea glass '... I'm uninspired. Have some baklava.' She took a piece in her fingers and bit into its sweet nuttiness. 'Mmm...' Then, suddenly aware of Jensen's eyes on her mouth, she bent her head and dabbed at her lips with a paper napkin.

He helped himself to a square, chewing slowly, and she watched his throat move as he swallowed.

'Thank you.' He lifted his coffee cup, tiny and delicate in his broad hand, and took a mouthful. 'The pharmacy is round the corner from the barber and it doubles up as the clinic, two days a week. Today is one of the days.' His brows drew together, the line between them furrowing.

'Is it still painful?'

'A bit.' He replaced the cup on its saucer and folded his arms. 'Thank you again for last evening. I didn't realise you were planning to come to the village today.'

Beth swallowed a mouthful of tea, keeping her eyes on the table, which was, she thought, much smaller than the one at which they'd sat last night. Even though they were outside, it suddenly felt rather intimate. 'I wasn't. But the Internet connection at the villa wasn't working this morning and I needed to...'

'Job hunt?'

'Yes.'

He removed his shades and rested his forearms on the table, leaning in towards her a little. His dark eyes were serious. 'You don't seem enthusiastic about it.'

'I'm not.' She tapped her laptop. 'As you can see, I've given up, for the day.' Beth shifted on her chair. Her pink linen dress, usually so cool and airy, felt clammy. She ran a hand across the back of her neck and patted her hair, checking it was still secure.

Jensen's eyes followed the movement and then he looked past her, across the square. 'If you want to talk about it...?'

'Oh, no. Thank you.' Inwardly, she shrank from the idea of Jensen reading the dull catalogue of her working life to date. She began to think inviting him to join her had been a mistake. He was too close. The small shifts of expression on his face were intriguing, the silver threads in his dark hair gleamed in the bright light, and, at this close range, his eyes were navy blue.

Awareness, unfamiliar and tantalising, seemed to spark between them, making her skin heat more quickly than if she'd been sitting in the Turkish sun and her lungs to feel squeezed, so that her breath became a little shallow. She ran a finger around the neckline of her dress.

From being two people at odds with one another, determined to keep themselves isolated, she suddenly felt as if they were being pulled towards each other in some magnetic way. She leaned against the back of her chair, but the sun caught her directly in the eyes, around the edge of the shade cloth, and she had to lean forwards again. She wondered if he felt it, or if it was entirely in her own imagination.

Fleetingly, she saw a flash of what she'd seen last night. A look of uncertainty flickered in his eyes, as if he'd thought he knew the answer to something but suddenly doubted himself. She wanted to ask what was bothering him, but hesitated, unsure of how to frame the question. A forceful, independent man like him was not going to admit to any insecurities, to a woman he barely knew.

This had been a mistake. He'd probably only agreed to sit down with her out of politeness. The best thing she could do, for both of them, was leave.

'Where's your bike?'

The question took her by surprise. 'It's leaning against the wall around the corner. Why do you want to know?'

'I can see you're trying to think of how to leave, although I'd like it if you stayed a little longer. Let me wheel it around here for you.'

'Would you?'

'At least finish your tea.'

She peered into the glass, then topped it up. 'It's just…' Beth felt flustered by his intuition. What else about her was so obvious to him? 'I don't like to leave it too late because it'll be hotter for the ride home.'

'Of course.' He inclined his head. His expression was implacable again, showing no trace of emotion.

She drained her glass and pushed her chair back.

Jensen stood and went to get her bike while she slipped her laptop into its bag, put on her sunglasses and dug in her purse for money to pay for her tea.

'Thank you,' she said when he returned. She put a banknote on the table, dumped her bag in the basket at the front of the bike and took hold of the handlebars. 'I hope you get good advice at the clinic. Let me…' She'd been going to ask him to let her know what happened, but she remembered that they didn't want to see each other.

'Shall I let you know what they say?'

She nodded. 'Yes, please. And…' she drew in a deep breath '…if you need any help, you know where I am.'

'Thank you, Beth.' He smiled, his eyes crinkling at the corners. 'I think I'll be just fine.'

Beth smiled back at him. She watched his long, tanned fingers unwrap themselves from around the handlebars of her bicycle and then his hands disappear into his pockets. She puffed out a long breath. She'd made the offer and it was up to him to decide whether he needed her help or not. She didn't expect to see him again, any time soon, and she'd also be just fine with that.

After all, neither of them wanted to spend time in each other's company.

Jensen watched Beth cycle away, her pink dress billowing around her legs, then he sat down again at the table, taking another piece of baklava in his fingers. Ela appeared in the darkened doorway, and he reached for his wallet, adding the cost of his coffee to the note Beth had left, plus a hefty tip.

If they could keep their encounters brief and light, like last night and this morning, they might enjoy spending a little time together, if she wanted that. He explored the feeling of mild annoyance that came with acknowledging it was what *he* wanted. For months, all he'd wanted was to be alone, to sort out his mind and find answers to the questions that plagued him. He shouldn't want Beth to intrude.

The image of her standing, alone, on the terrace last night had stayed with him. He'd noted that her green dress was a shade or two darker than her eyes. This morning, he might have missed her in the shade outside the café, but she'd stood up and come towards him, with that wide smile, and something inside him, which had been held tight for a long time, had loosened. He didn't understand what it was, but it felt good.

He hadn't thought twice about accepting her invitation to join her.

As he stood up, something beneath the table caught his eye. It was the charger cable for her laptop. He bent to pick it up, turning it over in his hands, looking in the direction of where she'd exited the square in case she'd realised her mistake and come pedalling back.

There was no sign of her, and if she'd kept going, she'd be too far away by now for him to catch up with her on foot. It occurred to Jensen that she wouldn't miss the cable until the next time she needed it.

He coiled the cable up and pushed it into one of his cargo shorts' pockets. He'd visit the clinic, buy his bread and olives, and then head back down to the harbour, where he'd left the RIB tied up at the jetty. Beth would be home by the time he'd motored up the coast back to the cove and climbed the twisting path to the villa. His fist closed around the coiled cable in his pocket. The fact that he felt pleased to have a reason to visit her again was irritating, but he pushed that aside.

* * *

Beth left the village behind her and kept pedalling. She tackled a hill at full tilt but had to slow down part way up it. The sun beat down on her bare head and she wished she'd remembered to bring her straw hat.

The day-to-day order of her thoughts and life had encountered a blip. There was something about Jensen, who stood so tall and seemingly steadfast, that kept snagging her attention. Having only recently allowed herself to admit to her own vulnerability, she thought she recognised a stubborn refusal to acknowledge the existence of it in himself. Behind his façade of manly strength and endurance, through the flashes of uncertainty he'd allowed her to glimpse in unguarded moments, she sensed the presence of hurt and confusion.

There was a tentativeness about him, which suggested he held himself in constant expectation of things going wrong.

It takes one to know one, she thought grimly, as she freewheeled down a slope, enjoying the breeze in her face.

She thought back to her confused, bewildered self of two months ago. She might still have a long way to go. After all, she remained homeless and unemployed. But she now had the clarity of thought to recognise how far she had come, and that was what she had to focus on, in order to keep moving forward, with her life, both personal and professional.

Her narrow, restricted existence was in the past. Having the ties that had bound her forcibly cut had been terrifying at the time, and although she didn't know what shape her life would take in the future, at least she was free to make her own decisions.

Something momentous had driven Jensen to sail, single-handed, back to the place where he'd expected to find solitude and solace. Beth wondered if, or when, he'd realise that reaching that goal was only the very beginning of the journey.

She crested the top of a slope and stopped for a breather. A slight breeze at the top of the hill cooled her skin as she enjoyed the glimpses of the sparkling blue sea and the dramatic views of the mountains in the distance.

She set off again, but as she reached the bottom of the hill the bicycle lurched beneath her and pulled to one side of the track. Tugging on the brakes, she skidded to a stop in a cloud of dust. The front wheel was completely flat. Bending to examine it, she found a thorn protruding from the wall of the tyre. She sighed. She'd have to walk the rest of the way, pushing the bike. The hill rising up in front of her was steep and shadeless and she thought she was only about halfway home. The journey, usually enjoyable, was turning into an ordeal.

Pushing a bike with a flat tyre was harder than she'd anticipated. Every stone sent a jolt through the frame and she had to fight to keep going in a reasonably straight line. Her flimsy, rope-soled espadrilles had been designed for wearing to the beach, not for hiking through the harsh Turkish landscape in the almost-midday sun. She could feel the rub of a blister forming on her right heel and a rivulet of sweat trickled down her back, between her shoulder blades.

After several stops to rest, when she tried to regain her breath, she trudged to the crest of the hill. If swimming was going to keep her fit, she'd have to dedicate more time to it. Down in the valley on the far side she could see a single, stunted tree.

The tree provided even less shade than she'd hoped, but she laid her bicycle on the stony track, making sure that her laptop was safe in the basket, then she sat down on the dusty ground, leaning against the tree trunk. The bark was rough and scratchy against her back.

Her parched mouth and throat longed for a drink of water. Dust coated her feet and legs and the heat intensified as the sun climbed towards its noon-day high point. It was no use berating herself for the position in which she found herself. She should have had a hat and water, but there was nothing she could have done about the punctured tyre.

She'd rest for an hour and then tackle the remainder of the journey.

The phone in her bag was useless. Even if a signal existed out here in the wilds, there was nobody she could call for help. It was a sobering thought.

She closed her eyes, but a rustle in the undergrowth nearby made her shoot bolt upright again, staring at the dry, crackling grass that moved, inches from her right hand. Rigid, she waited, wondering if it was a snake. Not daring to blink and hardly daring to breathe, she shifted slightly further away and watched as a scaley, blunt-nosed head appeared, swinging from side to side. Then she breathed out as a small tortoise, leathery neck stretched from its bumpy shell, emerged from the scrub. Ignoring her, it lumbered its slow, measured way across the track.

Beth rested her head against the tree trunk and prepared to wait.

CHAPTER FIVE

THE BOTTOM OF the RIB scraped on the shingle as Jensen beached the craft. He climbed out, pulled it further out of the water and looked around.

He'd wondered if Beth, knowing he was in the village, might have come down for a swim. But the heat was scorching, and he thought she was probably resting in the shade of her terrace, enjoying a siesta.

It was already mid-afternoon. After a long wait at the clinic, buying food and water and making the journey back to *Sundance*, he was later than he'd expected to be.

There was no trace of Beth at the villa, either. The sun lounger was empty, and the sliding glass doors were locked. He circled around the house and tried the front door. The door to the lean-to storeroom was open, and he looked in, seeing a beach volleyball net, two paddle boards but no bicycle.

A finger of disquiet traced up Jensen's spine and he rattled the brass handle of the front door again. The silence in the oppressive afternoon heat suddenly felt unnatural. Beth should have been home long ago.

He stepped back, getting his bearings. He could remember vaguely, from before the villa had been built, where the track began, and he soon found it, winding downhill into the trees. He was pleased that he was wearing his boat shoes. They might be battered, but they would provide a good grip on the rough surface.

As he stepped into the trees he heard a mechanical squeak, and the sound of stones on the track being dislodged. He paused to listen and heard irregular footsteps and uneven breathing from below him.

Beth came into view, rounding a bend in the track. She was pushing her bicycle, limping and her cheeks were as pink as the dress she wore. She stopped, swiped a forearm across her forehead and blew out a long breath, looking up at the final slope ahead of her.

'Jensen?'

He started down towards her. 'What's happened? Are you all right?'

'What are you doing here?'

'Looking for you.'

'Why? We aren't supposed to want to see each other.'

Jensen took the bike from her. 'Let me do this. You're limping.'

Beth let go of the bike and wiped her palms across her face. 'The front tyre has a thorn in it. Pushing a bike with a flat tyre is hard work.' She looked up the hill. 'Almost there. And it's only a blister.' She grimaced. 'A big blister.'

'Have you got water with you?'

She shook her head. Tendrils that had escaped from the knot of her hair flew around her face.

'I forgot to bring my water bottle.' She planted her fists on her hips. 'And my hat.'

'That was…'

'Stupid. Yes, I know.'

'I was going to say "unfortunate".'

'I don't forget things. Not usually.'

'I'll take the bike.'

Beth nodded. 'Thank you.'

They emerged from the trees into the glare of the afternoon sun and Jensen bumped the bike across the dry grass towards the house. 'Get yourself a drink of water. You may feel like swallowing a gallon, but take a few sips, at first. Otherwise you may feel sick.' He wheeled the bike into the storeroom.

When he went into the house she was in the kitchen, a glass of water in her hand.

'You haven't told me why you're here.'

He put the bag containing her laptop on the kitchen island and pulled the charging cable from his pocket. 'You dropped this under that table at the café.'

'Ah. Thank you. I'd probably have thought I'd dropped it on the track somewhere. I'd have retraced my steps, looking for it. Not an attractive idea, right now.' She sipped from the glass. 'How was the clinic?' She limped across the floor and slid open the glass doors onto the terrace.

'I've been given meds for what seems to be a mild infection.' He looked down at Beth's feet. 'There's blood on the heel of your shoe.'

'I know. I've tried to take it off, but it's stuck.' She kicked off the other espadrille. 'I'll have to soak it in water.'

'Do you need help?'

She shook her head. 'No, thank you. I might have to grit my teeth, but I'll manage.'

'I'll have a look for a puncture repair kit in the storeroom while you do that.'

She turned quickly to face him. 'Will you be able to mend the tyre if you find one?'

He nodded. 'Sailing teaches you to be handy and resourceful. If I can't mend it, I'll take the wheel to the village in the RIB tomorrow. Someone there will be able to do it.'

'That will cause you even more trouble than I have already.'

He folded his arms and regarded her steadily. 'Maybe, but what will you do the next time you need to get to Sula? It's almost too difficult for you to ride, in this heat. It's definitely too far to walk.' He glanced down at her feet. 'Especially with an injured foot.'

'I'm resourceful, too. I'll think of something.' She returned to the kitchen and pulled a plastic bowl from a cupboard, filling it with water.

Her back was poker-straight as she limped across the tiled floor and into the spacious, open-plan living area. Deep sofas, covered in cream linen, were grouped around a low, marble-topped table, facing the terrace and pool through a wall of glass. At one end of the room the up-to-date kitchen gleamed with porcelain tiles and polished appliances. Cool white walls and cream curtains pulled the scheme together, creating a room that combined elegance and charm with a laid-back informality.

Over to the left, Jensen noticed a wide, open fireplace in the end wall. The idea of a log fire when the mercury was climbing towards forty degrees seemed like madness, but he knew how cold it would be here in the depths of winter, when icy winds from distant, snow-covered mountain peaks in the north roared over the headlands.

The presence of this villa intruded on his solitude and spoiled his memories. He wished the land had been left wild and undeveloped. But he had to admit, unwillingly, that if he had designed it, this was exactly how he would have wanted it to be.

If the villa weren't here, Beth wouldn't be here either. Would that have been the perfect scenario he'd dreamt about? It didn't feel so attractive anymore. Being with her somehow soothed him. The knots of tension he'd carried for months seemed to unravel a little. It shouldn't be like this, he told himself, watching her sit on the sofa and lower her injured heel into the bowl of water. He should be on *Sundance*, grappling with how he was going to find some sort of life for himself.

Was that what Beth was doing, too?

CHAPTER SIX

BETH EASED THE shoe away from the injury on her heel. The skin was raw and red. As she stood up, Jensen walked back into the room.

'I can repair the tyre. I've found a kit in the store.' He bent his head to peer at her heel. 'How's the blister?'

'Thank you. I'd really appreciate that. And the blister is not great. I need to put a dressing on it.'

'Is there a first-aid kit in the house?'

'Under the sink, I think.' She eased herself back onto the sofa. 'Could you get it?'

Jensen carried the box across the room and put it on the marble table in front of her.

'Can you manage? It looks a little nasty.'

Beth laughed. 'I think I can deal with my own blister but thank you for offering.' She heard the rasp of his palm as he pulled it across his jaw, and she looked up. 'I'm used to taking care of myself.'

'Maybe, but that doesn't mean you can never accept help.' Jensen took a step back, away from her. 'I know your privacy is important to you. You didn't ask me in. I followed you, so I should go. The walk must have tired you out.'

Beth shook her head and a tendril of hair escaped from its untidy knot and flopped forward over her forehead. She pushed it back. 'I think I might be too much of a coward to put on the antiseptic.'

'If I'd found you sooner, I wouldn't have let you walk.' He nodded towards her foot. 'I would have loaded you onto the bike and pushed you all the way home.'

'I would have resisted, for sure.'

Beth took a tube of antiseptic and a pad of cottonwool from the first-aid box. Frowning and biting her lip, she returned her attention to her heel.

'Shall I do that? It's a slightly awkward angle for you. If you turn around I'll be better able to see your heel.'

'Would you? Thank you.' Beth shifted her position, turning towards the back of the sofa to expose her heel and resting her head on her folded arms. 'Are you a doctor?' she asked suddenly, looking back over her shoulder at him.

'No, I'm not. Why do you ask?'

Beth turned her face away again. 'Injuries don't seem to bother you.'

'Like I said earlier, sailing means having to develop all sorts of skills. I've dealt with way worse things than this, sometimes in the teeth of a gale, on high seas, at night.'

'Really? Like what?'

'Oh, fingers trapped in winches, heads smacked by the boom whipping across unexpectedly, twisted ankles…'

'It sounds like a violent pastime. Ow!'

'Sorry. Almost done now. I'll put a dressing on it but you're going to have to keep it dry for a couple of days.'

The crackling rip of an Elastoplast dressing being unwrapped sounded loud in the quiet room. He pressed it to the back of her heel and removed his hands.

Beth hadn't been at all sure she'd be able to bear having him touch her foot, but his calm ministrations and matter-of-fact manner had made her forget the way she shrank from contact these days.

She had no memory of straightforward affection. Her

mother was a vague shadow who had faded away before Beth's memories of her had been properly formed. She thought her father had remarried quickly to try to replace her, both for himself and for his small daughter. If he'd ever regretted it, he had never said. He seemed to shrink in her memory, after that, and the figure of her stepmother and then her baby half-sister grew large and overwhelming. Physical displays of affection or words of praise became forbidden.

It had been years before Beth had realised that not all families behaved in that way. She had felt like an intruder in her own home, an unwanted member of her own family. When she hadn't felt invisible, she'd been criticised. Her hair was unruly. It must always be kept tied back, tightly. Bright colours did not suit her. The clothes bought for her were dull and unflattering. She'd grown into a young woman who believed herself to be unattractive.

Later, her usefulness had been in working hard to keep the household running. It had only been after the death of her stepmother that she'd learned there hadn't been a shortage of money. She could have gone on to study botany and horticulture if her stepmother had allowed it.

And then, although her father had extracted a verbal promise from his wife to leave the house in Islington to her, she'd left it to her own daughter instead, who intended to sell it, depriving Beth of the home she'd had since birth.

She twisted round and pulled her feet up under the skirt of her dress, hugging her knees. Jensen's dark head was bent over the first-aid box, those long fingers reordering the contents, clicking the lid shut, folding the cloth and towel.

'That means no swimming.' She frowned. 'I'll have to do more gardening, in the early mornings. And I'll have to cycle into the village for entertainment and exercise.'

'I wouldn't put a closed shoe on until the skin has healed,

or you'll risk rubbing it raw again. And I wouldn't advise cycling in flip-flops.'

'Not that I have to listen to your advice.'

'No, you don't.' He shrugged.

His easy response surprised her. All the men she'd worked for had assumed that their opinions should be accepted without challenge.

What would working for Jensen be like? she wondered. Was he as calm and considerate in the workplace as he'd been when applying a dressing to her blistered heel? He gave the impression of being a good leader; one who would use quiet example rather than unreasonable demands. Beneath his measured exterior must lie a fierce determination, though, and an expectation of being obeyed, if he could command the respect and obedience of a crew at sea in dangerous conditions.

What had brought him to this remote part of the Turkish coast, alone?

'Is that what you do?' As soon as she'd spoken, Beth realised her words would have no context for him. She had become so familiar with her own internal monologue she'd forgotten that she hadn't spoken it out loud.

Jensen moved to the nearby armchair. 'Do what?' The lines between his eyes deepened. He propped his folded arms across his knees and turned his head to look at her.

'Sorry. I…was wondering what you do. From what you say, you're used to sailing with a crew.' She pressed her face to her knees, before looking across at him. 'I apologise. It's nothing to do with me. I just thought you might be a professional sailor.'

'For me, sailing is purely recreational. And therapeutic. It's not a job. It's an indulgence.' He tapped his fingertips on the marble table. 'Sailing alone is the perfect way to banish

everyday worries, and even bigger ones. The level of concentration needed is intense. It eclipses everything else.'

'But you're not sailing now. You're anchored in the cove,
going nowhere.'

A thrumming silence stretched between them.

'That's because…' He took a big breath. 'It's because
things have happened in my life which I need to address,'
he eventually said, slowly. 'For a long time, I dreamed of
getting back here. It felt as if only here would I find the
space and the silence I needed to sort things out. Not just
physical space and silence. I suppose peace and headspace
would describe it best. But…'

'But you finally arrived, only to find me—and the
villa—here, in your special place.'

He sat back, clasping his hands behind his head, balancing an ankle on a knee. 'Yes, but I think I'm discovering
that…you…are not really the problem.'

Beth smiled. 'Always good to know I'm not a problem.
But if it's not me?'

He turned his head away, looking out through the glass
doors towards the pool and the trees. 'This may sound
crazy…' He shook his head. 'I don't know if you'll understand.'

Beth saw that self-doubt take hold again in his dark eyes.
She thought back to the person she'd been when she'd first
arrived in Turkey, weeks ago. She'd felt hollowed out, invisible. Sure that nobody needed her and certain that nobody
wanted her. Her childhood home and precious garden were
being sold and she'd walked away from the job that had
given her identity and purpose for twenty-five years. It had
been the place where she felt she belonged, and, lately, was
appreciated for herself, rather than her organisational ability.

For days, she'd wanted to stay curled up in bed, the air
conditioning blowing cold, the blinds keeping out the hot

Turkish summer. But hunger had drawn her out, and each time she'd ventured into the bright living space downstairs, the outdoors she could see through the wide glass doors had worked a little more of its magic on her. Bright birds had swooped over the pool and congregated in the rosemary bushes that grew wild along the edge of the terrace. A striped lizard had blinked slowly, its head raised, basking in the sun.

One day, she'd slid open the doors and felt the warm, dry air brush against her face, and the scent of the grass and pine trees tickle her nostrils. Janet's voice had come to her, so clearly that she'd almost looked over her shoulder, expecting to see her standing inside the front door.

'The house will stand empty if you don't go and live in it. You'll be doing us a favour.'

'I can't accept it. It makes me feel like a hopeless case. Homeless and unemployed.'

'If you go and live there you won't be homeless. And you can use the time to search for another—a *better*— job. And if you still feel you owe us, please use your horticultural skills and do something about getting the garden started. Omer, Emin's cousin, will tell you where to get plants in Sula.'

It had been a slow process, but from that moment she'd had a purpose.

'You could try me, Jensen. You never know. I might just understand.'

He seemed to pull himself back into the room from somewhere distant. A frown, almost of puzzlement, creased his forehead and drew his brows together. His eyes, filled with doubt, found hers.

'The journey was tough, sometimes. But I liked those times best. I felt powerful, managing the boat, reading the weather, trying to predict the waves. There was no one else to rely on. Just me. I had to keep control, of everything, because disaster was always waiting to strike if I let my attention stray.'

Beth nodded. 'It sounds frightening.'

'It would have been if I'd allowed fear into my head. But I refused. Fear is corrosive. I thought I'd won the battle before I even reached the destination where I'd intended to fight it.'

'Here?'

He nodded. 'Here.'

Beth tucked her legs up onto the sofa and smoothed the skirt of her dress over her feet. 'And when you arrived…'

'It took a day or two, but then I found it wasn't like I thought it would be. I'd reached my goal. I'd stopped, at last, and could relax and think about what to do.'

'But?'

'But I can't relax and I can't think. That power I thought I had was an illusion. I could control *Sundance*, use my knowledge to make the best of the wind and the weather, but I cannot control my thoughts or my emotions. I'm confused and doubtful that I'll ever sort things out. And most of all, I hate the idea that this might all have been for nothing.'

'I don't think,' Beth said, carefully, 'that anything is for nothing. Things happen for a reason. You may not be able to see the reason yet, but you will eventually. When I first came here, I had lost all purpose. My life had spun out of control, and it felt as if everything I'd ever known or valued had been snatched away.'

'What happened?'

She shook her head. 'Knowing that wouldn't help you, Jensen. Just as knowing what has brought you here is irrelevant to me. What I discovered is that reaching the destination is only the beginning. The journey is still ahead of you. It may seem impossibly difficult, and you may not know where it's leading, but if you take one day at a time, you'll get there.'

Jensen rubbed a hand over the back of his neck. She kept her eyes on his face and he met her gaze with his own. She smiled at him.

'Thank you, Beth. I thought I wanted solitude but talking to you helps to put things into some sort of perspective. I didn't think I'd be able to say this, but I don't mind the villa, with you in it, nearly as much as I did.'

An unfamiliar mix of emotions stirred behind her breastbone. Muted pleasure, at his words, and satisfaction that her own experience, to date, might have helped him a little. And something else: a faint frisson of anticipation of the beginning of a tentative friendship between them.

'I've taken up most of your day, Jensen. Thank you for your help'.

'You're welcome, Beth. I was pleased to help, even though you denied needing it, and I've enjoyed your company.'

Silence stretched between them, but it was companionable and comfortable. Beth felt it could be left like that. They didn't need to fill it with words.

He'd said he didn't mind her being here. That did not mean they were going to become new best friends.

She pressed her bare feet to the cool tiles and stood up, walking to the glass doors, keeping her back to him. 'You've been very kind and I owe you thanks.' She inhaled a deep breath, trying to control the tremor in her voice, which would give away how anxious she was for him to accept what she said next. 'I'll owe you even more thanks if you repair the puncture. May I cook dinner for you tomorrow as a thank you?'

CHAPTER SEVEN

BETH HAD TRIED to keep her voice steady. He could tell that by her straight spine and pulled-back shoulders, but she hadn't quite managed it. It reminded him that, while she might look and sound strong and positive, there was a vulnerability beneath the façade she was presenting to the world.

He stood up and moved to stand next to her at the glass doors. 'I wouldn't be comfortable accepting your invitation if your only reason for issuing it is to discharge a debt of gratitude.' He cast a quick sideways glance at her profile, noticing her chin lifting in something like defiance. Or perhaps it was self-defence. She opened her mouth, about to reply, but he held up a hand. 'If, on the other hand, your invitation is to share a meal with me and perhaps enjoy my company as well, then…'

She turned abruptly towards him, her hands clasped together, her gaze direct.

'I've been on my own, here, for weeks. I've never socialised much, but now I'm well and truly out of the habit.'

He nodded, filing that information away to examine another time. 'I'm not much different. I was pleased to help you today, but I don't need repayment, of any sort.' He stepped away from her, aware of the tension radiating from her body. 'I'll get on with fixing your bike.'

He could mend the tyre and walk away from Beth—from this unsettling need to spend more time with her; to try to find out more about her—and return to the solitude of *Sundance*'s deck.

That seemed to be what she wanted, and he was not going to push her for reasons.

He worked methodically, completing the repair and re-inflating the tyre. With the bike returned to its place on a rack in the store, he packed away the tools he'd used and emerged into the late afternoon sunlight.

Beth stood on the rough grass, pink flip-flops on her feet.

'Before you use the bike again check that the tyre is still properly inflated.'

'Jensen?'

He'd been about to walk away, but he stopped.

'Yes?'

'Thank you. But…'

'But you don't want my company. That's fine, Beth.'

'That's not what I was going to say.' She lifted her hands, palms upwards. 'What I mean is, I've enjoyed your company, too, and I think I could enjoy more of it.'

He smiled at her, keeping his distance.

'You think? What,' he asked, 'are the chances of you finding out for sure? One in ten? In fifty?'

'No chances,' she replied. 'I've decided. I'd like you to come for dinner. That is, if you don't already have a dinner party planned on *Sundance* tomorrow evening.'

He shook his head, welcoming the glimpse of humour that sparkled in her eyes. 'No, I don't. I just happen to be free.'

'Good. Would seven o'clock suit you? It'll probably be pasta.'

'Excellent. I'll bring a bottle of wine.'

'Does that mean you have to go back to the village to-morrow?'

'I'll raid the cellar on *Sundance*.'

'You have a cellar on *Sundance*? Is that ballast?'

'It could be if the need arose. And it's not really a cellar, obviously. It's a few bottles of wine wedged into the cubby holes above the main berth.'

Yesterday, this had seemed like a good idea. She'd enjoyed Jensen's company and was grateful for his help in mending her bike and dressing her blistered heel. The awareness that had sparked between them at the little café table had faded by the afternoon, she thought, allowing her space to begin to relax in his company. With that had come the realisation that perhaps he might need help in confronting whatever demons had brought him here.

She had no idea what those might be, but she could listen, if he wanted to talk.

Why, then, when she'd woken from a restless night, had inviting him to dinner seemed like the worst idea in the world?

Beth turned off the shower, wrapped a towel around herself, and thought about the contents of her wardrobe, wondering what to wear, then reminded herself that she was cooking a simple supper of pasta, not a four-course dinner party with four different bottles of wine. Stressing over her outfit was not necessary.

She pulled on a pair of cream linen crops and a loose-fitting top with elbow-length sleeves. Before stepping into the shower, she'd made a sauce from the fresh tomatoes, peppers, garlic and onions she'd had in the fridge, adding a few sprigs of herbs from the pots she'd planted up around the terrace. A rich aroma now floated up the stairs.

She rubbed condensation off the surface of the mirror and studied her reflection. She'd caught the sun the previous day, on her long walk from Sula, and her cheeks glowed more than she'd have liked. Jensen had made it plain that friendship was what he sought, so the nerves jumping in her tummy were ridiculous and annoying. It was, she told herself, because she hadn't cooked a meal for anyone other than herself, for months. Her skills as a hostess were non-existent.

Why had she done this to herself? It hadn't been necessary to put herself under stress.

Then she reminded herself how far she'd come in the past few weeks. Certain things might still make her anxious, but serving pasta and tomato sauce to one other person should not be one of them. It wasn't as if she planned to bare her soul to him. Her heart and soul were carefully locked away, where they couldn't be damaged any more than they had been already.

Get a grip, she told her reflection, already blurred by more condensation.

A slick of lip gloss took away the dryness that over-exposure to the sun had caused, and she towelled her hair vigorously before blow-drying it roughly and reaching for a scrunchie. As the whine of the dryer died away, she heard the knock on the door. Her stomach plunged. Of course he was early, and she wasn't ready.

'Beth?'

Why hadn't she locked the door?

'Beth?' His voice was steady, calm, coming from the foot of the stairs. 'Are you okay?'

Beth dropped the scrunchie and combed her fingers through her hair, trying to tidy it into vague orderliness, as she walked down the short passage to the curving staircase, knowing that curls would be falling around her shoulders in an unruly mass. Too bad. This wasn't a work dinner. She didn't have to entertain an important client. This was the wild Turkish coast and she wasn't obliged to look perfectly groomed.

The marble floor was cool beneath her bare feet, her footsteps silent. She rounded the curve in the flight of steps and found Jensen looking up at her.

She decided, again, that this had been a bad idea. Her fingers tightened on the iron railing that curved up around the stairs. He looked cool and fresh, his hair slicked back, his navy eyes calm. Not at all as if his appearance had just delivered a potent kick to her abdomen.

'Hey.'

'Hello. You're…'

'I'm a little early. I apologise.'

'I wasn't quite ready.' She lifted the hand that wasn't gripping the banister and ran it over her hair.

'Something in the kitchen smells delicious.'

He had swapped his shorts and faded tee shirt from yesterday for jeans and a pale blue shirt, slightly crumpled, open at the throat and with the sleeves rolled to the elbows. She wished she felt as relaxed as he looked, a bottle of wine in one hand, the other in the pocket of his jeans.

'Oh,' she said, 'thank you,' wondering again what had made her do this. Perhaps if she'd put her hair up she would have felt more in control of the situation. Of *herself*. A sleek French pleat was the image she liked to present to the world: severe, remote.

Don't even think of crossing my personal boundary.

'Your hair looks beautiful.'

'Beautiful?'

'Yes,' he said. 'Beautiful. Now, I don't know about you, but I'm hungry and thirsty and this bottle of wine won't open itself.'

She didn't understand why she felt so anxious about this evening. It should have been so simple. She took a deep breath to steady herself so that she could at least walk down the stairs towards him without wobbling, but she needn't have worried. He'd turned away and was strolling towards the kitchen.

Beth had a sudden, vivid flashback to her old life, where chairing a meeting or arranging a client dinner had been something she did every day, without a second thought. What had become of that version of herself? It had vanished the day she'd walked out of the office, her reason for being taken away from her and the future she'd imagined in tatters.

She blocked the memory and made herself think, instead, of how a sense of purpose and self-worth had begun to creep back into her consciousness when she'd decided to start planning Janet's garden and nurturing the plants she'd bought for it.

Jensen's dark, steady gaze seemed to be able to see into her, beyond the image she presented to the outside world, to question things about her that she'd rather keep secret. He made her feel vulnerable again because he made her...*feel*.

She didn't want to return to that sort of feeling. She'd had enough of the cold weight of shock and devastating hurt that lodged in her stomach whenever she allowed herself to think about the turn her life had taken. Being surrounded by the peace and beauty of this place had enabled her to keep those damaging emotions under control, choosing when and where to examine them. She knew she had to examine them, in order to move on, but it had to be done at her own pace, when the time was right. No longer, she thought, did she sometimes have to fold an arm across her abdomen, giving in to the sensation that it was the only way to keep herself together.

Jensen was opening drawers in the kitchen, humming under his breath. No doubt he was searching for a corkscrew.

Shaking her hair out over her shoulders—had he really

said it looked beautiful?—she filled her lungs, exhaled strongly, straightened her spine and walked down the stairs, putting on her formal, PA face. It was her best defence and, under these circumstances, her only weapon.

Jensen located a complicated corkscrew in the second drawer he opened. He sliced around the foil covering the cork and peeled it away, positioning the device over the top of the bottle. Then he looked up and saw Beth coming towards him.

He breathed a quiet sigh of relief. He'd had the feeling she'd had second thoughts about this evening and wanted to disappear upstairs, but he wasn't at all sure what he would have done about it if she had. He couldn't have gone after her. He could have waited, hoping she might change her mind or offer an explanation, but he might have waited a long time.

Her rigid posture made her movements jerky and he saw the tip of her tongue run quickly across her lower lip. Suddenly and inappropriately, he imagined how her soft mouth would feel beneath the rough pad of his thumb.

She looked ready to shatter into a thousand sharp pieces of herself. He did not want to be the catalyst for that event. He wanted her to feel comfortable.

He smiled, hoping that it looked easy, and that Beth wouldn't notice the tension he felt. 'Could you find some glasses?'

'I don't want...'

He paused in what he was doing. 'I'm sorry. It was presumptive of me to assume you'd want wine. What else have you got? Would you prefer something soft?'

'No. No, thank you.'

She stopped on the far side of the marble-topped kitchen island. The pale green colour of her loose-fitting top was the perfect foil for her eyes, he thought. And her hair really was beautiful, with its streaks of faded gold threading through darker amber. But her expression bordered on fierce, faint lines creasing the wide space between her brows.

He forced himself to take his eyes off her and go back to opening the bottle, working slowly, twisting the metal screw into the cork and pressing down on the two levers to remove it smoothly, with a muted, satisfying pop.

He glanced round the kitchen and saw glasses lined up in neat rows on shelves. 'Ah, there they are. Sure you won't have wine?' He squinted at the label. 'I bought it on a sailing trip in the South of France a couple of years ago. I've been waiting for an occasion to try it.'

At last, Beth nodded. 'Thank you. I'd like some.'

Jensen decided not to ask her what she'd been going to say. He didn't understand what had happened to make her so nervous, but probing would only make it worse. He selected two stemmed goblets and set them on the marble countertop, pouring the golden wine from the bottle.

He held a glass out to Beth, noticing the slight tremor of her hand as she took it. 'Shall we sit on the terrace? It's a little cooler now.' Perhaps she'd feel more relaxed on the terrace.

Without waiting for an answer, Jensen slid the glass doors open and stood back, allowing Beth to go ahead of him. The air was warm with no hint of a breeze. The cicadas, which had been in full cry in the earlier heat, had fallen silent and in the west the sky still held the pink glow of sunset. Soft pools of light from concealed solar lanterns glowed in the garden. Two candle lanterns stood unlit on the wooden table.

'There're matches in the kitchen.' Beth turned back into the house, colliding with him as he stepped through the door. He put his free hand on her shoulder, to steady her, but she jerked away from him.

The connection between them lasted only a few seconds but it was long enough for Jensen to feel, not only the softness of her body against him, but also the taut muscles of her upper arm beneath his hand. He caught the floral scent of shampoo, the clean smell of soap. How easy it would be, he thought, to slide his hand down around her waist and hold her against him for a little longer. How easy, but how impossible.

Even if she'd been willing to give him a quick hug, was that what he wanted? He didn't think so. Beth intrigued him. She was complicated and prickly and that combination piqued his interest, but friendship was the only thing he was prepared to offer her, or any other woman, right now, so if there was one thing he was hell-bent on doing, it was keeping a lid on the sensations that fired into unwelcome life whenever she was near. A hug, however brief and friendly, would not be helpful.

She returned with a box of matches. The quick scrape of the match head against the side of the box sounded loud in the silence. The small orange flame flared and she leaned over the table, lifting the glass chimney of one of the lamps and lighting the candle. The wick caught, sending up a tall lick of dancing flame, before settling into a steady burn, light pooling around it on the table.

'Thank you for inviting me.' He raised his glass and she nodded, doing the same, and then taking a mouthful of the honey-coloured wine. 'I don't have to stay long.'

She almost smiled and he thought that somehow what he'd said had ticked a mental box for her. Was she pleased he wouldn't stay long? Or had she told herself he'd eat and be gone?

'This wine is exceptional. Thank you.' She put her glass on the table. 'I'll put the pasta on.'

* * *

Beth reminded herself how easy she'd found his company the day before. The best way to get through the evening was to try to recapture that feeling of relaxed companionship between them. The fact that the silence felt charged and awkward was entirely her fault. She'd used up all her reserves of emotional energy preparing for him to be here and now she had none left for making conversation.

Frustration bloomed inside her. Why couldn't she relax and enjoy the evening for what it was? Two people, possibly both lonely, sharing simple food and finding pleasure in each other's company. She couldn't relax because she was afraid of the emotions that might escape from the locked-down state in which she kept them. She couldn't afford to drop her guard. She never would, again.

'How is your heel?' Jensen had pushed his cleaned plate aside and now sat, leaning his folded arms on the table.

This was safe territory, Beth thought. Her heel was the reason he was here at all.

'It feels good, thank you.' She nodded, smiling. 'I've washed my shoes and they'll be wearable again.'

'Just don't put them on before the skin has healed completely.'

'I won't, but staying out of the water for a day or two is going to be a challenge.' She reached for his plate, stacking it on top of her own. 'How is your leg?'

'Definitely improving. Twenty-four hours on the antibiotic and I can tell it's going to be fine.'

'Luckily I haven't needed to use the clinic but it's good to know there is one.'

'That was delicious. Thank you. Who taught you to cook?' He took a mouthful of wine, watching her over the rim of the glass.

'Oh, I'm self-taught,' she replied. As far as safe topics of conversation went, cooking must surely come second only to the weather. She could move on to the midday temperatures and strength of the breeze, when there was one, if the conversation flagged.

'You mean you didn't have an Italian grandmother or aunt, teaching you the wizardry of combining ingredients, from an early age?'

'No grandmother, or aunt.' She took the paper napkin from her lap and folded it in half on the table, smoothing the crease with her thumb.

'None at all? Italian or otherwise?'

She shook her head. 'None.' In the silence that followed she folded the paper oblong she'd created into a square. Perhaps now was the moment to comment on the brightness of the stars, or the lack of light pollution.

But she'd reckoned without Jensen.

'Did you teach yourself to cook, Beth? Was it something that interested you?'

Beth thought of the years she'd spent planning and shopping for economical and nutritious meals for her stepmother and half-sister, cooking when she'd come home from a hard day at work to find they hadn't washed up their breakfast dishes. And then discovering she'd been duped and none of it had been necessary. Her father had left a lot of money, just not to her. He had simply been manipulated by the woman he'd married and had been too weak to stand up to her. And then, when circumstances had set her free, and a beautiful, exciting future had seemed to be within her grasp, it had all come crashing down.

'No,' she replied, slowly, picking up her glass and swirling the dregs of wine in it. 'I didn't particularly want to do it. In fact, now I wonder why I did. I could have just walked away, if I hadn't promised my father...'

That was one of the problems of living alone. Sometimes she talked to herself, and this was one of those times. Was she losing her grip on reality? What had she said? Too much, probably. She tipped up the glass and swallowed the last few drops. Jensen stretched an arm across the table and held up the bottle, raising his eyebrows. Recklessly, she allowed him to top up her glass.

'What did you promise your father?'

'My life story is rather dull. You said you didn't want to stay long, so don't feel—'

'That's not what I said at all. I said I didn't *have* to stay long. Not that I didn't want to. And you've told me just enough of a story to keep me interested.'

Beth kept her eyes down, looking at her replenished glass. Did it matter if she told him what had happened? It wouldn't count as baring her soul. Once they went their separate ways they were never going to see each other again and he'd forget about her, and her sad story as soon as he'd sailed *Sundance* out between the headlands.

She could clam up, but that would lead to more glaring gaps in the conversation. It would be easier to fill them with the irrelevant details of her background. It might also keep Jensen happy. There were questions about her personal life that she would not be happy to answer.

'My father died of cancer when I was sixteen. He asked me to look after my stepmother, Ava, and half-sister.' She raised her glass and took a sip of wine. 'He'd always said the house would be mine, but he changed his will a few days before he passed away. I'd promised to care for them as he seemed to think they were incapable of caring for themselves. I soon discovered that absolutely wasn't true.' She looked across the table to find Jensen's dark eyes on her face.

'Is that when you could have walked away?'

Beth shook her head. 'No. I was still at school, but soon

I was running the household, on the limited funds I was allowed. Ava said my father had left very little money to live on but if I fulfilled my promise, she'd told him she'd bequeath the house to me, as he wouldn't ever want me to be without a home.'

'And that didn't happen.'

'No. I eventually became Ava's main carer, as well as working full-time. When she died a few months ago, she left the house to Sherri, my half-sister. She's ten years younger than me.' She paused, sitting back in her chair. 'You could say I was easily manipulated, but I'd tried to please my father all my life and I continued after he'd died, keeping my promise to care for his wife and daughter. I think he remarried quickly, after my mother died, because he wanted to replace her, both for himself and for me, and eventually Sherri came along, the baby sister I'd always longed for.'

'Only it wasn't like he imagined?'

'Or like I did. His new wife—my new mother—for whom I was meant to be grateful, never intended to be a mother to me, but I had to do a lot of growing up before I realised that. When I left school she told me there was no money for me to go to university.'

She watched as Jensen raised his glass, then replaced it on the table without drinking from it.

'What did you hope to study?'

'Botany and horticulture. I wanted to be a landscape designer. The garden in Islington…' She swallowed a mouthful of wine. 'Well, it was my escape, in a way, when I had the time.'

'So what did you do instead?'

'I went to secretarial college and got my job. I don't know why I'm telling you this. You can't be remotely interested, but that was when I could have walked away.'

He shook his head. 'Don't assume you're not interesting. Was that the job you had until...?'

'I worked for the same company until I...left, a few weeks before coming here.' She noticed that the moon, a perfect crescent, had risen over the trees, wisps of cloud trailing across its face. 'My father was foolish,' she said, steering the conversation away from the subject of her former job. 'He should have tied things up more tightly, legally. I just assumed he had, but I think he changed his will under duress and there was nothing legal to say the house would eventually be left to me.' She shook her head. 'I prefer to believe he would not knowingly have left me without a home.' She saw the muscles of Jensen's jaw tighten, even under his stubble, and his eyes narrowed. 'When Ava died, I discovered there'd been a lot of money in my father's estate. I could have studied further. There'd always seemed to be enough when Sherri needed something.'

'What's she doing now?'

Beth pressed her fingers to her temples, shaking her head. 'She became a successful estate agent in London. After her mother died, she told me she was moving in with her fiancé and selling the house.' She heard Jensen suck in a long, controlled breath.

'Your stepmother's behaviour was outrageous and dishonest.'

'Maybe, but not illegal, and Sherri has promised me a percentage of the value of the sale. There was nothing I could do to stop it. Janet and Emin lending me this house has been a lifesaver. Being somewhere so different, away from all my familiar routines, has meant I can be more detached from what happened.' She looked out at the darkened garden. 'And making a garden here for them has been my motivation for keeping going, sometimes. They refused to let me pay rent, but Janet said if I wanted to repay them in some way, I could design the garden. It's what I've been doing today.' She didn't say she'd worked herself to a stand-still, in the heat, digging, weeding and planting. It was how she'd kept her anxiety about cooking him dinner at bay.

'Where have you bought the plants? I noticed the newly planted pomegranate yesterday.'

'Omer, at the shop, told me where to get them. There's a small nursery on the outskirts of Sula. He delivered them for me, in his van.' She smiled. 'I couldn't manage more than a few pots of herbs and pelargoniums in the basket of the bike. I was defeated by the pomegranate sapling.'

'And your job, which you'd worked so hard at for so many years?'

Beth met his eyes across the table. His stare was search-ing, intense, but she was done with sharing. The memories of that awful day were still too recent, too *raw*. She cringed when she remembered how she'd walked to work that morn-ing, feeling as if she were floating on a cloud of happiness. Sherri's announcement that she was selling the house had shocked her at first, but then she'd seen the possibilities it opened up. She'd been freed, by Ava's death and Sherri's decision. When Charles heard what had happened, surely he'd immediately suggest moving in together. She'd resign, find another job, and the secret of their relationship, which she'd hugged to herself for a year, could be made public. They'd be a proper couple. At last, she could plan for the future she craved: a home shared with someone she loved. Someone who loved her back.

Afterwards, she'd wondered if anyone had guessed the truth about them. Who had watched her breeze into the of-fice that day, alight with happy expectation, only to leave again, two hours later, her face streaked with tears? Had there been gossip? Emails flying around the office, specu-lating?

She'd become anxious about interacting with anyone, never knowing who might be judging her or ridiculing her behind her back. The foundation on which her life had been built for twenty-five years had crumbled, leaving her free-falling through life.

She lifted her chin, stopping her destructive train of thought. 'I don't want to talk about that. I judged something badly. *Very* badly. I paid the price and I…left.'

'You mean you were fired?'

'No. I left. I was in an impossible situation. I couldn't have continued to work there, afterwards.' She watched him frown and look down at the table, rubbing at a mark on the wood with an index finger.

'Were you properly compensated? I could investigate it for you, if you like. Not now, but some time.'

Beth stared at him. 'I know you're not a doctor. Are you a lawyer?'

Jensen shook his head. 'I've retired from all my roles, but that doesn't mean I can't investigate something privately. At some point.'

'That's very generous. I've saved carefully over the years and with some money from the house I'll be able to take a little time about finding another job and somewhere to live. But even so, I couldn't afford to pay you and I don't think a supper of pasta and tomato sauce would cover it, some-how.' She pulled her bare feet up onto the edge of her chair and hugged her shins. 'And anyway, I've taken control of my own life now. It was controlled by others for so long, and I include my work in that. But even though I've lost the anchors that kept me grounded, I'm learning to appreci-ate the freedom that has given me.' She rested her chin on her knees. 'It has taken weeks, but I'm gradually finding a kind of acceptance of my new state. The future I thought I had planned no longer exists, but that doesn't mean I can't plan a different one. One thing I know for certain is that I wouldn't give up my new independence for anything.'

'I wouldn't expect to be paid for helping a friend.'

Did this mean they were now friends? wondered Beth. Only a few minutes ago she'd believed he'd forget all about her as soon as their ways parted.

'That would be pushing the bounds of friendship a little too far, don't you think?'

'Is that what you think? In your opinion, how far could they be pushed?'

This was exactly the sort of conversation she wanted to avoid. It was straying too close to...*feelings*...for comfort. The combination of the wine and food, the warm evening, the soft glow of candlelight and the relaxed atmosphere Jensen had somehow managed to conjure from her stiff initial reception of his arrival had lulled her into dropping her guard. She thought about how she'd bumped into him earlier, in the doorway. His body had felt hard and yet not hostile against hers. If anything, those few seconds of contact between them had made her feel shielded and protected. It hadn't felt as if he'd wanted to pull away from her, as she had done from him.

What would have happened if she hadn't? If she'd been daring enough to take that minuscule step of not recoiling? If she'd put the palm of her hand flat on his muscled chest, just for a moment, would that still have been within the bounds of friendship, in his opinion, or would she have stepped over the boundary into hostile territory where she'd once thought she understood the rules, but found she didn't even speak the language?

A cold finger of apprehension touched her spine at the thought. Never, *never* again would she put herself in a position of giving her heart to someone, only for them to break it and throw it back at her. Jensen seemed to be honest, kind, dependable—all the qualities which she'd thought she'd found in Charles. She'd thought she'd *known* him. She'd never make such an assumption again, about anyone.

She'd thought she was a good judge of character, but her experience had proved her to be utterly wrong. She'd lost all faith in her own judgement. It had been proved to be completely flawed. Had she been so desperate for love and attention that she'd fallen for a man whose only consideration was the satisfaction of his own needs?

If so, she could never risk another relationship. She'd never be able to trust another man, but what was worse was that she didn't know when she'd ever be able to trust herself again, either.

On that last day, when Charles had run his fingers down her arm, circling her wrist, just tightly enough to be uncomfortable, it had suddenly made her skin crawl with a dread she hoped never to experience again. The words he'd spoken next had confirmed it.

'You must have misunderstood me, Beth. I've never given you any reason to believe this could be permanent...'

He'd let go of her wrist and she'd rubbed it, staring at him, but he'd turned away.

She wouldn't think about that. Not now. Not again.

'I...don't know. I hardly know you at all.'

'And yet, sitting here with you this evening, it feels as if I've known you for a long time,' he said, softly. 'How does it feel to you?'

Beth felt her heart thump and then pick up a faster rhythm. She pressed a hand to her side, trying to control it.

Her stomach swooped and she wished she hadn't had that extra glass of wine.

If feeling as if you could tell someone everything meant feeling you'd known them a long time, then yes, that was exactly how she felt. Trying to make sense of the emotions swirling through her was making her head spin, a little, and her hands shake. She had to wrest control back before she said or did something stupid.

Jensen was still, watchful, waiting for her answer and she knew he wouldn't let it go.

'No,' she said, knowing she was being untruthful. 'I feel as if I've known you for no time at all. But now I have a question for you.'

He raised his eyebrows a fraction and lifted his chin. 'You do?'

She hoped she could change the direction of the conversation. 'You don't usually sail alone. Why have you had this rather special bottle of wine in the locker above your berth for so long? Surely you must have had opportunities to drink it before now?'

CHAPTER EIGHT

JENSEN'S ATTENTION HAD been focussed on Beth's story, a slow-burning anger intensifying steadily at the way the behaviour of her possibly well-meaning but ultimately weak father had led to her being disinherited. If he had any spare mental or emotional space, he'd feel compelled to investigate the circumstances on her behalf.

But she'd made it clear that she had taken control of her own life, hinting that any interference wouldn't be welcome. He totally got that. She'd used her time here to confront her situation, choosing to make an attempt to shape a new life for herself. It couldn't have been easy, or comfortable, but she'd reached a point where she could at least consider looking for a new job.

From where he stood, that was great progress.

All this swirled in his mind while he studied her. She'd relaxed significantly as the evening wore on. She smiled more readily, and a lot of the tension seemed to have left her body. He didn't think the effects of the wine were solely responsible. When he'd first arrived and seen her, standing on the stairs, he'd been certain she'd been about to ask him to leave. Poised, wide-eyed, one hand on the banister, with her hair loose around her shoulders, she'd reminded him of something wild, on the point of flight.

But she hadn't fled. She'd faced up to whatever it was that

was troubling her and come downstairs and she'd seemed to decide she could cope with him, as long as he didn't overstay his welcome.

He'd thought that she was vulnerable, behind her façade of competence, and he was right. But she'd faced up to her vulnerability, accepted what had happened, and decided to move on. Having the determination to do that gave her the strength of titanium.

He'd like to ask her how she'd done it, but he knew she wouldn't answer any more questions. She'd said making the garden had given her purpose and, no doubt, a focus. Well, he couldn't make a garden on *Sundance*, but he could focus on making his beloved yacht absolutely safe and shipshape again.

He'd been putting it off. Each time he'd tried to concentrate on a task, a maelstrom of negative thoughts had ambushed him and he'd given up. He wondered if Beth had experienced something similar. Had digging the hard, dry earth distracted her enough and worn her out sufficiently so that she was able to sleep, and to wake with a clear head and renewed purpose?

'Jensen?'

His attention snapped back to the present, and the problem. She'd turned the tables on him. Up until now, he'd been the one asking the questions. There was no reason why he shouldn't have bottles of wine on *Sundance*, but he'd let slip that this one had been there for a while.

'Ah, yes,' he said, taking his time, stretching his arms before clasping his hands behind his head. 'The wine.'

'What has kept you so busy over the past few years that you couldn't find an opportunity to share it with friends?'

He pushed his fingers into his temples, massaging the skin in small circles. 'Last summer, and the summer before that, I didn't sail at all. I was occupied with business affairs.

It must have been, probably, two years before that when I bought half a dozen bottles of this in France. We were at Antibes for a few days and I took a trip into the winelands.'

'But you didn't drink everything you bought? I imagine storage space is at a premium on a yacht, especially for non-essential items, like bottles of wine.'

He smiled. 'That depends on your priorities, but you're right, there isn't a lot of space. Everything needs to be organised and tidy. This bottle was one that was overlooked.'

'And since then, you haven't been sailing with friends, or met any ashore? No one with whom you wanted to share it?'

Jensen shook his head. 'No. And I'm glad I didn't, because then I wouldn't have been able to share it with you.'

It hadn't been difficult to work out that she shied away from personal comments, compliments and questions. He hoped this would be enough to make her back off.

With mild satisfaction, but also a sharp twinge of regret, he saw that his strategy had worked. She straightened her knees, placing her feet under the table, and folded her hands in her lap.

'I've enjoyed the evening,' she said, formality creeping back into her voice, 'and thank you for choosing to share the wine with me.'

Jensen felt a little of his own tension release. 'At the end of that summer I left *Sundance* in a marina at Piraeus, in Greece. I picked her up again about five weeks ago.'

'Alone.'

'Yes, deliberately so. I needed a challenge. I hadn't sailed solo for a long time, and I'd begun to think that, at almost fifty, I was too old. Perhaps not fit enough. I wanted to prove I could still do it.' He sat forward, releasing his hands from behind his head and pressing his palms flat on the table. 'Now, let me help you tidy up and I'll be on my way.'

'Has it been hard?'

Her eyes were on his face and he didn't think he'd get away with anything less than the truth. And besides that, she deserved honesty.

'Sometimes, yes. Sometimes I thought I was going to have to admit defeat and give up. The need to be constantly on the lookout, the fatigue, wears you down and feels relentless at times. I tried to plan the trip so that I could be in a safe anchorage each night, but it wasn't always possible. There were nights when I could only snatch an hour, or less, of sleep at a time. But I kept going. It was important to me to do it. Crucial, actually. For a long time I'd known that I needed to get back to this place to think about things. Work things out. If I'd given up, I would have sacrificed a lot more than simply the journey.'

'Like what?' Her eyes were steady on his face, searching.

He huffed out a breath, suddenly aware that his breathing had become very shallow. How candid did he need to be? How much could he say without it being too much? His mind began to slide towards that familiar but dreaded downward spiral. He braced his hands on his thighs and breathed in, filling his lungs with the pure, sea-salted air.

'My self-belief,' he said, at last. His voice felt rough. 'Over time, there'd been circumstances that had tested it to the limit and I needed to re-establish it, rock-solid, in order to build…to rebuild…'

Jensen stopped. He was in danger of giving himself away. He tried to inhale deeply, again, past the knot that formed in his chest, when his stress levels mounted and his lungs felt squeezed. He stood, scraping his chair back on the tiles. He needed to leave.

He heard Beth follow him into the house as he carried their plates across to the kitchen. Would she question him further, or pick up on the fact that he didn't plan to say any more?

'Would you…?'

He turned towards her, still holding the plates, the cutlery piled on the top one in an untidy heap.

'I need to go…'

She stopped a few paces away from him. 'I was going to ask if you'd like a cup of coffee. A nightcap?'

The plates rattled as he placed them on the marble worktop. 'Oh…actually, no, thank you.' He pushed a hand through his hair, ruffling it. It hadn't been this long for thirty years. 'You must be tired after your long walk yesterday and gardening today. It's very warm.'

'I'm fine, thank you. And I'm grateful for your help yesterday.'

He smiled, relieved the questions had stopped. 'I was glad to help you. Thank you for an enjoyable evening.' He extended a hand towards her.

Whether it was because neither of them seemed in a hurry to break the contact between them this time, he wasn't sure, but somehow Beth was drawn towards him. He was conscious that her lips were slightly parted, her wide eyes pools of dark, shimmering green, and that he wanted to kiss her more than he'd wanted to kiss any woman for a very long time.

But he knew kissing her would be unforgivable of him. She'd given him no encouragement at all, and he'd be crossing a very strongly drawn boundary if he took that liberty. He'd ruin what could be a warm friendship, and for what? A few seconds of gratification taken at someone else's expense. That was not the sort of man he was.

He gave her hand a light squeeze and broke the contact.

'Goodnight.' Her voice was quiet.

'There was something else I meant to say.' He stepped back, towards the door. 'I've been thinking about what you said yesterday, and I think it'll help me to move on.'

Beth folded her arms, her head on one side. 'What did I say?'

He put his hand on the brass doorknob behind him. 'You said reaching the destination is only the beginning of the journey. For me, that's absolutely true, but if you hadn't said it, I don't think I would have realised it.'

Beth pushed the heavy door closed behind him and leaned her forehead against the cool wood. She wished she'd stepped up on her tiptoes and kissed him goodnight. His eyes, with that slight frown between them, had been on her mouth and she didn't think he'd have objected. But what if it hadn't been what he wanted?

Someone had tried to kiss her, once, against her will, and she remembered how angry she'd felt. It had been a drunken attempt by Steve, from Accounts, at the office Christmas party, who'd thought he'd caught her off guard under a bunch of mistletoe. She'd shoved him away before he'd even got close and the next day made it known that in future anyone behaving in a similar fashion would be reported to HR.

She thought the incident had cemented her in the role of ice maiden queen of the City.

Beth poured herself a glass of water and leaned against the kitchen island, tapping the glass against her lips.

What planet was she on? Perhaps the sun and spending all this time alone really had affected her ability to think logically and see straight. Romance was firmly off her agenda. She'd begun to get her life back under control and to at least see a way into the future. She did not need any complications. Definitely not a holiday fling. She packed the plates and glasses into the dishwasher and dropped the empty wine bottle into the bin.

The lesson that fairy tales did not come true had been a hard one, but she'd learned it well.

* * *

Jensen dragged the RIB across the beach, into the sea. He climbed in, not caring that his leather boat shoes were saturated with seawater. Then, instead of releasing the outboard motor down into the water, he pulled the oars from the bottom of the craft. He needed to expend some of his frustration in physical exercise. Manoeuvring the RIB so that the bow pointed towards the dim shape of *Sundance*, riding the slight swell in the middle of the cove, he put his back into the first stroke. The dinghy surged forwards with a satisfying leap, and he pulled again.

He'd been floored by the desire to kiss Beth. Her mouth had looked so soft and inviting, her eyes deep green pools, harbouring a question he couldn't interpret.

Could he have managed a friendly, goodnight peck on the cheek? No, he told himself, he couldn't. If his lips had so much as brushed her skin he'd have wanted it all, but she would not. He had nothing in the world to offer her, and he knew neither of them was the sort of person who would indulge in a holiday fling.

A woman like Beth—beautiful, intelligent and with new-found freedom and independence—could have her pick of men, when she chose to. And if she ever discovered his true circumstances, the reason he was hiding from the world in a remote cove in Turkey, she'd want to put the width of the Mediterranean between them.

She'd get another job, with someone who appreciated her dedication and loyalty, and, with the right advice, he thought she could successfully claim something from her stepmother's estate.

Whereas he... There was no certainty, at all, that he'd ever recover. There was no way back to his old life and he hadn't yet figured out a way forward into a life where everything had changed.

She'd said the journey could only begin, now he'd reached his destination. He had to hang onto that belief and find the start of his new path. He just wasn't sure he believed it existed yet.

So what the hell was he doing, even thinking about kissing Beth? He'd sworn off women. They'd all proved shallow and disloyal, deleting him from their lives as soon as things had gone wrong.

There was no reason, at all, why Beth would be any different.

Glancing over his shoulder, Jensen altered his course slightly and nudged the RIB up to the platform at *Sundance*'s stern, leaping aboard and securing the mooring. He climbed up the short ladder to the cockpit and then onto the deck. He waited for the familiar feeling of safety and comfort to envelop him, but this evening it was absent, adding fuel to the frustration that simmered through his veins. The trip across the water to *Sundance* had not been nearly long enough. It would take a couple of miles of hard rowing, at least, for the exertion to have a therapeutic effect on his mind or exhaust his body enough to enable him to crash out on the deck and sleep.

It was a relief to ease his feet out of his wet shoes and strip off his jeans and shirt, welcoming the slight, cooling breeze that hummed softly in the rigging and whispered across his heated skin. He stared back at the shoreline, where the trees were a darker, more dense mass than the surrounding headlands and sky, but tonight, as every other night, there was no glimpse of a light from the villa that he knew was there, sheltering a woman who, rightly or wrongly, was someone he thought, in spite of all his angry protestations, he wanted in his flawed life.

There was an odd sort of relief in admitting that. Stretching out on his unrolled mat and pulling a cotton sheet over himself, gazing up at the dark sky and dewy stars, he tried to get his thoughts into some sort of logical order.

He wanted her in his life, in whatever form possible. But the words that flashed, in neon-bright colours, in his brain were: You can't have her.

CHAPTER NINE

TWO LONG DAYS LATER, Beth was buzzing with unexpended energy. Her routine of swimming in the morning and evening had been wrecked by the injury to her heel. Gardening was limited by the heat. The mornings and afternoons had merged into one, time dragging in the stillness.

It was tempting to blame Jensen for her unsettled spirit. She'd been happy in the rhythm she'd established before he'd arrived, but she knew she had allowed his presence to disturb her more than she should have done. She wondered if he was all right. Did he need help but was too proud to ask for it?

She should have been pleased that he appeared to be staying away from her. It was what they'd both said they wanted, after all.

Why, then, did her eyes keep returning to the gap in the trees where the path from the beach emerged? Was she subconsciously willing him to appear?

As the shadows lengthened towards the second evening, she poured herself a glass of pomegranate juice and carried it out onto the terrace, risking the heat even though she knew she couldn't cool off in the pool. But she'd removed the dressing from her foot and from tomorrow nothing would keep her out of the water.

Early the following morning, listening intently, she could not hear the telltale tapping of *Sundance*'s rigging, but there was not even the trace of a breeze, so that wasn't a guarantee that the boat had gone. But perhaps he had left, leaving her well behind him. She sipped her morning coffee, and knew she had to find out.

She'd dressed in her bikini, in anticipation of her first swim for several days, and she pulled her kaftan over it, picked up her sunglasses and slipped her feet into her flip-flops.

The cove was at its peaceful best. Glassy ripples pushed onto the beach, lit by the low sun, and the rocks cast long, dense shadows onto the limpid water.

Sundance lay at her anchor, like a vision from another age, her graceful lines immaculate. The scene was so perfect that Beth caught her breath. She slid her feet out of her flip-flops onto the sand, which was still cool under her feet, and pulled the kaftan over her head, leaving it with her sunglasses at the edge of the trees. Then she walked down to the water's edge and waded in.

This was the time they'd agreed she would use the beach, and from today she intended to claim it. A new confidence and energy lightened her step. Jensen was free to leave, if he didn't like her presence on the beach, or if he needed anything he could seek her out.

The silky water was just cool enough to raise goosebumps across her skin. She stood, ripples lapping around her thighs, and then took a deep breath and dived in, surfaced and struck out in a steady front crawl across the cove.

When she reached the overhanging rocks around the rim of the bay, she stopped and rolled onto her back, floating. The morning sky had lost the rosy tinge of dawn and was deepening to its summer azure. Golden sunlight lit the crest of each ripple around her. The only sounds were those of the sea, the only movement the water.

She rolled over, relishing being back in the sea, and

began swimming towards the beach in a measured breast-stroke. A slight splash behind her made her turn her head, and Jensen emerged from the water, flicking his hair from his eyes.

'Hey.'

His voice carried clearly across the water and she raised a hand to acknowledge his greeting, finding she was back within her depth, the shingle tickling the soles of her feet. Jensen swam towards her, his powerful arms cutting through the water with barely a splash.

Beth waded onto the beach. She wanted to carry on walking until she reached her kaftan and sunglasses, both of which would provide cover, but she knew he'd reach her first. And anyway, she decided, she was over trying to hide herself away. Recognising the uncertainty he'd allowed her to see in him had added a layer to her own confidence. She squared her shoulders, turned, waiting for him.

He pushed his hair back and wiped a hand over his face.

'Hi.' She folded her arms. 'Your leg looks better.'

'It is, thank you. I'll return what's left of the comfrey. It worked wonders on the bruising.' He looked down at her feet. 'Your blister must have healed.'

'I'm celebrating with a swim in the sea.'

'According to our plan. I apologise for being here. I no longer expected you to come down to the beach. But I'm glad you have.'

'How are the repairs to *Sundance* coming on?'

His smile was a little crooked. 'Do you mean when might I be leaving?'

'That's not what I meant at all, although in this still weather I can't hear the tapping of the rigging so I don't know if you're here or not.'

'I've finally managed to settle down and get on with the list of things that need doing. The repairs are going well, now. The past two days have been pretty busy. I need to take her out for some gentle sea trials.'

Beth looked beyond him, to where *Sundance* drifted serenely on her anchor. She wondered if she was as beautiful below decks as she was above. Was there a neat galley and a cosy saloon, or was it stripped back and spartan?

'If you take her for a sail, could I come with you?' The words were out of her mouth before she'd even thought them. She felt shocked at herself. 'But you won't need a novice on board when you're testing things out. I might be...' She stopped in mid-sentence. Jensen was regarding her with such surprise that it made her smile. 'What?'

'Nothing.' He shook his head, looking bemused. 'That is... I wasn't expecting that. But I... I'd love to take you sailing. Have you ever sailed before?' The corners of his mouth lifted and her stomach turned over. It was such a gentle smile. 'Is there any particular reason why?'

'Just...for fun? And I imagine it's cooler out on the water.'

'It is. And it would be fun.'

'I must warn you that I don't know how to sail. When I was little my father used to take me to the Round Pond in Kensington Gardens to watch the model boats. I thought it looked difficult.'

He laughed, his hands on his hips. 'You don't have to be able to sail to come out with me. Not even a model boat. It's not difficult. I'll do the work. All you'll have to do is enjoy yourself.'

'I might be sick. Or afraid. The only boat I've ever been on is a cross-channel ferry from Dover to Calais and I was ill.'

'If you feel queasy, I can give you a motion sickness tablet, and there is no need to be afraid. I've been sailing for most of my life, and I haven't lost a man overboard in...let me see...ever. If you really want to come, I hope very much that you might enjoy it.'

She gripped her hands together and raised her eyes to look beyond him, out towards the sea.

'Where would we go?'

'We'll go out between the headlands and, if the wind is favourable, turn south-west.'

'And if it's not?'

'If it's not, we'll turn north-east, but the south-west will be more interesting.'

'Oh…why is that?'

'You'll see when we get there. When would you like to go?'

'When could you?' Beth felt a mixture of excitement and apprehension dance in her stomach. She could hardly believe she'd instigated this, but the idea had taken hold now and she knew she wouldn't back out. It would be a new experience, to push her out of her comfort zone and test her resilience.

'There're a couple of things I still need to check, but by tomorrow morning she'll be ready to go.' He turned and began to wade back into the sea. 'I'll pick you up in the RIB on the beach at around eight if that's not too early for you.' He spoke over his shoulder. 'Bring a hat and sunscreen, and a tee shirt in case you want to cover up,' he called, before diving into the water.

She'd half hoped he might say today. But was the idea of having to cling to a tilting deck while being splashed with seawater and probably feeling sick a good one? On the other hand, if it meant spending the day with a handsome man in whose company she felt comfortable, and who seemed to enjoy hers, it couldn't be a bad one.

It was just before eight o'clock when Jensen steered the RIB through the calm early morning sea. He scanned the beach, but he couldn't see any sign of Beth. The bottom of the dinghy scraped on the shingle and he jumped out, holding onto the mooring rope.

The sun was up but the morning shadows were long and the air still held a breath of freshness. The heat would ramp up during the day, but out on the water they'd be kept cool by the sea breezes. He was looking forward to feeling *Sundance* come alive beneath his feet and hands again, and to the sensation of freedom, which setting sail always brought to him. He hoped, very much, that Beth would feel a bit of it, too.

A movement caught his eye and he saw her emerge from the line of trees behind the beach. He blew out a long breath, finally allowing himself to admit that he'd been afraid she might not show up.

She was wearing the embroidered cotton kaftan that reached to mid-thigh and her hair was pulled into a ponytail, which swung as she walked. It was a compromise between the severe, pinned-up style she usually favoured, and the loose-around-the-shoulders relaxed look that he thought was beautiful. A cloth bag hung from her shoulder.

'You came. Good morning.'

'Did you think I might not?' Her gaze met his, holding a faint challenge.

'I would have come looking for you, if you hadn't.'

Ripples of water curled onto the shingle, but as they'd washed in they'd lifted the RIB and it had bobbed a little further out and it was now floating, a few yards away. Jensen tugged on the rope to bring it closer in. He held out a hand.

'Pass me your bag.'

He waded through the water and deposited the bag in the boat. Then he held the RIB steady with one hand. Beth was beside him, stepping into the boat. She wobbled and put a hand on his shoulder, steadying herself, and then she sat down on the wooden plank, which formed the seat.

'Okay?' He had to work at keeping his voice neutral. The rosemary and lavender scent of her hair had swamped his senses, and the soft touch of her hand on his shoulder felt like a caress.

She nodded. 'Yes. Thank you.' She pulled her bag towards her and took out a pair of sunglasses, putting them on. 'I'll need these.'

Jensen climbed in, taking care not to splash her, and started the outboard motor. As he turned the boat and set a course towards *Sundance*, Beth's hands came down by the sides of her hips and her fingers curled around the edge of the plank, but her back remained straight. This might have been her idea, but he could see she was out of her comfort zone. The fact that she'd deliberately put herself there sent his admiration of her climbing several notches.

He hopped onto the platform at *Sundance*'s stern, secured the tow rope and held out a hand to Beth. Lip caught between her teeth, she straightened her knees and stood, wobbly and unsure, and clung to his fingers. As she negotiated the transfer from the dinghy to *Sundance* she swayed and he caught her, holding her encircled in one arm.

'You're okay.' That perfume assaulted his senses again. 'Up that little ladder and you'll be in the cockpit, where it all happens.'

He would not let her see how her nearness affected him. She'd put herself in his care, doing something new and, no doubt, scary, and he'd never, ever take advantage of that. She looked unsure and conflicted, but she hadn't backed out of the trip. She had courage and determination, which he would do his best to emulate.

Beth climbed the few rungs of the ladder and swung herself into the cockpit. She sat down hurriedly. Even at anchor, the gentle sway of *Sundance* beneath her feet was disconcerting. It suddenly felt as if all her usual points of reference had been altered or removed. She felt untethered, and very vulnerable. She was, she admitted to herself, on a boat with a man whom she hardly knew, and completely dependent on him for her safe return to dry land and the villa.

Nobody else in the world knew where she was.

Although the thought might have been alarming, it was also oddly liberating. She felt empowered by her decision to try out something completely new and different. It was an opportunity that might never present itself again and she needed to savour it, even if in the end she didn't enjoy it.

Jensen had joined her in the cockpit.

'Now you're wondering what you've done.' He sat down on the bench a few feet away. 'Alone at sea with a strange man.'

She nodded. 'Exactly. Somehow, I've allowed this to happen.'

'By the end of the day you won't want to go home.' He flashed a smile at her. 'Let me show you *Sundance*.'

Beth could feel that Jensen was in his element. He moved with ease around the complicated cockpit, his footing sure, his big hands familiar with all the strange pieces of equipment that mystified her.

She followed him up two steps onto the varnished deck. He led her towards the bow and pointed to where cushions were arranged against the side of the projecting roof above the space below the decks.

'Make yourself comfortable here.' He dropped her bag onto the deck. 'You'll be able to see where we're going. We'll be motoring out between the headlands, but you'll be out of the way of the boom once I put the sail up.'

'Where *are* we going?' Beth dropped to her knees before settling herself, cross-legged, on the cushions. 'Have you decided?'

'It's a perfect wind for sailing down the coast. Have you heard of Kekova Island?'

'No.' Beth shook her head and adjusted her sunglasses.

'We'll head that way. It's a small, uninhabited island where the ancient city of Dolichiste once stood, until an earthquake, one morning in the second century, sent it sliding into the sea.' He propped one hand against the foremast. 'Now most of the ruins are underwater, although some can still be seen on the shoreline and the rocky slopes above.'

'It sounds a bit creepy.'

'On a storm-tossed winter's night, it might be, but in the sunshine on a day like today it's interesting. Shall we go and take a look?'

Beth heard the quiet hum of *Sundance*'s engine starting up and watched as the anchor chain hauled the anchor from the seabed. As the yacht passed between the two headlands that sheltered the cove, almost hiding it from the open sea, she wondered how Jensen had navigated his way through this narrow passage, in the dark, on a damaged boat. The knowledge that he must be a skilful sailor gave her confidence a boost.

The creaking in the rigging and snapping of the mainsail as it unfurled from the boom and rose up the mast was unnerving, but then the big sail filled with the breeze, the sound of the engine died, and *Sundance* was rising and dipping gently, a creamy wave curling away from the bow as she cleaved through the aquamarine water.

It wasn't anything like Beth had expected. It was serene and beautiful.

Jensen appeared at her side and she glanced towards the stern, a little wave of anxiety pulsing through her.

'Shouldn't you be steering, or something?' She remembered the big, spoked wheel in the cockpit.

'Don't look so worried, Beth. There's a self-steering rig,

but I won't leave the wheel for long. I'm only going to raise one sail today. It'll be less lively that way.'

He disappeared towards the stern and Beth relaxed in the cushions, determined to enjoy the experience and the view of the coast, with its inlets and coves, rocky slopes and scrubby hills. The slap of the water against the hull and the occasional hiss of a small wave cresting and breaking was rhythmic and soothing. She settled herself more comfortably and propped a cushion behind her head, against the mast.

If this was sailing, she could definitely get to like it.

She woke with a start, remembering where she was and sitting bolt upright. It was quiet. *Sundance* was barely moving through the water and the sail had been furled.

Jensen crouched in front of her, his face creased in a smile. He'd taken off his tee shirt.

'Good sleep? You must have been tired.'

Beth rubbed a hand over her face, trying to pretend she hadn't noticed his broad shoulders and the sprinkling of dark hair, mixed with silver, over his chest. 'I didn't sleep too well last night.' That was an understatement. She'd hardly slept at all, nervous anticipation stalking her waking moments and her restless sleep. 'But it was so peaceful, and the sounds of the water were soothing. I didn't mean to drop off, but…'

'That's Kekova Island, on the starboard side. We'll motor closer in and you'll be able to see the ruins, if you like.'

Beth nodded. She glanced up at the sun, now high in the deep blue sky. 'I'd better put on some sunscreen.'

'Would you like me to do your back?'

'I'm not going to take my kaftan off…' too late, she saw the teasing lift of the corner of his mouth '…since I'm not planning to go swimming,' she finished. 'But I could do yours.'

'We can't go swimming. Swimming and diving have been forbidden here. Too many visitors were taking artefacts home as souvenirs. And yes, thank you, you could.'

'Have we anchored?' She pulled her bag towards her. 'I'll find my sunscreen.'

'No, we're drifting, for a minute.' He stood up. 'Come astern to the cockpit. There's sunscreen in the locker. You can do my back while I find us somewhere to anchor for lunch.'

She followed Jensen back along the deck, down into the cockpit, where his tee shirt lay on the bench seating. With one hand resting on the wheel, he reached into a locker and pulled out a tube of sunscreen, handing it to her. He replaced his hand on the wheel and stood with his back to her, bronzed bare feet planted on the deck, his powerful thighs braced apart.

Beth looked out at the quiet island as the coast slipped past them. It was more beautiful than she'd ever expected. Somehow, getting here on Jensen's yacht made the whole experience more empowering and satisfying; so much better than being on a tourist boat, with a loud commentary in several different languages. It was exhilarating to stand on the gently moving deck, her hand on the rail, and watch the scenery slide by. At that moment, she didn't think she'd have changed places with anyone in the world.

Was she really the same Beth who'd arrived in Turkey, her spirit crushed, her confidence at rock bottom, and fear of the future overshadowing every moment?

That version of her would have been horrified at the idea of putting sunscreen onto Jensen's back. She'd never put sunscreen on anyone but herself, and the thought of running her hands over his muscled shoulders would have been terrifying.

But none of those emotions troubled her now. How hard

could it be, to squeeze cream from a tube and spread it onto skin? She smiled at the realisation of how far behind she'd left her previous self, acknowledging, at the same time, that her interaction with Jensen had helped her. He'd demonstrated kind consideration towards her, and talking to him about her family relationships had been therapeutic. Afterwards, she'd realised with surprise that she'd never discussed them with anyone else at all.

She stood still, holding the tube in one hand, and let go of the railing with the other.

'Beth?' Jensen glanced over his shoulder. 'Are you okay?' There was a gentle note of intimate teasing in his voice, as if he thought she might be wishing she hadn't volunteered for this task.

'I'm fine. Just loving the view.' Two could tease. She flipped up the lid and squeezed some of the cream from the tube into the palm of her hand, and launched herself into another new experience.

His skin shivered as she dabbed the cream across his shoulders. 'That's cold.'

'Your skin is so warm.' With care, she smoothed the palms of her hands over his tanned skin, feeling the muscles bunch and flex beneath her touch. 'That's why it feels cold.'

'It's also good. Thank you.'

The flat blades of his shoulders pulled down alongside his spine as his upper back moved in. She rubbed the cream into his skin, her confidence growing. His chin dipped towards his chest as her fingers massaged the base of his neck and then fanned out, moving down over his ribs, her thumbs circling each individual vertebra. She added more cream, wondering at how simple and curiously natural it felt to be standing behind a man, on a yacht, massaging cream into his back.

Suddenly, Jensen's head went up and he stepped sideways, away from her.

'Thank you. That feels great.'

'I haven't quite finished. There's still some left to rub in.'

'I need to drop the anchor,' he said, an edge of urgency sharpening his voice. 'We're getting too close to the rocks.' He left the cockpit and strode along the deck, out of her sight.

Beth pressed the cap back onto the sunscreen and replaced it in the locker. If he hadn't said how good it was she'd have thought he hadn't liked it.

Jensen gripped the railing at *Sundance*'s bow and leaned forwards. He ducked his head and took several deep breaths of the salt-laden air, trying to exert some degree of control over the off-the-scale reaction of his body.

There was a straightforward explanation, he told himself. He hadn't felt a woman's touch for so long that naturally he—*his body*—was bound to overreact. But when, he wondered, had he ever felt anything more sensual than the gentle, firm, caressing strokes across his back that Beth had administered?

Had she genuinely no idea of the effect it had been having on him? Was that what had made it so erotic? He'd had to clench his jaw, straighten his spine, try to move away to lessen the pressure of her fingers on the most sensitive places on his back. But her hands seemed to know where every single pleasure zone was, and nothing he'd done had stopped the electrifying, white-hot darts of sensation that had arrowed straight down to his lower abdomen, creating all kinds of havoc.

Where had the anxious, defensive woman he'd met on the beach that first morning gone? She seemed to have vanished without trace, to be replaced by this new version. She even looked different. Some of her hair blew around her face, having escaped the ponytail she wore it in today. Her tense expression had softened into one of enjoyment and happiness. But most of all she exuded a new sense of quiet self-confidence and positivity.

Had he changed, too? He remembered how angry he'd felt when he'd discovered that a house had been built above *his* secret cove; that a woman was living in it, who claimed the beach and cove as her own. He'd felt cheated; as if his long, sometimes dangerous voyage had been in vain; as if the world, which had already dealt him the worst possible hand, were laughing at him for thinking he might still defeat the odds.

He hadn't been able to escape defeat. When he'd stopped moving, instead of finding solace, he'd been overcome with negativity and destructive thoughts, revenge uppermost in his mind. But those had faded. Perhaps the place had exerted its magic, after all, with a subtlety he'd been unaware of. But perhaps, with her acceptance of him at face value, Beth had shown that only a small part of the world despised him. Not everyone needed him only for what he could give them, and when that had turned to nothing, they'd all deserted him.

Beth had told him that his journey was only just beginning, without knowing the impossible path he was on, but he'd realised she was right. He'd had to stop running and allow everything he was running from to catch up with him. Then, when he'd examined his demons, he'd found they didn't stand up to detailed scrutiny, after all. They were mostly in his head. Rather than trying to block them from his mind, he had to admit them, and then let them go, without attaching any value to them.

That was how to rob them of their power.

Over the past few days he'd found a measure of peace,

and the space that had created in his head was allowing him to appreciate this day, in the moment. Beth wanted nothing from him at all, and in return he found he wanted to give her everything.

He'd wanted to abandon the wheel, turn and take her in his arms but that was beyond impossible. He thought she was beginning to trust him, otherwise she'd never have put herself in this vulnerable position, alone with him. She'd feel threatened and trapped if he touched her. He would do anything to nurture that trust.

Sundance had, he noticed with a shock, now really drifted too close to the rocky shore for safety. Trying to gather up the shreds of his self-control, he forced himself back into action. Not only had he allowed his body to almost overrule his mind, but the consequences of his lack of control had put them in a position of possible danger.

He'd told Beth he was a competent, safe sailor. Landing them on the rocks was not going to happen. He released the anchor, hoping it would secure them at the first try, and then returned to the cockpit.

'Jensen?' He heard her call before he saw her. She was standing before the wheel, peering forward to see where he was.

'Yeah. I'm here.' He leapt down into the cockpit, took the wheel and motored forward, over where the anchor should be, before cutting the engine and allowing *Sundance* to drift astern until the chain pulled taut.

'Are you okay? Did I do something wrong?'

From somewhere he conjured up a smile. 'Of course not. What could you have done wrong?'

She'd done everything right.

'You just seem a bit…distracted. Is this where we're having lunch?'

Distracted was one way of putting it. Body on fire, brain turned to sponge, heartbeat out of control was another.

'It is. I'll go below and get some food. It's very simple.'

He disappeared down the companionway into *Sundance*'s spacious galley.

'Do you need help?' Beth's face appeared in the hatch above him. 'Can I come down?'

'Turn around and come down backwards, at least the first time. It's steep.'

He stepped back as Beth's feet appeared, her right heel still red where the blister had healed. Now he wondered how he'd managed to apply that dressing without self-combusting. Her long, shapely legs followed, her skin a pale, polished gold. He pushed his hands into his pockets to prevent them from reaching out and resting on her waist, to help her down the last two steps.

'It's so beautiful. And so tidy!' She looked round, wide-eyed. 'I had no idea it would be so…luxurious. Will you give me a tour?'

Jensen followed her through the dining area to the adjoining salon with its panelled walls and dark green leather seating.

'There're two cabins through those doors, and a bathroom.' He thought she might have seen enough, but she pushed the door open and carried on. 'The master cabin and bathroom are in the forward section.'

'It's amazing. I love it. Everything has a place.' She ran a hand over the gleaming wood, her eyes shining.

'It's really important to keep things tidy below decks. And everything has to have a secure place so that nothing goes flying in rough weather.'

Beth bent to look through a porthole. 'That's hard to imagine, on a day like today. I wouldn't like rough conditions.'

'You might surprise yourself. To pitch yourself and your craft against the wind and the sea is exhilarating.'

She'd reached the master cabin. 'This looks super comfortable.'

The wide berth was made up in fine cotton bedlinen, with deep pillows and a knobbly cotton throw folded across the foot. The glimpse into the en suite bathroom showed gleaming chrome, tiles and porcelain.

Jensen stood at the door. 'I suppose it does.'

'Is this where you sleep?'

He shrugged, putting a hand up onto the doorframe above his head. 'No.' He shook his head. 'I…sleep on the deck. I prefer to be in the open.'

He hoped she was too star-struck by the cabin to probe him for reasons. He also wanted to get her away from that soft, wide bed, before his wayward brain began to imagine uses for it that did not involve sleeping, and his body, just recently talked into submission, called in reinforcements and rebelled again, testing his determination to the limit.

Beth walked past him, back towards the galley, her hips swaying beneath her loose kaftan and her ponytail swinging as she moved. Jensen rubbed a hand over the back of his neck before following her, wishing he could stop acting and reacting like the teenager he'd been over thirty years ago.

'This is all so tasty. Thank you.' Beth wiped the last piece of flatbread around the bowl of hummus and popped it into her mouth before reaching for a piece of rose-scented Turkish delight from a small tin. Powdered sugar clung to her lips as she bit into it, finding the soft sweetness studded with crunchy pistachio nuts. 'Those olives are the nicest I've ever tasted, and this is the perfect dessert.'

She'd let Jensen persuade her to have a glass of wine and she felt deliciously relaxed. Eating al fresco on board a yacht was a brand-new experience and possibly about to become her favourite pastime. She pulled up her knees and leaned against the bulkhead, watching Jensen stack the bowls and plates.

'Ready to look at the ruins?' He disappeared, carrying the remains of their lunch down into the galley before re-appearing and getting ready to get under way again. Beth joined him in the cockpit, leaning over the side.

In the depths of the crystal-clear water, the ruins of the ancient city, which had slipped down the mountainside al-most two thousand years ago, floated into ghostly view. The steps of a staircase, carved from stone, curved down into the water and disappeared in the shadows far below. The foundations of a house were clearly visible, and what had been a harbour wall jutted out from the shore.

'It's extraordinary,' she said, her voice low. 'All this, de-stroyed in a few moments of volcanic upheaval. There were people living here, going about their lives, when suddenly everything changed for ever…' He saw her brows draw to-gether in a frown. 'It really brings home that thing about second chances.'

'What thing?'

'You know, how we all believe we'll have a second chance at something if we mess up the first time around. There'll always be a tomorrow to improve on today. But for all these people—' she trailed her fingers in the water '—it never came.'

Above the waterline were the ruins of houses, water channels and pipes.

'Dolichiste was an important trading hub in the ancient Mediterranean,' Jensen said, slowing *Sundance*'s engine to an idle throb. 'Its catastrophic destruction must have had far-reaching effects.'

'It's like a living museum. I'm glad swimming and diving

have been prohibited. Even looking down at the ruins from here feels almost intrusive.' Beth straightened up. 'Thank you for bringing me. It's something I'll never forget.'

Jensen squinted up at the sun. 'Not quite over the yard-arm, but I think we should make our way back. The wind is freshening and we'll be sailing into it. It'll be a longer journey.'

Beth looked out across the water. It was calm in the lee of the shore, but a little choppy. White waves danced out in the main channel. Anxiety lurched in her stomach.

'Oh. Will it be rough?'

'Not rough. Just more brisk than it was this morning. If you don't like it, you can go below and make yourself comfortable in the salon or on one of the berths. The wind will be stronger up on deck this afternoon. We'll be sailing on a close-hauled reach and then coming about and motoring back through the headlands under the power of the engine.'

'Most of that sounds like a foreign language to me, but I think I'd prefer to stay up here with you. I like to know what's happening.'

'That's good. I'd like you to stay up with me.'

The wind held steady as Jensen set a course that would bring them opposite the entrance to their cove. With the sail pulled in tight he aimed to sail as close to the wind as he could. *Sundance* responded swiftly to the adjustments he made and she heeled away from the wind, picking up speed, her starboard beam close to the water.

Jensen pulled a towel out of a locker and tossed it to Beth. 'Wrap yourself up in this. There'll be some spray coming into the cockpit.' He glanced at her face. She was chalk-white and gripping the edge of the seat with both hands. 'Are you feeling ill?'

Beth shook her head. 'Not ill. Just…scared.' She ducked as a sheet of spray arched over them.

'There's no need to be afraid, but I understand it's scary if this is your first time on the water.' He braced his legs against the kick of the deck as *Sundance* slapped back onto the surface after cresting a slightly larger swell. 'Move up this way.' He nodded to a corner of the cockpit. 'It'll be more sheltered.'

Beth released the death grip she appeared to have on the seat and shuffled along, pulling the towel over her shoulders and drawing her knees up underneath it. He reached out with one hand and tucked the edges of the towel around her neck, briefly cupping her cheek in his palm. He hoped the gesture might reassure her. 'I'll get us home as quickly and as comfortably as I can,' he called. 'If you can relax you might enjoy the ride.'

He hoped she would. He'd watched her unfurl today, opening as a flower opened its petals to the warmth and light of the sun, and watching it happen was addictive. He wanted more. He wanted her to love this day, to remember it as one of the best days of her life and to feel the excitement he felt as *Sundance* skimmed over the water. He didn't want it spoilt by her anxiety or fear.

He kept the yacht on a steady course, not allowing her to heel over too much. It was a beautiful, breezy, sun-filled afternoon, the best kind of day for sailing, and they were making excellent headway. For the first time in many months, a sense of exhilaration and freedom took hold of him. It was more—far more—than physical freedom. It felt, at last, like freedom of the soul.

Another burst of spray fanned out over the cockpit and he heard Beth gasp. Expecting to see her cowering beneath the towel, he was surprised to find she'd let it slip around her shoulders and that her face was lit by a smile.

'The spray was filled with rainbow colours,' she exclaimed. 'We were under our own rainbow. It's magical.'

A rush of relief made him laugh out loud. Beth had begun to enjoy herself again. 'Not so bad?'

'I think it's not so bad at all. In fact, it's very, very good.'

He laughed again, throwing his head back, feeling his over-long hair blowing in the wind and noticing that Beth's ponytail had come undone and her hair was dancing around her shoulders. She was learning to trust him, and it was the best feeling in the world.

'Once we get into the lee of the hills, closer to the shore, it'll be calmer.' He looked over his shoulder, and when he turned back he was surprised to find Beth standing up, keeping herself steady with one hand on the rail.

'Jensen?'

He leaned towards her, concerned. 'Are you okay?'

'Will you show me how to steer *Sundance*? Just for a minute. I really want to see how it feels.'

'Of course.' A rush of feeling, a mixture of relief and joy, washed over him. He wanted to share this unique, exquisite sensation of living in the moment, for the moment, with her, and he loved that she wanted it, too.

'Are you sure it'll be safe?'

'I won't let anything bad happen to you, Beth. Trust me.'

It felt odd, suggesting she should trust him. Trust was a luxury that had been taken away from him the moment he'd been accused of the theft of funds from the charity of which he was the CEO. The sense of disbelief that such an accusation could be levelled at him still took his breath away when he remembered that chaotic day. He'd been suspended, barred from the office, left with nothing to do but protest his innocence. Even then, he'd believed it would all be okay. A mistake would be found. An apology made. Everything would return to normal.

Nothing would ever be normal again. As soon as the shadow of suspicion had fallen on him, he'd been viewed with distrust. His friends, colleagues and, worst of all, his family, had distanced themselves from him, as if they themselves might be tainted by association with him. The court case had been a nightmare, which still revisited him frequently in his sleep. The aggression of the prosecution had floored him, and the verdict bewildered him.

The determination of the one friend who'd kept faith in him had kept him from sinking into the depths of depression. James had rallied support, mounted his own investigation, never given up, and Jensen had been proved innocent, after all.

Perhaps other friends would be willing to bury the past now, but would he still want them as friends? No, he would not. The only person with whom he wanted, desperately, to engage was his fifteen-year-old daughter. The knowledge that Emily had refused to speak to him ever since he'd been accused was too painful to confront or accept. What if she never changed her mind? The thought felt like something sharp, which twisted in his chest and almost made him gasp for air. Anyone else could go to hell, but Emily... He was, he admitted, too afraid to try to make contact with her, in case she rebuffed him. He didn't know if he could bear that.

Beth knew none of that. If she trusted him, it was without prejudice, on the basis of what she'd learned about him in a few days. This time they were spending together would be perfect and unspoiled by any of his history.

He guided *Sundance* into calmer waters as the twin headlands appeared on the port bow. Their speed dropped a little, and he hauled in the sail more tightly. Then he put out a hand to Beth.

She took it, wobbling a little, the towel dropping to her

feet. He pulled her towards him, making space for her between his body and the wheel.

'Put your hands here, and here,' he said from behind her, and then placed his hands over hers. 'Hold on like this, not too tightly, and get the feel of the boat. Don't fight it. Control it, but with as light a touch as possible.'

Her shoulders and arms were rigid, her jaw tense.

'It feels as though it's fighting me, not the other way round.'

'Try to relax your shoulders and arms, or tomorrow you'll feel as if you've done a weights session at the gym.'

'I've never lifted weights, so I won't recognise that feeling.'

He was pleased she felt relaxed enough to joke, and he saw her making an effort to release the tension in her muscles. Her hands softened a little under his, and she flexed her fingers.

'That's better. Much better. Do you see that headland beyond us? Try to keep the bow lined up with that. That course will bring us to the right place.'

Sundance's bow plunged into an unexpected trough and Beth swayed on her feet, clutching at the wheel and pulling her slightly off course.

'Sorry. That was wrong, wasn't it?'

'That was fine, Beth. Don't beat yourself up. Nobody gets it right the first time. You can't predict or fight the sea. You just have to learn to go with it.' He moved closer to her, so that if it happened again she'd feel safe from falling. His arms closed round her shoulders and her back pressed against his chest. 'You're doing really well.' He bent his head to speak into her ear and she half turned towards him. His mouth brushed against her cheek.

He expected her to pull away, or flinch, but instead she tilted her head to look at him.

'I'm not sure I can steer with you so close. It does funny things to my sense of direction.'

'Just keep your hands on the wheel. I'll steer for both of us, if you want me to?' He waited for her nod of assent and then lifted his right hand and wrapped his arm around her waist, pulling her gently against him and holding her there.

'I think I do,' she murmured. 'As long as you keep holding me like that, and don't ask me if we're going north or south.'

'I would like to.' His voice felt impeded. 'But I'm going to have to drop the sail and start the engine.' He tightened his hold on her for a moment, then took the wheel in both hands again, turning *Sundance* into the wind. She slowed almost to a stop, her sail flapping above them. 'Hold her there, Beth, and I'll be right back.'

When he returned, putting his arms around her again felt like coming back to a safe place. The sail was safely furled and he pressed the ignition button, feeling the vibration of the engine starting up below the deck.

'I won't be able to steer through the headlands, Jensen. You'll have to do it.' Her voice trembled slightly.

'It's okay, I'll help you. Just stay where you are.' He rested his chin on the top of her head, for a brief second. She stepped back a little and he felt her curves pressing into his thighs. His breath jammed in his throat. 'Beth...'

'Mmm?'

'That's...almost too much.'

He felt lit up and properly alive for the first time in a year. She wanted to be with him, not because of who he had been, but simply because she enjoyed his company. The fact that she might make him buzz with need and, yes, desire, did not seem to occur to her.

The experiences of the day had been liberating for Beth. She couldn't remember another time—apart from her final day at work, and she'd rather forget that—when she'd deliberately done something outside her comfort zone, and the buzz it had given her had been incredible. Over the course of a few months, she'd lost her home and her job, and with it her self-belief. She'd been left with no anchor, no safe space, until she'd made a temporary one in the villa in Turkey.

But today she'd discovered she no longer needed to be bound by those insecurities. She'd dared to let herself go and found she hadn't been sucked into a frightening, unknown vacuum. She'd met challenges and enjoyed them. She felt ready to meet more.

Jensen made her feel safe. Infinitely safe. It was a deeper level of emotion than anything she'd ever experienced. It should have been frightening, but it simply felt exciting, something she was eager to explore further. He was kind and honest, a rock of a man who held her and promised no harm would come to them, and she believed him.

The pressure of his hands on hers as they guided *Sundance* through the narrow channel between the headlands felt sure and solid. She turned her head, looked up at him, and smiled, loving the way his eyes crinkled at the corners, the way the corners of his mouth lifted, as he smiled back.

The water in the cove was calm, the low sun sending golden shafts of light across the aquamarine sea. Jensen cut the engine so that the only sound was the lap of the ripples against the hull and then the splash of the anchor.

Beth didn't want to move. She wanted to hold onto this moment for as long as possible, the warmth of Jensen's body pressed against the length of her back and thighs, the feel of his steady breath brushing against her cheek. He lifted her hands from the wheel, folding them in his. Her breathing became shallow, her heartbeat loud in her ears. He brought his hands to her collarbones, his thumbs brushing along them, and then stopping over the point where she could feel her pulse racing at her throat.

He made a sound that sounded like a soft groan. 'Oh, Beth,' he muttered, 'have you any idea what you're doing to me?'

She twisted in his arms, pulling her hands free and she thought she saw that flash of anxiety, or perhaps doubt, in his eyes again, but she put her hands flat against his chest, the roughness of the hair there deliciously abrasive against her palms.

'No, Jensen,' she whispered, finding a boldness that she didn't recognise as belonging to her. 'I don't think I do. Would you like to show me?'

It felt like long minutes before he reacted. His dark eyes, serious and deep, roamed over her face, as if he was trying to commit it to his memory. They returned, to meet her own gaze, with an intensity that rocked her to the core. An overwhelming sensation, which she dimly acknowledged as desire, swept through her, carrying all reason away with it. She needed him to hold her and kiss her. That was all she knew.

He bent and brushed his mouth across her forehead, but that wasn't ever going to be enough. Somehow, without her knowing how, her hands found their way around the back of his neck, her fingers burying themselves in his hair. This was so easy, she thought, when you didn't resist it.

The first touch of his mouth on hers felt like something she'd been waiting for all her life. She sighed and he moved away, his lips hovering a whisper from hers, his eyes searching her face for something.

'Beth,' he murmured. 'Are you sure? Do you want this?'

Her answer was to draw his head down towards her. This time there was no hesitation from either of them. Their lips fused and the force of the emotions that took hold of her was irresistible. Beth gave in to them, feeling herself pulled into a vortex of need and exquisite sensation and not caring where it took her.

His lips moved gently, coaxing her, lifting briefly to utter a whispered 'yes' as he changed the angle of his mouth, before returning, this time with more pressure, urging her silently to open to him. When she did, a moan of pleasure sounding deep in her throat, the exquisite warmth of the tip of his tongue stroking across her lips sending a jolt of sensation so pure and elemental through her body, she gripped his shoulders and cried out.

'I'm sorry, Beth. Are you all right? Do you want to stop?'

'Don't stop. Please.'

After that he seemed to hold back a little, his kiss deepening slowly, thoroughly, his tongue, just a flicker at first, becoming bolder and exploring every part of her mouth, urging her to do the same for him. One hand slid around the back of her neck, his strong fingers cupping her head, while the other moved in long strokes down her spine, finally resting in the small of her back.

She hesitated at first, unsure, but his gentle encouragement reassured her and then his taste, his warmth, the closeness of it, were so new and exciting that she craved more and more, fusing her body to his, longing to feel his touch all over her, lost in the sheer magic of it.

When it ended, and they pulled apart, breathless, he laid her head on his chest, brushing her hair from her forehead. His heartbeat was quick and strong under her cheek, his breathing ragged. He smoothed a hand over her shoulder blades, holding her to him and she didn't want him to let her go. She looped her arms around his waist, leaning against him, limp and spent.

'Let me take you home,' he whispered. 'It's been the best of days. Thank you.'

CHAPTER TEN

WHEN JENSEN WOKE, he rolled onto his back, throwing a crooked arm across his face to block out the slanting rays of the morning sun. Thoughts of Beth ambushed him and he groaned. Her scent still lingered in his senses, the taste of her skin on his lips and tongue. The memory of the way she'd moved her mouth against his, pleading wordlessly for more, sent renewed heat barrelling through him.

Would she have stayed if he'd asked her? A part of him hoped not. It would have been too much, too soon, but now he wished she were here, in his arms.

It was a long time since he'd experienced anything approaching happiness and he explored the unfamiliar emotion carefully. In Beth's company he felt deep contentment, and now, added to that, electrifying desire. He'd tried to convince himself that it was because he hadn't had female company—*had sex*—for so long, but deep down he knew this was more complicated than that.

Their conversations had never touched on previous relationships, but he couldn't believe that a woman like her hadn't had any. He wanted her, and she'd shown how much she wanted him. It should be simple.

He could offer her nothing. His life lay behind him, destroyed, his reputation in tatters. While he'd begun to move forward, while he worked at putting *Sundance* back in order, he was only at the very beginning. The future was still a foreign country through which he'd have to try to navigate a route. Sometimes it felt like a nightmare, sometimes like a devilish game for which the rules had been torn up.

Beth did not need someone like him in her life, holding her back, weighing her down with his own baggage.

Her life had been torn apart, but she had the strength and courage to see positivity in the ruins. She seemed to share the values he'd always stood for—honesty, integrity and truth—and circumstances had conspired to rip up those principles, forcing her to take stock, try to work out how to rebuild a life from the fragments left to her.

His presence in her life could be the last thing she needed, but what if he asked her for help? He'd been hell-bent on doing this on his own. He'd cut himself off from the world, certain that nobody wanted to be associated with him, but she'd shown him something different. With her, he could be the best version of himself and he hadn't been that for more years than he cared to remember. He thought she trusted him, and he could feel himself beginning to trust her, too. What if he could build on that trust and learn to stop running and begin to build something solid in his life again?

Going below, he splashed cold water on his face and rubbed a towel over his jaw. Then, studying his reflection in the mirror above the basin, he made a decision. It was time he stopped hiding from himself, as well as the rest of the world.

It was mid-afternoon by the time he leapt out of the RIB and crossed the beach. He felt energised. As he climbed the path to the villa, he wondered how he would find Beth today. Had she slept well, woken refreshed and enjoyed the quiet routine of her day so far?

When she woke, had she thought about him and the magical day they'd spent together, ending in that spectacular embrace?

He'd taken her ashore last night and they'd walked up through the trees to the villa hand in hand. It had felt as natural as breathing. But at the door he'd simply brushed his lips against her forehead and turned away. Any more than that and he would never have left. His body had sung with desire and anticipation, but he'd walked away.

Had she tossed and turned in her bed, as he had on his mat on the deck of *Sundance*, thinking, wondering, what it could have been like?

She was stretched out on a sunbed, in her red bikini, reading.

'Beth?'

He hadn't startled her. She lowered the book and turned her head towards him, as if she'd been expecting him. He crossed the grass to the terrace and stood looking down at her. She hadn't reached for her towel or beach wrap to cover herself. His hungry eyes devoured her, moving from her hair, which was loosely caught on top of her head, exposing the slender curve of her neck, down to the tips of her toes.

The red bikini moulded to her shape, accentuating the curve of her hips and breasts, the dip of her waist. His mouth went dry.

Her pale golden skin gleamed and there was a bottle of sunscreen lying on the tiles beside her.

'Jensen.'

He dragged his attention back to reality and tried to smile. 'I could do your back if you'd like.'

She looked at him and sat up, swinging her feet to the ground, pushing her sunglasses onto the top of her head.

'You've...changed?'

He spiked his fingers through his hair, still surprised by its new, shorter length.

'I've been to the barber in the village. A Turkish barber, in Turkey.' He smiled down at her.

Beth stood and raised a hand and her fingers hovered at his cheek before brushing lightly across his smooth jaw.

'You look different, and yet the same.'

'Do you mind?' He thought she looked faintly bemused.

'Mind? Of course not. Although I quite liked the stubble...' Her forehead creased and she studied him through narrowed eyes. 'You just remind me...no, sorry. Ignore me.' She shook her head. 'It's nothing.'

He reached up for her hand and tugged her towards him until they were almost touching. Almost. She lifted her face and he took it in both hands to kiss her.

It was everything he remembered from yesterday, and more. He loved the feeling of his newly shaved skin against her soft cheek. He imagined how it would feel against the satiny skin of her abdomen. Her thighs. His tee shirt and the red triangles of fabric that were her bikini top and bottom felt like a flimsy barrier between them, and yet getting past them felt impossible.

He didn't dare to close the gap but with a small, impeded sound, Beth pressed her body against his, her hands running down his back and then up under the hem of his tee shirt to spread across his shoulders. He had a brief, vivid memory of the feeling of her hands rubbing the sunscreen onto his back yesterday before his mind narrowed and all his blood went south. His focus shrank to the point of what was happening right here, right now.

She pulled away from his mouth, breathing hard. 'Jensen. I think I...want you.'

He ran his hands down her arms, taking her hands in his and bringing them up to cup them against his chest. His forehead rested on hers.

'I want you, too, Beth. So much. But that's not why I came.'

'Why, then?'

'I came to ask you to dinner. Will you come out with me, on a date?'

'A date?'

'Yes. You know, when two people agree to go out together. It's called a date.'

'I… Jensen, this isn't a teasing matter. I know what a date is. I just don't know where we'd go on one round here.' She looked around. 'Unless it's to the café in the village, but I don't know how late they stay open. Or perhaps you're going to cook me dinner on *Sundance*?'

'It's more special than that.'

'More special than *Sundance*? Impossible.'

'There's a village up the coast where the little restaurant in the harbour has a big reputation. The only reason it's not packed every night is because it's only accessible by boat.'

'So we're going on our date on *Sundance*.'

'The sea is going to be like glass this evening. It'll take twenty minutes in the RIB.'

'Are you sure?'

'Positive. You won't even get your feet wet. That is, if you say yes.'

'If I say yes, will you tell me what made you get your hair cut and a proper shave?'

'I promise.'

'Yes, then, I'll come. I'm eaten up with curiosity.'

'Be on the beach at six. I'll pick you up.'

Beth showered and washed her hair. She dried it in shiny waves and carefully smoothed some pink lipstick onto her mouth and a hint of eyeshadow to her eyelids. Of the three dresses she'd brought with her, she chose the one Jensen hadn't seen. It had a row of tiny mother-of-pearl buttons down the front, from the deep vee neck to below the waist, and the pale lavender cotton fell in soft pleats from the dropped waist and swirled in soft folds around her calves. She added a spritz of perfume. A restaurant, however big its reputation, could not be too formal if all its clientele arrived by boat, she told herself.

Half an hour later, as they motored into the tiny harbour and found a place to tie up at the quay, she realised that depended entirely on the kind of boat.

Several superyachts were anchored in the bay, the owners evidently ferried ashore by their skippers in sleek, gleaming speedboats, which now bumped together gently alongside the pontoons.

'Will we get a table?' She hooked a hand through Jensen's arm, feeling suddenly unsure.

'I asked Omer at the village shop to call them this morning to make a reservation.'

'Oh. So you planned this. And you were confident I'd agree to come on a date with you.'

'Not confident. Hopeful.'

Their table was tucked away at the end of the terrace with a view over the harbour. Candlelight flickered in a glass lantern on the blue-checked tablecloth. The darkening water reflected the last of the sunset and as lights came on around the edge of the bay and on the yachts anchored further out, the scene took on a dreamlike quality.

'Thank you for bringing me here, Jensen. It's magical.'

'How would you rate your date, so far?'

'A perfect ten. I can't see how it could get any better.'

Jensen took her hand, brushing his thumb across her knuckles. 'Want to bet?'

'You'd lose.'

His thumb moved to trace a light circle on her palm. 'I don't think so.'

The food was simple and exquisite, with fish as fresh as it could be, buttery little potatoes and crunchy salad. The wine Jensen chose from the small list tasted like honey and sunshine on her tongue.

Beth settled back in her chair. 'I think that counts as a perfect meal. These little pastries are sinfully good.' She licked her fingers. 'There's only one thing you still need to do.'

'Oh?'

'Mmm. Tell me what happened to the pirate I sailed away with, yesterday?'

Jensen propped his folded arms on the table and nodded. He looked out over the small harbour, then back at her. His eyes had lost their navy in the dim light and turned almost black.

'Yeah. I did say I would. I thought you might have forgotten.'

'No.' Beth smoothed the skirt of her dress over her thighs, sensing his hesitation. 'But if it's something you don't want to discuss, that's fine, too.'

'I've been…stuck,' he began, slowly. He dropped his eyes to the table, lifting his shoulders, then he dropped them and looked directly at her. 'I thought when I got to where I was going, I'd feel different. Unburdened. That I'd be able to come to terms with things, make a plan and move ahead with my life in a direction of my own choice. Rather like you.'

'I…'

He held up a hand, broad palm facing her. She wanted to wrap her fingers around his and hold him, but she kept her hands in her lap, aware that he needed to speak without distraction.

'I thought my head would be clear and I'd be able to think, but I couldn't. Things caught up with me and held me back. I couldn't shake them off. I wanted to be on my own, but you were there. Then I wanted to spend time with you, but I resented that want. It wasn't how things were meant to be.'

'I felt much the same at first. I wanted you gone. You've fixed *Sundance*, so I suppose you will be, soon. Only now…' She swallowed, emotion clogging her throat. 'Is that what you were going to tell me? That you're ready to go?'

'Not at all. I think what I'm trying to say is that I'm ready to stop; to stop trying to outrun my life. When you said that thing about the journey only just beginning, it made so much sense to me. I thought I was at the end of it, and I couldn't figure out why I didn't feel better. Accepting that this is just the beginning somehow set my mind free. Yesterday, with you,' he said, reaching across the table and pulling one of her hands from her lap, enclosing it in his, 'was the best day of my life. Seeing how you opened up and enjoyed it made me so…*happy*. And the way we kissed was…' His inbreath was shaky. 'It was beyond words. I wanted you. And when I woke this morning, I wished I'd asked you to stay.'

'I didn't mind that you took me home. I knew you'd come back. I was happy to wait for you.'

'But this morning I also thought about how far I still have to go, and whether I'll ever feel worthy of someone like you. And I wondered if you might be able to…help.'

Beth felt tears prick her eyes. She blinked them away. She could only imagine how difficult it was for Jensen, a strong, independent, self-reliant man, to ask anyone for help. He was used to solving problems, making things work, finding a way, and yet he'd stalled, held back by whatever it was that had happened to him. He needed her help, not her pity.

'I'm honoured,' she said, lightly, 'that you've asked, and of course I'll help, if I can, but you still haven't told me why...'

He released her hand and sat back, running his fingers through his hair. 'I was coming to that. I decided that a good start would be to stop hiding behind my appearance. If I'm to get anything of my life back, it must not be as a man badly disguised as a pirate.'

'Okay. I get that. But I think, if I'm going to be of any practical help to you, I need to know more about your past.'

His beautifully curved mouth, until this morning hidden from her behind his scruff, flattened into a straight line, the lips she'd been thinking about kissing again, all evening, thinned. He shook his head and pressed his fingers to his temples.

'I don't think I'm ready for that.'

CHAPTER ELEVEN

AT FIRST THE moon was just a pale smudge of light on the horizon but within minutes it had hauled itself out of the sea to sail free in the night sky, leaving a silver wake across the water.

'It was the perfect setting for a date, with perfect food and wine. Did you order the moon, too?'

'I might have tried.' With his hand on the tiller, Jensen guided the RIB between the headlands. The low lights he'd left burning on *Sundance* glowed invitingly. He slowed the engine to a throb so that the craft rode quietly on the still waters of the cove. 'Since it has appeared on cue, how do you feel about rounding off our date with a moonlight swim?'

'Have you been planning that, too? All part of the perfect evening?'

'You bet me it couldn't get any better. Remember?'

'Mmm. I do. It sounds like an amazing idea, but I think my bet is safe. I don't have my bikini or swimsuit with me.'

He opened the throttle a little and guided the RIB to the platform at *Sundance*'s stern.

'If I'd planned it, I would have suggested you bring them with you. I could lend you a tee shirt. If you like.'

In the light from the cockpit just above them, Jensen watched conflicting emotions chase across her face. Her growing, but still fragile confidence wanted to say yes, he was sure, but her insecurities were urging her to refuse. If sailing had been out of her comfort zone, then swimming with him in the moonlight would be on a whole different level.

He moored the RIB securely to *Sundance*, busying himself with the few things that needed to be done to make it safe, deliberately not meeting Beth's gaze or pressing her for an answer. Standing up, with one hand on the platform to keep them steady, he held out the other to her, helping her to step across.

He heard her inhale deeply and then breathe out.

'Yes.' She probably didn't sound as positive as she'd hoped.

'Okay.' He kept his voice light. 'You can change your mind if you want to. It's allowed.'

'I don't want to change my mind, but the idea does make me anxious. A week ago, a moonlight swim would have been so far out of my usual range of experience... I can't believe I'm even contemplating it.'

'Shall I get a tee shirt? While you think about it?'

There was a brief silence and he turned to look at her. She nodded. 'Yes, please. But I think you'd better hurry, in case I change my mind, after all.'

'That'll be fine, too. There's no pressure. It's meant to be fun. Come up on deck. There's a ladder down the side. It's the safest way to get into the water.'

Jensen handed her a tee shirt through the hatch and disappeared. 'I'm going to change,' he called from below.

Beth undid the buttons of her dress with shaking fingers and slipped it off her shoulders, quickly pulling Jensen's tee shirt over her head. Her courage failed her when she thought about removing her underwear, so she kept it on. Was this, she thought, the most foolish thing she'd ever done? It was so out of character for her that she wondered if her senses had been corrupted by the exoticism of the whole evening.

Mentally, she corrected herself. It was out of character

for the old Beth: the one who never did anything new, or challenging. For her remaining time in Turkey she would be the new, best version of herself, who seized opportunities to test her courage and made the most of this fragile, exquisite bubble of happiness in which she found herself, in Jensen's company.

She stepped out of the pool of lavender cotton at her feet as Jensen emerged from below decks, wearing his board shorts.

'Still up for this? You don't have to, you know.'

Beth nodded, afraid that her voice might give away just how nervous she felt. It's just a swim, she told herself. You're a good swimmer. No, it's not, her old voice reminded her. It's a swim, in the sea, in the moonlight.

With a rugged, handsome, caring man who had kissed her with reverence, as if she was the most precious thing he'd ever held.

She watched him swing himself over the rail, onto the ladder. Seconds later she heard the soft splash as he entered the water.

Taking a deep breath, she followed him.

He was waiting for her at the bottom of the ladder. The water was silky against her skin as she sank into it. It was cool but the gasp she gave was from pleasure rather than cold.

'Oh, this is…exquisite.' She turned, finding Jensen close behind her. 'It's the most incredible feeling.'

She swam a few strokes, then stopped, suddenly anxious about moving too far from *Sundance*.

'I'll stay close to you, Beth. You must get out as soon as you feel cold.'

Beth rolled onto her back, gazing up into the velvet depths of the starred sky, feeling her body supported and held by the water.

They swam together around *Sundance*, crossing the path of moonlight that stretched across the bay and turned their limbs silver, and the drops of water they splashed into glittering crystals.

'I think we should probably get out now, before the cold sets in.' Jensen put a hand in the small of her back, urging her towards the ladder. 'If you love it so much we can always do it again, another night.'

'Yes, but it'll never be like this again. I think I've lost the bet.' She turned towards him, laughing, and wrapped her legs around his waist.

'Beth…no.' He seized her hands and held them against his chest, as if he needed to stop them from touching him anywhere else. 'I need…we need to get out.'

A sudden breeze ruffled the surface of the water as they climbed the ladder. Back on the deck, Beth shivered.

Jensen picked up one of the towels he'd brought out and wrapped it around her shoulders.

'Come on. A hot shower will warm you up.' He pushed her gently towards the hatch and helped her onto the ladder.

She glanced over her shoulder. 'My dress…'

'I'll get it for you in a minute.'

The shower in the en suite bathroom was the more spacious, so he ushered her towards it, opening the door. Her teeth chattered and he swore under his breath. This had been reckless. Seeing Beth face challenges and overcome anxieties was hugely rewarding but now he felt he had pushed her too far. She was cold and probably mildly shocked. He reached into the shower, turning on the water and adjusting the temperature.

Beth stood shivering, clutching the towel at her neck. 'I'm n…not cold. I'm just…' Another bout of shivering blurred her words.

Jensen prised the towel out of her fists and dropped it on the floor. He gripped the hem of the sodden tee shirt and lifted it over her head. Even though he knew he had to get her into the hot shower and warmed up as fast as possible, he stopped, the tee shirt hanging from one hand, his breath caught in his throat, as he gazed at her.

Why had he thought she'd wear sensible underwear?

The wet, lacy garments enhanced rather than hid her nakedness, holding her perfect, rounded breasts captive and defining the vee at the apex of her thighs.

Her name was a groan in his throat as he put his hands on her hips and guided her under the steaming spray.

She tilted her head back and gasped, then twined her arms around his neck and pulled him towards her.

He pressed his cheek to the top of her head, sliding his fingers under the thin straps that ran over her shoulders.

'Beth…are you sure?'

'I've never been more sure…of anything,' she whispered as his mouth found hers.

His hands cupped her face as he kissed her, exploring her lips and mouth with slow thoroughness, then letting his mouth follow his hands, over the frantic pulse at her neck, down to the ivory and pink perfect orbs of her breasts, and on to her curved hips, hooking his fingers into the lacy thong and dispensing with it.

He felt her tug at the waistband of his shorts, and he eased them over his hips, kicking them out of the way. Then he wrapped his arms around her and held her still, loving the feel of her body pressed against the length of his and feeling like a man who'd been dying of thirst finding an oasis of sweet water in the desert.

He turned off the water and wrapped her in the robe that hung by the door, and carried her out into the cabin, setting her down and slipping the fluffy fabric from her shoulders, drinking in the sight of her as he laid her on the wide bed and covered her body with his.

CHAPTER TWELVE

'I'M SORRY.' Jensen's fingers traced over her cheek and jaw. His voice and the kiss he gave her were soft but the hard, bunched muscles of his shoulders, under her hands, told her he wasn't relaxed, at all.

'What for?'

He rested his face in the hollow of her shoulder. 'That wasn't the best…it's been a while.'

Beth smoothed her hands over the hard planes of his back, feeling his muscles shiver. 'For me it was perfect.'

'Next time…'

'There'll be a next time?' She spiked the fingers of one hand into his hair, massaging the base of his skull, while the other traced feather-light circles in the small of his back.

He lifted his head and smiled against her mouth.

'All too soon, if you carry on doing that. I'm not *that* old.'

'Mmm.' She increased the pressure, surprising herself, again, at how easy it was to be with him. Everything felt as if it was meant to be. There had been no self-consciousness or awkwardness. 'Promise?' She shifted beneath him, hooking a leg over the back of his thigh.

'Can you…keep still?' He cradled her face between his hands and kissed her. 'Just for…a minute?'

'No. I…'

'Beth.'

* * *

Eventually, they slept. Beth woke in the dawn half-light with the weight of an arm across her waist.

She turned her head carefully to look at Jensen. His expression was peaceful, his breathing quiet. He moved his head a little; his profile, clear and unblurred, was etched against the light creeping into the porthole beyond.

Something in Beth's brain clicked into place. She blinked, but he'd moved, and the memory slipped. She turned over and he tightened his arm, pulling her into the curve of his body and resting his chin on her head. She thought he murmured her name. She slept again.

Jensen slipped out of the master cabin. He pulled on an old pair of shorts, made himself a strong cup of his favourite coffee and carried it up onto the foredeck.

It was the best time of day. The sun had just risen above the horizon and the air still felt cool, the only sounds the creaking of *Sundance*'s rigging and the quiet slap and suck of water against her hull. A seabird swooped low over the water on silent wings.

He slid down onto the deck, leaning his back against the mast. It was the first time he'd slept indoors for weeks. In Beth's arms he had forgotten how intolerable he found sleeping in an enclosed space. She'd still been deeply asleep when he'd woken, and he hadn't wanted to disturb her, just yet.

The magnetic attraction between them had been there from the start, although he had denied it. He smiled as he remembered how they had tried to avoid one another; the rules they'd—*he'd*—laid out about using the beach, protecting their privacy, giving each other as wide a berth as possible.

None of it had worked. They'd been drawn together and

now it seemed that every second they'd spent in each other's company had led, inexorably, to the bed, where Beth now slept, below the deck, and the unfathomable joy that she had given him, and, he hoped, he had given her.

Apart from joy, she'd given him something else. A flame of hope flickered in his heart. She made him believe that things could change for him and would be different from now on, as they opened their hearts to one another. The certain knowledge that he was a different person—a better man—when he was with her made that hope grow stronger by the second.

He could hardly wait for her to wake so he could tell her how he felt.

When Beth next woke, Jensen was gone. She put out a hand and found his pillow was cool, in the indent where his head had lain. She felt bereft, still feeling the imprint of his body along her back and thighs.

She listened for signs that he might be moving about in the galley, or in the shower, but there were none. She'd expected to wake, slowly, and find herself still cocooned in his arms. She just couldn't imagine being anywhere else, right now.

Then she remembered the quick snapshot her brain had called up in the early hours of the morning. It had lasted half a second and then vanished but now that she'd thought about it again, it persisted.

She pushed herself upright, more detail added to the memory as sleep receded. Apprehension propelled her out of bed. She pulled on the soft robe in which Jensen had wrapped her after their shower, only to slide it off her again minutes later, before lifting her onto the bed. Wrapping it around herself, she padded towards the galley.

A faint smell of coffee hung in the air and the sky was a

square of pale blue morning light, through the open hatch at the top of the companionway.

Jensen was not in the cockpit. Perhaps he'd gone for an early morning swim, but there was no sign of him in the waters around *Sundance* as she climbed up to the deck and worked her way forward, towards the bow.

He was almost hidden by the foremast, but she could see his bare, bronzed feet on the deck, his elbows resting on his drawn-up knees. His big hands were wrapped around a coffee mug. Last night she'd discovered how those slightly rough hands, which were adept at fixing so many things, were also capable of infinite gentleness, and of eliciting un-dreamt-of pleasure from her body. As she approached, she could see he was resting his head against the timber mast, his gaze fixed on something distant.

She watched him for a long moment, sharply aware that she stood at a crossroads, making an agonising choice. She badly wanted to retreat softly, slide back into bed and wait for him to return to her. She need say nothing.

But Beth knew, even before she'd formed the thought, that she could not go down that path. Jensen deserved her honesty; of that she was certain. It might destroy the frag-ile beginning of something beautiful and precious, but it might also make it stronger. Whatever happened, she could not deceive him.

Sucking in a deep breath, she stepped forward.

'JJ?'

The quick twist of his head as he turned to stare at her was all the confirmation she needed.

She was right.

She'd asked him to take her back to bed, but he'd refused. Instead, he'd made her a mug of coffee and brought it up onto the deck for her.

'You didn't drink yours, Jensen. It's cold.'

He shrugged, resumed his place in front of the mast, and patted the deck beside him.

But Beth positioned herself between his knees, shuffling backwards until she could lean against his chest, cradling the warm mug in her hands. Jensen combed his fingers through her hair, teasing out some of the tangled evidence of their night of lovemaking. 'How long have you known?' he asked, after a long silence.

She reached up and stilled his hand in its restless caressing of her hair. 'Since early this morning, although yesterday, when you'd been to the barber, something...' She sipped the coffee. 'This morning, I glimpsed the outline of your profile in a particular light, not blurred by that stubbly beard and long hair, and it jogged a memory.'

'I tried to avoid the press.'

'You did well. In the few pictures I saw, you'd shielded your face. But there was one...'

'Yes, I know.' He dragged a hand over his face, shaking his head. 'It was the day I was sentenced.'

Beth put her coffee on the deck and reached for his hands with both of hers. He let her take them and she pulled his arms over her shoulders and kissed his knuckles, settling against his chest again.

'I'm sorry.' Her voice was husky. 'It must have been dreadful.'

He took a couple of breaths, hoping to control the shake in his voice. 'I didn't know it was possible to feel—*to be*—so helpless. You know you're innocent; that you've done nothing—*nothing*—wrong, but twelve strangers decide you're lying. And there is nothing...*nothing*...you can do about it.'

He stirred, needing to move, unable to keep still and remember, but Beth kept him anchored against her.

'But now you're free and declared innocent.'

'I'm free, yes, from prison. But I'll never be free of the stigma of having been there. That's not something anyone is going to forget.'

'Your friends and family must have believed in you, though. And they've been vindicated.'

Jensen laughed, but even he recognised the harshness in the sound. 'Someone like you, Beth, with your loyalty and honesty, might find it hard to imagine how quickly friends, and even family, will put a safe distance between themselves and disgrace.'

She twisted her head and looked up at him, her expression of shock confirming his words.

'Your *family*?'

'Yup. My wife—'

'*Wife?*' Shock jolted through her. 'Jensen—'

'*Ex*-wife. And my daughter. I haven't heard from them, since.'

'You have a daughter?'

He nodded. 'Emily. She's fifteen. And beautiful. I...' In spite of his iron control, his voice broke.

'But it was declared a miscarriage of justice. Surely now they'll...'

He rolled his head against the mast, liking the sense of solidity and permanence it gave him. 'Even if they did, would I want them in my life again, when they'd believed I was guilty of stealing from a children's charity?'

'No. But your daughter is at an impressionable age. She must have been influenced by what other people said. She's not old enough to have made a sound judgement. She'll want to be a part of your life now. And your friends...'

'One friend. James and I go way back. He's a lawyer. He wouldn't accept the judgement and he made it his mission to expose the truth. It's thanks to him that I'm free.'

'What a good friend. You must have had quite a celebration with him when you were released.'

Jensen closed his eyes, forcing himself to think about those first hours and days of freedom.

'No,' he said, feeling tightness in his throat. 'When I was released, I went to my apartment to collect a few things and then I went straight to Heathrow Airport. I didn't see or speak to anyone except the cab driver and staff at the airport.'

He felt Beth go still.

'But you've spoken to James since? Surely...'

How could he explain that desperate need to be on his own, doing whatever he wanted, after months of regulated prison life, every minute of every day, and some of the nights, regimented and allocated to something or other? There'd been no peace, or quiet.

'No,' he said, eventually. 'I've spoken to nobody. I turned off my phone, let the battery die. You're the only person who knows where I am.'

'But...people...must be worried about you. You should make contact with someone.'

'No one cared about me when I was locked up. Why should they care now?' The familiar taste of bitterness was strong in his mouth.

'James cared. He must be beside himself with worry about you.'

'James knows me, and so he will know that I'll get in touch when I want to. He won't try to find me until I'm ready to be found.'

'Jensen—I don't think I can call you anything else.'

'No, please don't. JJ was my name—Jonathan Jensen Heath—in *that* life. I'm no longer that person.'

'Could you bear to tell me about that life?' The stroke of her thumbs across his knuckles was soothing. 'I'd like to understand what happened. But if it's too difficult for you, we can wait until another time.'

Jensen's breath quickened, and his heart hammered, at the thought of relating the story. Beth must be able to feel his heartbeat against her back, but she gave no sign. When he'd walked out of the prison gates, a free man, he'd tried to put it behind him.

He hadn't always been successful. But he wanted Beth to know. He didn't want her to have any doubts about him, even though knowing who he was must now have thrown up the biggest doubt in her mind.

The best gift he could give her would be the perfect memory of this time together.

He bent his head and brushed his cheek against hers.

'I made my money—an obscene amount—as a hedge-fund manager. I loved the life, but the stress was insane and I knew if I didn't get out, I would burn out, so I quit while I was ahead. It turned out that my…ex-wife…loved the life, too, and she wasn't ready for the change of pace. She missed it—the parties, the restaurants, the chalets in Gstaad and St Moritz and the helicopter skiing—all the things I liked the least about it.' He shifted his thighs, tightening them around Beth's hips. 'The way I relaxed, once a year, was to take *Sundance* on a sailing trip, but she hated that. In the end we split. She took Emily and married another city high-flier.'

'But you still saw your daughter?'

'Oh, yes, there was no problem about access, especially when she wanted the freedom to go off on a fancy trip somewhere. Emily and I had great times together. I tried to be the best father and I miss her…'

'I'm so sorry.' Beth pressed her mouth against his hands. 'I can't imagine how you must feel.'

'Lonely, regretful, guilty. All those things. And…hurt. It hurts to think Emily believed I was a criminal.'

'I feel sure,' Beth whispered, 'you'll be able to put things right with her. She'll need time, but it'll happen.'

'I wish I shared your confidence. Anyway, I wanted to do something worthwhile with my time, and when the opportunity came up to be the CEO of the charity, it seemed like the perfect solution. I loved the job, but I admit there was a time, during the divorce, when I took my eye off the ball. I wanted to make things as easy as possible for Emily and I lost focus, briefly. That's when it happened.'

'Someone framed you?'

'Essentially, yes. Money disappeared. A lot of money. As the CEO I was ultimately accountable, but I was astonished by what had happened. I couldn't understand it. I was arrested and the finance guy—the CFO—took over. They appointed one of the most aggressive prosecuting lawyers in the City, and they got their conviction. I'd still be there if it weren't for James' work.'

'He found new evidence?'

Jensen nodded. 'The verdict was overturned, and I was released. The new investigation is ongoing, but I've been out of touch, so I don't know what progress has been made, if any, in identifying the culprit.'

'What did you do when you got to Heathrow?'

'I took the first available flight to Athens. By that night I was in the only place I wanted to be: on *Sundance*. I sailed out of Piraeus the next morning, early. I think you know the rest.'

'Mmm. You sailed alone, with the aim of getting here. That must have been tough.'

'Sometimes. But being free and master of my own destiny again was so mind-blowing, I didn't mind how tough it was. In fact, the times I sailed through the night were the best. When I had to devote all my powers of concentration to the wind, the sails, the sea, it stopped me thinking about anything else. And after a passage like that, I was exhausted enough to sleep.'

'And you got here and found me. What a let-down.'

He almost smiled. 'A surprise, yes. A shock, maybe. But not a let-down, and soon a tentative kind of pleasure.'

'And now?'

'Now?' How could he tell her what he felt now? 'Oh, Beth, I've loved being with you. Seeing you face challenges, overcome anxieties, take delight in new experiences has been transformative for me. It's made me believe that I can have hope. Maybe things can be different. You make me *feel* different because you've made me feel again. I was numb with pain, disbelief, anger, for so long, but you've unlocked something. But…'

'But?'

He tightened his hold on her. 'But now the past has caught up with me…with us. I would have told you eventually, but I wanted you to get to know me better, first. I wanted you to learn to trust me. I hate the thought that you might doubt me, or not believe in me.'

Beth moved away and turned to face him. Their knees touched and she still held onto his hands.

'I need to look at you and hear you say that, and then I need you to explain how this works, Jensen. We enjoy each other's company. I find you so easy to be with and that's a whole new experience for me. And last night…' She stopped and took a breath that stuttered in her throat. 'Last night was more wonderful than I could ever have imagined it would be.'

'Beth…'

'Are you saying you think I'll walk away from that? Because I need to tell you that I don't know how to.'

Her green eyes were huge, her teeth fastened over her soft lower lip and he could see the pulse thrumming at her neck. He wanted to put his mouth there and feel her life force.

'I'm saying that if we don't I'm so afraid of ruining the rest of your life.'

Beth let go of Jensen's hands and scrambled to her feet. The towelling robe swung open and she grabbed the edges of it, wrapping it around herself and tying the belt in a fierce, tight knot.

She stared down at him. 'What do you mean?'

Jensen unfolded himself and stood up, stepping past her. He put his hands on the rail and dropped his head.

There were marks on his back she must have made last night. She wanted to stroke her fingers over them, or touch her lips to them, but she pushed her hands into her pockets, balling her fists.

He straightened, looking out over the sea. The day had started to warm up and Beth would have liked to find some shade, but she felt stuck where she was, waiting for his answer.

At last, he turned, his expression grim and distant.

'I mean,' he said carefully, 'that my reputation for truth, integrity and compassion—everything I believed in—has been destroyed. My life, as I knew it, is in ruins. Even though I've been exonerated of the crime for which I was found guilty, it will take years to cast off the shadow of that conviction and jail term.'

'I don't care…'

He held up a hand to stop her.

'You should. You *must* care, about your own future.' He looked down, then raised his eyes to her face again. 'You have so much potential. You can make your future whatever you want. What you don't want is to be associated with someone like me.'

'What is someone like you meant to be like?'

'Beth, I've lost all credibility. Nobody will want to work with me.'

'So because I now know who you are, you think I won't want to be with you?'

Jensen nodded.

'That's ridiculous. Everything that has happened between us happened before I recognised you.'

'I know, but we can't undo it. Now that you know who I am, you should be running as fast as possible in the opposite direction.'

'Well, I'm not.' Beth slid her hands around his waist. 'Last night you asked for my help. Well, I'm asking for yours now.' She laid her cheek against his chest, feeling the thud of his heart speed up as she pulled him against her. 'Just please don't do this.'

Jensen's cheek pressed against the crown of her head. His chest rose in a long, slow breath.

'Beth, this is crazy. How can I possibly help you?'

'You can help me to understand what I need to do to support you, Jensen. Meeting you, having you care about me, knowing you enjoy being with me, and wanting to make love to me have been the best things that have ever happened to me. I'm not giving all that up. I'm strong enough to fight for both of us and that is what I'm going to do.'

'Beth, let me take you home. When you have space to think clearly, away from me, you'll realise I'm not worthy of you.' He bracketed her face, stroking his thumbs across her cheekbones. 'You'll have to find somewhere to live, find a new job, rebuild your life. You won't want me...'

She raised her chin. 'I may be a homeless, unemployed, forty-five-year-old woman who doesn't know what the future holds, but for the first time in my life I'm free to make my own choices, and I'm choosing to be with you.'

His next breath shuddered in his chest and then his mouth came down over hers, hard and uncompromising, his tongue probing the seam of her lips until she opened to him with a soft moan in her throat. His kiss was hungry, devouring her mouth like a man starved. Those strong hands held her head still while he plundered her sweetness, sending wave after wave of sensation whipping through her, a flame licking its way along her limbs until a fiery need had been ignited in every cell of her body.

She wondered how she could ever live without this now that she'd tasted it. She'd feel as if half of her were missing, if Jensen took it away from her, the half that had been missing up until she'd met him. He'd rescued her from her life of shrunken horizons and self-imposed boundaries and shown her how to fly free. How could he believe she'd choose to crash back to earth, wounded, alone, without him?

Breathless, her lips bruised and swollen, her heart pounding like a drum, Beth dragged her mouth away from his. 'Jensen, please…'

His breathing was quick and harsh. 'I'm sorry. I've hurt you. I was rough.'

'No.' She shook her head. 'It's okay. Please,' she pleaded. 'Please take me back to bed.'

Afterwards, Beth couldn't remember how they negotiated the companionway, half falling, in each other's arms, into the galley, or how they stumbled along the passage to the master suite. It was a blur of entangled limbs, kisses that neither of them could stop, and words of need and love, gasped and whispered. He tore the robe from her shoulders. She tugged at his shorts.

Jensen had been gentle before. Now, he made love to her with a desperate urgency, as if he believed it was the last time and he was utterly intent on making every movement, every meeting of lips, every stroke of his clever fingers, one that neither of them would ever be able to forget. Afterwards, as they clung together, drifting in and out of sleep, he raised his head and lifted a strand of her hair, smoothing it away from her forehead, and whispered to her.

'I wish things were different, but I can't wish away what happened to me. Because if none of it had happened, I wouldn't have met you.'

CHAPTER THIRTEEN

JENSEN STOOD UP from the table on Beth's terrace and stretched.

'Thank you for breakfast.' He stacked the plates and cutlery and dropped a kiss onto her head. 'Sun, sea and...'

'Sex?'

His face creased in a smile. 'If you say so. I was going to say surfing. Sun, sea and surfing will work up an appetite.'

'We haven't been surfing, but we have had brilliant...'

'Sex. Yes. You'll wear me out.'

'Actually, I was going to say we've had brilliant times in the sun and the sea, but I'll concede your point. And I don't want to wear you out. What would the point of that be?'

'Then you'd better indulge me this morning.'

'I thought I had, already. More than once.'

Jensen replaced the crockery on the table, took her wrists and pulled her to her feet. 'When last did you wear anything other than your bikini, or nothing?' He dropped her wrists and wrapped his arms around her. 'Not that I'm complaining.'

'Three days ago.' She planted a kiss on his bare chest then rubbed her cheek against his skin. 'I think there're a few more grey hairs here than there were yesterday.'

'Does that surprise you? Like I said, you're wearing me out.'

Beth smiled. 'All right, then, I'll give you a break. How would you like me to indulge you, except in the obvious way?'

'That can come later. Will you come down to the beach this morning?'

'You mean you're willing to share it with me?'

'Since we've shared just about everything else, I think we could give the beach a try.'

'Jensen... I don't think that's a good idea.'

'But you haven't heard my idea yet.' He splayed his hands over her ribcage, running his thumbs along the edge of her bikini top.

She caught her bottom lip in her teeth, hissing in a breath. 'Since you've had a one-track mind for the past three days, I think I can hazard a guess about your idea.'

'Speak for yourself, Beth. And from what I'm seeing, your mind is still running on that same track.' He looked down at the burgeoning triangles of her red bikini top and his attention narrowed and focussed.

She'd gone very still, her breathing deep and slow. Her body was warm, her curves, which he'd come to know so well, mesmerising. He knew her mouth would taste of the honey she'd had for breakfast, and her hair smelled of lavender and rosemary. Being with her filled him with a depth of happiness he'd never experienced before. She reached his very soul. A while ago he'd thought he'd never smile again, definitely never laugh, but she made him do both, often.

They talked about the past and what had happened to their lives. Somehow, Beth managed to shine a light of positivity onto the darkest of times. She'd lost her job, but looking back, she said, with the perfect vision of hindsight, she could see how stuck, how bound by convention she'd been, in the only job she'd ever had. He thought the edge of bitterness that had sharpened her words when she'd originally spoken about her work had blunted.

She'd lost her home, too, but at least she no longer had to share her space with her toxic stepmother and spoilt stepsister, she said. What could be better than a clean slate? To start afresh?

When she returned to London, she'd have to find a job and all she'd been able to imagine was trying to find one exactly like her old one. Now she felt free, and able to think about looking for something different. Something connected to gardening, which was what gave her joy.

And just because she'd lived all her life in a large Georgian house in Islington didn't mean she couldn't live somewhere different, as long as she had a garden. Jensen noticed the regret that crept into her voice when she talked about the garden she'd made behind the family home. It was, she said, the one thing she missed from her previous life.

He didn't deserve her. That thought beat a constant refrain in his head, marking time, it seemed, until the moment would be right for it to slide into a discordant cacophony of noise, which he'd be forced to take notice of and act upon. Sometimes it was loud, sometimes an insidious whisper that ambushed him in the dark hours of the early morning, when he looked down at her, asleep in his arms.

He tried to drown out the beat, kissing her awake so he could make love to her again, or swimming, hard and fast, across the bay, pushing himself until his muscles ached and his lungs threatened to burst.

If he didn't deserve her, she sure as hell didn't deserve him, with his prison record, disgraced reputation and a teenaged daughter who hated him. But being with her helped. Very slowly, he was beginning to see a glimmer of light at the end of the tunnel he seemed to have been stuck in for so long.

He dropped his eyes and gazed down at her. Her chest rose and fell slowly, deeply, and her eyelids, fringed with dark lashes, fluttered down over her eyes, her gaze and focus, he knew, turning inwards.

Her fingers traced a pattern across his lower back, but he didn't think she realised she was doing it. She ought to know by now what that did to him. Perhaps she did. Perhaps...

With difficulty, he hauled in a big, deep breath.

'Hey.' Resolutely, he removed his hands from her ribs, feeling goosebumps shiver across her skin as he drew them away.

'Mmm?'

'Come back, Beth, from wherever those thoughts have taken you.'

'Not far,' she murmured. 'Just upstairs...'

'Later. Will you come to the beach in half an hour?'

'Your plan?' Her voice was sleepy, dreamy.

'You'll find out when you get there. And no, it doesn't involve sex on the beach.'

When Beth walked onto the beach thirty minutes later, Jensen was already there. Just above the waterline lay a bright blue windsurfer board and he was engrossed in setting up the sail.

'What are you doing?'

He glanced up. 'Sorting this out. Want to have a go?'

Beth frowned and nudged the board with a foot. 'Where did you get it?'

'It was strapped to the deck on *Sundance*. Hadn't you noticed?'

'When I'm on the deck of *Sundance* there are other things that I find more distracting. And no, I'm not sure I do want to have a go. I wouldn't know how to begin.'

Jensen put the yellow and red sail down and dropped an arm around her shoulders. 'I haven't noticed that stopping you, lately. You could add windsurfing to the list of things you hadn't tried before.'

She raised her eyebrows at him. 'Such as?'

'Sailing? Swimming in the moonlight?'

'So this is where the surfing, as in sun, sea and...*surfing*...comes in.'

'Precisely. *Now* would you like to have a go? I'll be right there with you. The worst that can happen is that you fall in. Over and over again.'

An hour later, Beth had lost count of how many times she'd toppled off the board to hit the water with a shriek and a splash.

The sea in the cove was warm and calm and falling into it was fun, but not being able to master the technique was infuriating.

'There's not really enough wind,' Jensen called, before diving under the water and surfacing next to her. 'It's like riding a bicycle. Easier to balance if you're moving. Impossible if you're not.'

Beth laughed. 'How diplomatic of you to blame the conditions rather than my obvious ineptitude.' She rolled onto her back, floating, squinting against the sun. 'But it's the most fun I've had since...'

'Since?' His eyes narrowed.

'Well, I was going to say since you let me take the wheel when we were sailing *Sundance* back from Kekova, but then I remembered...'

'This morning, right? And last night, and...' He ducked below the surface as Beth's hand sent a shower of sparkling drops arcing in his direction, then came up behind her.

'Then I remembered the evening we spent at that restaurant up the coast. It was *so* much fun.'

'Mmm.' His voice hummed low in her ear. She turned, about to splash him again, but his dark gaze captured hers and she stilled, watching, as his eyes travelled down her body. His arms slipped around her waist and he pulled her closer. She wrapped her legs around him, gripping his hips.

She felt his fingers move over her back and stop at the clasp of her bikini top.

'Jensen,' she murmured, thinking that drowning in the deep pools of his eyes was a real possibility, 'you said your plan did not include sex.'

'Incorrect, Beth. Try to pay attention.' His breath was warm across her cheek. 'I said it did not involve sex on the beach.'

'So...' She gasped as her top floated free and his hands splayed over her ribcage, his thumbs teasing her skin.

'So look around and you'll see that this isn't the beach.' His lips hovered a fraction away from hers. 'It's the sea.'

Later, they lay on their backs in the sun, loose-limbed, their hands linked.

'Beth?'

'Mmm?'

'I need to go into the village this afternoon. Omer promised to find me some nylon rope to replace one of the downhauls on *Sundance*. It's one of the last repairs I have to do.' He lifted her hand and kissed the palm. 'Shall I bring back dinner?'

Beth yawned and rolled onto her stomach, propping her chin on her hands. 'What shall we have?'

'Kebabs?'

'Sounds perfect. I'm easily persuaded.'

'I know.' Jensen bent up his legs and propped himself up on his elbows.

'Don't be presumptuous. One day I'll say no.'

'Really?' He ran a finger up her spine, watching how her back arched and her head lifted. 'I'll consider making you change your mind a challenge. We could take bets on how long it would take.'

Beth shook her head. 'I've given up gambling. I lost the last bet.'

'You did. Big time.'

She laughed. 'It was a bet worth losing.'

'I'm glad you think so.'

'I'm sorry I wasn't better at windsurfing. Perhaps it was the teaching.'

Jensen sat up. 'I taught my daughter. She did really well, so I don't think so.'

Beth let the silence stretch. She'd been hoping he'd talk about his daughter, but she'd wanted it to come from him. She'd resisted the urge to raise the subject herself.

Then she reached over and clasped his hand softly in hers. 'How old was she? When you taught her?'

'Seven. We were on holiday in Crete and I hired a special small board for her. She could swim like a fish by the time she was four, and she'd been begging me to let her have a go. She was always so daring and quick to learn.' He shook his head. 'I thought she'd disappear over the horizon. I panicked. But she came back, asking me why I was being so slow.'

'She sounds like you. Is she?'

'She…well, I haven't seen her for a while, so I don't really know now. But she was.' He turned towards her, tracing a circle on her palm with his thumb. That hurt and doubt was in his eyes. 'I think she'd have liked to stay with me, after the divorce, but my lifestyle made it difficult. At least I saw her often, until…'

'Until you were accused.'

'Yes. After that, her mother wouldn't let me near her. She said her schoolfriends would drop her if they knew. But they must have known anyway. It all became very messy and public.'

'Did she want to see you?'

'I don't know. I hate to think she believed I was guilty.'

'You don't know that she did.'

He frowned, propping his head on a hand. 'She must have, obviously.'

'No. She might have believed fiercely that you were innocent. Little girls love their fathers. She might have been utterly loyal. And now that you're a free, innocent man, her mother can't object to her seeing you. She might be desperate to hear from you.'

'I feel afraid to try to contact her. What if she doesn't respond?'

Although Beth hated that he feared contacting his daughter, hearing him admit to his fear made Beth's heart sing.

'You'll never know if you don't try, Jensen. And it seems to me to be a terrible waste of a relationship. It's absolutely worth fighting for. You have a daughter—your own family. Don't let that slip from your grasp because you're afraid of failure.' She squeezed his hand and pulled it towards her, brushing her lips across his fingers. 'I'll give you the Wi-Fi code for the villa. Then if you feel like sending her an email, you can.'

He stood and held out a hand to her and she let him pull her to her feet.

'Will you come back to the villa?'

He shook his head. 'I'll take the windsurfer back out to *Sundance* and then head to the village in the RIB. Would you like me to walk up with you first?'

'No. The quicker you get to and from the village, the quicker you'll be back with me.'

He caught her around the waist and tipped her face up to him with his thumb and forefinger. 'I don't like being parted from you.'

She stretched up on her toes and kissed him lightly. 'Then hurry. I don't like being parted from you either.' She swept an arm out. 'Remember how we had to negotiate with each other about when we'd use the beach, separately?'

'And you didn't keep your side of the bargain.'

'What? I did...'

'No, you didn't. You never came to the beach, even when it was your turn.'

Her forehead creased. 'I didn't like the idea of you watching me from *Sundance*, making sure I didn't overstay my time slot.'

'But if you'd come I would have wanted you to stay longer. I think, even then, I wanted to be with you.'

'When I began to enjoy your company I refused to admit it, at first. I was determined to want to be on my own. I thought it was what I needed.'

Jensen laughed. 'As we've discovered, we don't always know what's good for us.'

'Oh, I think I do now. And whoever said you can't have too much of a good thing was absolutely right.'

CHAPTER FOURTEEN

BETH SCATTERED CUBES of feta cheese over a plate of sliced tomatoes studded with glistening olives and carried it out to the table on the terrace. 'I'll get the flatbreads. They're warming up in the oven. Oh, those look delicious.'

The smoky aroma of barbecued kebabs rose from the platter Jensen carried towards her. 'Ela made them,' he said. 'All I did was light the barbecue and cook them.'

'We're ready to eat, then.'

'Before we do, could I have that Wi-Fi code?' he asked. 'I've charged my phone. I thought I'd just check my news feed…'

Relief loosened muscles Beth hadn't realised were tense. This was a huge, positive step, but she had to make it feel like something perfectly normal.

She smiled at him, trying to keep her voice light when she replied. 'Of course. It's here somewhere.' She pulled the information file from the bookshelf in the kitchen. 'Second page, I think.'

'Thank you.' He held a smartphone in his hand.

'Are you going to read your emails?'

'Not my emails. There's nobody I want to hear from.'

'What about James?'

'James won't have emailed. He'll wait to hear from me first.'

'Okay.' She pushed the file towards him, across the

kitchen island worktop. 'Why don't you go and sit on the terrace while you do that? I'll get the wine.'

She slid the flatbreads, fragrant with warmed spices, from the oven and went to the fridge. She hesitated over choosing the wine, reading one label after the other before finally pulling a bottle of chilled Pinot Grigio from the rack and heading for the door.

Jensen sat with his back to her, an ankle balanced on a knee, one of her favourite poses to see him in. It meant he was comfortable. Relaxed. She paused in the doorway, just to look at him. His broad shoulders in the faded tee shirt, thick dark hair streaked with silver, now neatly cut, long fingers tapping the screen of his phone, all made her heart turn over in her chest.

The feelings he aroused in her were almost too big for her heart to contain. If she weren't holding a cold bottle of wine and a basket of bread, she'd put her arms around his neck and…

'Beth?' He half turned his head, looking over his shoulder. 'This was a good day to reconnect with the world. It says here that my former CFO has been questioned and the prosecuting lawyer in the case against me, Charles Denby, is being investigated, following an allegation of jury intimidation.'

The bottle of wine slipped from Beth's suddenly nerveless fingers and crashed to the tiles, shattering into a million shards of razor-sharp glass.

Jensen leapt from his chair, causing it to tip over backwards. He dropped his phone, sending it spinning across the table, and swung round. 'What happened? Are you okay?' He took in the wine spreading across the tiles and the jagged pieces of glass. 'Beth, don't move.' He swore beneath his breath. 'Your ankle is bleeding.'

Beth remained motionless, frozen to the spot. Jensen reached out and took the basket of bread from her, putting it on the table. 'Beth?' He glanced around the terrace, looking for something to use to pick up the glass. 'You've gone very white. Do you feel faint?'

She raised her hands to cover her mouth, the movement jerky, and shook her head.

'No.' The word was a hoarse whisper through her fingers. 'No, I don't feel faint. I feel… I'm…*shocked*.'

Jensen relaxed a little. 'It's only a bottle of wine, Beth. I'm sure there're more in the fridge? Let me clear this up and we'll start again.'

'That's not it.' Her voice shook. 'It was what you said.'

'Something *I* said?' The accident had wiped what he'd said from his mind. He made an effort to think back. It was the news about the CFO and the prosecutor he'd relayed to her. He reached towards his phone.

'My ankle…'

Jensen grabbed a paper napkin from the wire basket on the table and bent to press it against the wound, but Beth took it from his fingers. Gingerly, she raised her foot and rested it on the nearest chair, bending to dab at the injury.

'I said the prosecutor from my case…'

Her hair swung forward, obscuring her face. She pushed it back with one hand. 'You said his…*name*.'

'I did. Let me do that.'

But she shook her head. 'It's okay. Not deep. It was just a shock, hearing his name.'

Jensen's eyes moved from studying her ankle to her face. He drew back a little, moving his feet out of the path of the white wine, which trickled across the floor. He felt confused, struggling to make sense of what had just happened. Their barbecue dinner had been thrown into chaos, but it should be easily fixed. The food was on the table, the glasses ready to be filled. If he could clear up the broken glass and spilled wine, find another bottle, their evening would be restored.

But something had gone wrong; something that was much more fundamental than a broken bottle of wine. He could see it in the expression on Beth's chalk-white face as she straightened up. Incongruously, he noticed that the scattering of freckles across the bridge of her nose stood out in stark contrast to her pallor. She was chewing on her bottom lip, a sure sign of stress.

What was it she'd said?

His name. It was a shock, hearing his name.

Why would a name have shocked her into dropping a bottle of wine?

'I did,' he said, carefully. 'I said his name. Charles Denby.'

Beth released her bottom lip. She folded her arms across her chest and before she buried her hands in her armpits he saw that they were shaking. She raised her chin and stared at him, her gaze unwavering.

'Charles Denby,' she repeated, her voice trembling. She took a breath, noisy and harsh. 'Charles Denby was the prosecutor in your case?'

Jensen nodded and a cold finger of fear snaked up his spine. The happiness he and Beth shared was so fragile. Many things could happen to derail it, but this wasn't one of the ways he'd imagined. He had a sudden image of it being snatched away from them and broken beyond repair, just like the green glass bottle, which lay in dangerous fragments around their feet.

'Yes, he was,' he said, forcing the words out, fearing that once they were out everything would change, irrevocably. 'Why?'

Beth nodded, once, her chin dropping and then lifting

again, higher, as if she was grappling with something, determined to do the right thing, but unsure what that might be. Her shoulders dropped and her spine lengthened as she exhaled and then took a long shaky breath.

'Charles Denby,' she said, her tone flat, devoid of all expression, 'was my boss. He was the reason I left my job.'

He had never had the air punched out of his lungs, but now Jensen thought he knew what it felt like. He tried to breathe, to allow the steady inhalation and exhalation of air to calm him, and his brain to function, but it felt as if there were a great weight pressing onto his chest. That's from the punch, he thought, before remembering there had been no physical blow. Only Beth's words had struck him. He stepped back, but the table behind him dug into his thighs, blocking his retreat. He moved sideways, feeling along its solid edge with his fingertips.

At last his brain, which had seized on the words '*my boss*', repeating them over and over again in his head, lurched into action. It hurt to breathe, his heart hammered against his ribs and a clammy chill swept over his skin.

'Did you know?' he asked, quietly, forcing out the words.

'*No.*' The whispered word was barely a breath of sound. 'No, I didn't, Jensen.'

'How could you have worked for him and not known?'

'I'll explain, but I can't do that marooned in a sea of broken glass and sticky spilt wine, with a cut on my ankle.' She gestured to the area around her feet. 'Help me out of this, and then please listen to me.'

He wanted to turn and walk away, but he had to listen to her. He had to know that his sweet, beautiful Beth hadn't been hiding something from him.

He found a brush and dustpan in the cupboard in the laundry. He swept up as much of the glass as he could see, retrieved Beth's flip-flops from beside the sun lounger, and dropped them next to her feet. Then he found the first-aid box and carried it outside, putting it on the end of the table.

He couldn't bear to watch while Beth spread antiseptic ointment over the cut with shaking fingers and stuck on an Elastoplast, remembering how he'd dressed her heel with such care.

Beth closed the lid of the box and walked towards him, but he held up a hand. He didn't want her close. It was too dangerous. She could so easily convince him, with her gentle hands and lips and beguiling scent, that she was telling the truth.

She stopped. 'Jensen, I swear to you that I didn't know. Why wouldn't I have told you?' She pressed the heels of her hands into her eye sockets, rubbing them, and then pulling her palms down over her face. 'Your reaction makes no sense.'

'From my point of view, it's your reaction that makes no sense. And for the record, you are the only thing in my life which has made sense for quite some time.' He pinched the bridge of his nose between a thumb and forefinger.

Beth gripped the edge of the table. 'The man I'd been PA to retired suddenly due to ill health and Charles Denby was brought in to replace him. He was seconded from the New York office.' She pulled out a chair and sat down. 'Please sit down, Jensen. It'll make it easier to talk.'

Slowly, he skirted the table and pulled out the chair opposite her, sitting down and leaning forwards.

'Go on.'

'I heard he made unreasonable demands, but he came with an impressive track record.'

'Huh. Mostly achieved through dubious practices.'

'Maybe.'

'*Maybe?* He's the one being investigated, right?'

She pressed her fingers to her temples. 'You said I should go on. May I?'

'Please do.'

'I was assigned as his PA partly because he was replacing the man I worked for, and partly—I suspect mostly—because I had a reputation for being able to manage difficult people.' She ran her fingers through her thick hair, to the tips, and let it fall around her shoulders. 'A talent which doesn't necessarily make for an easy life.'

He watched her hair tumble to her shoulders and anguish twisted around his heart. He loved that she'd stopped pinning it up in tidy, restrictive styles. He loved feeling the weight of it in his hands, and the way it swung so freely around her shoulders when she walked.

'When was this?'

'It was over a year ago. After your case had been heard. I vaguely knew about it, from the press, but to be honest I hadn't taken much interest in it. My stepmother was ill and I was juggling a lot of things, between home and work. Then she was moved to a care home, and I had more time...' She pushed a lock of hair off her forehead. 'I became aware that he...noticed me. He noticed me in a way I wasn't used to. A way other men never had. For the first time in for ever I didn't have to rush home to care for my stepmother or cook dinner. My stepsister had moved into her own place and took very little notice of her mother.' She inhaled, her breath stuttering.

'Beth,' he said, quietly, 'would you like me to get you a drink?'

'No. No, thank you.' She gripped her hands together, her knuckles bone white. 'He...paid me a lot of attention and I...*loved* it. It was so new and exciting, and it made me feel *seen* for who I was, *needed*, not for what I did. Nobody—' she lifted her eyes to his '—had ever needed me before, in that way. I felt alive and interesting and... I... I *loved* him.' She shook her head. 'We had an affair, for a year.'

'You had an affair with a senior partner, for a year? How was that possible?'

'Oh, it had to be kept secret. That was part of the excitement of it, I suppose. We could never let anything show. But he took me to restaurants, and away for weekends. And back to his flat. Often. He travelled to New York a lot, and to the other international offices, but I was always waiting for him, when he came back to London.'

Jensen's dark eyes stayed on her face. She wished he'd look away. It felt as if he was witnessing the shame that she'd never been able to admit to anyone.

'What happened, Beth? How did it end?'

'My stepmother died, and I was free, and then I discovered I would shortly have nowhere to live. I told Charles. I genuinely believed he'd be ready to make our relationship public. I said I could resign, find another job, so it would all be okay. We could be a proper couple. But…he looked at me as if I'd lost my mind. He said he was going back to the States, to his…*wife*. I said, "You're married?" He said, "Yes, but you're not. That's why we've been able to do this."'

Jensen swore. 'Beth, how come you've hidden this? Why didn't you tell me? I thought we'd shared everything.'

She shook her head and gave up trying to blink back her tears. They spilled down her face and she scrubbed at them with her knuckles. 'The only person I've told is Janet. Why would I tell you?'

'Because you trust me? Or perhaps you don't.'

'Afterwards, I heard that the reason he'd returned to New York was because a case he'd prosecuted had been found to be an unsafe conviction. That was yours, of course. He didn't want to be too available, although that wouldn't stop him being investigated. He would have felt safer with the width of the Atlantic between him and possible trouble.'

'Coward.'

'Maybe.'

It was a long time before Jensen spoke again. When he did, his voice was quiet. 'Beth?'

She loved the way he said her name. It felt like a caress, even now.

'Yes?'

'Is that what you wish? That you were still working for him, still keeping his bed warm? That I...' He swallowed and sucked in a noisy breath. 'Do you still love him, Beth?'

Her eyes closed briefly. She looked exhausted. When then they opened again they were filled with pain—the kind of pain that told him just how much she'd been hurt, how much she was still hurting.

He crossed his arms over his chest, breathing hard and fast. He'd tried to convince Beth that she needed to be free to make new choices, meet new challenges, form new friendships. An association with him would hold her back, prevent her from becoming the person she deserved to be, but she refused to accept it. She wanted to fight for their relationship.

Now he wondered if he knew her at all. How could he not have known about this hurt that she carried in her heart? He'd shared with her the pain of his failed marriage, how he'd tried his best to save it. He'd revealed how his daughter refusing to speak to him or see him had torn his heart in two.

There'd been so many opportunities for Beth to tell him how she'd been hurt, but she'd never taken any of them. Why had she waited until now? She'd once talked of a relationship she'd had when she was at college, but she'd brushed it aside, as if it had meant nothing. She'd allowed him to believe it was the only other relationship she'd had.

He could think of only one reason why she'd kept this

hidden. She hadn't been open and honest with him because she didn't think he was trustworthy. Was it possible that, deep down, she did not even believe in his innocence? The feelings of inadequacy that had plagued him came crowding back, making him question whether she felt anything for him at all. Was their attraction for each other just something he'd grown to believe in because he so badly needed someone to make him feel good about himself again? Over the weeks he'd grown to believe they shared a unique connection, but he was suddenly plunged into doubt. She'd been so deeply traumatised that she couldn't bear to talk about it. She'd buried it, desperately holding onto the memories and the pain, rather than addressing them, as she'd advised him to address his own trauma. If she no longer had feelings for Charles Denby, why hadn't she been able to open her heart to him?

He'd asked her if she still loved him, and she hadn't denied it.

The chair grated on the stone terrace as he pushed it back. He stood, moving slowly, deliberately, his brain and his limbs not fully co-ordinated. He stared at Beth's tear-stained face—tears that were for the loss she'd suffered.

His wife had left him, even before his reputation had been trashed. His daughter had cancelled him from her life. The friends he'd thought were loyal had withdrawn.

Now he wondered why Beth would be any different. He'd told her he felt unworthy of her. He'd never felt more positive that he was right.

Beth's eyes still shimmered with the sheen of tears. Jensen kept his arms folded, his hands pinioned in his armpits. He would not, could not, do what his mind screamed at him to do. He would not step forward and wipe them away with the pads of his thumbs or fold her against his chest and tell her it was all okay.

It would never be okay.

He turned on his heel and began to walk towards the line of trees, to the place where the path to the beach began.

'Jensen.' Her strained, choked voice reached him and compelled him to turn round. 'How can I make you understand that I...?'

'Beth.' He said her name one last time. 'I think I understand very well.'

This time he kept walking. When he reached the safety of the sheltering trees, he broke into a run.

CHAPTER FIFTEEN

MOVING ON AUTOPILOT, her mind numb, Beth cleared away the remains of what should have been a beautiful evening. She filled a bucket with water and sluiced the spilled wine from the terrace. It had turned sticky and had already attracted a wasp. It flew up angrily, and with the small, functioning part of her brain she half wished it would sting her. At least that would be a distraction from the awful, heavy pain in her heart.

She swept up some remaining splinters of glass and pushed the salad and cold kebabs and bread into the fridge. The idea of eating made her stomach heave.

It seemed impossible to stop her eyes from straying to the gap in the trees, where the path led down to the beach, expecting to see Jensen appearing there any second. He'd have that wry, self-deprecating look on his face, be pushing a hand through his thick dark hair and apologising for being too quick to judge her.

Surely, he'd come back.

She stretched out, exhausted, on a sunbed. It was fully dark, the only light coming from the solar lamps in the garden. A lighter patch on the horizon showed where the moon would eventually rise. The day, which had started with such joy, was ending in anguish and crushed hopes. How could the tenderness Jensen had shown her this morning have turned into such angry bitterness this evening?

If she hadn't encouraged him to reconnect with the world…if she hadn't given him the Wi-Fi code…

But she couldn't allow herself to think like that. She'd done the right thing. She'd promised to fight for them both, and she'd been trying to do that.

Foolishly, she'd allowed herself to begin to imagine a future with him, instead of taking one day at a time, as she'd advised him to do. But just as the dreams she'd had as a young girl, of meeting her soulmate and falling in love, had never been allowed to come true, so was this dream destined to turn to ashes.

Much later, she retreated inside, slid the glass doors closed, and lay on the sofa, her knees pulled up and her arms wrapped around herself, and slept fitfully.

Milky dawn light woke her. The promise of sunrise lay in the band of pink and grey light along the horizon in the east, and a few bright stars still hung in the deep blue of the sky. Beth uncurled, stiff and tired, and walked out onto the terrace. The pre-dawn air was crisp and fresh but once the sun rose, she knew it would grow hot again.

Through the wakeful hours of the night, she'd rerun last night endlessly through her mind. The turn of Jensen's head, his voice speaking *that* name, the splintering of the wine bottle at her feet. Her memories were confused, blurred with shock. She'd tried to recall what she'd said. What *he'd* said.

Now, in the pearly light of dawn, she remembered something else. Jensen's voice, quiet and steady. *'Do you still love him, Beth?'*

What had she said? She struggled to remember. The question had shocked her. She'd tried to explain her feelings. But a cold certainty spread through her, making her shiver in the warm air. She hadn't answered him. Not properly. Her heart had cracked, but she'd tried to keep the feelings in. It was as if she didn't want to admit, even to herself, how she really felt about Charles Denby.

She listened for the reassuring tapping sound of *Sundance*'s rigging. Silence echoed around her. It would be a while before the cicadas began to tune up. Not a breath of breeze stirred the leaves of the trees, and she pressed her folded arms across her stomach, trying to crush the insidious coil of dread. The rigging would be silent today, the sea a sparkling kaleidoscope of blue, turquoise and green.

Her kaftan lay where she'd abandoned it yesterday afternoon, on the back of a chair, when she and Jensen had swum in the pool. She'd grown so used to wearing only her bikini that she hadn't even thought of covering up again. Now she pulled it over her head, wriggled her feet into her flip-flops and walked across the dry grass.

She had to talk to Jensen.

The light beneath the tree canopy was still dim and she trod carefully, picking her way over roots and stones. As she emerged onto the beach the sun broke free of the sea on the horizon, unfurling a path of light across the width of the bay.

Beth shaded her eyes against the sudden glare, searching the water with increasing desperation.

Sundance had gone.

Jensen paced the deck in the dark. His habit of searching the trees for a light at the villa persisted but as always there was no sign of life up on the hillside. He drank three mugs of ferocious black coffee, laced with whisky, so at least he could blame the caffeine for the way his hands shook and his heart thumped in his chest.

The battle he fought with his body was fierce. He imagined himself climbing back into the RIB and racing back to the beach, running up the rough track. What would Beth have done, after he'd left her standing alone at the edge of the terrace? Was she sleeping in her bed—the bed he'd shared with her, where he'd held her, *loved* her?

He stopped, gripping the rail. How would she have reacted if he'd told her he loved her? Would she have admitted she was still in love with someone else? Someone who'd treated her so badly?

At the first glimmer of pale light in the east, he started *Sundance*'s engine and winched up the anchor, turning the wheel to set her on course for the narrow channel between the headlands. He tried, and failed, not to think about the last time he'd stood in the cockpit, with his hands over hers, when she'd asked him to show her how to sail. As he'd turned her in his arms her beauty and uncomplicated joy had stolen his breath and the kiss that had followed had robbed him of his heart.

He swore and opened up the engine. *Sundance* responded, gathering speed.

Once out in the open sea, he raised both sails and felt her come alive beneath his feet. He'd sail hard and hope for a freshening wind, until he found himself in that sweet spot, where the necessities of keeping *Sundance* hauled tight and cutting through the waves, perfectly trimmed and balanced, would absorb all his attention and he wouldn't be able to think of anything else.

In his pocket his forgotten phone pinged. He dug it out to turn it off, glancing at the screen. His unwanted emails had downloaded automatically but he had no intention of reading them.

But the one at the top of the screen caught his eye. Dear Daddy...

He pressed the off switch, and the screen went black. He couldn't think about Emily now. Beth had wanted him to try to contact her, and he'd decided he would. He pushed the thought away.

He set a course that would take him east of Kekova Island, into the wide, open sea, way from the shelter of the land. The wind would be fresher there, the sailing more challenging, he thought, grimly, glancing at the sky. High cloud streamed in the distance, and he nodded. Weather was approaching, which was just what he needed.

Sailing so hard for so many hours was taxing, and being alone, he knew, it could be extremely hazardous, but Jensen pushed on, hour after hour, taking *Sundance* to her limits and keeping his mind relentlessly focussed on what he had to do to keep her there.

Cloud bubbled up in the east, climbing through the sky and eventually obscuring the sun. The wind turned gusty as it transformed from a steady blow into a gale, pushing the sea into short, steep swells capped with white foam. Some of them broke over the bow, streaming across the foredeck. *Sundance* hit a trough, juddering, and Jensen fought with the wheel to keep her on course, drenched with cold spray, but relishing being able to battle with the elements rather than his thoughts.

He knew the sensible thing to do would be to reef the sails and slow down, but he did not feel like being sensible. He wanted to push himself to the very limit.

There was a loud crack, and the vessel swung violently off course, beam-on to the breaking seas.

It was three days before Beth ventured down to the beach again.

A restless wind had sprung up the day Jensen had left, bending the treetops and curdling the sea into an opaque, choppy green. The time had passed in a blur of empty days spent swimming laps of the pool trying to tire herself out and nights spent tossing in the wide bed where they'd lain in each other's arms, but which now felt far too big for her.

The memories of Jensen, his wide shoulders and broad

chest golden against the white linen, opening his arms to her, twisted in her heart like a knife. His citrussy scent lingered on the pillows and imagining the scrape of his unshaven jaw against her skin in the mornings was a bitter torment.

Every corner of the villa held a shadow of his presence, and the beach was no different. The wind had died and the bay looked empty and abandoned without the graceful shape of *Sundance* swaying gently at anchor. Memories ambushed her on the gritty sand where they'd lain, hands entwined, drying in the sun, their skin sparkling with salt crystals, and in the place in the water, overhung by rocks, where they'd made love.

There was no escape.

She followed the curved edge of the beach, where the tiny ripples of water filled her footprints behind her, and then turned and trudged towards the trees and back up the path to the villa.

The place that had been her sanctuary now seemed lonely and vaguely hostile. It no longer felt like hers and no longer felt safe. There were too many hard surfaces and sharp edges and too many echoes in the silence.

She carried her laptop to the table on the terrace and logged on to the Internet.

Jensen wasn't coming back.

He could have come back to her, but she could not go after him. What was the point of waiting any longer, hoping each day to hear the sound of *Sundance* in the bay and to see him appear through the trees? She knew that the only thing keeping her there was the possibility that he might.

She had the power to end the waiting and hoping, and she decided to use it.

She booked a flight for the following day, then she cycled cautiously to the village to say goodbye to Ela, and to ask Omer to arrange for someone to water the garden, and a taxi to take her to the airport.

CHAPTER SIXTEEN

IT WAS A tall Victorian house near the river in Putney, with a blue door.

Jensen took the front steps two at a time. His suit felt a little tight and he rolled his shoulders. Perhaps he'd built muscle, sailing alone, or perhaps it was because he hadn't worn anything as restrictive as a suit for so long.

The woman who opened the door, after he'd rapped once on the brass door knocker, wore a navy linen skirt and striped top. A tall teenaged girl appeared in the passage behind her.

'Who is it, Mum?'

The woman raised her eyebrows. 'Can I help you?'

'Janet?' Jensen held out his hand. 'Janet Ayhan? I'm Jensen Heath.'

Beth stepped off the riverboat at Cadogan Pier and made her way towards the Chelsea Physic Garden, a green space on the embankment, since 1673. It was a journey she'd made twice before in the previous three weeks, and she looked forward to the sense of peace she found there. She loved imagining the ranks of apothecaries who'd trained there over the centuries, in their outdoor teaching garden.

The courses available were now limited to day-long experiences, but she'd already signed up at an adult education centre to take evening classes, which would lead to a horticultural qualification. Meanwhile, she was using her visits to this four-acre garden, which held four thousand five hundred species of medicinal, herbal and useful plants, to learn as much as possible.

It was a five-minute walk to the Embankment Gate, where she stopped for a moment between the pillars, breathing in the scent of green grass, herbs and flowers, before taking a roundabout route, which would lead her, eventually, to the pomegranate tree. It had been a surprise to find it flourishing here, in London, but she liked to look at it and hope that Omer had organised someone to water the garden at the villa and that the pomegranate she'd planted was flourishing there, too.

She moved on, past the Gardens of Edible and Useful Plants, to the seven recently restored glasshouses.

The scent of the pelargoniums was almost overpowering. She closed her eyes, brushed her fingers through the leaves, and inhaled.

Instantly, she was transported back to the heat of a Turkish summer afternoon. She could almost hear the singing of the cicadas, feel the warmth of the sun on her skin and the cool water of the sea washing around her ankles.

Perhaps, she thought, one day she'd be able to remember all those things without the pain that accompanied them, that accompanied *her*, wherever she went.

She'd explained to Janet the reason for her abrupt return, without adding any detail about Jensen Not much had to be said between such old friends and Janet had demonstrated her sympathy in actions rather than words: the posy of flowers which her daughter—Beth's goddaughter—Myra, picked for her; the homemade biscuits in a pretty tin; a copy of one of her favourite author's latest books.

This garden was a place where she could allow herself

to remember. She wanted to keep her memories safe, and here, with the scents of tropical plants surrounding her, felt like a safe place for them. One day she hoped the memories of her time in Turkey would lose the power to hurt her. She hoped they'd soften, and she'd remember the beauty and the peace, and the kindness of the people. Most of all, she hoped she'd be able to remember the wonder of falling in love with Jensen, without the pain of how he'd left her. Their time together would be something she'd cherish. One day she'd examine the memories and be glad of them.

She allowed herself to feel faintly optimistic about the future. It was, she told herself, infinitely better than the one she'd previously imagined. She had the power to shape it, perhaps not into what she wanted, so deeply, but into something positive that would feed her creativity and give her satisfaction of a different kind. The knowledge was empowering.

She took one last, deep breath.

'Memories, Beth?'

His voice was soft, but roughened, as if clouded with deep emotion. Beth's heart lurched, then picked up an uncomfortable, fast beat. The hot rush of adrenaline raced through her, making her head spin. Her eyes flew open, and she saw the toe of a polished leather shoe behind her. She straightened and turned, looking up.

She barely recognised him. His charcoal-grey suit skimmed the wide shoulders she was used to seeing uncovered, or filling a faded tee shirt.

A white cotton shirt and pale silk tie contrasted with his deeply tanned face, his expression watchful, his dark, dark eyes uncertain. He reached out, as if to brush a strand of her hair away from her face, the gesture achingly familiar, but then his hand dropped to his side, his fingers curled into his broad palm.

She watched the movement and then her eyes went back to his face. His thick dark and silver hair was brushed smoothly back from his forehead, strangely formal. Beth curbed the urge to reach up and ruffle it, to try to make him look more like the Jensen she knew: relaxed and slightly windswept, bare-chested in his worn board shorts.

'Jensen?'

'I'm sorry. You probably don't want me to touch you.'

'What are you doing here?' She stepped back, putting more distance between them.

Jensen pushed his hands into his pockets to stop them from reaching for her. He wanted to hold her, drink in the scent of her hair and her skin, make that shocked look disappear from her face and stop her from chewing her bottom lip. But he knew, more clearly than any of those things he wanted, that he had to try to get this right.

He'd left her, heartbroken and in tears, without giving her a chance to finish her story. He'd leapt to the conclusion that hurt him the most, because he hadn't wanted her to hurt him first. That was what he'd come to expect from life, and in his shock at her revelation he hadn't been able to believe that anything had changed.

He needed to apologise, ask for her forgiveness for the way he'd treated her. Then he would have the courage to ask the question again, even though he knew the answer might rip his heart to shreds. If she told him to leave, he would. It would be the hardest thing he'd ever have to do, but he'd listen to what she said and to what she wanted.

'How did you find me?' She sounded bewildered and shocked.

'If you still want to talk to me, after I've said what I need to say, I'll tell you.'

'What? What do you need to say? I thought you had nothing to say to me. You...left.'

'I've come to say sorry for leaving you like that. I want... *need*...to apologise for how I behaved, that night. I'm deeply sorry, for abandoning you when you were shocked and upset. I should have stayed to make sure you were all right. I should have asked...the question I asked you, again. I'm not sure you heard me the first time. You didn't answer...'

'I heard you. Jensen...'

He pulled a hand from his pocket and held it up. 'No, please let me finish. In my defence, I was shocked, too, but that is no excuse for how I behaved. The thought of you... my beautiful, tender Beth, being manipulated...'

'I was a willing victim. I said I loved the attention.'

He dropped his head and pressed his fingers to his forehead. 'Is there somewhere else we can talk?' Other visitors had entered the glasshouse, chatting loudly. 'That is, if you want to talk to me.'

Beth indicated the door behind him. 'I'm not sure that I do. I appreciate your apology, but if that is what you came to say, I think we're done.'

Panic fluttered somewhere behind his breastbone. There'd been time for her to reflect on their relationship and maybe she'd decided she didn't need him in her life. He'd told her that, often enough. If she sent him away he'd go, but he'd come back, fighting. He looked over his shoulder. 'There's a café. I saw it on my way here. Would you like a cup of tea?'

He watched the hesitation simmer in her eyes, but then she nodded. 'All right. If you have more to say it'll be easier over tea.' She pushed past him and led the way to the door.

The cup rattled against the saucer as Beth put it down. The café was busy, but Jensen had found a table in the corner, at the edge of the paved area. She still felt a little shaky after the shock of his sudden appearance. His apology had been sincere, she was sure, and a week ago, she thought, she would have rushed into his arms, but recently she'd felt some of her strength, fought for and built up during her time in Turkey, returning. The memories of Jensen were painful, but at least she'd been able to examine them. And rather than blaming herself for the way he'd left, she questioned his abrupt departure.

She'd been distraught, her ankle cut by flying glass, and he'd walked away. Not only had he walked away, he'd sailed away, and he hadn't come back to check that she was okay.

'Thank you for the tea. What else was it you wanted to say?' She glanced at her watch.

'Are you in a hurry? What time does the garden close?'

'Five o'clock but I want to catch the next boat back to Putney.'

She watched him pick up a spoon and turn it over in his fingers. The memories of the exquisite sensations those long, strong fingers could provoke in her made her shiver involuntarily, and she looked away.

'Beth,' he said, replacing the spoon beside his cup, and capturing her eyes in his direct gaze, 'I've apologised for how I behaved the night I left you. Whatever becomes of us, however you feel about me, I will regret that for ever. I'm truly sorry.'

She nodded. 'It was…horrible. I waited for you to come back. And the next morning, I found you'd sailed away.'

'It was thoughtless and unkind. But I'd asked you a question, and you hadn't answered me. I was afraid that, if you did, I wouldn't like the answer. I ran, again.'

'You must understand now that I know what running away feels like, especially from something that is not your fault.'

He nodded. 'Yes. I do. It is not the solution.'

'No, it's not, but it's not easy to get to that understanding, either. When I remember how I was when I first arrived at the villa, and look at myself now, even after you'd left me, I feel like a different person.'

'How?'

'I'm strong, Jensen. I was strong in my job. I was known to be determined, iron-willed and inflexible. But inflexibility snaps easily. There's greater strength in being flexible. You're more likely to bounce back up if you're knocked down.'

'Is that what you've done?'

'No, but I think I might be able to. One day.' She bent to pick up her bag, keeping her head down, not wanting him to see how difficult this was for her to say.

'Beth, before you go, I need to know the answer.'

She raised her head and stared at him. 'I was shocked by your question, Jensen. I couldn't believe you'd need to ask it, after everything we'd shared. If you could believe that of me, I thought perhaps I didn't know you at all. But the answer is no, I do not still love him.' She stood up, needing to escape before she cried. 'In fact, I know now that I never loved him at all. Being with you taught me that.'

He watched her walk away, her back straight, her head high, her lovely hair blowing around her shoulders, and he remembered her saying she was going to fight for them both.

She wouldn't need to now. He would be doing the fighting.

He had to queue to pay for their tea. He couldn't go after her. It was the longest wait of his life, or so it felt. She'd vanished by the time he came out of the café and he had no idea which way she'd gone. Whichever way was the way to the river, he thought, desperately, looking for signposts.

He was the last person to board the boat. He'd run, and decided he wasn't as fit as he could be, as he bent to put his hands on his knees and catch his breath. When he straightened, he couldn't see her anywhere. Had this been a mad, pointless idea, to follow her and try again? He'd promised he'd do what she wanted, but she hadn't actually asked him to go away, had she?

He threaded his way through the covered section, searching for a glimpse of that bright hair or that emerald-green cardigan. It was cool on the river. Surely she'd have chosen a seat inside?

But she wasn't there. His heart, still beating painfully fast after his dash along the embankment, refused to slow down, even though he'd got his ragged breathing under better control. He pushed through the doors onto the open rear section of the boat. It was deserted.

Then suddenly, there she was, tucked into a corner against the rail, out of the wind, looking out across the river, with her sunglasses on and her hair blowing behind her. His heart lurched, remembering her on *Sundance*, loving the experience of sailing, challenging herself to try new things, her example challenging *him* to become a stronger, better person.

She turned, evidently sensing his presence behind her. 'Jensen? You followed me.'

He frowned down at her. 'I ran,' he said, 'but this time it wasn't away from something which scared me. It was towards you. Please, Beth, will you give me another chance?'

Her green eyes studied him for what felt like much too long. Then she reached up and ruffled his hair. 'There,' she said. 'Now you look more like yourself.'

He smiled in relief, daring to slip an arm around her shoulders. 'And you simply look more beautiful than ever.'

They left the boat at Putney. Beth stood on the embankment, clutching her shoulder bag.

'It's a ten-minute walk from here, along the river. How did you get here?'

'My car is parked near Janet's house, if it hasn't been towed away by now. Janet suggested looking for you at the garden.'

'You can walk with me, then. It's this way.'

They walked in silence, their shoulders bumping against one another. They'd hardly spoken on the boat, either, spending what was left of the journey standing, with Jensen's arm around her shoulders. It had felt strange, out of context, but also achingly familiar.

Outside the house, Beth turned to him. 'You haven't told me how you found me,' she said.

'Yes, I did. Janet suggested I try the garden.'

'That's not what I meant. How did you find your way to Janet?'

'That story is too long to tell on a doorstep. Will you come out for the day with me tomorrow?'

This felt like a parting of ways. In one direction lay the safe path. In the other, a path that led somewhere unknown and challenging, possibly rough in places. She knew what she should choose.

'Yes, please,' she said, letting go of the safe Beth, the Beth everyone knew. Only Jensen knew the other version of her.

CHAPTER SEVENTEEN

THEY HAD A picnic on Parliament Hill, sitting on a rug with the city spread out below, the Thames a thread of silver winding through its midst. They walked on Hampstead Heath, occasionally linking hands, talking about their time together in Turkey.

They dashed back to Jensen's car when sudden rainclouds threatened to drench them. Jensen turned to her, seeing the bloom of colour in her cheeks, which had been missing the day before, and the smile he'd longed for.

'Let me show you my apartment. This rain looks set.' He peered through the windscreen at the downpour. 'But if it lets up you can see my roof terrace, too. I could do with some advice on what to grow. It was neglected while I was in prison.'

Beth nodded her agreement, noticing the new ease with which he referred to the time he'd been imprisoned. It had been an awful time for him, but the bitterness with which he usually spoke of it had faded.

Now, she stood looking out at the futuristic landscape of the City of London, the Thames wide and grey many floors below, the gleaming dome of St Paul's Cathedral visible between the soaring, thrusting skyscrapers. She heard the soft pop of a cork being extracted from a bottle, and then Jensen handed her a glass of wine.

'Thank you.' She sat at the end of the enormous sofa,

which faced the view, while Jensen occupied an armchair opposite. Awareness had been building between them all day, every touch of a hand or smiling glance increasing the tension. She was pleased he'd chosen to sit a distance away from her. She wanted to listen to what he had to say without the distraction of his physical closeness.

'I said I'd tell you how I found you.'

'What happened, Jensen? I really need to know.'

'Before I start, I have something for you.' He lifted a package from the table and handed it to her. 'You forgot to pack this when you left.'

Beth pulled one of her pink flip-flops from the wrapping.

'What?' He smiled at her incredulity. 'How...?' She turned it over in her hands. It still smelled of salt and the sea. 'I couldn't find it when I left.' Her hands stilled and her eyes widened as realisation dawned. 'You went back, Jensen. You went back to find me.'

'I sailed hard. Too hard, as it turned out.' Jensen put his glass on the coffee table between them. 'I was half out of my mind with despair and anger and all I could think of doing was pushing *Sundance* to the limit so that anything else would be pushed out of my brain. I went east of Kekova Island, because I knew the wind would be stronger on the open sea. It was, and it picked up all afternoon. I was tired—I'd hardly slept.'

'I hardly slept, either. I went down to the beach as soon as it grew light. I was desperate to talk to you...'

'I'm so sorry, Beth. I... I just felt bitter and angry. In my shock, I thought that because you hadn't denied it, you still loved him. I thought it was no less than I should have expected. Nothing much had gone right in my life for a while, apart from you, and a part of me wanted to protect myself by leaving you before you could leave me.'

'What happened? Is *Sundance*…?'

'*Sundance* is fine. But she's not a new boat and I asked too much of her. The backstay broke, leaving us in danger of losing the main mast, in a heavy sea. I dropped the sails and tried to rig up a temporary repair but sailing on your own there's not a lot you can do, safely. I started the engine and that was when I realised I'd made another, very basic error. I had very little fuel. I'd planned to get more but…like I said, I wasn't thinking straight. I tried to conserve the fuel by sailing under the mizen sail, but I couldn't make much headway in such a heavy sea. Early the next morning a fishing boat spotted us. The storm had blown over, but the swells were still big, and *Sundance* was being steadily washed towards a rocky shore, which would not have been…it wouldn't have ended well. They towed us to a sheltered anchorage and left us there. They picked us up again on their return journey, two days later, and took us around to the leeward side of the island, to a small marina on an isolated peninsular of the mainland. It was safe, but I knew it would take days to get *Sundance* repaired.'

'Is that where she is now?'

He nodded. 'She's perfectly safe, but I'll have to get the right fittings shipped out and have help repairing the damage.'

'Okay. That's good, but it must have been scary…'

'It was, and I only really appreciated how close we'd come to disaster once we were safe. But it was good, too.'

'*How?*'

'I was shaken, and very tired, but after having something to eat and catching up on sleep I had time to think. Lots of time. And I remembered, very clearly, something we'd talked about.'

'What?'

'About the ruined city. How people must have been going

about their lives, when suddenly, in a flash, everything changed for ever. How you never know what tomorrow, or even today, might bring, and it's important to live every moment in the best way you can because things we take for granted in life can be snatched away in a moment. It's rare to get second chances, when things go wrong, but that's what I've had, and you, too. And us.'

'Jensen…'

'Let me finish. Please.' He swallowed a mouthful of wine. 'I've spent the past year believing I'd lost everything; that my life was wrecked; that nothing I could do would bring it back. But I've been exonerated and now I have the chance to start again and build a life, which I hope will be better than the old one.'

Beth nodded. 'That's a positive step to take.'

'I'd lost the foundations on which I'd built my life and, waiting for that fishing boat to come back for me, I realised I was afraid that I'd lost you, too. I walked away because I was afraid of what you were going to say. I thought about how I'd known I loved you and I'd never told you. We always think there'll be the chance to do the things we want or plan, but sometimes that chance doesn't happen. Suddenly, with desperate clarity, I knew I didn't want that to happen to us, and I knew I had to get back to you, at least to tell you my true feelings.'

'Jensen…'

'Shh. The place where I left *Sundance* is only accessible by boat. I thought about trying to make a temporary repair to the backstay, but decided I'd already been foolish enough. Luckily the RIB had survived the drama without being washed off the platform at the stern, so I set off in that. The wind had dropped, and it was calm but it still took hours and hours. I had to stop once at a small harbour to refuel.'

'Did you stop at Sula? Omer and Ela knew I'd left.'

'No. I kept going. I was desperate to get back to you. But when I got to the villa I knew at once you'd gone. It was locked up and deserted. The only trace of you I found was your flip-flop. I motored back down the coast to Sula and Omer told me you'd left that morning.'

'I'd waited for you for three days and then I couldn't bear to wait any longer. I had to make something happen, so I left.'

'I was panic-stricken. I thought there was no way I could find you. Because I'd been so stubborn about using my phone, we'd never swapped contact details. Returning to *Sundance* and making her secure took the best part of a week, and then I managed to get a taxi to the airport at Antalya and a flight back to London.'

'You must have been exhausted.'

'I was. The whole experience taught me that my solo sailing days are over. I won't be doing that again.'

'I'm glad. My journey home wasn't exciting at all. Just sad. I've been staying with Janet, again, but I'm looking at a small flat tomorrow. And I have a job interview, at a nursery garden, next week.'

'I thought you'd be with Janet, at least at first.'

'But you haven't told me how you found *her*. Last night, she wouldn't tell me, either. I think she wanted to make sure that I didn't change my mind about today.'

'Once I sat down to think, logically, I remembered that you'd said Janet's husband was Omer's cousin.'

'Ahh. It's starting to become clear.'

'I went to find him and he gave me their address in Putney. Janet didn't know where you'd gone yesterday, but she said I should try the Physic Garden. She said it's your favourite place.'

Beth nodded. 'In London, yes, it is. She and Myra were excited to meet you yesterday.'

'I was torn when I got back. Part of me wanted to find you immediately, but I thought perhaps you needed time…' He stood up and paced to the window. 'It was torture, knowing you were here, but waiting, and not knowing if I was doing the right thing.' He came around the coffee table and sat on the sofa, leaving space between them. 'Also, there were a couple of things I wanted to do first.'

'Have you seen James?'

'I have. That was one of them.'

'Did you tell him where you've been? Explain your silence?'

'Yes. He'd guessed I'd have headed off somewhere on *Sundance*. He understood my silence, especially when I told him *something* about what I'd been doing…'

'Jensen.' A faint flush crept up over her cheeks.

'When he meets you, he'll understand even better.'

'You have plans for us to meet?'

'Not just James. There's someone else I'd like you to meet if you want.'

Beth's brows drew together. 'Who?'

'When I logged onto your villa's Wi-Fi my emails downloaded. I decided I should read them while waiting to be rescued. Well, one of them, anyway. It was from Emily.'

'Your daughter?' The delight in her voice was obvious.

'Yes. She wanted to see me.'

'Oh, Jensen, I'm so pleased.'

'She'd like to meet you.'

'You *told* her about me?'

'I told her I'd met someone very important and special, but I'd screwed up, big time. I said I needed to find you to fix it.'

'What did she say?'

'She rolled her eyes and said, "Typical." And then she said, "Go and find her, Dad." So I did.'

'That's the best news I've heard in just about for ever, Jensen.' Beth blinked back tears. 'I'm so, so happy for you both.'

'Beth, sweetheart, don't cry.' He reached for her, and she felt herself pulled towards him.

'They're happy tears.'

But he didn't let her go. She felt the solidity of his body against hers, breathed in the scent of him, which she'd last inhaled on his pillow in the villa, trying to keep his memory whole. He skimmed the tears away from her cheeks with his thumbs and his big, weather-roughened hands framed her face. 'Can you ever forgive me for hurting you?'

'You said once you couldn't regret what had happened to you, because without it you wouldn't have met me. Do you remember?'

He nodded. 'Yes, I do remember. I also remember the sense of wonder I felt at the realisation, because it was so utterly true.'

'After you left me, the one thought I had was that, however sad it made me, I would never, ever regret what we'd had together. And I don't.'

His arms encircled her, and she felt infinitely safe. One broad hand splayed across the small of her back and the other drifted up her spine to cup the back of her head, tipping her face up towards his. His fingers tangled in her hair and she felt his breath ghost across the top of her head.

'May I kiss you?'

'Mmm.'

Jensen's arm curved round Beth's shoulders, pulling her against his side, his other hand smoothing her hair behind her ear and then resting on the place above the tip of her collarbone where he could feel her pulse fluttering. Her breathing was still quick.

'Hey.'

'Mmm.'

'I didn't mean that to happen. I was going to open a bottle of wine and show you the view, sit and talk and then take you out for dinner, properly, on a date.'

'The view from here is quite good.' She glanced up at him, and her smile did something strange to his heart. 'Not sure the London skyline can compete.'

He laughed softly and kissed the top of her head. 'You still have a tan.'

He brushed his lips over her mouth and rested his forehead against hers. 'Please, Beth, will you agree to stay with me? Be my soulmate? I love you more than I'll ever be able to express in words.'

He knew by her smile that her tears were still happy ones.

'When you turned up on my beach—' she slanted a look at him through her lashes '—all we each wanted was to be alone, but fate had other plans for us. Being loved by you is the best, most amazing thing that has ever happened to me, and all the love I have, which nobody else has ever needed, I want to give to you.' She stroked a hand across his chest. He captured it in his, turning it over and kissing her palm.

'Thank you. In the midst of thinking I'd lost everything, I found you, and you are all I need. You *are* everything to me.'

EPILOGUE

BETH'S AIRCRAFT CIRCLED over the glittering sea before making its final approach to land at Antalya.

She spotted Jensen in the crowded concourse quickly. He looked faintly anxious, his dark eyes scanning the faces of the passengers who streamed through the glass doors from the arrivals hall. His spontaneous wide smile, when he saw her, sent warmth and pleasure racing through her.

His arms were strong and tight around her, his kiss firm. 'I'm so pleased you're here.'

'Did you think I might change my mind?'

'No, but… I just don't like being apart from you.' He took her cabin bag, keeping a protective arm around her. 'Let's go. *Sundance* is as good as new.'

Beth had been hesitant at first, when Jensen had suggested she return to Turkey and sail *Sundance* back to Greece with him. But he'd spread a map out on his dining table and described, gently, how they could island-hop all the way, sailing during the day and stopping at an island each evening. If the weather was poor, they could afford to wait a few days. There was no rush.

'We'll be back in good time for you to start the horticulture course and by then you might have heard from the Physic Garden about the volunteering job.'

'I'm really looking forward to studying again. Being

able to do something I've wanted almost all my life feels like a gift.'

'That's what you are to me.' He'd pulled her against him. 'A very rare and precious gift. I still can't believe I have you in my life. And I've had positive feedback about the programme I'm planning to set up. Apparently, mentoring prisoners to prepare them for life back in the community is massively under-resourced and I'll be able to make a real difference. That's all I want to do—help people less fortunate and less able to help themselves.'

Jensen held Beth's hand as she stepped from the pontoon onto *Sundance*'s deck. 'Welcome back aboard. We've been waiting for this day. She's fit to sail again. We'll take her out for a trial this afternoon. But I'll be treating her gently from now on.'

Beth put her arms around his waist. 'As gently as you treat me?'

He dropped a kiss onto her mouth. 'If that's what you want. Sometimes I'm not so sure.'

She laughed. 'Perhaps I'll schedule some trial time, too.'

'No need to schedule it. We've all the time we need. Well, four weeks, and that's more than enough time to sail back to the marina in Piraeus in a sedate and leisurely way.'

'I'm not sure about sedate…'

'No, nor am I. There was not much that was sedate about you the night before I left.'

'Speak for yourself, Jensen. I was expecting a lie-in the next morning.'

'And that's what you had. A lie-in, with me.'

'I did.' Beth yawned. 'Not this morning, though. I had to get up insanely early to catch the flight. I think I need a siesta.'

'I also had to get up early to meet you. The sea trials can wait until tomorrow. I've booked a restaurant for this evening.'

* * *

They sat in *Sundance*'s cockpit later, after dinner, watching the last of the daylight drain from the sky and the sea turn from deep blue to burnished pewter. Jensen pulled Beth tightly against his side. He hadn't expected to feel nervous, but his voice shook slightly.

'I want to do this properly, Beth.' He took a deep breath. 'I love you with all my heart and soul. Please will you marry me?'

Her green eyes flew wide and he loved that he'd been able to take her by surprise.

'Oh, Jensen, of course I will.' Then she gasped as he took a small box from his pocket and eased the velvet-covered lid open. 'Oh, it's the most exquisite ring.'

He slipped it onto her finger and turned her in his arms to kiss her. 'I wanted to surprise you. Have I?'

Beth put a hand up to his cheek and the solitaire diamond shone in the soft twilight. 'It's the best surprise I've ever had. I love you, so much. Thank you for loving me. This is the perfect way to start our journey into the future together.'

'As long as we're together, whatever we do will be an adventure. And our love will grow stronger, with each one.'

His kiss was warm and demanding, her response urgent.

'Yes,' she whispered, 'starting now.'

* * * * *

COMING SOON!

We really hope you enjoyed reading this book.
If you're looking for more romance
be sure to head to the shops when
new books are available on

Thursday 26th September

To see which titles are coming soon, please visit

millsandboon.co.uk/nextmonth

MILLS & BOON

MILLS & BOON ®

Coming next month

ALWAYS THE BRIDESMAID
Ally Blake

'Are you serious? You will actually be a pretend best man at the wedding of a person you do not know, for me?'

Shut up, Charlie! Just say thank you, then, maybe have him swear a blood pact.

By then Beau had pushed his chair back, and also stood. He tossed his napkin to the table and said, 'It seems so.'

Charlie felt as if a pair of hands grabbed her by the waist, lifted her from her chair and propelled her around the table then, for suddenly she was leaning over Beau, flinging her arms around his neck and hugging the life out of him.

Her body a comma curled into his. The heat of him burning through her clothes, till his heart beat in syncopation with her own.

Her inner monologue cleared its throat, waking her from the heady fog. And she pulled away, pushed more like. Once clear, she tugged at her t-shirt, and attempted a smile.

'Thank-you,' she managed. 'I mean it, Beau. This will be life-changing.'

In a good way for once, she hoped with all her might.

Continue reading
ALWAYS THE BRIDESMAID
Ally Blake

Available next month
millsandboon.co.uk

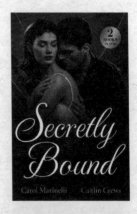
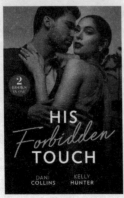
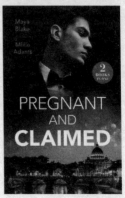

LET'S TALK
Romance

For exclusive extracts, competitions and special offers, find us online:

f MillsandBoon

X @MillsandBoon

⬚ @MillsandBoonUK

♪ @MillsandBoonUK

Get in touch on 01413 063 232

afterglow BOOKS

Afterglow Books is a trend-led, trope-filled list of books with diverse, authentic and relatable characters, a wide array of voices and representations, plus real world trials and tribulations. Featuring all the tropes you could possibly want (think small-town settings, fake relationships, grumpy vs sunshine, enemies to lovers) and all with a generous dose of spice in every story.

♪ @millsandboonuk
⊙ @millsandboonuk
afterglowbooks.co.uk

#AfterglowBooks

For all the latest book news, exclusive content and giveaways scan the QR code below to sign up to the Afterglow newsletter:

SCAN ME

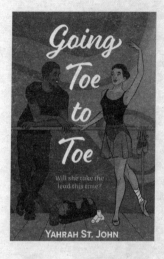

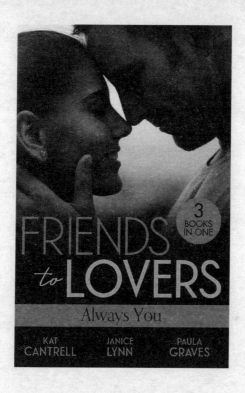